C+
P

Inappropriate
Men

STACEY BALLIS

currently serves as Director of Education and
Community Programs at The Goodman Theatre
in Chicago, *Time* magazine's pick for Number One
Regional Theater in the U.S. She holds a B.A. in
English literature and American studies from Brandeis
University in Waltham, Massachusetts, and an M.A. in
education from De Paul University in Chicago. She is
also the president and founder of Dayton Associates
Consulting Group, specializing in strategic planning, arts
administration and educational consulting for businesses,
cultural organizations and educational institutions.

She has been a writer for as long as she could put
pen to paper, with reams of poetry and short fiction
taking up space on her hard drive. *Inappropriate Men*
is her first full-length novel.

She lives on the near-northwest side of Chicago and is,
at time of press, still taking applications for Mr. Right.

For more information, log on to www.staceyballis.com.

Inappropriate Men

Stacey Ballis

**RED
DRESS
INK**
™

First edition April 2004

INAPPROPRIATE MEN

A Red Dress Ink novel

ISBN 0-373-25055-X

Visit Red Dress Ink at www.reddressink.com

Printed in U.S.A.

ACKNOWLEDGMENTS ·

There are dozens of people without whom this book would have been impossible, so the work is dedicated with all my love to:

My amazing family, whose unflagging support and encouragement in all areas of my life is an inspiration to me always: most especially my parents, Stephen and Elizabeth Ballis, who are the living embodiment of all the finest aspects of love; my grandmother Harriet "Jonnie" Ballis, whose strength, courage and humor are always safe haven; and my sister, Deborah Ballis, my best friend, my best confidante, my truest hero and the most perfect gift my parents ever gave me. Plus all of my extended family, both genetic and honorary, who are too numerous to name here, but no less dear.

My wonderful circle of "family by choice," the extended Gault, Adelman, Srulovitz and Heisler clans, who have been with me in all of my best and worst times for my whole life. The combined force of their laughter and love over the years has been a tremendous blessing.

My extraordinary circle of friends in its entirety, with special mentions for Kate, Donna, Erin, Jonathan, Ora, Larry, Susan, Scott, Hollis, Cassie, Chloe, Joanna, Steven, Harry, Rachel, Sarah, Kevin, Alyson, Joel, Judi, Gary, Mark, David F., David C., Andra, Jamie, Darren, Rita and Dan. The rest of you know who you are and how much I love you.

My colleagues at The Goodman Theatre, who feed me creatively, make work feel like play and the office feel like home, especially Roche, Bob, Steve, Kathy, Deb C., Cindy, Tom, Louise, Rachel, Jeff, Marty, Henry, Chuck, Anthony, Peter, Les, Shera and the best lunch pals a girl could have—Jodi, Deb G., Julie and Rob.

My associate and friend Megan Welch, who keeps me sane, makes me look good and puts up with all of my day to day craziness.

My exceptional agent, Scott Mendel, who hit the ground running based on a phone-call handshake, and helped make my wildest dreams come true. My cousin Susan Sussman, who knew that he was the one. Bob and Sonia Reich, who always told me that I could, and deep down believed that I would.

And, of course, Margaret Marbury, who began it all.

Finally, in loving memory of Kimberly J. Massey, who continues to be a source of light in the universe.

For Mom and Dad, who are, as ever, *beshert,*
and make me believe in true love always.

For Deborah, who makes me laugh the hardest,
especially "running south on Lake Shore Drive."

chapter 1

poets and madmen

QUOTES OF THE DAY

There is a pleasure sure
In being mad which none but madmen know.
—John Dryden

There is a pleasure in poetic pains.
Which only poets know.
—William Wordsworth

Geoffrey M. Fahl, Esq. is holding my hand.

Now I know that this may seem a rather insignificant detail to you, but to me, this is the probably the best, and certainly most unexpectedly fabulous thing that has happened in a very long time. I suppose that what I am finding interesting about this little bit of random human contact with the esteemed Mr. Fahl is that it is forbidden and wrong on so many levels that I am loath to admit to myself that I am awfully intrigued about what it might mean.

Perhaps I should begin with the fact that Mr. Fahl is, at this moment, sitting on my right in the last occupied row of a small movie theatre, and that the hand holding mine bears on its fourth finger a wedding band. I did not place it there. Additionally, it may be worthy of note, on the end of my left arm is a hand that is tingling and dewy, jealous of the attention my right hand currently enjoys, and that this hand too feels the weight of a thin band of gold, a small diamond solitaire, representing years of living with a man who is most definitely not Mr. Fahl. Mr. Fahl seems reasonably casual about this entire situation, and yet is not coming off as a practiced Lothario. He just seems bored by the film, bold enough to make contact, and right now his thumb is making lazy circles on the fleshy pad below my thumb, and my thumb is gently stroking the first joint on his pointer finger, and the whole arrangement seems to be the most exhilarating and intimate of activities.

Several thoughts cross my mind all at once. I am the luckiest girl in the world. I am an evil seductress. I am making a huge mistake. I am a slut. I am having the best time. Nothing will ever be the same.

As it turns out, the statements are all true.

Of course I don't know that at this moment, I am concentrating only on the feel of his hand in mine, the way our arms are touching along their length with an easy pressure. The way our legs are aligned, connected at the knee. The feel of his pulse beneath my fingers. The light scent of his cologne, the rhythm of his breathing. I am trying to remember how it happened, what made it okay, why we ended up here, like this, connected and disconnected, full of strange promise.

It is blurry.

I remember wanting to see the movie, and that my husband was out of town. I remember my girlfriend Pam blowing me off, and the decision to go alone. I remember arriving at the theatre to discover that the listing in the paper was wrong and that I was an hour early. I remember sitting at a table in the café next to the theatre, and perusing *The Reader,* Chicago's weekly alternative paper, even though it was last week's, and I had already read the really important bits, like News of the Weird, and Savage Love. And I remember the voice breaking into my concentration.

"Sidney?"

I looked up into a face I recognize from all the Fun events (Functions and Fund-raisers and Funerals), which I have occasion to attend with my parents. A face I had always found strangely appealing, despite its quirky crookedness. Despite its age. Despite its being attached to the personage of a partner in my dad's law firm, married to a woman who serves on three different boards with my mother, one of which happens to be the Women's Auxiliary Board for the college where I happen to teach. I think it was the eyes. Really lovely blue, twinkly sparkly starkly blue, with the tiniest squinty quality, as if he is always pondering something important, which may be why you don't really notice the eyes till you are right up on them. He is smiling hopefully at me, and his brow is furrowed in a way which makes me think that it is somehow important to him that I remember who he is.

"Mr. Fahl, you startled me. What an unexpected pleasure to bump into you, how have you been?"

He seems chuffed, and lowers his head a bit.

"Geoff, please. I have been very well, thank you, and yourself?"

"Can't complain, really. Busy as usual. What brings you to the neighborhood?"

"Movie next door. Paper got the time wrong, so I am early and came in here for a coffee and to waste an hour."

"Ditto. Please, join me? Save me from reading the personal ads?"

"Absolutely. And I promise not to tell your husband you were reading the personals."

"Tell him if you like, just don't tell him I am thinking of PLACING an ad."

Mr. Fahl—Geoff to his friends—which apparently now includes myself, laughs.

"Your secret is safe with me. Will he be joining us?"

"He is out of town on business for the week. And Mrs. Fahl?"

"She is also away."

"If we were the suspicious sort we might think they were having an affair!"

"I suppose they could suspect the same of us, especially after the slumber party incident."

"This is a good point." We laugh together.

BACKSTORY

So a little over a year ago, maybe a year and a half previous to tonight's fateful movie house meeting, my mother calls me with a completely strange proposition. Did I want to spend a night in the Shedd Aquarium? Now, on the one hand, my love of all things aquatic might make this a logical offer, were it not for the fact that I am not TEN YEARS OLD, and there is something really bizarre about a thirty-one-year-old woman with a husband and a Master's degree spending the night in a sleeping bag at a museum with god knows how many strangers. Sigh. My mother means well, she is a totally fabulous batty lady whom I dote upon, but here and there she gets these really ridiculous ideas, which usually involve me, a portion of my limited free time, and an event that is deeply tedious. As I am for all intents and purposes an only child, (my sister Naomi is eight years my senior, and lives in New York with her husband and kids, and we see each other once a year at most, and my brother Adam, two years my junior, is living and working in London for the time being) I have no siblings available to take up the slack when it comes to dutiful child responsibilities. All the "great things" parents have a tendency to volunteer you for because they think you would have such a "good time." The parking lot duty for the art fair, filling the last empty seat at their table for any number of rubber chicken dinners in support of diseases, the arts and Jews in general (sometimes in support of diseased Jewish artists for a grand slam), donating myself at silent auctions to lead book discussions or give one-on-one workshops in the writing and performance of poetry.

I love Mom, she means well, it is easier to acquiesce, so I am scheduled for a Slumber at the Shedd event, complete with seafood buffet dinner which is (a) a little creepy considering we are at the aquarium and the fish will be watching us chow down on their cousins, and (2) annoying, because I don't eat seafood.

At least I can drag my husband Mark to this one, and eerily enough he seems excited about it, which, for whatever reason makes me irritated with him. I suppose it is important to acknowledge that of late, most of what he says and does makes me irritated with him.

And by "of late," I mean for the last couple of years or so.

But that is not particularly relevant at this moment; we will deal with it later.

Long story short, we go to the aquarium, find a good spot to camp out near the seahorse exhibit, hit the buffet, (where I show solidarity with my fine-finned friends by eating only salad and rolls, and Mark calmly eats his way through about three pounds of shrimp, crab legs, mussels marinara and baked cod as if he has never seen seafood before) and begin to wander through the exhibits, all of which have been lit to show us what happens to the seas and rivers at night. A great deal of it is very interesting, or would have been, except most of the guests are families with small children, and these little people are out past their bedtime, and many are behaving badly. Mark is tired, (probably from all the strenuous digestion) so we head over to our little nook and try to sleep. Sleep is impossible. Ever notice how your house or apartment makes those strange noises you can only hear when you can't fall asleep? Well, imagine the racket an entire museum makes. Around 2:00 a.m. I get out of my sleeping bag and go for a walk. They have limited the "camping" areas to the gallery spaces, which leaves the central tank and its surrounding grottos blissfully free of dozing patrons. I find a small cave and wander in to watch the parade of the nocturnal ocean life, at this hour consisting primarily of sharks, rays and one sea turtle. I adore sharks. They are truly fascinating creatures. So serene, yet with an underlying dangerous quality. So clearly perfectly designed for their environment. So, so very, well...

"Elegant."

There is a tired-looking man sitting behind me in my little hideout. "Excuse me?"

"Elegant. The sharks, they are the most elegant fish in existence, don't you think?" He looks very familiar to me but I can't place him, and the pale blue-green light from the tank settles in the lines on his

face, and the shadows of the big fish as they pass by glide over his fea-tures making them so much jumbled nonsense. Plus, I took my contacts out when I thought sleep was a possibility.

"It is a perfect word for them, yes, awfully sinisterly elegant. I was just trying to put my finger on it."

"Can't sleep?"

"Not a wink, you?"

"My wife planted us near the otters. Not only was that a prime spot for families with kids that are scared of the fish, but apparently—little known fact—otters snore."

I laugh, imagining those sweet furry faces, peaceful in dreaming, lithe brown bodies tangled in a heap, gently snoring away.

"Don't laugh, it is a real racket. Can't get a wink. Plus, I am too old for this sleeping bag on a mat on the floor business."

"Poor Methuselah, is your rheumatism acting up?"

"Oh I see, a comedienne. If you're not careful, I'll tell your dad you were teasing the fish and tapping on the glass."

Mental smack in the head. One of Dad's partners. Had only ever seen him in a crowd before; by himself he is all out of context. Then again, I never saw him in his pajamas before either, but I have to say he seemed to wear them like a business suit.

"Oh please, don't tell Daddy. He paid so much for these tickets."

"I was wondering how you got roped into this?"

"Mom bid on it at some auction and passed it off to me. And you?"

"My wife's best friend is on the Women's Board here."

And so it began. We walked from grotto to grotto, wandered into the Great Lakes gallery, which apparently wasn't exciting enough for any-one to want to sleep there, and chatted easily about nothing in partic-ular. At around five-thirty he suggested we go to the oceanarium and watch the sun come up over Lake Michigan. It was a perfect sunrise, and we sat in silence, hearing only the clicks and whistles of the Pacific white-sided dolphins and the beluga whales. And then we left in search of a few hours of exhausted sleep. It was a strange and lovely night. We didn't spot each other at the breakfast (lox and bagels—have these peo-ple no souls?) and after a week or so, I completely forgot it had even

happened. Then about a month later, Mark and I were at my parents'
table for somebody's annual gala, and the Fahls wandered over to say
hello. Mrs. Fahl asked if I enjoyed the salmon, and before I could reply,
Mr. Fahl said:

"She doesn't eat fish."

My parents, my husband and his wife all turned to him, perplexed.
I looked down at my half-eaten dessert, feeling vaguely guilty, and not
knowing why.

"Really? Is that true?" she asked me.

"'Fraid so."

"Astounding. Geoffrey, are you suddenly psychic?"

"Not at all. I bumped into Sidney at that thing we went to at the
Shedd, and asked if she had enjoyed the buffet and she informed me
that she didn't eat seafood."

"I am sorry Sidney, I don't remember seeing you there." Then, turn-
ing to her husband, "Where was I when you two were chatting?"

"Asleep."

There was an awkward silence, which I decided needed to move past
strange into mortifying, so I piped up with…

"I couldn't sleep and went for a stroll, and Mr. Fahl couldn't sleep
either, so we bumped into each other at the main tank in the mid-
dle of the night and kept each other company for a bit." Which might
have landed better if either one of us had mentioned this little ad-
venture to our spouses, which clearly, we had not. Blissfully, my dad
changed the subject quickly to some big case the firm was dealing
with, and Mrs. Fahl and my mother began discussing someone's de-
clining health, and Mark and the gentleman on his other side con-
tinued their political debate, while I looked sheepishly at my panna
cotta as if it was going to speak to me. When the dancing started,
we three couples all retreated to the floor, but once, over the shoul-
ders of our swaying spouses, we locked eyes for a moment, and he
winked at me.

Meanwhile, back at the ranch…

Over coffee (my Grande Skim Cappuccino and his Venti
Decaf House Blend) we chat about nothing in particular, but in

a way that makes us both laugh, and when it is time to head over to the theatre, he offers me his arm like a gallant gentleman of old, and I take it, liking the feel of his crisp shirtsleeve, his surprisingly strong forearm. He purchases my ticket, waving off my proffered money with a wink. I don't know why this makes me blush, but it does. We find seats toward the back of the theatre and after the usual twenty minutes of previews and Snapple ads, the movie begins. The house is completely empty behind us, maybe two-thirds full in front of us, and the film quickly bores Geoff. He leans over every two or three minutes to make some clever comment, and I laugh quietly at his jokes. It is easy here with him. Strange and familiar, awkward and comforting. It is inexplicable. About a half hour into the movie, something strikes him as bizarre, and he smacks his forehead dramatically, sighs, and drops his head onto my shoulder for effect. Instinctively, I let my own head lower to touch his, and despite the fact that we both tense, neither of us moves for thirty seconds or so. His hair is surprisingly soft under my cheek. And he smells really good.

Then everything seems to slow down. Our arms, sharing the armrest between us, get heavy. And I don't remember our hands so much moving, as realizing that our pinkies were touching. And then of their own accord, those rogue pinkies interlocked with each other, like they were making a childhood promise. I wanted to cross my heart.

Geoffrey M. Fahl, Esq. is holding my hand. And I like it.

Gradually this hand-holding escalates until the length of my forearm is entwined with his, resting lightly across the tops of his thighs, and now both his hands are there, the left one in its original place clasped around mine, the right one now crossed over and resting with a firm pressure on my forearm. My arm is most pleased. Quite beside itself really. And it suddenly wants a large martini and a cigarette, which is a new sensation for an arm. My left arm is still pouting, and has decided to fall asleep to punish me. It can play with the pins and needles all it wants,

I can barely breathe for fear that something I do might spoil the thing entirely.

And then, too quickly, the movie is over. We rise, he assists me with my coat, and we walk out through the lobby and into the night air, which has a delicious chill about it. He walks with me almost silently to the parking garage.

"May I escort you to your car?"

"Certainly."

We do not speak, Geoff and I. At my car he says only, "Thank you for the distraction."

"Anytime."

He leans in and kisses me on the mouth, lightly.

And then is gone.

I ponder the events of the evening on the drive home. The whole thing seems surreal. I find myself thinking of all the times Geoff and I have been in the same place at the same time, how frequently we have been seated at a table together at an event, how often I have spotted him at the lectures and luncheons and readings that seem a consistent fixture in my life. How many times I have taken note of his form across a crowded theatre lobby or hotel ballroom. He had never made more than friendly small talk, had never seemed to take particular notice of me, certainly not in the way so many of my father's friends and colleagues have.

I think men in their early fifties have a certain affinity for me. I find that now that I am in my thirties, I get a great deal of attention from these middle-aged men—gray at the temples, slight softness of the skin below the chin, the twinkling eye contact when they speak to me, full of benign and embarrassed flirtations. I think it has to do with the fact that while I am young, I am not ridiculously so, and my innate intelligence and maturity has an appeal very different from the twentysomething Twinkies that these men sometimes fall prey to. I am married, which makes me a little safer. They get to have some harmless banter with a younger woman, which feeds their need to think of themselves as virile still, and I get the rush of power that comes from knowing you are having an effect on a member of the opposite sex, that silly tingle of ego-boost that never seems to get old. When I am feeling especially wicked, I may flirt a little more shamelessly—touch an arm to make a point, lower my eyes a bit, and then raise them again to meet a gaze with a small smile playing around the corners of my mouth. I love the way these men blush when I do this, the slightly fevered look behind the eyes, the tiny questioning move of the shoulders as they try to figure out if I am indeed available to them, the small nervous backward step as if I might lean in for a kiss. I know it is sort of wrong, but what can I say, it is harmless fun for me. But Geoff and I have never had one of these moments or exchanges. I never really thought he paid me much attention at all, which makes tonight's adventure that much more interesting, that much more titillating.

At home, I get undressed, wrap myself in the thick blue fleece robe that is my least attractive and most comfortable garment, and don the silly slippers I found in a crazy boutique in New York, all velvet and silk and suede in a harlequin pattern, like something one might find in the boudoir of a fairy-tale Indian princess. There is a message from Mark saying his trip is going well and asking me to remember to have the oil changed in his car. I make myself a cup of green tea with spring cherry blossoms, indulgent with three teaspoons of raw sugar and a splash of milk instead of the usual Equal packet, and sit down at the computer to write the evening into tangible explication before the sense of it leaves me completely.

I conjure the moment of first contact with my eyes closed, wonder if it would be a solitary footnote episode, or if it might not have meant something more. If it might not have been a start to something. A prologue of sorts. My fingers on the keys begin to move.

Beginnings?

it is exquisite
in a dark movie house
next to a man who fascinates you
a man who maybe is a little fascinated by you too

the music starts
epic dance of subtlety
no one wanting to appear to make a first move
and yet, somehow
infinitesimally
hands touch
knees touch
do not shift away

it is safe
in its danger
little communications
whispered jokes
shared secrets
like two children
bored in church
making the most of their enjoyment of one another
of the mutually perceived possibility
of an unnamed something
that might mean nothing
and yet
might not

they test their new connection
slight pressure is applied
is equally returned

a head on a shoulder
made welcome

fingertip caress
matched stroke for stroke

and now there is
behind the comfort
beneath the friendly casual gestures
there is
electricity
tiny pulse of current
hearts do not race
but beat louder in the veins
breath does not quicken
but deepens
skin awakens to touch
nerves unfurling to embrace the minutiae of sensation

it is not a seduction
there is no manipulation
no dishonesty
there is simply
       yes
in the dark
because deep down
they might have been
inevitable

it is not love
there is no inclination for that
they are not monumental
there is simply
       yes
in the private way two people can speak without words
in the back of a movie house
surrounded by strangers who do not know that the story
is unfolding behind them

I write this poem in a fury, frenzied, it pours out of me like blood from a wound and then is done. I like it. The event seems adequately captured for the time being. I do not change anything, but save it, finish my tea, now tepid, and shut down the computer. I make my simple evening toilette, hang the robe on the hook behind the door, climb into bed and read for a few minutes. Or try to read, but the lines of the book swim before my eyes like so much insensible cryptic code. I give up, shut off the nightstand lamp, and lay in the dark, wondering what it meant, and why it happened and why I wanted it to happen. The memory of his head on my shoulder, the smell of his hair, the tiny good-night kiss, and I am touching myself with the hand that held his and saying his name in the darkness when I come, just to feel the weight of it on my tongue.

chapter 2

venial, cardinal and deadly

TODAY'S MEDITATION

> Six things there are, which the Lord hateth, and the seventh his soul detesteth:
> Haughty eyes, a lying tongue, hands that shed innocent blood. A heart that deviseth wicked plots, feet that are swift to run into mischief. A deceitful witness that uttereth lies, and him that soweth discord among brethren.
>
> Proverbs 6:16-19

I am most intrigued by the idea of sin.

Jews don't think of sin in the same way that Gentiles do. Essentially Jews are supposed to obey the Ten Commandments, tithe ten percent of their earnings and send at least one son per generation through medical school. No heaven, no hell, just make the most of your time and God will be pleased. Gentiles, on the other hand are in varying degrees obsessed with the idea of sin. They have devised different categories of sins, and ways of being punished, both earthly and in the afterlife, for the commission of those sins, or in some cases, the omission of counterpoint virtues. This is all terribly interesting to a non-practicing cultural Jew, who tends to identify as a humanist agnostic. Especially as I am about to be involved in committing actions which incorporate several sins of varying degrees of morbidity, as well as the breaking of at least twenty percent of the Decalogue. (Maybe more, I am no comparative religion scholar.) At least, I hope I am. If not, I shaved my legs for no reason at all.

When the phone rang, I was lounging. Languishing. Lying on the couch, too bored to watch TV, too tired to read, too lazy to get off my ass and get dressed, I was literally paralyzed by inertia. I was contemplating the previous evening, wondering if it might not have been a dream, when the dulcet tones of my cordless phone beseeched me from the pocket of my bathrobe to engage in dialogue with the outside world.

"Hello?"

"Sid? It's Geoff."

Well, I'm up now.

"Geoff, hi. How are you?" Please let me sound casual, like it is no big deal that he is calling.

"Fine, and you?"

"Fine, just having a lazy day."

"Me too." There is an awkward silence at this point, then he speaks again.

"So, do you have a radio there?" This strikes me as an odd question.

"Yep. Sure do. Why?"

"NPR is running the two-hour joke special hosted by Paula Poundstone, I thought you might want to listen."

This may be the lamest excuse for a phone call in the history of phone calls. If Alexander Graham Bell had said these words over that first scratchy exchange, we might still be using drums and smoke signals. I am finding him unbearably cute.

"Well, thanks for the heads up, I will have to turn it on."

"I have been enjoying it myself."

"A lovely way to spend a quiet Saturday."

"Indeed." Now there is more silence. Obviously he needs help here.

"So do you have big plans for the rest of the evening?" Okay, this is unsubtle, even for me, but for some really bizarre reason, I want him to know that there is a door open here. The implications of opening that door I will deal with later.

"Not really, you?" Bingo.

"Not a thing in the world."

"Would you want to get together?" My heart feels like it is going to bust right through my chest.

"Sure, if you want." The picture of nonchalance.

"Maybe have a drink?"

"Sounds good to me."

"Like, eight-ish?"

"Fine. Where?"

"I don't know. Any ideas?"

"Well, it is likely to be a madhouse most places—whenever St. Patrick's Day falls on a Saturday, the natives get doubly restless." The angler tests the air with a moist fingertip, adjusts the lure, lets fly the cast, and—

"I forgot about St. Patrick's Day. I suppose, well, it might…I mean…you could come over here if you like." —hooks him. This one looks like a keeper, boys. Weigh him and fillet him.

"Sure. Where is here?"

Geoff gives me his address and driving directions, we exchange one or two other pleasantries, and say goodbye. I get up, turn on the radio, and tune in to NPR. At least with the jokes, I have an excuse for the grin on my face.

A couple of hours later, I begin the preparations. It has been a very long time, but just like riding a bike, this is the way we prep for a date when we think we may end up in bed. Now of course, I am a rare sort of bird…a woman who can go from asleep to showered, dressed, made up, hair done, in the car in T minus twenty-five minutes. Eighteen if I wear glasses instead of contacts, and minimal face goop. And to be frank, I usually despise the sort of women who take hours to get ready and keep everyone waiting. It always seems silly to think about the countless hours wasted in daily cosmetic routine and tortured hair ritual. However, when I have no one waiting on me, and hours to kill before an event, even I can be more over-the-top-self-indulgent than a gay man getting ready for a first date with the guy from high school he always wanted to fuck but thought was straight. Once I decided on the outfit, casual black skirt and gray sweater, sexy but not slutty, comfortable underthings that were cute enough for a late night showing, the real work began.

SIDEBAR

Actually, this is something of a lie. Any woman will tell you that choosing the right clothes for a first date, even a sort-of date, requires at least an hour of teeth gnashing, hair-pulling, screaming at the bulging closet that seems to contain only items that are too large, too small, too casual, too fancy, too unflattering, too last year, anything but what you need. And in a situation like this one, i.e. a spontaneous, unplanned adventure, whatever your one great never-fails-you outfit is, it is destined to be at the dry cleaners when the call comes.

I am nothing if not a regular gal, and I will confess to something that very few regular gals will confess to. When it comes to needing the right outfit, if it ain't in the closet, it must be at the store. I know, the purchase of new clothes for such an objectively minor event seems completely irrational. Especially when we all know that there are literally dozens of perfectly serviceable outfits already in one's possession. It is a position I cannot defend, I am the same sort of mass of inconsistencies as anyone else. So after nearly forty-five minutes of trying on and discarding half of my wardrobe, I jumped in the car and ran out to find something that would suit. Now, in my very small defense, I do have a rule about such things. I won't buy anything too terribly expensive, and I won't buy anything too trendy. I limit myself to items that I will be able to get some good use out of, preferably separates that will go with other things I already own, usually in some neutral color. And luckily for me, there is a Lane Bryant only five minutes from my house, so it only took me a half hour to get there, find the skirt and sweater, both on sale, and get back home. Now, since I have just given a fairly snooty

*and intolerant stance on hair and makeup routines by some of my sis-
ters, telling you now that I actually went out and bought new clothes
for this date, especially clothes I am hoping to be wearing for a minimum amount of time, well, I should get some points for honesty at the
very least.*

Meanwhile, back in my bathroom...

While you have been making whatever judgments you care
to make about my little shopping spree, I have been languorously
getting ready for whatever lies ahead in my evening. It is really
just a sort of exponential explosion of a normal toilette, all the
pieces one might spread out over a week or so condensed into
a few hours of lavatory excess. Shower with all the basics, pat
down to get the water off, lotion on arms and legs, oil everywhere else, perfume on the pulse points, and into the carefully
chosen undergarments (black satin, classy but not chaste). Feet
covered in lotion and slipped into cotton socks to get soft,
bathrobe on...and then we tackle hair.

And I do mean tackle. I have an abundance of dark brown,
naturally curly, naturally thick hair. A ridiculous amount of hair
for any one human being. Completely unmanageable 357 days
a year. Which is why, for much of my life, I wear it twisted up
into a loose bun, or pulled back in a ponytail or barrette. Now,
down is sexier, but harder to control; one wrong move, too
much or too little of one product or another, and I become a
walking shrubbery by midnight, or worse, crunchy or sticky
curls that don't ever lay right and leave residue on the hand of
anyone who might touch them. If I am going to attempt it, the
key is patience, step by step, follow the rules and don't get creative. And if I am lucky, soft, touchable springy ringlets that stay
out of my face and do not take over the planet.

Today, I am very lucky.

Makeup is far less time-consuming. I get some color on my
cheeks, some earth tones on my eyelids, three coats of mascara,

and a little smudge of color and shine on the lips, nothing to inhibit a possible kiss, things are smooth and quick. Two-and-a-half hours, and I am as cute as I can possibly get in broad daylight with sober people around. Which hopefully means that unless Geoff's house is done in fluorescent lighting, once he gets a drink or two in him, I am going to be one significantly adorable chick to look at.

Here again, sin pokes its nosy way into my head. I am a married woman. I am on my way to the home of a married man. Both our spouses are out of the zip code. There are drinks planned. There has already been flirting and contact. I am making every possible preparation to have sex with this man. There are condoms in my purse. I have been meticulously over every inch of my body to make it smooth, remove unwanted hair, scent it lightly, ensure that it is pleasant to the eyes and nose and hands and mouth. I have consumed an entire liter of pineapple juice that someone brought to my house for brunch last week and never opened, because I read somewhere that if you drink pineapple juice two to six hours before a man performs oral sex on you, it gives you a pleasantly sweet taste. (I cannot believe that I actually did this, let alone admitted it to you.) And not once have I given more than a fleeting thought to my husband of eight years, my partner and lover of fourteen years, the man I vowed to honor and cherish and be faithful to for the rest of my days. And I know this must make me seem callous and unfeeling or even a bit like a slut. But the simple truth is that the passion and excitement went out of my relationship with Mark a long time ago, and I have about given up on getting it back. There is a very fine line between comfortable stability and total stagnation, and we have crossed that line. So while I know that what I am readying myself for falls solidly in the realm of the reprehensible, I cannot help the part of me that is swept up in the sheer unexpected romance of it all. And so, for the moment at least, I am feeling no guilt, no shame, no regret about what I am preparing to do, and am flooded with a sense of exhilaration that I have not felt in years. And realizing that if he doesn't make a pass at me tonight, I will cry from disappointment, not relief. I am, officially, a big-time sinner.

For here are the seven deadly sins, along with their virtuous opposition:

Pride (two and a half hours of making oneself into an object of desire, or at the very least a possible object of desire seems to fall under this category) vs. **Humility** (which today I apparently possess none of)

Covetousness (Avarice) (of another woman's husband, seems the obvious choice here) vs. **Liberality (Generosity)** (if I sleep with him, I am known for being a generous lover, but I doubt I will get any bonus points for that)

Lust (well, taa daa!) vs. **Chastity** (well, it is possible I won't sleep with him…but only if he doesn't want to, in which case I am chaste by default which I doubt is what is meant here)

Anger (Wrath) (now here I seem to be okay for the moment) vs. **Meekness** (this is where I wonder if you lose status for not possessing the virtue, even if you don't commit the sin…because meek doesn't exactly match up either)

Gluttony Well, well, well. It was bound to come up….

SIDEBAR

Surprisingly enough, this may be the big one here. The ultimate of my litany of sins. For this is where I admit to being fat. Not fat in quotation marks or parentheses, fat in actuality. Not that girly, "I am so FAT I had to buy a medium and not a small T-shirt!" Not movie fat of like twenty extra pounds that two weeks of diet and exercise can erase just in time for the "big makeover reveal" scene—that isn't fat, that's bloat. Not even "beach novel" fat, where some strange miracle or tragedy occurs that suddenly makes the pounds melt away without having to diet or attend meetings or eat tiny portions of shitty food or even really feel like it is at all a hardship, after which the fabulous man that loved *her in spite of her size is able to watch her float down the wedding aisle toward him in a size six Vera Wang gown. I am not large, I am not zaftig, I am not voluptuous. I am fat. Marilyn Monroe may have been a size 14, but I haven't been a size 14 since I **was** 14, and even then it was clear I was no Marilyn Monroe.*

I am a size 24 on a good day. I am five-three and I weigh anywhere between 258 and 265, depending. According to doctors, this is technically morbidly obese. Let that roll off the tongue for a moment. Morbidly obese. Doesn't have quite the same ring as Rubenesque, does it? And yes, there is a genetic predisposition towards obesity in my family. There is also a predisposition to sit in front of the television at three in the morning and eat a whole pint of Cherry Chip Ba Da Bing ice cream with a side of potato chips. Yes, there were some bad eating habits instilled in my youth, but my youth was in the seventies when the culinary rages were fondue and fancy French food and casseroles made with Campbell's Cream of Mushroom soup and the only diet drinks were TaB and Fresca, and no one knew what their cholesterol level was.

Now, I am a woman of major league intelligence. Just shy of Hawking-level genius on the IQ charts. I have worked with nutritionists, I have read the books, I own the treadmill and the Dynabands and the videos and the motivational CDs. I am fat for two reasons only. I eat a lot. I exercise very little. I take food in copious amounts at varying levels of nutritional soundness and digest them, and while I lead a pretty active lifestyle for a fat person (walking, hiking, swimming, snorkeling), these activities are taken at a pace which causes the least amount of sweating and discomfort possible. And are inevitably followed by a good meal and maybe a cocktail. It comes down to this: I love food, and I hate exercising.

I am a self-taught gourmet chef, and the creation and eating of fabulous meals is a tremendous passion. With a different metabolism, or an interest in any physical activity that raises the heart rate for an extended period of time, I might be okay. But alas, I am blessed with neither. Thus, I am a woman of significant physical amplitude. I am not an hourglass, I am a dayglass. Maybe a day-and-a-half glass. I wear a 44 DD bra and you could park a Volvo in the shadow of my ass. When

I sit cross-legged I look a lot like Buddha in drag. I am somewhere between fat Liza and Camryn Manheim.

And I am one sexy beast.

No I am not kidding. I am totally cute. When Armistead Maupin wrote about "The Most Beautiful Fat Woman in the World" in the fourth or fifth collection of his Tales of the City *series he knew whereof he spake. I may be big, but I am genuinely beautiful. This is not bravado, and yes I am aware that I am losing more of those Humility points as we speak, but what the heck. I have a beautiful face. Big blue/green/gray eyes with flecks of gold and long dark lashes. Clear fair skin, with a smattering of freckles across the nose when I am out in the sun. A fabulous smile (thanks to five years of orthodontia). Full rosy lips, the aforementioned hair...I am, for a fat chick, a real hottie.*

Remember when Delta Burke gained all the weight, but never lost her looks? I am that kind of fat. Luscious. Luxurious. Abundant. I am the fat girl the guys who aren't usually chubby chasers go for. Which I suppose is at least one good reason why I have never had too much motivation to get serious about losing weight. Sure, there have been plenty of guys who didn't want me because of my size, and kids have been cruel, and there have been moments of genuine depression and despair. But overall, I have had a pretty good life, and more than my fair share of high quality men. I am done making apologies for being fat, as if it is some sort of social disease. Would you want to see me naked under a halogen lightbulb? Nope. But moonlight and candlelight do okay by me. Are my tits going to be in my armpits when I lie on my back? Absolutely. But between us we have four hands to move them to somewhere more accessible, and they are soft and creamy and most men I know are not above reveling in an embarrassment of riches such as this. Will I be able to hook my ankles behind my head for your sexual titillation? Not in a million years. Am I a fantastic lay? You bet your boots.

If you want to read the book about the fat girl who gets everything she wants while the extra weight magically disappears, return this book to Barnes & Noble and find someone else. If you are expecting me to win the lottery, hire a trainer and discover an untapped but deeply rooted

love of tofu, nonfat yogurt, and spinning classes you will be sorely dis-
appointed; Borders will process a refund happily. There are no fat-girl rev-
elations to be contained in this book, except that there is more to any
human being than one characteristic, be it skin color, religious belief, sex-
ual preference or size. I find the whole fat discussion boring. I am who
and what I am in more complexity than any single label, and the story
I tell is about that complexity. If I get the guy, it is because of who I am,
and if I don't the same applies. Success, failure, happiness, misery, they
will all be mine in some measure, and none is avoidable or achievable
based solely on the numbers the scale flashes. Amazon.com will be happy
to recommend the fat-girl-gets-thin genre to you, complete with reader re-
views and suggested musical selections.

Don't get me wrong, this isn't some fat-girl manifesto either. I am not
recommending obesity as the next edgy trend. There are a lot of things I
would like to do that I cannot because of both my size and lack of phys-
ical fitness. Places I cannot go. People who will dismiss me out of hand,
and say awful things behind my back. For every man who has loved me,
there are dozens who would put me on their "not in a million years"
list. I can guarantee that while I have a lovely large circle of good friends,
there are plenty of people who find me tedious, and when I irritate them,
you can bet that they refer to me as a "fat bitch" not just a "bitch." And
while I am in very good health at the moment—no heart problems or
diabetes, no cholesterol issues or fatty liver disease—the longer I stay fat,
the better chances that I will cause permanent, irreparable damage to my-
self, and shorten my life span.

But that is not the topic of this book. This book is about life and love
and joy and heartbreak. If you buy ten copies to give to your friends and
my publisher makes a bunch of money and hires me to write the sequel,
then I may have to pen the saga of the search for the diet and exercise
program that don't make me feel like I am losing more brain cells than
fat cells. In the meantime, make a choice before you move forward. If you
are interested in me, Sidney, and whatever adventures lie ahead, then stay
with me. It isn't that the weight issue won't come up again, but it may
be a while, as there are more important things on my plate. (Pun in-
tended.)

Meanwhile, back in Sunday School...

So **Gluttony** it is, ridiculously so, vs. **Temperance** (see preceding pages)

Then we have **Envy** (this is not a big thing for me yet, but stay tuned...) vs. **Brotherly love (Kindness)** (now this stuff I have in spades—at last a winner!)

And finally, **Sloth (Apathy)** (and while my previous rant about exercise might belie this, I don't count this one on my sin list. I lead a very active life, both career-wise and socially, and I do not need to be surgically removed from my couch.) vs. **Diligence (Zeal)** (here again, I am going to give myself some credit, especially as I am already far gone on the Pride path)

Of course I have other sinful problems as well. The following two weigh somewhat heavy on me as I drive to Geoff's: **delectatio morosa,** i.e. the pleasure taken in a sinful thought or imagination even without desiring it; and **desiderium,** i.e. the desire for what is sinful. I sound even more reprehensible in Latin.

Geoff (and, to be clear with myself, his WIFE) live in a beautiful two story in historic Oak Park. There is no street parking, so I leave my car in the public parking lot of a building up the block for a mere $15. So we are beginning already with the little machinations of protective camouflage; I do not park in the driveway of Geoff's house, nor do I enter the building's front entrance, but rather the back door. The service entrance. After all, I am here to service him, if he is so inclined.

The house, while pure arts and crafts on the outside, is like a contemporary art gallery inside. White walls, minimal furniture in chrome and leather and dark woods, and a truly eclectic but impressive collection of both paintings and modern sculpture. I spot an early Miró, a Hopper, and a pencil sketch that I am pretty sure is a Picasso, as well as a huge felted piece by Calman Shemi, and a small Vasarely, tiny halogen pinspots illuminating everything perfectly. An abstracted nude bronze languishes on a black granite pedestal. And that is just in the formal entrance and living room. But even at this first glance, I can see that while it is the antithesis of my own apartment and style, I like it, and am intrigued about the rest of the place.

Geoff is casual in linen slacks and a button-down shirt of woven olive green, with the hint of a white T-shirt visible from the unbuttoned collar. He looks happy to see me. Takes my coat. Gives me the grand tour of the house. These old places are always so deceiving, they look small on the outside, but seem endlessly huge inside. Through the aforementioned living room to one side is the den, wood paneling and shelving, built-in entertainment cabinet, eggplant purple chenille couch and a strange green velvet chair with matching ottoman. Leather tile flooring, which is about the coolest thing I could imagine. Through the other side of the living room is the dining room, done in an Asian style, oval table of a heavily lacquered wood, black chairs with deep red upholstery, a sideboard which looks to be an antique, inlaid with an intricate pattern in ivory and abalone, a huge pair of verdigris bronze dragons flanking it ominously. In the center of the table, a tall stem of white orchids, growing like a miracle of weightless gravity from a wide shallow dish. The kitchen is surprisingly small, and seems to contain what must be the original cabinetry, green granite countertops, brushed stainless appliances.

The back hall serves as pantry space and access to both backyard and basement (it was through this hall that I had originally entered), as well as having a narrow staircase to the second floor. A door at the end of this hall leads into a powder room, and a second door just to the right leads back into the den. The finished basement seems to be used only for working out; there is a treadmill, a recumbent bicycle machine and some free weights, all facing a television which is mounted to the ceiling.

Behind a wall there is storage, the usual furnace and air-conditioning equipment, and what appears to be an enormous side-by-side refrigerator, which turns out to be climate-controlled wine storage.

Upstairs, Geoff takes me first to the large master bedroom suite. There is a fireplace, a small sitting area and dueling walk-in closets, old architectural prints on the walls. I had no idea there were so many shades of beige. The bathroom is surprisingly girly, a big tub with elaborate arrangements of bathing products, a separate shower in travertine marble, the seemingly ubiquitous double sinks with his and hers accoutrements. But the cabinets are sort of faux baroque, there is a huge dried flower arrangement over the door, peach hand towels trimmed in lace. I am having a difficult time picturing Geoff in here. Across the hall, an afterthought of a guest room and guest bathroom, functional, but surprisingly underdone considering the care with which the rest of the house has clearly been designed. Next to the guest room, an office—obviously Geoff's—big antique roll-top desk with one of those sleek little computers that seem too fragile to be useful. Tall, deep, leather desk chair that calls to me to sit in it and spin around. Except that I am a grown up. Sort of. A battered leather love seat that was apparently his first major purchase out of law school. His diplomas from NYU and Columbia, old black-and-white family pictures.

Throughout the house there is almost too much art to describe, and while I am no expert, I know I saw a Pollock, another Miró, a Chagall, a Basquiat, and two stunning small pieces by Mexican surrealist Remedios Varo, as well as several pieces which I thought I might recognize but couldn't find names for. Still, there is an air of serenity and open space about the whole place. Everything seems to have been chosen out of genuine admiration, as opposed to "smart acquisition." Back downstairs, Geoff makes me a drink, and we sit side by side on the purple couch, facing each other.

Have you ever noticed how the discussions you have with

someone you are interested in are never terribly interesting to anyone but you? You know that you are having this great time chatting with someone, you know that the conversation is easy and pleasant and that there is laughter and honesty, and that the nature of the dialogue makes you believe with your whole heart that this is a person with whom you have significant connection. But if you were to repeat the discussion word for word, anyone else would be bored to tears. Suffice it to say, Geoff and I talk for some two-and-a-half hours about life and family and history and current events and literature and movies. Some of the older art pieces were from his mother's collection, he got his passion for it from her. The love of fine wine he got from his dad. Both of his parents passed away when he was in his forties. He has one surviving sibling, an older sister who lives with her husband in the family home they grew up in, back in Connecticut, and two deceased siblings, a younger sister who recently passed away from breast cancer, and an older brother who was killed in Vietnam. Eventually we get around to marriage.

His first marriage, to his college sweetheart, lasted fifteen years, and ended badly due to mutual serial adultery, a fierce work ethic (his) and a small addiction to painkillers (hers). In a terribly "it only happens in the movies" way, he came home early one afternoon to pick up a brief he had forgotten, and caught her in bed with the neighbor's husband. Two divorces ensued, and once final, the adulterers married. The details about the two children from this first union, both daughters, neither of whom I had been previously aware of, bring a tear to my eye. The older daughter, three years older than myself, had effectively never forgiven him for leaving her mother, and had asked that he allow her stepfather to legally adopt her when she was sixteen. They had barely spoken since, and all he knew of her was that she was currently living with her lesbian partner somewhere in Oregon. His younger daughter, a year my junior, had been born severely retarded, and had lived her whole life in a facility near his ex-wife and her husband outside of Boston.

It was shortly after the divorce that a case brought him to Chicago and connected him with my dad, who was opposing counsel. Impressed with each other, and discovering a mutual love of both good whiskey and a lively game of squash, my father persuaded him to move here full-time and join the firm. For a while, apparently, he was the toast of their social set; after all, it isn't every day that an eligible thirty-eight-year-old lawyer moves to town. He bought the house two years later—apparently it was a mess—and spent ten years fixing it up himself. After a year on the dating-go-round, he embarked on several long-term relationships, one of which involved living with a woman for five years before she left him. He didn't say why. He and Sandra were fixed up on a blind date by a mutual friend, were engaged within six months, married within the year. They have been married for eleven years, which means that actually, Mark and I have them beat as to total time together.

We share the embarrassing secrets, admit to faults, and make each other laugh. We are neither of us happy or fulfilled in our relationships, nor miserable enough to be actively seeking a way out. It may seem cold and calculated, immoral or unethical, or just plain mean, but there it is. Sometimes it isn't about the big things, just years of little things that add up to apathy. We aren't two soul mates trapped in cruel loveless marriages to evil spouses. We aren't being physically, verbally or psychologically abused. Geoff is very clear about how hard he has worked over the years to stop being the guy he was in his first marriage, and that while he is obviously imperfect, the semi-compulsive cheater he was in his youth is long gone. Mark and I are going the therapy route, to little avail, Geoff and Sandra went for a brief time a few years ago, and it nearly ended their relationship. Geoff doesn't say whether that might not have been a better option. We are simple and frank about where we are in our respective lives.

Then we are silent.

"Is this okay?" he asks me, a hand lightly on my shoulder.

"Yes, it is," I reply, suddenly surprisingly calm.

When Geoff leans toward me, my whole spirit moves forward toward him, utterly open. And then he kisses me.

Geoffrey M. Fahl, Esq. is kissing me. And I like it.

First kisses are without a doubt the most intoxicating feeling in the whole world. Better than any drug, better than any wine, the most powerful and mysterious Magick. I read an article once about relationships, and it contained the results of a poll of people in serious relationships of anywhere from one year to fifty years. The only thing that all these people agreed on was that the thing they miss most about being single is first kisses. All of the anticipation that leads up to that moment, the combination of nervousness, excitement, lust, fear, exhilaration, the moment your lips first touch the lips of someone else is a spark to the fuse. When Geoff reaches for me, when his lips touch mine, softly closed at first, then with increasing pressure, until our tongues begin to make their timid way into acquaintance, I have a feeling of the most sublime, earth-shaking wonder. It actually occurs to me that I should will myself into instantaneous death this very moment, for nothing in the world will ever feel this good again. But then he kisses me a second time, and surpasses the first, and then the kisses take a life of their own, each one escalating in intensity, duration, and divine sensation until I think my head may very well explode under the overloaded strain of so much perfect pleasure.

I can't tell you now how long we kissed, there on his couch, only that it felt at once endless and brief. I can't recall the exact moment we came into mutual awareness that we were both possessed of hands, only that once we began touching, everywhere a hand was placed was glad of the connection. It was like dreaming, everything in the world was soft focus except for the razor-sharp connections of lips and teeth and palms and fingers. Things intensify to near madness of pace and fury, then there is a gradual denouement to slow exploration. There are times of shocking sexual fierceness, and just as quickly a sense of playful innocence. And after what might have been an hour, or only ten minutes, Geoff pulls back.

"Either we should have another drink and go straight to hell, or maybe we should stop."

Straight to hell. There is that sinning thing again.

"I suppose that is for you to decide. I am fine to continue, drink or no, or to leave, whichever will make you happiest."

"I think maybe it will be smarter for you to go."

Yeah, right.

"If you like." I am calm. I have been here before. I get off the couch, straighten my clothes, push my hair off my face. Geoff stands and takes me in his arms and holds me, swaying slightly. Then he kisses my forehead right at my hairline, and I can feel him inhale the scent of my hair. I allow the touch to pull my face up to meet his, look deep into his eyes, and smile softly. He leans in and kisses me on the mouth. The kiss gets deeper, and I allow my hands to run down the length of his back to rest lightly at the top of his buttocks. He begins to kiss my neck and I whisper in his ear.

"Or you could just take me to bed."

He looks at me, nods, takes my hand and leads me up the narrow staircase to the bedroom.

There will be times when I will describe for you in voyeuristic detail the activities of my lovers and me. I will give all the ammunition for your own imaginings and rememberings that you could possibly need for a vicarious thrill. But this is not one of those times. For the first time you make love with anyone is as sacred as your very first time, and belongs to the two of you only. It would cheapen it to try to put into words what goes on in those minutes together. I will say only this. It was the most amazing two hours I had ever spent with anyone, and every caress, every sensation, every shared breath or sweet sound is burned into my brain like a memory tattoo, and I will be forever grateful to the universe for allowing me to have them. As Shakespeare said, the rest is silence.

chapter 3

QUESTION OF THE DAY

If someone tells you they are a really bad liar, how can you believe them?

I am a good liar. A very good liar. And it is a good thing, because I am having an affair. At least, I think I am having an affair, it is somewhat unclear at the moment.

Geoff and I have just spent a lovely couple of hours in his well-appointed bedroom, alternately making love and talking and laughing and cuddling as if we have been lovers forever. It is our second "date," ten days after the first night, and in a strange déjà vu, we are having the same conversation we had ten days ago. They are temporarily interchangeable, so for the sake of time, assume them identical, second verse same as the first, and they go a little something like this: I said I could spend the night if he wanted me to, and he said he didn't think that was a good idea.

"This may never happen again." Which is not exactly the

most romantic way to begin a post-coital chat, but I couldn't blame him for his paranoia.

"It's okay," I replied understandingly.

"I mean it was wonderful, and special, and I like you very much, you are a good friend and I am attracted to you, but it is very complicated and not a good idea, and if anyone found out there are all sorts of repercussions...." I placed a finger gently on his lips.

"Darlin', it's okay. If it never happens again, I will be always fond of this memory. And if it does, we will deal with that when it happens. No worries."

"Thank you."

"Thank you." And then he kissed me again, and rose naked to go to the bathroom.

I am really liking his body, which is interesting because it isn't particularly notable. He is not terribly tall, probably only five-nine or ten, thin, with not much definition between shoulders and waist, narrow hips, slim legs. Great hands, with long, tapered fingers, and truly lovely feet, which, if you knew me, is a ridiculously monumental thing to say, because I hate all feet, including my own. A light dusting of gray hair mostly on his chest, but with one of those sexy trails of down on his flat stomach, really great ass, and (here is where that voyeuristic thing is kicking in for you), the prettiest, most perfect cock I have ever seen. Long, straight, smooth, pink, perfectly centered with no pull to the right or left, nestled in a thatch of very thick dark hair, over tight, smallish balls. A paragon of a penis. Not so big as to be uncomfortable or freakish, but large enough to announce its presence with authority. Sublime ratio of length to girth. A well-shaped head with a gentle flare, not too veiny, no odd curves. He could make a fortune as a dildo model. I do not mention this to him. I do, however, rejoice in looking at his naked ease as he returns to the bedroom and begins dressing, despite my smiling attempts to get him to come back to the bed. He leans over and kisses my forehead and leaves to fetch us cold cans of fizzy lime-flavored water. I get up, get dressed, feel the pleasant achy emptiness between my legs and meet him in the den for a quick drink and an illicit, slightly stale cigarette from his secret stash. We are still easy together, with that little hum that comes from truly earth-shaking sex, and soon I rise to leave.

"Thank you for another truly lovely evening." He is holding me gently at the side door.

"Thank you, this was really wonderful," I reply, thinking that I could be quickly persuaded back to the bedroom.

"I'll talk to you soon, we'll have dinner or something."

"I would love that."

"Get home safe."

"Of course. Good night…"

He kisses me softly. And I leave.

This is how things go. But here is where we diverge on what happens after.

Now, after the first night, it went a little something like this…

BACKSTORY

On the ride home, my head is spinning. I am giddy. I can still feel his lips on mine, I can still taste him, I can still feel his body beneath my touch, I can smell him on my skin. I have never been so sated. He is, without question, the best lover I have ever had. And now I am weeping, hot salty tears staining my cheeks, guttural sobs filling the car. For what I have done and felt tonight cannot be taken back, cannot be erased. And for the first time I am afraid.

I am afraid he won't call.

I am afraid Mark will find out.

I am afraid my parents will find out.

I am afraid that no man will ever make love to me like that ever again.

I am afraid that a gauntlet has been thrown down in front of my feet, and the challenger is me.

I am afraid that it will become a sordid affair.

I am more afraid that it won't.

Stacey Ballis

Deep breath. You are just a normal, human girl-person in a weird place, and you have just had two of the best evenings of your entire life, however morally ambiguous. Be Scarlett O'Hara for a night, and think about it all tomorrow. Because tonight, you were electric. And you got everything you wanted and more. Relish it the tiniest bit. Tomorrow is another day.

I get home, wash the tear trails off my face, and look at myself in the mirror. Despite the crying jag, I look pleasantly rumpled. There is a sparkle in my eyes, and a flush to my skin that has been gone so long, I had stopped noticing. I get undressed, and into my bathrobe. I know I should shower, but I cannot bring myself to wash Geoff away, not quite yet. I know I won't find sleep for some time, not with my head so full, and my publisher called yesterday wanting an ETA on my next book, so I retreat to my office, turn on the computer. One good thing about whatever this is, it serves as intriguing inspiration for the work.

The screen jumps to life. Microsoft Word loads automatically. The clear blank digital page appears. I re-read the piece from last night, pleased with it as a starting place, pleased with tonight as a starting place. I think about what has happened between us, the move forward, the inexplicable connection I feel to him, my own unconscionable lack of remorse.

Next Steps

a woman in purgatory
may see heaven
and not enter

a woman in hell
may have heaven in her hands
and not feel it

a woman in heaven
knows what she has
and how to keep it

a woman on earth
will extend her wild grasp for heaven or hell or purgatory

just to feel something

women want out loud
our need screams silent in our ears
we cannot hear reason
we make such elaborate plans to be casual
take such pains
to be quiet

we are such liars

the ritual expands exponentially
shower, lotions, oils, scent
carefully chosen clothes
painstaking application of makeup
tedious management of hair

all for the
what if
that lingered in the air
the
perhaps
that haunted the dreams
the sudden anticipated sweetness
on lips unkissed

"Thank you for the distraction."
was how it was left
explained
excused

I had never wanted to be a distraction
unwieldy
unwelcome

and yet

I wanted to drive him to distraction

at eighty miles an hour
windows down
radio loud
on a black stretch of highway
with no destination
other than
a beginning

because it somehow makes sense
in its insanity
the very reasons to turn
to flee
make it okay
because life is complex
ridiculous
messy
difficult
wonderful
because we are good together in spite of ourselves

It goes on for three more pages like that, but I am going to try to be good about not inundating you with every little word that comes out of me—you get the general idea. It does not make me feel better, this poem. In some ways it makes me feel worse. Because it is, at its core, something of a false attempt to be what I have claimed to be. I was never good at potential. I always turn a little bit of potential into a whole lot of fantasy. And then I crash into reality and get bruised. I look over the words, which, as always, have come out of me mostly of their own accord, channeled through me from somewhere else, and I hear the self-consciousness in them. The unwillingness to admit that despite what I have said about welcoming the impermanence inherent in what was begun, it is not what I want. I want the fantasy, the fairy tale. I want to fall in love, and have someone fall in love with me, and live out our happy years together.

Of course I also want to win the lottery, get tenure, write an inau-

gural poem for someone I really want to be president, have a late onset growth spurt getting me to my true height of five-eight, and learn to speak Italian one night in my sleep. It is good to want things.

I look over the two poems back to back, and realize that what has begun is a journal. I date them like diary entries, save them as one file, and shut down my computer. Maybe I'll pitch it to my editor as a possible next book, the Diary Poems. Journaltry. It is a thought. It is one of too many thoughts.

I do not shower after all, but retreat to the bed in the cocoon of Geoff's cologne, which lingers on my skin, and sleep, dreamless.

Meanwhile, back in the real world...

Maudlin, isn't it? Whiny, boring, self-indulgent, self-important, crapola. Today I am a new woman. Today I am not paying attention. Today I am purposely ignoring all that romantic idiocy I am so prone to, and enjoying the wicked pleasure of being a bad girl. I am having an affair, a deliciously illicit relationship, sort of, with a man who is very, very wrong for me. The level of my own excitement surprises me. I cannot stop smiling.

A week went by after that first night, and I got over my initial sadness, let go of my guilt, and chalked it up to a strange and wonderful little memory. I tried not to think about it, and went on with my days, teaching, editing the book, hanging out with friends. And then he called. And we made plans for dinner a few nights later (both spouses conveniently out of town yet again, and you thought it was a bad thing to be married to someone who travels for work all the time), a charming little French bistro located two blocks from his place. We sat over pastis and shared a salad, and ate lightly grilled chicken paillard with lemon and herbs, and strawberries macerated in eau de vie, and talk-talk-talked for nearly two hours until there was nothing left to say, and then walked back to his house.

Here is the couch. And here is the kissing, as powerful in its impact as those first kisses of ten days ago. The quickening, the escalation, the rise, the move to the bedroom. I cannot get his clothes off fast enough, cannot keep my hands and my mouth from his skin, cannot ever remember a time I felt such urgency, such overwhelming need. We sprawl across the bed, luxuriate in each other, there is moaning and gasping and hearts pounding and simultaneous—joyous release. Well, not exactly simultaneous, that really only happens in the movies unless you are both consciously agreeing to attempt it—but damned close for real life, me first and him right on my heels and then truly luscious collapse into entangled bliss of after-glow. He is superhuman. Preternatural. I am the sexiest woman alive. We are nearly ridiculous in our excess. His stomach rum-bles and we giggle, and he strokes my hair and shoulders, and I kiss his chest, and we hold each other tightly and sigh. And soon, much sooner than one would have imagined for a man of fifty-five, he reaches for me again, and it is almost no sooner begun than ended for him.

"I don't know whether I should be embarrassed or impressed with myself!" He is laughing.

"Be impressed, by all means—I certainly am."

"Sorry about that, I just couldn't hold back."

"Nor would I want you to. Makes me feel irresistible."

"That you are."

"I am so glad you noticed."

"I noticed." And with that, he started to notice in very spe-cific ways, and as his grinning face disappeared beneath the cov-ers, I remember thinking that I was a very lucky girl indeed, and then I couldn't think about anything at all.

And now we are back. You have heard what happened next. (I can wait while you return to the top of the chapter if you need to refresh your memory.) The fact that he still didn't want me to stay over was somewhat disappointing, but understandable. A line he said he couldn't cross. I nodded sympathetically. He repeated his mantra about not having expectations. I acqui-esced. After all, I am irresistible. The rest will take care of itself.

In the pale light of my computer this fine early morning, I find that I like tonight's little journal entry much better than the last. It is stronger, which I am. More real, which I am trying to be.

genesis of desire

will my tongue consume
this slender liquid secret
gentle blue burn
in the splintered mind
would your arms around me
ignite or quench
would one kiss extinguish me
one caress
slide of skin off bones
slow dissolve from the me to the we
just a quick dyslexic reverse
does vow
become now
could I stop you
would I want to
can an infant revert to a breathless life
after the first taste of air
and do we struggle together
or does my soul wrestle
isometrically
tell me I trouble you
tell me you think of me
tell me you recognize
the sweet insanity
in what I want
in what I need
in wanting and needing you
to want
to need
this possible festival of moral ambiguity
blinded by the light of the morning

unable to see tomorrow
unwilling to compromise tonight
lost in the blue of your shirt
the blue of your eyes
the blue of the dawn
that comes to us separate but links us together
outlaws in training
renegades in the making
we wait only for the push
to be lawless

Okay, I know I said earlier that I wasn't going to give you every damn thing I write, but I really like this one. And I love that he sparks such words in me. I love that I am feeling inspired to the page by his presence in my life, by my own presence in his bed. I love that he makes me feel so beautiful, so sexy, so completely femme fatale. I always fancied myself as a femme fatale, all mystery, smoky eyes and dark allure. In an odd way, he makes me feel like an adult. I think that making a life with someone you first met as a child, keeps you in some ways a child with them always. But Geoff will never think of me as a child, and I will never think of myself as anything but a full-fledged woman in relation to him.

Mark returns tomorrow. So tonight, I shower, put fresh linens on the bed, hand wash the evening's undergarments to remove telltale signs of misbehavior, check myself thoroughly in the mirror to ensure there are no marks on my skin, no little signposts that announce that someone has been here. I am fresh as a daisy. Outwardly unmarred. And when my husband returns, and asks what I have been doing in his absence, I will lie. Facilely, glibly, utterly sincere, terminally plausible, I am a very good liar.

A very good liar indeed.

And it is a good thing, because I am having an affair. At least, I think I am having an affair, it is somewhat unclear at the moment.

chapter 4

wilting

QUOTE OF THE DAY

All love is sweet,
Given or returned. Common as light is love,
And its familiar voice wearies not ever.
They who inspire it most are fortunate,
As I am now; but those who feel it most
Are happier still.

—Percy Bysshe Shelley
Prometheus Unbound. Act ii. Sc. 5.

Geoff and I are lying entwined on a hammock in the shade of an enormous tree at my parents' weekend place in Wisconsin. The remains of a picnic are strewn around on the ground, a couple of bees drunkenly buzzing around the remnants in the wineglasses. Geoff is aimlessly playing with my hair, my hand is rubbing his chest and stomach, we are half-dozing, and the sun is warm, and the breeze is cool, and there is a small wolverine biting my toes....

And now I am awake. One of the cats is playing in my hair, and the other is nibbling on the part of my left foot which has crept out from under the blankets. I am all twisty inside the sheet like a mummy, and one of my pillows has migrated between my legs, and I kick halfheartedly at the silly feline who has interrupted my lovely dream. She, of course, thinks this means we are going to play, and attacks my foot with even more ferocity, and I try to roll over to get away from the sharp little nips, but the sheet is really wrapped around and under me. I start to squirm around and make little body-hops to try and get the sheet untangled, and it gives too suddenly, and in one large, un-graceful flop I find myself on the floor beside the bed, legs akimbo, with all my bedding sliding on top of me. Since I slept naked, anyone looking at this scene would be presented with the significantly unfortunate sight of my huge, white, bare ass flailing in the morning sunshine. The whiskered monster who started it all jumps on my chest and begins purring loudly. And I start to laugh.

I get up, throw on my robe, and go to the phone where I call information, then dial Geoff's home number. The machine picks up, I leave a brief message and go to get dressed. I regret the message immediately. It wasn't revealing—I really only said hi and that he should call if he wanted—but I wish I hadn't. The dream had been so lovely, the evening that preceded it such a perfect span of hours together; I actually missed him, wanted to hear his voice. But I knew instinctively that I shouldn't have called. It felt like pressure, and if there is one thing a tax lawyer having an extramarital affair with the 20-plus-years-younger married daughter of his business partner cannot stomach, it is pressure. And I don't want to scare him off, I really like the idea that we might be starting something of at least some sustain-ability. Someone to be with on a sort of ongoing basis. Main-tenance, if you get my drift.

I forgot about it in the shower when I stood under the scald-ing water and felt the twinge of my thigh muscles, sore from exuberant sexual escapades. As the hot water made its way over my body, I thought of the previous night, the way he kissed me, the feel of his skin beneath my touch, the way his hands tangled in my hair. I closed my eyes and remembered the low "mmm-mmm-mmm-ing" noises he made while his face was buried between these same thighs, and just the memory makes me so excited that I am able to bring myself off, furtively, very quickly, standing there in the shower, one hand against the cool tile, one foot propped on the side of the tub. It makes me dizzy. He makes me dizzy. Deliciously dizzy.

SIDEBAR

I am assisted in this particular endeavor by the most ingenious toy, a gift from a good friend who knows of my delight with all things bath-related. It is a yellow sponge, spherical, maybe the size of a large soft-ball. Cleverly hidden inside is a small, waterproof, vibrating egg. It is the best sort of toy, one that can hide in plain sight, and perfect for those weekends when the in-laws are visiting, and one only need create an excuse for a shower in order to have some quality time with herself. And while I occasionally make a voyage to The Pleasure Chest to find such items, if you are in search of erotic enhancers of any kind and are too shy to find the nearest adult store, I have to put in a plug for www.goodvibes.com, a really great, easy-to-navigate site, with simple, non-threatening explications of all of their products. They deliver in plain wrapping, and will not sell your information to anyone, nor will you start getting unwelcome mailings or e-mails. Four stars.

After the shower, I call my brother, Adam, to check in on his life.

"Adam Stein."

"That's a very professional way of answering your home phone."

"Sidney! Force of habit, I answer that way all day long at work, it follows me home. How are you?"

"Okay, you?"

"Liar."

"Am not."

"Are too. I am a gajillion miles away and I know you are not okay."

"I'm fine."

"Really? How's Mark?"

"Okay, I am mostly fine."

"See. Told you so. What is going on with him?"

"You know Mark, traveling all the time, I barely see him." Not that I am missing him much, especially these days.

"And when you do see him, is it getting any better?"

"Not really, to be frank."

"Have you talked to Mom and Dad about it?"

"I think they know there is some trouble, but I don't want to have the conversation with Mark, so how can I have it with Mom and Dad?"

"Whatever the right choice is, you will make it, of that I have no doubt. Talked to Naomi lately?" Our older sister has always been something of an enigma to both Adam and me, and the fact that we are so close to each other makes the gap even bigger.

"Not really. You?"

"She called on my birthday, but we ran out of things to say after about five minutes."

"I know. God bless her, I love her, but we have no common ground."

"Exactly. Think she was adopted?"

"Absolutely. Or switched at birth."

"You mean we might have some fabulous funny older sister out there in the world somewhere without a major pole up her ass?"

"Be nice. We love Naomi."

"Especially from so far away."

"Touché. How is everything going for you?"

"Good, busy. Work is crazed, but frankly I prefer it that way. The flat is fine, I don't need to remind you that you still haven't been to see it, all in all, despite the British weather, things are good. No birds at the moment, but a friend is fixing me up next week, so we will see."

"Birds? I'm sorry, did you just refer to women as BIRDS? Out loud?"

"Give a bloke a break, Sid…something has to rub off!"

"I suppose. When are you coming home?"

"Thanksgiving if I can."

"Thank God."

"Sid…"

"Yeah?"

"What are you going to do about the Mark thing? You can't let it go forever."

"I know. I am working through it."

"Mom and Dad will understand. No one will think you are a terrible person, Sid, I know you think you guys are keeping up appearances, but people notice that you aren't so good, you know?"

"I know. I'll figure it out."

"Whatever you decide, you have my support. I just want you to be happy." If he only knew how happy I have been of late….

"Thank you darling. You and Parker both—he tells me once a week to leave Mark." Parker is one of my very best friends, and he and Adam have developed a very interesting relationship.

"How is that sexy animal? You be sure to smack his bottom and give him a big wet smooch from his uncle Adam. And thank him for looking out for you." See what I mean? For a straight boy, Adam is very comfortable with flirting outrageously with all my gay boyfriends, which makes them adore him. He and Parker bonded over drinks one night at my place a few years back, and their interaction with each other is always over-the-top sexual. Parker is secretly dying to get Adam drunk and attempt a temporary conversion, but anyone who has ever met Adam knows one thing. However playful, he is 100% a ladies' man.

"Will do. Take care of you…and thanks for your support. I will keep you posted."

"Do that. Love you much."

"Love you back."

Adam always makes me feel better.

* * *

With a buttered bagel and a cup of tea, I do something I do very rarely these days. I sit in the front room on my big chair with a legal pad, and write longhand. It always seems somehow decadent and ritualistic and ancient to write this way, languid almost. But I am feeling languid this fine spring morning. The writing comes easily, as it seems to do of late, and I ponder the piece only briefly before slipping into a light doze there in the chair, the sunlight on the back of my neck from the window a soothing heat, the pad resting on my lap, my head full of liquid dreams of my lover and his touch and our improbable but no less desirable future together. The phone doesn't wake me, but the sound of my mother's voice leaving a message does.

"Sidney, this is your mother, I just wanted to know if you and Mark were coming for dinner tomorrow, and if it is okay that I have invited the Grossmans, because, you know, David's mother is with them now, and I think they could use a night out, you know how exhausting it is to have the eld- erly around for any length of time, I swear, you know what I always say, just send me off to the ice floes before I become a burden to anyone, I mean, who wants to think of it, God forbid, but you know, I mean it, I do, the first sign of drool- ing, and pack me off somewhere with a bottle of sleeping pills, it seems the only way to have any peace, and I know your brother will fight you on it, but whatever you do, don't let him attempt to take me in, because death by slow starva- tion and burial in dirty laundry would certainly be worse than Alzheimer's, and in any case, it won't matter unless Daddy is still alive, because you know, if he goes before me, I am going with him, I have no intention of being without him for one day on this earth, and if I go first, God willing, what you do with him once I am gone is entirely up to you, as long as you don't let him remarry any of my friends. Any- way, schnookie, we'll see you tomorrow around 5:30, the Grossmans like to eat early, and don't worry about bringing anything, but do ask Mark not to talk about politics, because David is a Republican, and we just need to have a nice meal. Love you."

Vey is mere. I am light-headed on behalf of my mother, who seems to need very little oxygen when speaking, and never ever leaves a message of less than two minutes in duration.

By the time Mark gets home in the early part of the afternoon, I have forgotten all about the regrettable call to Geoff, and while he busies himself unpacking, doing laundry, and re-organizing the materials from his trip, I make light, convivial conversation to keep him company. It doesn't occur to me to think twice when the phone rings, I am expecting to hear from my mother, wondering why I haven't called her back yet.

It is not my mother.

"Sid, it is Geoff." Oh my.

"Hi, how are you?" Trying desperately to sound casual, while Mark, who is always sure it isn't for him, continues his activity nearby.

"I am okay, but listen, you really shouldn't have left a message. What if Sandra had called in from out of town to check the machine?"

"I'm sorry, I didn't think, I just wanted to…" I trailed off. What the hell could I say?

"It's okay, but, I just, I don't think I can do this."

"I am sorry to hear that. But I am sure it couldn't possibly happen again."

"I like you, Sid, I really do, and I am very attracted to you, but this is too complicated, too dangerous. I have been here before, it just isn't a good idea."

"If that is what you think, I mean if you are sure…" I sound light and airy, but there is a lump in my throat. Where is the devil-may-care girl that I was last night?

"It is best. But look, I do think of you as a friend—we can still get together. I'll call you, we'll have a drink or something, okay?" No, it is most certainly not okay.

"Sure thing, that's great." Pants on fire. "Whenever."

"Okay, then. Look, Sidney, last night was really special to me. It isn't about that."

"Of course, I get it. I'll talk to you soon then." I hate this. Mark is looking at me. I make the face of someone who is on the phone with someone irritating who is talking too much, little hand puppet miming flapping jaws, eyes rolling. He laughs. I want to die.

"Okay then, I will talk to you soon." Such relief in his voice that I am not making a fuss.

"All right. Bye now."

"Who was that?" Mark wants to know.

"Risa. Madly in love again, after two dates." My sort-of-friend Risa is best taken in small doses, and Mark hates her, so she is a safe bet.

"Oy. I don't know why you even bother with her. Maybe we should get caller ID so you can avoid her." So helpful, my husband. I am nauseated.

"Maybe. I'll check it out with the phone company. When do you leave again?"

"Monday morning. I'll be back for one night on Wednesday, but gone again Thursday through Saturday. Then, I'll be home for a week or so unless something comes up."

"If you leave me your dry cleaning, I will be sure to get it back for Wednesday."

"Thanks, honey." He kisses my forehead. I am such a thoughtful wife, aren't I?

"I'm going to work for a bit, do you need anything?" I have to get out of the room.

"No, you go ahead."

"Okay, then. I'll be in the office."

"Okay."

I walk to the other end of the apartment, and go into my office and shut the door. I put Janis Ian on the computer CD player, since she is the only one who understands me in these moments of sheer womanly despair, and let myself cry. I am such an idiot. Why the hell did I call him? Why did I not hang up on the machine when he didn't answer? Why can't I just have what I want? When the tears stop, I turn to the computer. I know it will help, but I am uncertain. Sometimes, in moments like these, the work is so raw. I copy this morning's poem into the computer, and the memory of such hopefulness and joy makes my eyes prick with tears again. Why do I care so much? What is he, besides good sex? But I know I will not be able to will myself into resignation right now. I am mythological in my misery. What results is a poem rife with allusions to the ill-fated house of Atreus, and too sad to share with you here.

I am a very blue girl. Midnight blue. Navy blue. I am the blue-black of the moonless Montana sky blue. I am blue like a 2:00 a.m. torch song. I am the blue of the ocean trench, a mile and a half from sunlight, where the pressure is so great and the water so cold that very few creatures can survive. I am blue like Chet's low range, like Patsy's twang, like a bassoon. I am, in case you had not noticed, exceptional in my ability to wallow. And while I am quite certain that I must seem an immoral petulant to you at the moment, I am in all honesty too sad to care much what you may be thinking of me.

While I do have some very minor background as an actor, I know I will not be able to bounce back believably from today's debacle, nor can I hide out in the office for the rest of the evening. So I rely on the oldest, most tried-and-true high school gym class excuse in the universe, and I tell Mark I have PMS and that I am sorry for being cranky. He orders Chinese food to make me feel better, but gets the order just wrong enough that it only bothers me. I take a long bath, go to bed early, and when he tries to snuggle up behind me, I pretend to be asleep, and roll away from him.

chapter 5

things fall apart, or:
how i became a parrot

FACT OF THE DAY

Boredom can lead to madness in parrots. When caged by themselves and neglected for long periods of time, these intelligent, sociable birds can easily become mentally ill. Many inflict wounds upon themselves, develop strange tics, and rip out their own feathers. The birds need constant interaction, affection, and mental stimulation. Should a neglected parrot go mad, there is little that can be done to restore it to normalcy. In England, there are "mental institutions" for such unfortunate creatures.

I need to go back. You need me to go back before this becomes too unforgivable. I need to give you the pertinent facts so that you are fully informed as you make your personal judgments. Plus, the story won't make much sense unless you get some sense of the history. Or rather, herstory, as it were.

SIDEBAR

Even though I know it is ultimately inconsequential what you may think of me, I also know that I want you to continue to pay attention. Well, more than that, I want you to like me. It won't kill me if you don't like me, plenty of people don't, that is the way of the world. And maybe it isn't even so much like as it is understand. Comprehend. See, the thing about such situations, as far as my experience goes, is that nothing is original. None of my problems or circumstances is the first of their kind, just new to me. Whenever I have some problem or make some mistake, I am sure I am the one and only person to have faced it. But then I will share it with a friend or colleague, and they will commiserate and tell me about when they experienced much the same thing, or when their best friend did, and then at least I am not the biggest idiot in the world, just one of many. This makes me feel better. So I want to be sure that I present all the facts, in my own utterly subjective objectivity, so that if you have been here, you will empathize, and if not, perhaps you may at the very least sympathize the smallest bit. Then again, you may very well write me off entirely, which is your absolute prerogative to do, but I will have to warn you that coming up later is some stuff you might want to stick around for. Can't reveal too much, but thought you might want to be aware.

Meanwhile, back at Hester Prynne's house...

So, in light of my current mishegoss, I did a little bit of research, and as it turns out, there is some very interesting information out there regarding marriage. And somewhat surprisingly, when it comes to infidelity, not only are women as likely to cheat as men, the women who are MOST likely to commit adultery are in their 30s, well-educated, professional women without children. I am officially a statistic.

And which is worse, I am a cliché as well. Let me show you what I mean...

Mark and I met at Northwestern. It was love at second meeting. First meeting was when we accidentally slammed into each other while both walking backward, looking at the sweeping architecture of the lakeside campus during the pre-freshman visitation weekend. I knocked the breath out of him. His hand-me-down briefcase left a scratch on my arm. We both blushed, mumbled apologies, and turned to flee. The second meeting was when we slammed into each other again, in nearly the same spot, both of us reading course syllabi and walking at the same time. This time, in true sit-com fashion, all the armloads of shiny new books and papers flew into the air, and landed in a jumbled mess on the grass. We looked up with fire in our eyes, recognized each other, and began to laugh.

"We have to stop bumping into each other like this," Mark said, shyly, but with a very nice smile. I laughed.

"Perhaps we should trade schedule information so that we can avoid each other."

"Or maybe we should just walk everywhere side by side." It was the most romantic thing anyone had ever said to me. It turns out it was the most romantic thing Mark had ever said, period. He helped me gather my stuff. He offered to carry my books. We went to the snack bar in the student union and shared a wickedly decadent chocolate malt. Apparently the blow had jarred us back to 1954. And we talked for hours. Boy did we talk.

We couldn't have been more different, Mark and I. I was the city girl, streetwise, jaded. I had been bribed out of going to the East Coast for college with a shiny new Honda and a shared apartment off campus, since my parents wanted to keep me nearby. Mark was from a tiny town in southern Iowa and had a scholarship and work study to afford his dream of a real university. I was the short, round, loudmouthed Jewess from hell, and Mark was a tall, thin, fair Episcopalian. I was of solid Russian peasant stock, Mark was from impoverished aristocratic Aryan bloodlines. I had spent most of my high school days cutting class, getting high and sleeping around. Mark hadn't ever done a drug, had gotten drunk for the first time graduation night, was a straight A student, had one girlfriend from the time he was in seventh grade (and when he broke up with her before leaving for college, everyone in town gave him the cold shoulder).

We, of course, fell madly in love. I made him feel worldly, he made me feel safe. I taught him about city life, and he gave me a reason to stop partying. I was the second girl he had slept with—the first had made him wait till junior prom, and they hadn't ever had much opportunity to have sex in novel places like beds—so I introduced him to all sorts of new activities. He was a decent learner, if a bit plodding, but what we lacked in lustful electricity we made up for with intellectual compatibility. Surprising, as I was the artsy English major (with a minor in theatre), hoping to have a career in writing and teaching, and he was the serious Business and Marketing guy, taking classes like Economics and Finance while I took The Victorian Poets and Novels by 20th Century African-American Women. He essentially moved out of his dorm room and into my apartment within a few months. We were one of those "old married couples" you see on campuses…nineteen years old with a five-year plan and a shared pet. Well, two shared pets…the aforementioned cats, adopted in honor of our three-month anniversary. Sisters, from a litter of a friend's cat, one smoky gray, the other a calico, named Charlotte and Emily (Brontë, of course, pretentious as I wanted to be in those days).

We did what very few kids actually do these days, we stuck it out. We didn't fight, but we weren't those sickeningly sweet "Pookie Bear" and "Sugar Muffin" types either. We played house. We had dinner parties. We didn't cheat. We were solid and stable, and everyone knew we were destined for one another. We got engaged a couple of months after graduation, and decided to wait until we were done with graduate school before taking the plunge. A little over two years later, the ink barely dry on one MFA in Writing (mine) and one MBA in Marketing (his), we gathered friends and family for a small late-morning ceremony at Café Brauer near the Lincoln Park Zoo, followed by a lovely light luncheon, gallons of champagne and dancing. Mark's folks gamely allowed my cousins to hoist them up on chairs during the horah, but my new mother-in-law protested vociferously of her impending bilious attack, so it didn't last long. We honeymooned at the Four Seasons in a ridiculous suite for five days, courtesy of my parents, pretended to be tourists in our own fair city, and reported to work the following Monday like good little campers.

I convinced myself that a lot of people probably make love on their wedding night with a morose sense of obligation. Especially these days, when we all live together for years before taking those vows. Right?

We were also fine, if a little boring, during the four years I spent teaching composition and drama at a Montessori School near our apartment. I was working a great deal, had published several individual poems and two short stories in literary journals and magazines, and had put out a limited run of my first anthology with a small local press. I taught or wrote during the day while Mark was at his office, doing some incomprehensible marketing research hoo-ha, and when he got home we would make dinner and watch TV or read until bedtime. Four years. It was at once strangely quick and interminable.

And then it happened.

Columbia College called me looking for someone to fill in for their Beginning Poetry Workshop professor, who was taking a semester-long sabbatical, ostensibly to complete a major research text on Pablo Neruda, but actually to go through intensive rehab for alcoholism. I accepted the job immediately, began poring through my library to come up with an appropriate syllabus, gave notice at school, and ran round in a state of heightened glee for three weeks before classes started.

When I started teaching at Columbia, everything changed. Firstly, I was suddenly surrounded by interesting, articulate, intelligent colleagues and graduate students who reminded me that I love nothing more than long, passionate conversation. And since my classes and office hours were all in the afternoons, my life as a consummate night owl returned with a vengeance. Suddenly there were all these places to go, people to meet, smoky bars to sit in—the social butterfly that I had been in my reckless youth was resurrected, older, wiser, but full of life. I was quickly adopted by the theatre department, having been an occasional actor in high school and college, and since Columbia pulls their part-time staff from the best and brightest of the formidable Chicago theatre community, I quickly found myself in a whirlwind of free tickets, opening night invitations, and an ever-growing circle of friends. Mark, who got up at 5:30 in the morning to go to work, did not partake much in my new life. But he gamely sent me off to my soirees with good wishes and requested I try not to wake him up arriving home in the wee hours. I did my best. By the end of the semester I was offered a more permanent associate professor position, tracking between the English Department where I taught Beginning Poetry Workshop and Advanced Poetry Seminar, and the Theatre Department where I co-taught a course on Classical Dramatic Texts (I covered the analysis work while my professional actor co-teacher covered the acting basics).

Then Mark too got a fabulous new job. Regional Account Representative for the Midwest. It was a big promotion, with a lot more money. It required that he travel 75 percent of the time. They tried in the beginning to make his trips manageable, gone Monday-Friday, home for the weekends, but since we didn't have kids, he was always needing to accommodate someone else's calendar of recitals and soccer games and first communions so often he was on the road for weeks in a row, home for a day or two, then gone again. To be frank, I didn't really miss him. It was great to not have to worry about checking in. I could just live my life without worry or obligation. And to be more frank, I don't think he really missed me. Hotels are always clean, and I am at best an indifferent housekeeper. Hotel beds don't come home smelling of smoke and beer at 2:00 a.m. and hog the covers.

Don't get me wrong, there was—there is—much love between us. But it has morphed into a love of stability and companionship and history. What little passion we had once had for each other has long gone, and we have gone months at a time barely noticing that we can't remember the last time we made love. We are affectionate platonics. We are like brother and sister. We are in big trouble, and too protective of each other to say anything out loud. We aren't miserable, we just aren't happy. And we aren't really together that much, so it didn't used to seem to matter.

But it is starting to matter. It is starting to matter very much indeed.

We have our routine, which includes a serious discussion of something unpleasant about every four months, but other than that, we live in an easy stupor. I have my life, he has his, we overlap occasionally and no one asks questions. All the parents gave up on asking for grandkids the Thanksgiving Mark's mother asked me when she could expect a little bundle from us, and I replied (having indulged in several glasses of sherry) that as soon as I finished raising her son to do things like dress appropriately for special occasions, not play with his food, and to wash his whiskers out of the sink after he shaved, I would get right on spawning some grandchildren for her. No one was amused, and Mark, rightly so, gave me the very cold shoulder for the rest of the night.

After a while it became clear that I was no longer particularly attracted to my husband physically. Our sex life had gotten into the area of dull repetition very early for young people, so by the time we actually got married it was something we did less and less. With Mark on the road all the time, and me so busy with my new life, and the unspoken problems we were having, what little passion there was in me for him dried up completely. And his seeming inability or lack of desire to pay attention to my wants and needs and likes and dislikes didn't help. When he bothered to try and initiate sex, he invariably picked the wrong time, or the wrong way. More and more I found myself turning him down, and so he started asking less and less.

This is how we get into unfortunate and dangerous territory. The complete lack of sexual attraction to my husband did not mean a lack of sex drive. Again, in the first few years of our marriage, it wasn't such a big deal. When teaching elementary school, one is not exactly tempted by one's colleagues, and the schedule keeps you too exhausted to be out meeting people who might be intriguing. Teaching on the post-secondary level, however, does both of those things most handily, and while I have always thought of myself as a natural monogamist, recently I have found myself terribly tempted to stray. I certainly have rediscovered my ability to flirt, and this flirting now and again achieves some specific results. I have turned down advances from such sundry gents as a dreamy grad student from the comparative literature department, a student's father, and an out-of-town actor starring in a friend's show. But each time it was harder and harder to say no, and since we are in confessional mode, I did let the actor kiss me for about three minutes before stopping him. I was horribly guilty about all of these incidents, and would, for a time after, attempt to be more attentive to my husband whom I very genuinely loved, even if I suspected I had fallen out of love with him.

After a time we admitted that things seemed to be not so good between us. We figured growing pains, we had been together so long, we had met when we were so young, we just needed help finding out how to relate to one another better based on who we had become. So we did what many couples do, we began marital therapy. We sit once a week or so, depending on Mark's travel calendar, for one hour in Dr. Janssen's beige and benign office and talk pretty honestly about what is wrong with our marriage. The problem is of course that I am not honest about the current situation with Geoff. Mark talks a lot about his feelings of not knowing who he is, and trying to find out without my pressuring him to be what I want him to be. I do admit to sexual thoughts about other men when we are discussing the fact that we have entirely stopped having sex. And I really do mean entirely. At last count, it has been about a year and a half or so since we have made love. Time does fly. Mark never talks about other women. I have no idea if he has ever cheated on me and really do not care to know. Nor will I litanize his faults here, the things I dump on him in the sessions, the things he does that make me crazy, the ways he proves his indifference. The point is not to provide some sort of magical blend of facts that excuse my current behavior—it doesn't exist.

I know in most books the hapless heroine is entrenched in some truly awful marriage, which means you root for her infidelity as if it isn't reprehensible. But it is. I am. And which is worse, I do not feel badly. I do not have remorse. I do not regret what I have done, only that it appears to be over, and in my heart, I want more. I am thirty-two years old. I have spent most of the last fourteen years of my life with Mark. I am only now coming to the courage to say that I have not been happy for a reasonably significant number of those years. I think that the therapy is teaching me that we will never be fixed, and that Mark will never be able to be a partner for me in the ways that are most important. And this, this ended-too-soon-whatever-this-is-or-was, made me happy for a time. Deep down blissfully happy. And it is not over by a long shot.

After all, I am irresistible, didn't he say so himself?

I will not sit back and become some deranged parrot, plucking my own feathers out from spite and boredom. I crave attention, affection, romance, passion. Mark and I fit like old sweatpants. Very comfortable, suitable only for relaxing at home, and not remotely sexy. Be honest. When was the last time you looked at your partner or spouse in those stained and faded sweats with the baggy knees and the shot elastic and thought "Oh yeah, baby, I want you so bad…?" Our whole marriage has become those pants. The same qualities Mark possessed which troubled me in the early days of our living together, the ones I naively assumed would disappear with time and maturity, they persist. The absence of social graces which embarrassed me once upon a time, mortify me now, and I find him frequently inexcusable in his total lack of tact. His inability to be the tiniest bit romantic, to be at all in tune with who I am and what I want, by degrees we have smothered this union, barely aware of its passing. And now there is someone who has come into my life with fire and intelligence and an astounding inherent ability to do and say all the right things, and I have no intention of letting him go this easily.

Does it make me wrong? You betcha.

Does it make me immoral? More than a little.

Does it make me human? Abso-fuckin-lutely.

You want to know why I am so committed to this affair, and so willing to give up on my marriage? Well, so do I, believe me, so do I.

eden falling

if I offer you the apple of my heart
and you share with me
that fine sweet fruit
we will be cast out of the garden
to forge our way
in the cold world

but the knowledge will fill us up
keep us from harm
keep us from aching blindness

the safety of ignorance
isn't bliss
but brain fog
and in that darkness
there is no truth

so I choose instead
these open eyes
these open arms

awaiting the rapture
of our mutual exile

chapter 6

SONG OF THE DAY

I know what it means to be lonely
And I know what it means to be free
Now I want to know how to love you
Return to me
Return to me
I am here calling the wind
I am here calling your name
I am here calling you back
Return to me
Return to me

—October Project

So I take the bull by the horns. I wait a week, and then send Geoff a chatty little e-mail about some article I had read. He replies, equally chatty, having read the same article. I mention a night off. He mentions a little Cuban joint in Little Village which he loves, but which Sandra is too "suburban scared" to go to. Mark is going to be in town, but I am not really thinking about it. We make plans for dinner. And I decide to turn up the heat a notch. I get my hair cut and make my poor hairdresser blow it dry straight. This is a Herculean feat taking no less than forty-eight minutes, but the results are amazing. Perfectly straight, shiny, glossy, soft and silky with the slightest insouciant flip at the bottom. Pet me hair. Breck Girl hair. I go for a look of extremes, guaranteed to throw him off balance. Smoky, slightly smudged eye makeup with heavy mascara, but lightly flushed pink cheeks and just a nude gloss on the lips. Deep blue men's oxford with French cuffs, but unbuttoned to reveal ample cleavage. Simple, straight, tailored black pinstripe skirt, very business chic, and tall lace-up black boots that scream high-priced dominatrix. My sassy new hair is held away from my face on one side with a sweet little barrette of pewter flowers. My nails are Jungle Red. I am a mixed message in the flesh…professional and sexy, vampy and innocent, masculine power with feminine underpinnings. Poor thing. He is gonna want me so bad….

We meet at the restaurant, where he orders a half pitcher of margaritas for us to share and an appetizer of queso fundito. He comments on the new hair, and I run my fingers through it to play it up to full effect. I make a great show of the melted cheese, dangling the long strings from above my tilted-back head, and using my tongue to help them into my mouth. Licking my fingers. He is getting glassy-eyed. Boys are so silly when you think of it, how easy it is to push their buttons. By the time we have finished our entrées I know he is mine.

He walks me to my car and hugs me tightly, and I look up at him, still in his embrace, and say in my most husky and seductive voice, "Is Sandra out of town?"

"Yes," he replies, his voice catching a little.

"Do you want company?" I ask. He pulls me closer to him.

"God you make me weak. Yes, I do."

"Meet you there." I kiss him quickly.

SIDEBAR

Ladies, this little trick is pretty easy and guaranteed to give you a touch of the timbre that makes women like Kathleen Turner so smoking hot. When you are talking to the object of your affection, whether on the phone or in person, lower your shoulders. I mean actually push your shoulders downward while you are speaking—it is a surefire way to get

a half-octave or so lower without sounding unnatural. I used this trick
when recording my answering machine message, and in the first week I
got four messages that began "hey sexy," one "hubba hubba, nice mes-
sage," and one "darling, are you getting a cold?" (that was my mother).

Luckily at this hour, Oak Park is a surprisingly quick ride,
so barely twenty minutes later we are in his foyer. I reach over
and take his hand. He squeezes it. I turn to face him, stand on
my tiptoes, lean lightly against him, and kiss him softly on the
mouth. He smiles down at me. We hold hands all the way upstairs to the bedroom, then he turns to me.

"Would it be okay if we just got naked right away?"

He stops my heart, he really does.

"Yes, please." It is all I can muster.

He removes his suit jacket, puts his watch and wedding ring
on the dresser, empties his pockets of wallet and change, crosses
to me and takes me in his arms and begins to kiss me. He is the
best kisser on the planet. The best kisser of all time. I had never
conceived of kisses the likes of which I am now enjoying. Remember what I said about those magical first kisses? Those
nothing-ever-compares kisses? Okay, so while that is USUALLY
the case, clearly I have some wires crossed, because every time
this man puts his lips on mine, I get the same rush, the same
swoon, he has short-circuited my first-kiss pleasure radar, and
now I am all deliciously broken.

We begin to undress each other, a jumble of hands and buttons. His hands in my hair while I kiss his chest, my hands working the buckle of his belt, the zipper of his slacks. We take one
step sideways toward the bed, leaving everything but his cute
blue boxers and my red panties behind us, and he pushes on my
shoulders until I am sitting on the edge of the bed. He kneels
before me like a child in bedtime prayer, helps me slide my lin-
gerie off, and leans in to begin kissing that second mouth with
the same perfect skill as he demonstrated northerly when we
were still vertical. He might have invented this, it is so as-

tounding, so absolutely fresh and new for me. He needs no direction, no guidance, no encouraging words, and the only thing I can say is his name over and over like a mantra, and when I come, I completely lose myself in the waves of pleasure which wash over me. And for the first time in my life, I know what the damned writers always meant about waves of pleasure, because for me, even really great orgasms were more of a big bang, followed by a desperate need to not be touched at all. But this, this exquisite sensation, it is upon me like tide at the Bay of Fundy, rippling through my entire body.

And then the most astounding thing happens.

Instead of stopping, demanding quid pro quo or doing a victory dance like so many men before him…this amazing man beams up at me from between my still quivering legs, kisses the inside of my right thigh, turns his head and rests his cheek there, and very softly, almost imperceptibly, begin to lick me gently. And instead of making me shriek in discomfort and pull away, I find the touch so subtle, it is kind of soothing. And then it is tingly. And then it is really really shockingly fabulous, and then all of a sudden, in a surprising rush, I am coming again, maybe only five minutes after the last time, and it is so sweet and fine that I laugh aloud at the sheer, unexpected joy of it.

He clambers onto the bed, and I shift so that I am lying beside him, realizing that not only are we on top of the covers and not beneath them, and not only is it not dark in the room, but that I haven't for one moment wondered how I looked to him physically, not once thought that I should shift so that my stomach looked flatter. I wasn't scrambling to cover myself with the blankets, I was just lying full out nekkid next to my lover in the astonishingly bright light of the bedside lamp, reveling in sublime satiety. And what is more, I never have with him, not ever, not even our first time. What a rush. I am so pleased that he makes me not care that I feel the immediate need to thank him tangibly, and proceed to give him my super-duper-all-out-deluxe-come-so-hard-you-lose-consciousness blow job.

Ancient Chinese secret. And as this is not a sex manual, I ain't giving up the goods, you ladies will have to find your own secret weapons.

SIDEBAR

If you are looking for a sex manual, by the way, I highly recommend Sex Tips for Straight Women from a Gay Man, *not only for amusing readability, but for really solid, relevant advice. The chapter on hand jobs alone will make any man your slave.*

Geoff is awfully appreciative, and the two of us finally manage to get the covers situated, and snuggle up happily. He smiles down at me, shaking his head.

"I had really only planned for us to have dinner."

"I know, but I am irresistible."

"You are like nuclear power."

I don't exactly know what he means by this, but I take it as a compliment.

"Aren't you gonna tell me this might never happen again?" There is a smirk in my voice and on my face.

"I would, except clearly, I have no idea what is going to happen. Let's just say that we will continue to play it by ear, okay?"

"Okay."

"Now hush, I am an old man, and you have worn me out."

He places a hand on my head and begins to stroke my hair, and I snake my arm around his waist and snuggle very close next to him. We doze lightly, for maybe forty minutes or so, and he wakes me with kisses, and then rolls over and makes love to me in that languid, dreamy way that is usually reserved for the very early morning, except I am not allowed to be with him in the very early morning, so we move it up. We cuddle only briefly after, and our now familiar routine emerges, and within a half an hour, I am dressed, refreshed with sparkling libation, have smoked my one allowable cigarette, kissed my lover goodbye, promised him to drive safely, and left.

I, not wanting to go home and face my husband who might still be awake, head straight to the Four Moon Tavern, do not pass go, do not collect two hundred dollars. The Moon is a lovely little Roscoe Village pub which my theatre friends have introduced me to, half actors and such, half locals, all friendly and warm and casual. Reasonably priced drinks poured with a generous hand, great food, terrific jukebox, comfy back room with couches and tables, pool table up front. In the couple of years I have been coming here I have gotten to know the owners and waitstaff pretty well and feel very much at home. Upon arriving, I find a table of people I know in the back room, order a grilled cheese sandwich with bacon and a cup of their homemade tomato soup, since great sex always makes me hungry for comfort food, and zip into the bathroom to be sure I am not too rumpled. I have a lovely flush in my cheeks, and luckily having temporarily straight hair means that a quick finger-comb has restored it.

Parker shows up unexpectedly with some of his current castmates, and we play catch-up for a bit. Mid-mouthful of hummus he suddenly looks at me and cocks his head.

"What is up with you?"

"What do you mean?" I know what he means, but I am not yet ready to divulge any information about Geoff.

"You look sparkly. Why do you look all sparkly?"

"It is the hair. You know I always feel sassier with straight hair. Makes me all cute." I hate keeping a secret from him, and I know I will eventually come clean, after all, Parker is my best confidant in most matters. But there is something about the secret of this which feels important to maintain, at least for a while longer.

"All right, if you say so, but you have something going on. Is it Mark?"

"Trust me, Mark is not making me remotely sparkly these days."

"Is he in town?"

"Yes."

"Are you here to avoid him?" Parker knows me too well.

"Yes. I know I should have gone home early like a good wife, but these days all he does is mope around the house and complain about being exhausted from all the traveling, and frankly, I am getting less and less patient with him."

"You should end it." Parker is a big fan of making firm decisions.

"You know it isn't that simple. But Adam agrees with you, if that makes you feel better."

"Almost everything about Adam makes me feel better. Does he miss me?"

"Of course, he told me I should spank you and kiss you from him."

"Delicious. Sigh, I do wish they made that model in Gay."

" I know. If it is any consolation, if he were in any way inclined in that direction, I think you would be top on his list."

"Well, that is something."

"It says a lot. He will be in for Thanksgiving, so if you aren't going home to see the folks, we can get together."

"I have shows all weekend, so I will probably just hang out with my aunt for the festivities. Tell that big handsome boy I am his for the rest of the weekend."

"Will do. I am sure he will be thrilled."

"Okay then, I am unfortunately going to abandon you to this fine group of people, and head home. We have a put-in rehearsal tomorrow for an understudy who is going on tomorrow night, so I should get some sleep. Talk to you later?"

"Of course."

"And Sid? Some unsolicited advice?"

"Sure."

"Don't avoid home. If you want to fix it, you have to be there, and if you don't, staying away won't make the end any easier on either of you."

"Point taken."

Parker kisses me, says goodbye to the table, and leaves. I stay for a while, eating and chatting easily with the group, and once I am sure that Mark is deep in REM cycle, I leave and go home. I tiptoe down the hall, and pull the bedroom door closed. I sidle into the bathroom and run a hot bath. I sit in the dark, feeling the slight sting of the water on my bruised sex, chafed and tender from love. I wash the scent of Geoff off my skin, wash our mingled juices of passion off my thighs. It is a mikvah, a sacred cleansing bath that I might be pure enough to sleep in my marital bed. But sleep does not come so easily and I find myself at the computer just as the blue is beginning to brighten in the early morning sky.

the end of days

but oh how redemption
when unexpected
is sweet
for even quicksand
is survivable
if someone will throw you a line

to ask
and be granted
to offer
and be accepted
to want
and be wanted
without the excuses
without the protection
of the little details
that temper reason
for this specific joy
there are no words
yet
our tongues are far from still

but what do you do
with a minor miracle
when it comes to you
without being beckoned
for I did not wish for him
but for the idea of someone else

yet
I know now I wished wrongly
rashly
I did not think it through
did not know what I needed
until it came to me unbidden
snuck into my heart
sideways
found the dusty door in the back
the rusted key on the nail
oiled the lock
turned the knob
entered the chamber
where once a lover reveled briefly
leaving as promised
locking up carefully behind him
kissed my forehead
and was gone

when we leave childhood
the nursery which was our haven
becomes superfluous
and I was a child in his arms
in his love
and when my schooling was over
I left the locked door behind
without even curiosity
or sentiment
pulling me to revisit
the ghosts of joy which lived there

until there was
a new teacher
who made me a child again
in his embrace
a child in the way I trust
that he is safe
that he is for me
because I feel it
because I want it
a child in the way he is best and brightest
without filling out the paperwork
or passing inspection
the way he is innocent until proven guilty
a child in the way I accept him
whatever he has to offer
with complete openness

I know my place in this his world
precarious
and without promise
and I move forward
certain that the universe sends me treasures
that will challenge and delight me
sends me knowledge
that I must have faith in
even when it frightens me
especially when it frightens me

and oh but we are complicated
inconvenient

oh but the world might mock us
misunderstand us
brand us and malign us
and make of us
an object lesson

fuck 'em

it rests between me
and him
and the wide blue sky

I will follow my heart
not because it is safe
but because in its danger
there is truth
I will back these feelings
not because I know that we are perfect
but because we are right
flaws and all
because I prayed for so long
for the idea of someone else
and the gods heard
and sent me him

because logical or not
he is everything I never knew I always wanted

ain't it ironic
ain't it a kick in the head

he called me amazing
compared me to nuclear power
said I made him weak

and I don't know how to tell him
what he does to me
without raising hackles
without causing fear

I would be honest

if I wasn't so certain it would trouble him
make him reconsider

no one ever brought such music out of me with such ease
no one ever seemed to instinctively touch me
exactly when and where and how I need to be touched
no lover ever took me to that plane where you can see the face of
god
no one was ever so devastating
or knew how to balance the exhilarating sexual gymnastics
with the longed-for comfort and caring
how did he know that afterglow is brighter
if he will kiss me on the eyelids
that when loving is paused
a hand in my hair keeps me from floating away into the atmosphere
that sometimes
just his two closed lips
pressed gently against mine
are all I need
to keep my heart beating

he knows
my god he knows

so I say
it can't be purposeless
it can't be wrong
and I will fight for this connection
until I am sure
it is broken
until I am sure
the electricity
is off
until the universe which sent him
takes him back

tells me it is time
time to lock the room again
hang the key beside the door
and let the dust once more have place to light upon

chapter 7

FUNNY STORY

(Supposedly true, told me by a friend of the court stenographer, in an accent that defies description, but makes me roll with laughter. If someone publishes this, I swear I will do the bit for you at a reading if you request it. It probably isn't funny here, but I need the reference.)

A very distraught transvestite prostitute is giving testimony in small claims court. "Your honnah, alls I know is, when I went into da baidroom, da jeweleries was on da table. And when I came out of da baffroom, da jeweleries was gawne. Now, on my honnah, I do not know what had happ-ed, but something has got to be did!"

Something has got to be did. It is mid-July. Chicago is unbearably hot and humid. School is out for the summer, and I am concentrating on both finishing the editing on my current anthology, and moving forward on the diary poems, which keep flooding out of me in an endless river of words. I have been seeing Geoff for four months now. Our habits continue discreetly, and we have settled into a comfortable pattern. We chat via e-mail and establish which day of the week Sandra is out of town. Since we do not spend the night, I do not worry about Mark's travel schedule, which more often than not is accommodating anyway. We meet for dinner, either takeout at his place or at the same little French bistro where we are often the only people in the joint, and we enjoy good food, excellent company and are indifferent to awful service. Our conversations are those of good friends who don't know each other's histories entirely; sometimes we are sharing only current events and asking for advice on dealing with various work and personal dilemmas, sometimes we get nostalgic and talk about family and friends and childhood memories. I stay away from too much information about my parents, and he stays away from too much information about Sandra, and in general, we never have awkward silences or moments of boredom, just free and facile conversation.

Which is why I suppose I have been able to pursue this relationship for so long. Mark and I seem to only talk about the mundane daily information, work, his travel plans, my classes. Not in that "we have run out of things to talk about" way, but more in that "everything we could talk about is likely to really only be of interest to the person doing the talking" way. Plus, the hard thing that I am discovering about being in an extracurricular relationship, is that the better it is, the less effort you feel inclined to make at home. I think it works like this, if the new guy is so much more fun and attentive and interesting, it illuminates every flaw in your primary relationship. I assume it would be different if Mark and Sandra didn't both spend so much time out of town. But she is gone at least one or two days of every week, and Mark as much if not more, so there haven't really been any scheduling obstacles. And Mark being gone allows me to keep the things very separate in my mind. I have a husband, whom I live with intermittently, and a lover, who I see once a week, and they don't overlap too much, so I keep them in my little mental boxes and don't dwell.

I do really love being with Geoff, in all the ways that make Mark problematic for me. We have a ridiculous amount in common, Geoff and I. Music, movies, theatre, literature, politics—half of our conversation seems to be one of us saying things like "Exactly!" and "Me too!" to whatever the other person has just said. Now and again we finish each other's sentence, or say the same thing at the same time, and we both will smile and shake our heads. He will pay for our meal, I will thank him very genuinely, and we will walk the short stroll to his house. Sometimes we will sit and talk or watch TV before beginning to be physical, sometimes once we are inside the clothes are too burdensome to keep on. Sometimes we make out on the couch like teenagers before going into the bedroom, sometimes he will just kiss me once or twice before rising and leading me upstairs, sometimes we just head straight to the bedroom the minute we are in the door.

Whatever the machinations of the evening, one thing is clear. Our sexual compatibility continues to amaze and surprise me. No two nights are ever exactly the same, nothing is ever boring or routine, I don't ever think "Oh there is that signature move…." Every second I spend in his arms, in his bed, is a delight, a revelation. I have never been with anyone remotely this astounding. I may have mentioned a bit of sleeping around in my youth—I was always a pretty sexual gal, for which I make no apologies—and I have had some truly fantastic lovers in my day, but here are some myths I have debunked under Geoff's tutelage:

- Multiple orgasms are not an urban legend.
- Nor are orgasms during intercourse without additional clitoral stimulation.
- Men do not necessarily want to avoid sexual activity with you when you have your period, nor do they always believe that if they do deign to play with you during that sacred time of commune with the moon that everything is all about them.
- Sometimes, when you think, "I couldn't possibly come again," you can.
- Sometimes, when you say, "I couldn't possibly come again," they believe you and cuddle, instead of taking it as a challenge to their prowess.
- Sometimes, a man just knows by the way your body has responded to him which place you are in, and can instinctively

determine whether to continue or stop without you having to say or think anything at all.

- Sometimes, the man who should be the most wrong man in the world for you, turns out to be really right.

Something has got to be did. My little "take-the-edge-off fling" has become an actual affair. I am far more interested in the needs and desires of my lover of once a week than my partner of fourteen years. And Geoff is great about not romancing me; there are no flowers, no love letters, no trinkets. No exclamations of love, no assurances that he will leave Sandra. He is very careful to limit our time together to spans of three to five hours. He is very careful not to see me more than once a week. And he still insists that we not spend the night together. I, of course, acquiesce to all of his rules, and yet allow myself the secret pleasure of imagining a time when all of those things might be mine. When he might be mine. I find that the poems he inspires me to are the most intense and sensual and in some ways naively optimistic of my life. Too hopeful, too forgiving of him. Why should he not spend a night with me, after all this time, or a day even? Why do I not inspire the little tokens of romance? Why do we always read about the wooings of mistresses full of love letters and gifts and expressions of attachment? I know that discretion is of utmost concern, but hell, even Monica got a copy of *Leaves of Grass* to remember Bill by (even if it was a fairly trite and mundane offering), and let's be honest, Geoff is no leader of the free world. I feel bewitched and alternately ecstatic about our continued connection, and pissed off that he doesn't appear to be remotely as smitten with me as I am with him. I am supposed to be the irresistible young thing who reminds him what it is to love, not just some convenient alternative to jerking off while the wife is out of town.

It is these thoughts that drive me to the computer one night after leaving him, the mental rant begun in the car on the way home, where I have all my most important imaginary conversations with him. By the time I am sitting at the computer, I am feeling quite put out.

she comes undone

for there is fear in the knowing
in the being known
without the veil of pretty speeches
nimble tongued explanations
when the point was not the answer
but the question
my heart makes a small sound oh
in the dark where we live
separate together
I wrap myself in bitter longing
braced against mourning winds
those hours live outside of time
beyond the black sky to the source of the light
where every minute licks a wound
blood dances like the point of a knife on the tongue

and oh how we laugh
and how we play at unspoken loving with each other
as if we invented it
hoard it
little fat children afraid it will be finite
stashing our passion in every closet chamber of the heart
under the dirty clothes
and dirty memories
beneath the bed where you do not let me smile for you
until every open space of this world we share
is stuffed to overflowing with our excess
the heat of the bottom layers decomposing
feeds every new layer of understanding?
we are bathed in the warmth we generate
and do not miss the sun

oh
but you will beat me
break me
leave me
the love in corners will devour itself
disappear
and I will feed on my sorrow
revel in the sharp grinding against my gums
weep my fire hot tears to salt the ragged edges
where you have torn yourself from me

there will be no redemption
truth is a demon
who coaxes our souls into slumber
though I can read the future
I cannot change it
destined to finish this tango with you
legs shaking
waiting for little deaths to release us
into the life where we reap the reward of each other

the promise is kept
yet doesn't fulfill
I am left bruised
without reason
desiccated shell
begging at the feet of the devil
to fill me up

fill me up.

Even this cops out, even this attempt to make him the bad guy finds forgiveness. I don't know what it is that I am dealing with, the whole situation is nothing like I thought it would be. On the one hand, after such a short time, why is it I see such potential in him, and not in Mark? Does familiarity truly breed contempt? On the other, my ability to engage in this affair is only a symptom of problems with Mark that were in place long before Geoff and I found each other. Am I trying to make my contemptible behavior less so by investing my lover with attributes that lean me toward love? If I convince myself that Geoff and I have something rare and magical, then aren't I simply being open to fate, however complicated or messy the pursuance of that destiny might be? And if I don't end up in love with Geoff, then have I simply given in to my most base carnal desires, with no more self-control than a wild animal? I am pondering these very thoughts the next morning, facing the poem again to see if I might not infuse it with more acknowledgment of Geoff's faults, when the phone rings.

"Sidney, it's your mother." Like I don't know that voice.

"Hey Mom, what's up?"

"Just checking in, seeing how you are…"

"I'm good, just grading some papers. How are you?"

"You know me, busy busy. And now I may have to chair this Jewish United Fund luncheon alone…"

My mother and Sandra Fahl are scheduled to co-host a small luncheon reception fund-raiser in two weeks, which I will have to attend. Yippee. *"Congratulations, Sandra, on a lovely event. And I really adore the new sheets in your guest room, thanks. Geoff and I popped in there last week for a change of scenery, and the higher thread count feels so silky on the skin, you should really get some for the master bedroom as well. By the way, FYI, next time you and Geoff are making love, you might want to really spend some quality time licking his balls, because that seems to totally push him over the edge."*

"Why is that?" Half-hoping it is because Sandra will be embroiled in the beginnings of a divorce.

"She just called me, some big blow-up at her company in the Texas office. She will have to take over until they can find a replacement for the CEO of that branch, who they fired yesterday, and now she has to host some major black-tie event to put on a good show for the local board of directors. Apparently the whole thing is very upsetting—she and the guy have been working together for years, and the company made her give him the news. Poor Geoff didn't find out till this morning. She is completely thrown by the whole mishegoss, so much that she asked him to come, and he had to fly out to Houston to help her, and leave daddy all his work to cover, so now your father is Mr. Cranky Pants to boot."

"That is awful, I am sure she will be okay though." My heart is in my toes. The woman was probably totally wigging out in Texas while I was happily fucking her husband and wishing she would leave him so that I might actually get to wake up in his arms one of these days. I am a terrible, horrible, dastardly person. I am going to be a dung beetle in my next life. My mother is still talking about something, but I can't concentrate, the words are just so much whining white noise, so I manage to convince her that I have a pot on the stove, and hurry her off the line. After what happened last time, I couldn't possibly call him, so instead I sit down at the computer and send him an e-mail.

To: fahlguy1@aol.com
From: poetsid@aol.com
RE: checking in

Geoff—

My mother just informed me of Sandra's work worries, and your sudden departure for Houston, and knowing what a hassle it is for you made me want to reach out.

I have only myself, my friendship, to offer. Dubious prize that I am.

If you need me, if you want me, know you are needed and wanted in return. If you think I can help, if only to distract, you need only ask. And more than that, I ask you to ask. Because good friends are rare. Because good men are rare. Because I see both in you.

They say that new friends are the best friends, as they hold all tomorrow's promise in their smiles. Or maybe they don't say that. Maybe it is just me who says that.

In any case, you make it feel true.

I hope it isn't too strange or awful for me to say that I am hoping to see you soon. It is all I can do.

yours,

Sidney

It makes me feel better knowing I have reached out to him. And worse.

For now I am feeling guilty. Now I am feeling unforgivable. It would have been one thing to stray the tiniest bit, but I am getting emotionally involved to a serious extent. It would have been one thing to give in to momentary lust, but I am too invested already in Geoff, and that means that I have to face up to the fact that my marriage isn't just in a rough patch, it is in serious jeopardy. I am always within thirty seconds of calling it quits. The words "I am leaving you" have taken up permanent residence on the tip of my tongue. I fantasize about Geoff calling me from some luxury hotel suite downtown and telling me he has left her and to pack a bag and come join him so we can begin a life together. I am desperately afraid to have the discussion with Mark, afraid of hurting him, of losing his friendship, of his finding out.

Something has got to be did.

I have begun to pray a lot. Not actual go-to-temple pray, or down-on-one-knee-humbled-in-the-face-of-God pray, but just little muttered prayers. *Make him leave me. Make him end it. Let me not be the bad guy who calls it quits. Let him be the one to say it out loud.*

I get a brief reply from Geoff. He says only that he appreciates my thoughts, that he has no gift for flowery language, but ditto to everything. He says he will be home in a couple of days, and that we can have dinner in the later part of the week. I am thrilled, relieved, ecstatic, sick. What if I am actually falling in love with him? What if he turns out to be my soul mate? What if he isn't falling in love with me? What if he isn't my soul mate at all?

I try to examine my heart, I try to see if I can focus my energies in other directions. I superficially convince myself that my feelings are lustful, not love driven, and that we couldn't possibly be soul mates—we are too wrong for each other. I ignore what my deeper recesses might hold. We are friends, lovers, no more. We are a fine distraction, a lark. We are working through our spark of attraction, and soon it will fade away, and six months from now we will both be wondering why it ever happened. But he haunts my dreams. And I cannot shake this impending sense of fear and doom.

And I cannot stop wishing for Mark to leave me. I cannot stop thinking about a life without him, without his calm acceptance of the staus quo, without his deference. I cannot stop praying.

Sandra stays in Houston for two weeks getting the place organized, before the company promotes an Executive VP from the L.A. office to take over and she is able to return home, where she remains for a full three weeks before resuming her usual travel schedule. Geoff and I use the separation, the longest in our time together, to work up a seemingly insatiable appetite for each other, resulting in an unprecedented two dates in a single week, both of longer duration than our usual four-hour romps. And for the first time, at the end of the dates, Geoff doesn't even mention how wrong we are, how much he risks, how awful it would be to get caught. He doesn't threaten to end it, he doesn't remind me that it might never happen again. He is more tender than he has ever been, he looks at me with a strange mixture of pride and adoration. He looks as me like he is thinking it—me through. For the first time, I am thinking he might just have genuine feelings for me. I am over the moon. And my prayers continue unabated.

★ ★ ★

A mere month later, a miracle happens. Not a parting the Red Sea miracle. A small, everyday miracle. A little gift from whichever gods were hearing my pleas.

Mark arrived home mid-August after three weeks on the road with an announcement. His company was promoting him again. Junior VP. It required a transfer. To sunny Southern Californ-I-A. Minimum of two years. More money, less travel. He wanted it very badly. I think the look on my face said everything.

"You don't want to leave Chicago."

"No, I don't." I couldn't lie to him, Chicago is home, deeply home, ancestrally home. My family, my friends, my career. My lover, although I squelch the impulse to think about him. "No, I don't want to leave Chicago."

"I didn't think you would. But I really want to take this job. It is important to my career, and my career is what makes me happiest these days. If we were doing better, if I thought we were moving forward toward making a better life together, I would have a much tougher choice, but we are both so unhappy and uncommunicative and uninvolved, I can't help but want this job. I love you very much, but this is too hard."

There it was. It was out there. And I didn't have to say it.

"What do you think we should do?" The question was genuine, I had no idea what we were facing.

"I think I should take it. I'll move to California. It can be a trial separation. Some distance, some space, some clarity. We can talk, and I will come home for a weekend here and there and you can come visit me, and we will see if it makes sense to figure us out."

We cried really hard, Mark and I, because deep down we both knew that there was nothing trial about the separation we were agreeing to. We cried like little kids, blubbering, and snorting and hiccuping. And that night, for the first night in ages, we went to bed at the same time, and Mark held me very close, and we didn't roll apart in the night. Just before daybreak, Mark woke me in tears, asking if we couldn't take it all back, saying he didn't want the job. I held him, soothed him back to sleep. But I didn't say yes, and in that moment, I felt sadder and stronger than I had ever felt before.

In the morning, he called in sick to work, and we stayed home to make arrangements. We wanted everything settled before telling our folks. We figured out finances and belongings and assets and details. It took the better part of the day, we had to keep stopping to cry a lot. I didn't know so much crying was in me. Or in him. By early evening, we chucked it, ordered a pizza, had a couple of beers, started to let it be okay. I think it was then that we both knew we would be friends. Real friends. Good friends. That is when we stopped crying. We didn't cry when we explained it to our folks. We didn't cry when we were packing his stuff. We didn't cry again until we packed up the cats and put them in his car for the long drive to California. We felt like such bad parents, but it seemed best for them to go with him; I was never too good about remembering to feed them or clean out the litter box, and it felt good to think that in his new and unfamiliar territory that there would be something warm and fuzzy to come home to. Just like that. In all its simple complexity.

And then he was gone.

I am in a fog, a daze, in the weeks after Mark leaves. I come home every evening to a full answering machine. Wonderful messages from friends, love and support and well-wishes, all tinged with an underlying sense of relief that the machine has picked up and that they don't have to talk to me in person. No one calls at night except my family, and Mark. We speak every other day or so, keep things as light as possible. Things seem to be going well for him, and he is finding his way around. Neither of us mentions his coming to visit, or my coming to see him.

Geoff is awfully supportive of my circumstances. He has his own first marriage to reference, and so all sorts of sympathy for me, but he doesn't appear particularly inspired to consider a similar change for himself. We don't talk about it. I try not to think about it. I spend my free time rearranging the apartment, going out with friends, continuing the work on the new anthology, being in the world and testing my freedom. I begin to invite Geoff over to my place, but he keeps finding excuses to stay away, so our evenings together continue without alteration. It doesn't matter, really, I am just happy to have him in my life, knowing that someone wants me, that I am desirable. I am doing pretty well, all things considered, and finding that living alone suits me.

You know, it doesn't really happen quite like this, I mean, it isn't so smooth, and quick in hindsight is interminable in actuality, and there is a whole big jumble of events and discussions and long nights that I am leaving out. But in the end, things get to here, regardless of whether I share every detail or not.

In the end, I am suddenly single and alone. I am thirty-three. I have never dated in any conventional sense. I have a husband from whom I am legally separated, living hundreds of miles away. I have two ex-cats who I will probably never see again. I live by myself in a too-large, too-expensive apartment, too old to have a roommate, too settled to think about moving. I have a day job I am good at which pays just enough for me to live at a slightly nicer sort of hand-to-mouth, and an art form that pulls breath to my lungs which will never make me any sort of actual money. I have a married lover who I adore—who I am beginning to suspect will never feel for me what I am beginning to suspect I may be feeling for him, and yet because of him, no impetus to get out into the dating arena.

It's funny really, that I have never felt so possible.

And that after all these pages, this may be where the story actually begins.

chapter 8

wolf at the door

QUOTE OF THE DAY

Heroism is the brilliant triumph of the soul over the flesh, that is to say over fear:
fear of poverty, of suffering, of calumny, of illness, of loneliness and of death.
There is no real piety without heroism.
Heroism is the dazzling and glorious concentration of courage.

—Henri Frédéric Amiel

When we last left our intrepid heroine, which is to say, myself, she was poised on the brink of a life uncharted. Husband gone to the west coast, in limbo with lover, facing her future with brave face, eager heart, timid and trepidatious and hopeful. What will become of her? Is the marriage really over? Will Geoff leave his wife? Will she succumb to the attentions of some yet unnamed suitor?

Well, if I told you all that, what would be the point of reading further?

Have you ever noticed how sometimes life can fly so fast that you wake up one fine November morning to a blast of bitter cold, wondering where the hell September and October and autumn glory got to? Well, good morning to us all. It is, by my calendar, November 12. Mark left two and a half months ago.

It was the heat of summer when I helped him pack the ratty nine-year-old Saab that was his pride and joy, wondering to myself if it would make it to California without the transmission falling out. Fall, as fall is wont to be in Chicago, was brief and tenuous at best, shifting these past couple of months between hot and summery, and damp and rainy, with eight perfect days of crisp cool autumnal breezes, moving immediately into winter chill.

I labored on Labor Day, and suffered through both Rosh Hashanah and Yom Kippur with my parents, fending off the head-tilts from their well-meaning congregation of High Holidays Jews (try to get them into temple any other day and you would be laughed at most heartily). The breakup of a marriage, particularly one that had seemed on the surface so healthy, inspires the worst possible sort of attention from the friends of one's parents. Highlights from this fall's services included nearly eighteen versions of, "How are you holding up dear?" with the aforementioned head-tilt accompanying. At least four "Darling you look fabulous—doesn't she look fabulous honey?"s with appropriate and embarrassed nodding from uncomfortable spouses. Several women mentioned that they had someone to introduce me to, "once you're ready, darling…" because lord knows the first place I am planning to turn for eligible bachelors is the coffee-klatch set. A woman behind me at the Erev Yom Kippur service actually leaned forward to inform me that her niece was a lovely and currently single lesbian, and that she would be happy to make an introduction if I was leaning in that direction. DURING KOL NIDRE!!!!!

Luckily for me, my parents, despite being a sideline part of that circle, have been unbelievably supportive, not pressuring me, assuring me that they understand what happened and that there is no reason to be ashamed. Being at once comfortingly present and blissfully absent, and more than all that, simply treating me not at all different. Naomi calls now once a week to check up on me, but the conversations are stilted at best. We have never been particularly close, too far apart in age, and I think her own seemingly perfect marriage makes her feel guilty when we speak, as if I will be resentful of her life. Mark and I speak about once a week, and we have agreed that visiting by either of us seems a bad idea. He will have a conference in Chicago after the New Year, and we have decided to wait to meet then and make some decisions. I think we both know that it will be the official "file for divorce meeting." I will deal with that when the time comes. Adam sends funny little e-mails from London, and has promised to come home for Thanksgiving this year, and crash at my place instead of with Mom and Dad, both for his own sanity and for my support. He also swears that he is going to do his damnedest to get me laid during his nine-day tenure in my guest room. Bless his heart. I may have to tell him about Geoff, just to have a confidant.

Sigh. Geoff.

Yes, we continue. It has been eight months. We are in some ways just the same as we were, in some ways even more deeply connected. The old rules still apply, of course, once a week or thereabouts, no sleepovers, no romancing. Every other date or so, he threatens that it might be our last. It seems to make him feel better not to get my expectations up. Every fourth date or so he has some silly paranoiac spasm where he lectures me about how much he has at stake, and how awful it would be to get caught. I am very supportive of him in these moments, and try to put him at ease, knowing that whatever he may think, he is not ready to let me go quite yet, which is fine, because I don't want to be gone. On our last date he had one of these episodes, just as we were getting undressed to make love, and when he caught me smiling at him in the middle of his exposition, he berated me for not listening to him.

"I don't think you understand the severity of my situation."

He is so adorable when he is freaking out, I can barely keep from kissing him. Plus, he is prancing around the bedroom in purple-and-green plaid boxer shorts while expounding on the flaws in our relationship, so how on earth can I take him seriously?

"I think I do understand the severity, but I also understand that we are not in any sort of danger."

I am using my calm, stable, soothing approach, which usually works.

"I don't think you do. If we were to get caught, it would be the end of my reputation, and I have worked my whole life to attain the good name I now possess in both my personal and professional circles, and if I were to tarnish it, there would be no getting it back."

"We aren't going to get caught."

"We ARE going to get caught. People always get caught. And whatever problems Sandra and I are having, I do still love her. But if I decide to end it, it is going to have to be on my terms, and if we get caught, it will be on her terms, and I cannot have that."

I cannot believe he actually said the words "if I decide to end it…." I continue to placate him, despite the joy rising in me.

"Baby, it is okay. People get caught for two reasons, either they are really dumb and make stupid mistakes, or they sub-consciously want to get caught, and sabotage themselves. We are both very smart people, and we have done nothing ex-cept take every precaution to be sure that we are not linked to each other as more than just friendly acquaintances. And neither of us wants to get caught. Do you think I want to face my parents with this? Or put them in the position of being the subject of gossip? Do you think I want to make my dad the butt of jokes at the firm? Do you think I want Mark counting back months on his fingers to determine when I really began to pull away from him completely, won-dering if you had anything to do with it? I am scared too sometimes, it would be bad for me were we to get busted, but I know what we do and what we don't do, and I genuinely believe we are safe. We are very careful. We have been very careful for a very long time, and no one suspects anything. There is no paper trail between us, no phone records, we don't go anywhere we might be spotted except for Bistro Campagne, and even there, we might just have bumped into one another eating solo and joined forces. It isn't like we are affectionate in public. I know that it worries you, but take a deep breath, we are fine, and we aren't going to get caught. I promise."

I deliver this speech in my most gentle tone, walking carefully around the bed and crossing to him, sliding my arms around his waist, and looking deep into his eyes. He puts his arms around me and holds me tight.

"You know I am just a paranoid Connecticut Protestant, and sometimes I have to say it all out loud to remind us both. I know you know, but I have to say it anyway. And maybe I just needed to hear you say that you were scared too." And me all this time never giving voice to my own fears, thinking he was frightened enough for us both, thinking I had to be the strong one. Funny how the little revelations come when you least expect them.

"Deer in the headlights."

"Excuse me?" He looks perplexed.

"Deer in the headlights. What do you do? Deer in your path, no way to avoid hitting it, can't afford to swerve around, you might end up in a ditch, what do you do?"

"I dunno, brake hard and pray, I guess."

"Nope."

"Nope?"

"Nope. Wrong answer."

"I am sure you are going to tell me the right answer."

"Yep. That is, if you want to know."

My man looks at me, his hands lightly caressing my shoulder blades, and smiles humoringly.

"Of course I want to know. What do you do?"

"Floor it."

"What? You have got to be kidding?"

"Not kidding, pedal to the metal, baby. The deal is this, a deer is a big animal, and at speed, even lower speeds, it is gonna rack up your car. If it is in the road, paralyzed in your headlights, and you know you are going to hit it, you want to hit it as fast as you can, as hard as you can. If you brake, hit it slow, it might not die right away, so it will be in agony, and it will end up all tangled underneath your car, and really potentially send you off the road to your own death or injury. If you hit it hard and fast, you will likely kill it humanely on impact, and you will send it up and over the top of your car, which is hell on the windshield and hood, but ultimately a much easier fix."

"I am sure you have a point here."

"Sometimes, even though your natural instinct is to slam on the brakes, sometimes it makes a lot more sense to hit the gas."

"Very cute, your little convoluted metaphors."

"I am nothing if not cute."

"This is true."

"You be as paranoid as you want. You give me the speech however often you need in order to feel comfortable, I am happy to listen. But know this, every time it occurs to you to tell me that maybe we should call it quits, think about the deer."

"You are as big a pain in the ass as I am."

"It is why we pair so well together. Aw hell, lover, anyone can be adorable and charming and fun and sexy for three or four hours once a week. If the thought of us really makes you that crazy, hit the fucking gas. Spend a day with me, a weekend. Two dates a week, maybe three. No one can maintain that much fabulousness, at some point you will be exposed to my crankiness, my petulant outbursts, the way my hair sticks up all over in the morning, the fact that I hog the covers. I'll find out that you are a boring old lawyer who snores. You find out all the faults I can so cleverly hide from you in our current arrangement, I'll discover yours as well. We will get tired of each other, the sex will get dull, and we can move on. Simple really. You want us over? Step it up."

"Deer in the headlights." Shaking his head.

"Deer in the headlights." Grinning proudly.

"I'll give you deer in the headlights, you insane woman...c'mere, Bambi."

Geoff leans in and kisses me hard, then holds me tightly against him. I slide my hands down his back, and into the waistband of his shorts, cupping his butt gently with both hands, and nuzzling into his chest, biting his neck. I can feel him twitch slightly against my stomach, a small lazy animal stirring in sleep. I begin to kiss his chest, rubbing my nose in the surprisingly soft fuzz, lightly suckling his small brown nipples, dropping slowly to my knees before him, and gently prying open the front flap of his underwear. I love it when his cock is soft and small, just beginning to be aware of my touch. I love to take the whole thing into my mouth, gently licking, feeling it grow until it will not be contained any longer.

Geoff reaches down and grabs my shoulders, pulling me up again to him, kissing me even harder while shaking off his underwear, then pushes me almost violently onto the bed, entering me in one swift movement. Not satisfied to give up power so easily, I put both hands on his chest, push to the left, and roll him onto his back, and straddle him. He is grinning now, surprised and apparently delighted with my decision to take charge.

"You just lie there, my little nutcase, and let me fuck you the way I want." I cannot believe I just said that. I half expect him to laugh at me. Instead, his voice gets really husky, and all he can say is

"Oh, yes."

So I do. Ride him like a rodeo pony. Pin his hands down, and fuck him hard until I can hear him moan his crescendo louder and longer than I have ever heard from him. I roll off him, take his hand in mine, and we bring me off together, I cannot tell whose fingers are which, nor do I particularly care. We are holding each other, all tangled limbs, sweaty, sticky, utterly sated.

"That was so awesome." A wordsmith, my lover.

"Yes it was."

"We are going to rest a little while, and then I am going to lick you until you come, and fuck you again before you have to leave." Oh my. He has a filthy mouth. Which he intends to put on me, lucky girl that I am.

"Yes, dear, if you insist."

"I do. I do insist most heartily." He kisses me gently, and smiles.

Geoff is nothing if not a man of his word, and an hour and a half later I am dressed to leave, having had a second act of equally raucous sex (filled with some truly eloquent and utterly filthy dialogue), two more supremely delightful orgasms, and half of Geoff's beer while we indulged in the first twenty minutes of Leno. I am more of a Letterman gal myself (more on this later) but Jay doesn't bother me, and Geoff likes his schtick. Plus, frankly, he could put on the paint-drying channel as long as he let me be near him while it was on. The strange pacing creature he was at the start of the evening is gone, and I am surprised at the slightly wicked turn the whole thing seemed to inspire in him. We had never engaged in dirty bed-talk before, and to be honest, I don't know whether I am more surprised that we said what we said to each other, or that it excited me as much as it did. Not for everyday, to be sure, but perhaps now and again for spice. I am already making mental notes about which phrases really pushed his buttons, for future reference. It is always too soon when he looks at me and tells me he has to kick me out. But it isn't unexpected, and besides, it is a school night and I really am exhausted from our rigorous escapade.

He walks me to the door. .

"I am sorry about earlier, I just get really worried, you know?"

"I know, it's okay."

"I wish I could keep it in when I am feeling like that, but I can't somehow."

"I know."

"I think Sandra is going back to Houston on either Tuesday or Wednesday."

"I'll keep them both open until I hear from you."

"Okay, I should know on Monday."

"Great. Have a good weekend."

"You too. Drive safe."

"Good-night, lover."

"And Sid?"

"Yes darlin'?"

"Watch out for deer."

"I always do."

He kisses my forehead. I don't know why, he never seems to want to really kiss me goodbye, no lingering smooching before I go. Doesn't matter really, I like when he kisses my forehead, it feels sweet.

I think about his little episodes, and their consistency throughout our months together. It reminds me of the little boy who cried wolf. I think about this analogy all the way home, and by the time I arrive, I am in a panic to get the computer on. I sit and type, coat still on, purse dropped at my feet with things spilling out the top, my fingernails clicking a mad staccato on the keyboard.

(Okay, I am going to include this one, because I like it, but since I did promise to at least attempt not to bore you with too much poetry...romantics read on; if you have a minor attention deficit, please skip ahead seven pages.)

crying wolf

the few hours that separate me
from the coming dawn
will not be swift

the stillness of my tongue
sitting so thickly
in the cheek of the jury of your peers
the mind which reels in silence

I should be sleeping
I should be safe
I should not be so ravished by concern

but you do ravish me
devour my sensibility
break down my barriers
make me more myself
more the me I have so feared

and I cannot believe that
after all my self-protective maneuvering
all the pains I took to keep myself from being too open
too free
too available for you
you still managed to slide under my radar
cast your spell
became water to slip through the cracks

and just when I begin to own it
allow myself to believe it
to want it with all of the longing at my disposal
you make of yourself a thin smoke
and disappear

Oh, you wicked boy
playing tricks on my poor wounded heart
shame on me
for wanting too much
my genie is displeased
because I am greedy
and tried to wish for more wishes

there are no rules of order
for this debate
no structure
to support
or restrict

there is only the wide open space
of our potential
your need to contain it
make it manageable

I will not be managed
I will not be contained

I will not let you convince me
of our impossibility
I will but lie in the stoic night
and let the knowledge of what is good and right with us
keep me contented
even if you will not possess it
not acknowledge it
it doesn't make it untrue

just once in this life
I want to be the blind one
want to be the one
who cannot see the good
who cannot see past the distracting chorus

it must make one so light

it is not to be
not now
not with you
the now is for the asking
the hoping
that you are simply crying wolf at me
and will be changeable

the tale is supposed to be a cautionary one
the young boy alone
screaming his terror
pulling his family
friends
neighbors
from their lives
to his aid

hearts in their throats
they come
only to discover
he is safe

the moral of the story seems to imply
that one has limited access to rescue
that there is an unspoken quota
that if you ask too often when you don't have deep need
someday when you do
your allotment will be used up

I think that little boy
is awfully misunderstood
painted as an imp
a prankster
malicious and manipulative
I find the moral unsettling

I prefer to believe that he is simply scared
and lonely
and so unsure of his place in the world
that he cannot trust his own value
does not believe he is worth saving

he does not cry out to torment
he does not cry out for entertainment
but to test
to reassure
that if the danger comes
he will not face it alone

that when he has need
he will not be left to fend off the monster
with what poor resources he can muster
that they will
prove their love
prove their steadfastness
help him to find
the place where he has faith
that assistance will come
when it is wanted

and you can be that little boy

so suspicious of anyone
who might dare find worth in you
so disbelieving of your own virtue
of your ability to inspire genuine connection
in anyone sane
in anyone without ulterior motive
that you test me
threaten me
dangle the possibility
the probability
of our ending

bait for the wolf

push me to become the thing you dread
wait for my breaking with rationality
expect my head to spin on its axis
wait for my behavior to become neurotic
high maintenance
damaging
vengeful
afraid that I will ask for impossible attention
make the potential rewards inequal to the risks
somehow unable to believe
that I will not alter

I will requite you in every way but this

ask for support
favor
advocacy
relief

ask for reassurance
sustenance
respite

ask for love
affection
caring
respect

ask for kisses
caresses
hours of lovemaking
nights of comfort
long talks
longer silences

ask me to hold you
to hear you
to know you

to remind you a thousand times
of all the gifts you possess

ask
and you will receive all you ask for
to the limit of my ability to procure it for you

but no matter how hard you try
how frequently you assay
how much you push me
I will not hurt you
I will not abandon you
I will not give you reason to regret me
I will not leave you vulnerable

I will not break you

You can send me from your bed
or entreat me to stay and watch the morning

you can request my company daily
or fortnightly

you can offer me the moon
or nothing more than this
it will not transform me

make rules
I will follow without question
will capitulate to whatever you need to feel safe

lie sated in my arms and pour your deepest concerns into my ears
tell me every time we are together that it may be the last time

if it keeps your demons at bay

you cannot scare me
cannot make me believe you aren't worth it
you can cry for me
every hour of every day
for the rest of your life

I will always come for you

protect you
because you are in my heart
and no little boy
should ever have to fear
that when the wolf comes
he will be forsaken.

Tuesday. Maybe Wednesday. I will invite him over again, and maybe this time he will finally accept. Make him dinner. Bring him into my home where I might prove to him that he can be comfortable there, in my neighborhood, where no one knows him. Maybe if he finds that my apartment is a haven, perhaps he might consider a whole night with me, in my bed, which longs for him. In my arms, which long for him.

If he ends it, it will have to be on his terms. If he ends it.

I have no words for that prayer.

chapter 9

homecoming

QUOTE OF THE DAY

Home is any four walls that contain the right person.
—Helen Rowland

To: poetsid@aol.com
From: fahlguy1@aol.com
RE: meeting

Sandra is leaving Tuesday, but it looks like Wednesday night will be better for me, how about sixish?
G

To: fahlguy1@aol.com
From: poetsid@aol.com
RE: RE: meeting

Wednesday is perfect for me, I notice that there is a Bulls game on that evening, perhaps I can entice you to come to my

place for dinner and basketball, just a little change of pace...
Sid

To: poetsid@aol.com
From: fahlguy1@aol.com
RE: RE: RE: meeting

Sounds good. Just let me know how to get there. G.

Ohmygodohmygodohmygod.

He said yes. Just like that. He is coming over. It is Monday evening, and he is coming over on Wednesday evening. To my place. For the first time ever. I may have a heart attack. I am totally freaking out. What am I going to do? What am I going to cook? How am I going to be ready in time?

Ohmygodohmygodohmygodohmygod. OHMYGOD! Okay. Need a plan. Everything must be perfect. He has to like it here. He has to feel at home. He is going to hate my apartment, I just know it. Don't get me wrong, I have a fab apartment. I occupy the first floor and half of the basement of a three-flat graystone Victorian on an historic Chicago boulevard. Three thousand square feet, hardwood floors, ten-foot ceilings, amazing original woodwork and gorgeous built-ins. Despite the size, it is very cozy, and in my new state of singledom, I have arranged it to suit me admirably. But as I have described, Geoff's house is this very "done", very clean, very careful, mostly modern place, not quite minimalist, but just a shade off, and I am, shall we say, something of a collector. Okay, a pack rat. I might be distantly related to the infamous New York Collyers whose Harlem mansion collapsed around them under the weight of over 100,000 tons of accumulated crap. Every inch of this place is full of, well, STUFF. Interesting stuff, odd stuff, old stuff. The walls serve as display for such sundry artworks as old hanging calendar cookbooks from the '20s, antique music posters, yellowed costume renderings, pages from early nineteen-hundreds fashion magazines and black-and-white photos of the family. Every room is packed to the gills with furniture. I have something of an addiction to occasional tables, and every one of them houses a display of odds and ends and artifacts that I have collected over the years.

SIDEBAR

I will admit to owning twenty-one of them, and will say only that three thousand square feet is very big, and one needs to have small tables conveniently placed every few feet or so, otherwise you are always searching for a place to set a drink. I know. It is a sickness.

Every doorknob and drawerpull has some little silky tassel hanging from it. There are eighteen throw pillows in the living room alone. Candles everywhere. I am a maximalist. It is the house that eBay built. Geoff is going to have an aneurysm. My apartment is one enormous curio cabinet, and I just know that he is going to think it awful. But there is no time to pare down, and no storage available to hide things, so all I can do is make sure that it is spotlessly clean, and everything arranged as neatly as possible, and hope that if I feed him well and make love to him skillfully that he won't really notice. I cannot ponder the cleaning part, it is going to take me hours, so I tackle instead the menu, thinking that at least I will be able to make him a memorable meal. I am, after all, a gourmet cook, so it is just a question of figuring out which succulent morsels to tempt him with, besides my adorable self.

Okay, think.

Since we have only ever eaten at Bistro Campagne or ordered in Chinese or pizza at his place, I have little information to go on in terms of his tastes. But at the bistro he always gets an endive salad with fennel, so I will riff on that for the first course. The entrée needs to be good, but not too filling; after all, there will be bedroom gymnastics following, and one shouldn't have too heavy a meal preceding. Nothing that contains more than a moiety of either onion or garlic, to keep the breath sweet. We almost never have dessert, and I do not know if he has a particular liking for sweets, so I won't put too much emphasis on a final course, maybe just have some simple items around in case. Good bread, a given. His favorite beverages on hand. And I will have to cook in front of him. Firstly, so that he knows that I can do it, second, because it seems terribly romantic to think of him in my kitchen watching me play chef for him. To cook like that, a la minute, as they say, requires a ridiculous amount of preparation in order to go smoothly. Mise en place, everything in its place, prepped and ready for last-minute assembly so that meals get to the table hot and delicious.

Of course, the best way to do that is to have at least one item that can be prepared way in advance and thrown in the oven, so that you aren't juggling stuff on all four burners at once. I finally settle on my famous baked Dijon chicken, with pasta in a sherry artichoke sauce and French green beans, the aforementioned salad and good vanilla ice cream and biscuits on the off chance he is in the mood for dessert.

I then tap into my latent and situation-specific OCD, and begin to clean house. Now, I am not a slob, and I do have a lovely woman who comes every other week to vacuum and dust and mop, but as it is Geoff's first visit, and I hope not his last, I decide that pristine is the order of the day. Now, consciously I know that rooms such as the guest bedroom, the office, the rooms downstairs, these are likely to get just a quick once-over during the fifty-cent tour, but that doesn't stop me from attacking them as if the queen herself is moving in for an inspection. I manage to get through nearly two-thirds of the place in five hours before I cannot stand it any longer, at which point I collapse into a scalding bath. There I doze off briefly, waking to find that the book I had been reading is now waterlogged, sitting at the bottom of the tub between my knees, four times the size it was before I fell asleep. Thank God it was just a cheap paperback.

Tuesday evening after class I rush home to finish the job, put Django Reinhardt on the stereo, and when the place sparkles to my satisfaction, I light my favorite incense in every room in the house, so that it will have just a light lingering scent tomorrow, as opposed to the more pungent effect if I were to wait. (*Melissa Pear, from L'Occitane, completely unlike the heavy patchouli or sandalwood odors one normally associates with reggae and cheap marijuana.*) I throw my best set of bed linens into the laundry so that I can put them on tomorrow, and thank God that Wednesday is my free day, no classes. I usually try to devote the day to grading papers, preparing lessons and writing, but I know that tomorrow will be devoted entirely to preparing for Geoff's visit. I have left all the shopping, so that everything will be as fresh as possible, so once my final spurt of cleaning is done, I am free to relax. But the combination of the music, which continues to play on endless repeat, and my giddy anticipation inspires me to the page, where I tap into my former life as a high school jazz trumpet protégé, to scribble the following.

jazz

your smile
plays twelve-bar blues in my pocket
slides around the seams in an occasional minor key
slips though the stitches on the razor point of a sharp note
touches skin with an icy hot c above high c

sneaky backbeat
that accidental note
you be-bop on my tongue
like an Ellington riff
like a good whiskey
like the first smoke in the pack

you jazz me up
I move to you
I groove to you
you tell me that sad story on the backs of the triplets
I lose my breath on your pick-ups
in your polyrhythmic kisses
those syncopated eyes
flashing up and down the scales
showing off
every note solid in my spine

you make me remember the double tongue
triple tongue
flutter tongue

I can sing a staccato sixteenth
pianissimo
in your ear
way above the scale
and drop a pedal tone for a steady four bars until you catch your
breath

you think you know music
think you understand the why
and baby
maybe you do
but I could be your bandleader
think it
check it
treat it
follow me through the bridge
past the melody you play so well
to the place where it has to come
from somewhere else

it's not enough
just to hit those changes baby

I got to hear the wail
got to know we found that spot
anything less
ain't worth playing
and anything worth playing
has a coda
and those pretty little words that make us free
repeat as needed.

I like the rhythm of it, it feels almost like a pulse when I read it, and I think I might actually give a copy to Geoff to read someday. He has not read any of the work he has brought out of me, but has been most complimentary of the older stuff I have offered him. Although he is, by his own admission, completely perplexed by the art form most of the time. But he said he liked my imagery, and the way my poems at least seemed to tell little stories, and that they weren't violent or dark like so much contemporary work. I loved that he took the time to read my first anthology, which he found on his own bookshelf, autographed by me to him and Sandra, a thank-you gift from my mother for making a substantial donation to one or another of her pet causes. I wondered if I ever published the diary poems in a slim and heartfelt volume if I might be free to give it to him directly, to inscribe it to my muse or whether by then we will have abandoned each other. No matter. I cannot think of that today. For tomorrow, he will be here.

I sleep, fitful in my nervous excitement, like a kid the night before a trip to the amusement park, and awaken before the alarm, wanting with equal measure to spring into action and get more sleep. Sleep wins, and I manage another couple of hours before I get up. Knowing I will shower and dress before he arrives, I throw on some leggings and a jean shirt, and head out to make the rounds.

I love grocery shopping. Especially for special occasions when I can wander the city in search of only the best of everything. I hit Gepperth's butchery on Halsted for the chicken, two perfect boneless breasts with the skin on and the little wing drumstick still attached. Then over to the Whole Foods on North Avenue for produce. Charlie Trotter's To Go on Fullerton has the best bread, as well as the imported artichoke puree which is the cornerstone of my pasta sauce—not to mention an indulgent little lunch treat for me of his pork loin sandwich, baby white asparagus salad, and the most amazing white chocolate chip macadamia nut cookie ever.

Once home, I decide to abandon the dried pappardelle in favor of fresh, and mix up some pasta dough like an old Italian mama, one cup of all purpose flour and a half cup semolina pasta flour mixed with two eggs and kneaded until elastic, then put in the fridge to rest. I mince shallots, toast some pine nuts, chop flat-leaf parsley. I found some lovely baby carrots with the greens still attached, and peel them for a little appetizer to go with the gargantuan green Cerignola olives and roasted salted Marcona almonds, all of which should pair nicely with the scotch on the rocks Geoff is likely to want before dinner, and will give him something to nibble on while I cook. I wash and julienne fennel, endive, and celery hearts for the salad, which will get green apple slices and pea shoots at the end, and shave a pile of parmiagiano reggiano into large curls to garnish it before serving. I mix two tablespoons softened unsalted butter with a tablespoon of good Dijon mustard, and smear the mixture on the chicken breasts, which then get rolled in a mixture of equal parts toasted bread crumbs and grated pecorino romano cheese, and put in the fridge until it is time to cook them. Gourmet Shake 'N Bake. I am so fancy. I roll out the pasta dough on my hand crank machine, and cut it with my pizza wheel into inch-wide strips, which I arrange like little birds nests on a cookie sheet to dry out a bit. I set up the kitchen counter with everything I will need for cooking, so that my movements will seem unfrenzied and smooth. Then I go to make the bed.

Oh, the bed.

The best advice my grandmother ever gave me was this:

"You are going to spend eighty percent of your life working and sleep-ing. So buy a really good bed, and get a job that you love."

Bless her heart. I did both. The work you know about. The bed is, well, sort of ridiculous. My bed is really more of a princess-and-the-pea shrine to the gods of sleep. The thick box spring and mattress were a gift to myself after I published my first anthology. I top those with a baffled firm support featherbed, which essentially looks like a futon, only boxier, followed by an old fashioned soft featherbed (the ones that look like huge pillows). Next a down comforter, then a king size chenille blanket that feels like velvet. Two king-size down pillows, two standard-size down pillows, all for sleeping, one long bolster pillow for decoration and support while reading. Sheets with a thread count high enough to make cotton feel like heaven. When I fluff everything up, the bed stands about four feet tall and requires that I use a small footstool to get in it. Getting out of it is damned near impossible, and say what you will about being over the top, no human being who has lay down on it has ever been unhappy. Most offer to move in. Many ask for the contact information for The Company Store, which provides all my sundry bed luxuries. It does take nearly twenty minutes to make properly, but well worth the effort, and in honor of the guest who will be joining me in the warm depths tonight, I give a spritz of Verbena linen water between all the layers so that it has a nice fresh scent.

By six o'clock, I am showered, dressed in a casual navy skirt and soft light-gray sweater, long white waiter's apron with a side towel neatly tucked in the string. The oven is preheated to 350 degrees for the chicken, everything is sliced, diced, chopped and minced and measured and in little white prep bowls at the ready. The table is set with my best china, white linen napkins, my great-grandmother's crystal glasses. The pre-dinner nibbles are arranged at the small round café table in my kitchen, where

Geoff can sit and keep me company while I cook for him. The pasta water is on low heat so that it will boil quickly when the time comes. Six-o-five. Six-ten. Six-fifteen. He isn't coming. I know he isn't coming. My pulse is racing, my palms are sweating. He isn't going to come, and all my preparations will have been for naught. I am nauseated. The phone rings at six-twenty-two and I am near tears. I know he is calling to cancel.

"Hello?"

"Hi, it's me, got out of the office late, I should be there in ten minutes."

"Okay, see you soon."

"Okay, bye."

Sweet fancy Moses, that man makes me crazy!

I take a deep breath, double check all my preparations, pop an umpteenth breath mint, and wait. At six-thirty-five precisely, the doorbell rings. Geoff enters full of apologies for being late, off on a tangent about some case or other while I take his coat and briefcase and deposit them on a chair in the living room. Suddenly in the middle of a sentence he turns and looks at me, and stops cold. Then he smiles.

"I'm sorry, hi." He leans over and kisses me.

"It's okay. Hi yourself."

"Nice place you got here. How about a tour? And a stiff drink?"

"I can accommodate you on both counts."

I take him through the house, and at every juncture he offers some small compliment about the décor, the architectural details, how warm and comfortable it seems. I am beaming, grinning ear to ear. We get to the kitchen where he sees the preparations for dinner, and says he didn't realize what trouble I had gone to, and hoped that his lateness didn't throw anything off. I assure him that he hasn't caused any problem at all, and pour him a Johnny Walker Gold Label (his drink of choice these days) on the rocks with a tiny twist of lemon. He makes himself at home, nibbles on the little snacks I have laid out for him, and chats at me about his week while I put the endive, fennel, celery, green apple and pea shoots in a bowl, toss them with fresh lemon juice, extra-virgin olive oil, and sea salt, sprinkle on a generous helping of parmesan curls, and arrange bread in a basket. I take the chicken out of the fridge to come up to room temperature, turn the heat up on the pasta water, and we retire to the dining room for salad. He pronounces it delicious, can't believe how simple it is, and declares I must be leaving out some secret ingredient. He has two generous helpings, mopping the dressing up with pieces of bread.

We clear the dishes, and he asks for a beer, pleased that I have his favorite brand chilled already. I drizzle olive oil over the chicken and put it in the oven. The green beans had been blanched earlier, so I heat some butter over low heat to warm them through. I put a drop of olive oil in my large skillet and add finely minced shallots to wilt down. When they have sweated a bit, I add a scant cup of chicken stock and let the mixture reduce by half. I whisk in two generous tablespoons of artichoke puree, throw in some chopped artichoke hearts, a quarter cup of dry sherry, and salt and pepper. I put the pasta in the now boiling water, and add a knob of butter to the simmering sauce, swirling to incorporate it without letting it get greasy. The fresh pasta takes only a minute to cook, I drain it, add it quickly to the sauce in the skillet, toss a few times to coat, throw in a handful of toasted pine nuts, a handful of parsley, and a scattering of grated parmesan. I give the beans one last turn in the melted butter, and a sprinkle of sea salt, and turn all the burners off. It has been exactly fifteen minutes, so I pull the chicken out of the oven, burnished and sizzling. I arrange the pasta and beans on two plates, put a chicken breast on each, garnish with more chopped parsley, and turn to my lover, who by this time has stopped speaking.

"Dinner?" I ask, plates in hand, ready to return to the dining room.

"That was amazing."

"What?"

"It was like watching a cooking show, or being in the kitchen with a real chef. Where did you learn how to do that?"

"Come eat it before it gets cold, and I'll tell you."

"You don't have to ask me twice, everything smells terrific."

Over dinner, between huge sighs and grunts of delight from Geoff, I talk about learning to cook, walk him through the recipes, promise to write it all down for him to try himself, and generally have about the best time I have ever had in my own house. We leave the dishes and go to the living room to see how the Bulls are faring against the Knicks. They aren't doing well, and Geoff, a former Knicks fan (NYU undergrad, Columbia University Law School) who converted to the Bulls when he moved to Chicago, is distraught, shaking his head, and yelling at the television. It is really sweet. We sit close together, his arm in my lap, my arm around his shoulders, and after maybe fifteen or twenty minutes, he turns to me and smiles.

"So is that poofy bed as comfortable as it looks?"

"Why don't you come find out?"

I take his hand and walk him to my bedroom. I light a candle, turn down the bed, and turn to my lover, who is watching me carefully.

"This has really been a wonderful evening. Thank you for inviting me over. I can't remember a better meal, or more lovely company."

"Darlin', you ain't seen nothing yet!"

After nearly two hours of, as usual, astounding lovemaking, I find myself nestled in the crook of Geoff's arm, my head on his chest, listening to the gentle sound of his small snoring. He is really asleep, not the light dozing that sometimes happens when we are in bed together, but actually ASLEEP. He is comfortable enough, full of good food and exhausted by good sex, to really be asleep.

Wanna know how I know it is different than the other times he has sort of half-dozed off with me?

He farted.

Twice. Softly. Not the sort of farts that one tries to let out silently that make noise anyway, just the casual release of pressure without thought that only happens in one's slumber. Plus, he is a perfect gentleman, so if he were awake and such a breach of decorum occurred, he would certainly excuse himself immediately. I don't mind admitting to you that I have never in my life been so happy to be in the presence of a flatulent man, nor am I likely to be again. But those little puttering, muttering noises muffled beneath my blankets are somehow a sign of victory. He likes it here. Likes it enough to really let himself fall asleep. And even though I know he will wake shortly, get up, get dressed, and leave me, right now, all I know is that he is, temporarily, mine. All I know is, my bed has never been as comfortable as it is with him in it, that my life has never looked as good as it does right now. He may be leaving soon, but in this moment I know he will be back. A third eruption, accompanied by a luxurious sigh, escapes my sated lover, who then returns to his snoring, mouth open slightly, enveloped in the pillows, and registering in my heart as probably the handsomest man I have ever seen, even knowing that any stranger viewing him on the street would think him painfully average. The fourth expulsion nearly makes me giggle aloud, and I mentally note not to serve the boy raw fennel and green beans in the same meal.

Geoffrey M. Fahl, Esq. is farting in my bed. And I like it.

I know. I am one sick puppy.

chapter 10

QUOTE OF THE DAY

Our birth is but a sleep and a forgetting:
The soul that rises with us, our life's star,
Hath had elsewhere its setting,
And cometh from afar.
Not in entire forgetfulness,
And not in utter nakedness,
But trailing clouds of glory, do we come
—William Wordsworth

Geoff's birthday is tomorrow. We have a date planned for tonight because tomorrow he flies out to Lake Tahoe to meet up with Sandra for a birthday weekend. I am trying not to think of it. I have found for his primary gift a lovely leather-bound journal, which he will either love or hate, I cannot be sure which.

BACKSTORY

Tomorrow, Geoff will be fifty-six, four years younger than my father, whose sixtieth we celebrated last week with a huge fete at the Four Seasons. Sandra sent her apologies from Kansas City. I got a little tipsy and slipped the following note into Geoff's hand during the toasts, scribbled on the back of a postcard I stole from the lobby.

Ah, the dulcet tones of dull lawyers making speeches gets me so hot that one thing is now clear: at some point tonight, I will be lying on a bed, touching myself, and calling your name when I come. Will this happen 1) in your bed with your participation or B) in my bed without you? If you pick choice number 1, simply find me when you are leaving to say goodnight and ask me if I enjoyed the cake, I will follow fifteen minutes behind you. If not, well, at least you know I thought of it. By the way, I am also hoping to discover the reason behind the sudden and mysterious disappearance of my panties, which I am pretty sure I remembered to put on before I left the house. Spontaneous combustion? S.

Needless to say, he asked me how I had enjoyed the cake.

SIDEBAR

Now, I don't exactly know what it is about the idea of not wearing underwear that is so compelling to men, women certainly don't like to think about their guys going commando under their suit slacks, and I for one much prefer a thin barrier between my tender parts and the outside world. But, whatever the reason, just the thought of watching a woman walk around and being the only one who knows that she is sans drawers is a really exciting thing for guys. To be frank, when I wrote Geoff that I was flying without a parachute, I was stretching the truth more than a bit. I was, at the time, safely enclosed in not only panties, but a pack-it-all-in-so-nothing-jiggles girdle, and panty hose. Luckily, I knew my boy well enough to know that he wouldn't attempt to ascertain the truth of it until we were secluded in his house. So before I left the party, I spent a few minutes in the ladies' room removing both underwear and girdle, hiding them in my purse, and putting the panty hose back on, thanking the inventor of the cotton crotch panel most heartily. That way he got the fantasy, I got the pleasure of knowing that every time he looked my way the rest of the evening he was thinking of what he might do to me later, and yet, I didn't need to abandon my comfort level beyond the brief drive to meet him.

Meanwhile, back at my place...

He is coming over for a quick date after his dinner meeting, and I will try to give him a birthday eve that will ensure his thinking of me fondly the rest of the weekend. I am surprisingly stumped when I sit down to write the note, more than a little blocked as to how to express my feelings. How to phrase things? What to say? I stop and start at least six times before finally acknowledging that I need help. But the problem with an affair is that one cannot go to anyone for help, there cannot be a secret between three people, a lesson I learned the hard way in my youth. So divine guidance it would have to be.

I like runes. They are less gypsy than tarot, more me than the bible, not really occultish, and in general seem more about providing thinking points than foretelling one's destiny. Tonight, they are a blessing. And the words begin to come.

(Another note to readers, one of the dangers of getting involved with a writer is that we have a terrible tendency toward overly long means of expression. Plus, when writers write love letters, they are some of our best material, and since we are used to sharing our deepest thoughts and feelings, it only seems natural to want to include it here. But the truth of the matter is that Geoff is required to plow through all my verbiage, because he is sleeping with me and it is directed at him. Since you and I are on intimate terms of a much different nature, if you want to skip it, I think by now you know my mind.)

In either case, for the terminally curious and voyeuristic, here is what finally came out.

Geoff—

What to say to you on this occasion? The day is significant not because of the number, no more important than 55 or 57 in the measure of a life, but because we can choose to take from society's insistence that we mark the event a rare opportunity to reflect on where we have been and where we are going. Who we are and who we would like to be. To cel-

ebrate our achievements, honor our mentors, and give thanks for the blessings the universe has seen fit to send us.

But what to say to you on this occasion?

As your friend, I can only begin to touch upon what an unbelievable trea-
sure you are to me. How uncommon. How important. When I sat down
to write this, I found myself at a complete loss, no words would come. So
I did something that I do on rare occasion when I need tangible input from
the fates, I got out my runes. Not that I am some covert crystal wearing
new-age believer, sometimes I just want a little outside opinion. Casting
runes, you blindly choose three, the first represents the atmosphere you live
in now, the second the direction to take, the third is insight for the journey.
I trusted, let my fingers find the trio, and will share their meaning with you,
strangely prophetic, utterly sensible, the meaning undeniable.

The first was GEBO, the gift of harmonic relationships. Unity with
self and others. Something personal freely given away. Generosity. Syn-
ergy. A new unexpected relationship. We acknowledge our higher power,
in turn the higher power gives back to us. We have harmony, and a rep-
resentation of the workings of karma. Good things come in return for good
deeds. We are supposed to meditate on the magic of knowing our spiri-
tual forces, treating them with reverence as we seek a pleasing and facile
environment to allow us to prepare for good things to come. I have to believe there is purpose in discovering this friendship now, in what I feel, in
the trust and honesty I share with you.

The second was KANO, an opening. Open arms, open world, open
to self and possibilities. Renewed clarity. Intellectual pursuance of truth
lights the darks of the soul and dispels shadows. You are the center where
harmonic and beneficial forces meet, it is up to you to shape those forces.
When you are in darkness, an opening with light is the most gracious thing
to have bestowed upon you. It identifies this as a time for putting effort
into new opportunities. We are supposed to meditate on seeing out of
seemingly dark situations, for there is a way out of every dilemma if we
will but see it in front of us. We should focus on what the action should
be, invest energies into breaking through. This is the path to take, embrace
every open door, see where it gets us. I have felt the darkness all around

me. I have faith in the light ahead. You, I believe, are an important source of that light, and I hope that I can in some way offer you the same clarity you have so generously provided me.

The final was WYRD, the Unknowable, the only rune with no symbol. Total trust. Total introspection. Creative power. Potential. You may have to leap over a precipice into the void, do so empty-handed and with utter faith. Some dispute it as a true rune, but I do not. In a world of uncertainty one must accept the existence of nothing if we are to accept the existence of anything. The meaning is of the non-knowable nature. The black hole of knowledge. Zero by anything is still zero. It represents the nothingness we may come from and may return to. We must confront the darkest fears of our reality. I have come to terms with the unpredictability of life, with needing to take great leaps of faith if I want abundance and joy. For what has been valiantly fought for, hard won, is ultimately sweeter victory, and will be honored. I saw that this was the third rune, the position for the journey to come, and was reminded that outcomes are not knowable. That sometimes you embark on the journey without a name for your destination. I dread the uncertain road in front of me, as we all do. But I want to go forward. I will go forward. And I feel so much safer when I think of your guidance and support along the way, so I want to believe that wherever your path leads you, that you know you can count on me for a sympathetic ear, for the soundest advice I have, for unconditional support, for collegial company.

Whether you believe in such things, or simply believe that they are random, even silly, I nevertheless was unable to deny how much they seemed connected to this friendship, which seems to me at once brand new, and yet somehow ancient. Constantly unexpected, and oddly comfortable.

I cannot remember the last time someone invaded my heart with such completeness, with such instantaneous awe. Not that instinctive "oh we shall be great friends" that happens every so often, but more "where the hell have you been, I have been waiting for you for so long" that happens almost never.

What can I say to you on this occasion? That I am privileged to know you. That you are a gift beyond price. That I hope to be writing you birthday messages for the rest of our lives. That I wish you a day that brings *you whatever joys you need and want, for you are deserving of all good things. I thank you from the bottom of my heart for your time, and spirit, and the blessing of your friendship. For all the little things you have done or said that make me feel special. For everything you are, and everything I become when I am with you. For a million things I cannot name. At the end of the day, ironically at the end of these many pages, when it comes to telling you what you mean to me, I have no words.*

Except these.

I wish for you sunshine, and laughter, and music all the days of your life. And all the happiness and love the gods can bestow upon you.

I am ever, your friend,

Sidney

While I am waiting for Geoff, I realize with delight that next weekend is Thanksgiving. Adam will be here. I need to talk it through with him before I lose my damn mind. Last week I was at lunch with my mother and a couple of her cronies, and somehow the topic of Sandra Fahl came up, and for nearly forty minutes I was regaled with the most horrifying and unwelcome bits of information.

BACKSTORY

Now, I had always known that my mother didn't much like Sandra, she always had thought her cold, dishonest, false of feeling. Sandra was rude to people she thought beneath her, like waitstaff, or underlings at the various charities where she donated time and money. Sandra was self-serving and ungrateful, never thanked people (or else she gushed in a way that was so patently fake that she made the skin crawl). I had heard some of the rumors, helping my mother out at various events, or at big firm functions with Dad. Once, at the family holiday function hosted by the partners, I overheard the following exchange in the ladies' room.

"Did you get a load of Mrs. Fahl, playing lady of the manor?" (This was June, my dad's assistant, whom I adore for the mere fact of her central casting executive secretary look, and her killer rum cake.)

"Did I? I swear she hangs on poor Mr. Fahl like a lead weight. But not affectionate, you know, just like, 'see who I am?'" (This was Marcia, general receptionist, and a woman I have never liked much, but the memory of her disdain of Sandra is endearing her to me at the moment.)

"Well, I finally figured out how to get her to be really sweet to me." (This was Faith, Geoff's assistant, who, from my mother's reports, has always been treated with the utmost contempt by Sandra, despite her unbelievable competence and the fact that Geoff completely dotes on her.) *"All you have to do is get hit by a bus."*

The three laughed together. But it wasn't funny. Not one little bit.

You see, about four months prior to this eavesdropping incident, Faith actually was *HIT BY A BUS*. It jumped the curb, and plowed her right through a plate glass store window. Lacerated liver, lost her spleen, broke all sorts of bones; she was in a coma for nearly two weeks, and was still in a wheelchair at the party. The physical therapy was going well, and she had returned to work part-time, but it was as near death as anyone would like to get, and Geoff had been completely devastated. I remember my dad talking about how lost he seemed without her, how curt he was with the younger associates and paralegals, how impatient with the temp. So the idea that one would have to nearly be killed, to still be incapacitated by injury to get someone to be nice to them, well, I think it was funny to them because it was true. And the fact of its truth turned my stomach then, just as the litany of my mother and the other women at the table turns it now.

Meanwhile, back at gossip central…(aka the luncheon table)

"Do you know what my manicurist said she heard?" Mrs. Rachmann, another wife from Dad's firm, and occasional bridge partner of my mother's, all perfectly frosted blond hair and subtle face-lift, not to mention a cutthroat instinct at cards. "Sandra was getting a pedicure, and the girl commented on her earrings, you know, the tanzanite ones Geoff bought for her birthday last year? The girl then asked how her husband was doing, and Sandra apparently replied that he was boorish, boring, and bad in bed, but that he had great taste in jewelry. Maggie said she overheard it, since she was working on a client in the next tub, and that she had never heard such an icy and matter of fact comment about someone one was presumed to love."

Mrs. Gittel, a member of my mother and Sandra's committee at the JUF Lions of Judea, pipes in. "Well, at the ladies' luncheon this summer I went outside for a cigarette—I know! I know! Don't look at me like that, I am going on the patch after Rachel's wedding, I swear! Anyway, Sandra was outside having some intense discussion on her cell phone, and when she got off she asked if she could have a cigarette. I know! I know! I didn't know she smoked either! So I give her one, light it for her, and ask if everything is all right. She says fine, just her husband as usual. I didn't want to pry—you know me—so I didn't say anything. She looked at me and said, 'You know the first time a girl marries for love, the second for money so that the third time can be for fun.' I laughed and said it was probably a good point. Only after she went inside did I realize that Geoff is only her second husband!"

"She said a similar thing to me!" Having my mother weighing in on this conversation may actually make my head implode. "We were at the Lynn Sage Cancer Foundation benefit, and Sandra was a little in her cups, and she gave me a whole speech about her travel schedule being the best thing about her marriage, since Geoff looks so much better from far away, and that she does not have to deal with him day in and day out! I mean, the chill in her eyes when she said it! I feel so sorry for Geoff, he is such a sweet man, how could he have been taken in by Sandra, I wonder?"

"That's easy," replies Mrs. Gittlel "She has that horsy, outdoorsy sort of WASP-y cuteness that makes men crazy. She looks like she knows how to sail a boat and play croquet, as if Ralph Lauren and Laura Ashley got together and had a child."

"I know I shouldn't, but I really resent the work she does for JUF." My mother again.

"I can't blame you there," says Mrs. Rachmann. "I mean, she

converted to marry her first husband, whats-his-face, Rosen? Rissman?"

"Mankowitz. Michael Mankowitz. Dentist." Mrs. Gittel, idiot savant in the arena of Chicago Jews.

"Right, right, Michael. She was raised middle-class Methodist, converted to marry Michael, started coming with her mother-in-law to the events, and then kept coming after the divorce. I mean, it would be one thing if she had REALLY converted, if she went to temple or something, but I think it is just a networking thing for her. After all, it isn't like Geoff is Jewish. It just always seems so weird to me, her supposed commitment to "our people." I always want to say 'MY people. Not YOUR people, MY people. Go help the Christian Children's Fund, why don't'cha?" My mother looks guilty for even thinking such a thing, let alone having voiced it with such vehemence.

"Well, if what I hear is true, she does still like the Jewish men." Mrs. Rachmann pipes in.

"What do you mean?" My mother looks perplexed.

"I mean, I heard she was introduced to Sari Ketzelman's cousin Ira on one of her little trips to Dallas, and that they had dinner three times, and when Sari mentioned Geoff casually to him over the phone, it appeared that a husband had not been a topic of conversation at any of those dinners...."

"Listen to us, cackling like hens over a fence, poor Siddeleh, you must be bored to tears! Please, Becca, let's change the topic otherwise your daughter will never agree to have lunch with us again!"

Have I mentioned that I hate Mrs. Gittel? Just when things were getting specific.

"Don't worry about me, girls, I find the whole thing fascinating! The three of you should have some sort of intervention, schedule a meeting with Mr. Fahl and warn him that he is in the clutches of an evil gold-digging unfaithful ice queen!"

Three coiffed heads turn to look at me with shocked brows. It might be the face-lifts, but somehow I think I may have said the wrongest thing imaginable. I wonder if the waiter will bring me some A1 sauce for my foot.

"Ha ha, kidding!"

They all laugh unconvincingly, and move on to listening to Mrs. Gittel talk about the plans for her daughter Rachel's upcoming nuptials, while I play with my goat cheese and onion tartlet, and wait for the misery to be over.

As I prepare for Geoff's arrival, the memory of that lunch and everyone's sentiment regarding Sandra, has me spitting feathers.

Remember when I talked about the whole Envy thing way back in chapter two? Well, kids, guess what? Say it with me now, I AM SEETHING WITH ENVY! Forget green-eyed monsters, too tame. Think Jurassic-era Raptors. I want Sandra in a tattered safari suit, running for her life through the woods, with Jeff Goldblum and Sam Neill back at camp, wondering aimlessly where she might have gotten to while they futz with the computerized security system.

Why does she get to have Geoff and I am relegated to second-class citizen? Why does she get to sit next to him at the functions and dance with him at the galas and have the weekend in the fancy hotel suite in Tahoe for his birthday, and I have to celebrate with him on a two-hour date which will, if I know my loverman, consist of ten minutes talking on the couch, an hour-and-a-half exquisite schtup-fest, fifteen minutes of general birthday merriment while he opens his gift, drinks a quick beer and smokes his one cigarette from the pack I now keep for such occasions, and five minutes saying goodbye in a way that ensures I don't mistake what we have for anything real. Why does she get him if she is off in Dallas having some sordid affair with Sari Ketzelman's cousin?

I know—she is his wife, she has prior claim. He is honoring, to the best of his ability, her place in his life. And there is a part of me that prefers my position; after all, he chooses me. Makes conscious and deliberate movement in my direction. I am not some obligation or default position, and he does risk a great deal by continuing our relationship. But I want more of him, more from him. I know it is dumb, and probably impossible, but I am wishing for him so hard these days. And the more I wish for him, the less his marriage seems right. The more I hear from him how generally dissatisfied he is with Sandra, his off-the-cuff remarks about having been in a heavy-duty drinking phase when they first started dating which might account for thinking it was a good idea to marry her, the more I wonder if we might not have some sort of actual potential.

This is bad. This is very very bad. I may be in way over my head. I may be actually falling for him, which I cannot do because it will only mean heartache for me. I cannot, no, I WILL NOT fall in love with Geoffrey Fahl. He is a lovely distraction while I ease myself back into the dating world. He is a good friend and a wonderful lover, and a very temporary, transitional sort of thing until I am ready to find someone to be serious about. He is the gift from the gods to make up for the mediocrity of my sex-life with Mark, and I am just refilling the vault with the dozens of orgasms I should have been enjoying in my twenties.

INNER MONOLOGUE

Okay, I don't really believe this either, but I have to let myself think I believe it, because clearly I am not ready to face up to what I really think or feel, not yet. But I know you don't believe it, and you would think me a patent fool if I tried to pass myself off as really believing it deep down. I think it is sort of like my alarm clock. I set the time fast, because I love the luxury of those stolen minutes of sleep the snooze button provides. So I set the alarm for the time I am supposed to be up, knowing I can safely snooze twice without jeopardizing my morning. Now why, you might ask, don't I just set the clock right, and the alarm earlier? I have no answer for that. This is just the way I do it. I set the time fast and I tell myself that I am not falling in love with Geoff and smack the snooze button on the clock and in my heart, and deal with it again in seven minutes.

Geoff arrives. The aforementioned schedule is kept nearly to the minute. The conversation is light, the sex is lovely, heavily weighted toward items from Geoff's favorite sections of the menu in honor of the impending birthday, he adores the journal, saying he has always wanted one like it, and can't imagine what he is going to do with the silly old print I found of "The House of Fahl," some dark and dreary manse in the Lake District of England, no relation, but still funny. He saves the letter to read later, thanks me most sincerely for the evening and the presents, and assures me we will be able to see each other next Tuesday evening briefly, very briefly, as he has to get up early Wednesday and drive to meet up with Sandra at her sister's in Minnesota for the turkey day festivities.

I wish him a safe trip and a good time, and send him home with a lingering kiss, achieved in spite of his usual tendency to just peck and run.

And for the first time, after he is gone, I return to the bed which is rumpled and smells of his cologne and my perfume and sex and candle smoke, and bury my face in the pillow where his head lay, and weep. Because for the first time, when he left, I wanted to beg him to stay. And I am not so sure I am ready to deal with the implications of that desire.

I may be in over my head. It may be time to bring in an expert. Enter, Adam. Super-bro. Able to juggle three girlfriends at once, all of them working in the same office, with no hard feelings when things are over. The boy who slept with his professors in college, as well as their teaching assistants, in one legendary incident, at the same time. (And I do mean, the same actual time, not during the same time period, if you get my drift.) The man can have a long-term committed relationship in which he is completely faithful in word and deed, but the minute it is over, he is over it, and on to the next round of revelry. I asked him once how he rebounded so quickly, especially from the few girls with whom he had seemed to really be in love, and he said, "It is pretty simple really, I look at my pain and think, I am going to be over this eventually, why not now?"

Sort of devastating logic, if you ask me.

So then, Adam. Next week. He will help me think the whole thing through. He will tell me to end it. And I don't think I can end it. In which case, he may not be helpful at all. But I have to try. I have to do something. Don't I?

chapter 11

when Geoffrey met Sidney

Scene One: Three women sitting outdoors at a table in a restarant, nice view overlooking water and willow with sky-scrapers faintly visible in the distance

Marie:	I went through his pockets while he was in bed.
Alice:	Marie, why do you go through his pockets?
Marie:	You know what I found?
Alice:	No, what?
Marie:	They just bought a dining-room table. He and his wife just went out and spent sixteen hundred dollars on a dining-room table.
Alice:	Where?
Marie:	Huh... The point isn't where, Alice. The point is he's never going to leave her!
Alice:	So what else is new. You've known this for two years.
Marie:	You're right, you're right, I know you're right.

I am remembering a time when I would have been Alice in this scenario. I am, in fact, remembering several specific times when I have offered excellent and pointed advice to friends who have even been vaguely considering affairs with married or significantly coupled men. "Bad idea," I would always say. "They never leave their wives."

I was so coy and full of myself, so righteously indignant. So, this is what karma feels like.

There is a reason that they say—those ubiquitous and faceless "they" of the vernacular—that there is no such thing as a secret between three people. My mother used to sum it up simply, "Everybody has a nobody. And you can't ever be sure that the person who is your nobody doesn't have one that isn't you."

I have been a very good girl. I have told exactly no one, not my bestest friends, not my most fabulous and trustworthy hairdresser, not my colleagues, no one. I am busting at the frigging seams. I mean, it was easy not to talk to anyone about it when I was with Mark, I was so mortified at turning out to be "one of those women" that I couldn't admit it to a soul. But since then, I have nowhere to turn for advice, no one cheering me on or telling me to stop. No one telling me that he might be the real deal, or that he is a shit. No one congratulating me on having such raw and earth-shattering passion in my life, nor warning me of its likely eventual fade to boring routine. I still haven't told Parker; somehow I can't find the words. Plus, he's going to KILL me when he finds out I've been keeping a secret this long. So I have a plan. Today that is all going to change. For today, Adam arrives for Thanksgiving weekend, and I am going to make him my father confessor. I have sworn to myself to try and be honest about things, not romanticize them too much, not make Geoff out to be some Plasticine perfect paramour, nor me some unwitting accomplice. I am going to tell all, and see what he has to say, and try to actually hear him when he advises me. And then I can tell Parker, and just say I needed to tell Adam first.

It is going to be very difficult.

I am served in this endeavor by the fact that Geoff canceled our date last night because he had to work late, and had to drive to Minnesota early this morning, and just didn't feel up to it. I was very gracious, and played it off like it was no big deal. Then I carefully got out of the blue shirt that he loves, not to mention the fabulous black lace bra and panties I had purchased for the occasion, and packed up the turkey tettrazini casserole I had made for us in honor of Geoff's confession that one of the hardest things about Thanksgiving was missing his mother's day-after-use-up-the-leftovers treat.

And no ordinary canned cream soup plebian offering from me for my lover's delight, no sir. Homemade turkey stock, reduced and thickened with heavy cream, sour cream, butter, good sherry, fresh parmesan and celery salt. Turkey thigh and breast meat, poached with shallots, celery leaves, bay and peppercorn. Homemade wide egg noodles, freshly toasted breadcrumbs mixed with more parmesan and unsalted butter. It took me two fucking days to make a casserole that is a staple because usually you use leftover meat, Campbell's finest, and whatever noodles are lying around, resulting in, for a normal person, twenty minutes of labor for a hot meal the day after too much time in the kitchen.

One bowl, one pot, one cutting board and dinner is served. But since I am completely out of my gourd, I dirtied a whole cabinet full of pots and pans, ended up washing dishes and cleaning the kitchen till three in the morning, so that I could dish my man up a treat that showed not only that I care and can cook, but that I hear his every offhand wish and try to provide for him. And he was too tired to show up and eat it. Not to mention me. And no, I don't particularly care that it is a little graphic for some tender sensibilities—suck it up—I am too ticked off to pretty it up for you. That man gives the best head since the INVENTION of head, and I am not going to see him for another ten days since Sandra doesn't have another trip scheduled until the week after this long holiday weekend—not to mention the impending interminability of the SIX WEEKS we will be apart between mid-December and early February when Sandra is on her annual travel hiatus dealing with the end of the fiscal year. So you will have to excuse me for being somewhat curt and indelicate, but I may in fact be addicted to the way he makes me come so hard I think the top of my head has been blown across the room, so missing even one date, especially due to blatant laziness, ESPECIALLY right before a difficult scheduling period, really chaps my ass. Sorry, but that is how it goes.

To make matters even worse, I call Geoff's cell phone, and when he answers, I offer to come over and help him pack, try to tempt him with the idea of a neck rub and a blow job. Nothing doing. He is, as he says, awfully sorry to have to turn me down, and feels bad for canceling, but he has three briefs to go over before bed, plus the aforementioned packing, and the early-morning long drive to think of. He says several sweet things to me, none of which I can be bothered to recall in my disappointment, wishes me a really great Thanksgiving, and promises to make it up to me in a couple of weeks.

He had better.

Foiled, I spend the evening instead watching a marathon of old *Sex and the City* episodes, takeout Chinese in hand, followed by half a package of DoubleStuf Oreos (I assume some long-ago sister compulsive overeater consumed the missing second f in a fit of self-loathing anguish over a man). Feeling sick and ashamed of myself, I end up at the grocery store at 10:00 p.m., and by one in the morning have made a big batch of my famous pumpkin soup, which Adam loves, enough to feed the small army at my parents' place on Thursday, and still keep some at home for him to enjoy for the rest of the weekend. He likes to put a mug of it in the microwave and drink it scalding hot with crushed-up gingersnaps and mini marshmallows floating in it before bed. Bless his little fuzzy butt. I adore Adam even more than I adore Geoff, and these days, that is saying something indeed. Of course, since cooking soothes my spirits always, by the time it is chilling in the fridge, I have totally forgiven Geoff, and scolded myself for not being more understanding.

Essentially, I have become a complete and utter wimp. But I make one hell of a mean pumpkin soup.

Recipe of the Week
Sidney's Famous Pumpkin Soup

This is so simple, I have to share it with you, and easy enough that anyone can do it, even those of you who think you can't cook. Whip it out at your next autumnal meal, and wow the crowd. It freezes beautifully. I am not going to give you amounts here, since soup is one of those things best done by eye and taste, and unlike baking, hard to screw up. Plus, one never knows about the size of the pumpkins, nor how much meat is in them. You can substitute butternut squash for all or some of the pumpkin with no alterations necessary.

Take one medium pumpkin, cut into wedges, scrape out the seeds, and carefully slice the rind off with a sharp knife. Chop into fairly large chunks, so that they are all approximately the same size. In your stockpot, sweat a medium onion in a tiny bit of olive oil until soft, but not colored (a sprinkle of salt will ensure it doesn't caramelize on you), then put all the pumpkin pieces on top and pour in chicken stock to just barely cover the pumpkin. It is okay if some pointy bits stick out of the liquid. Cook over medium heat with a grating of fresh nutmeg until the pumpkin is very meltingly soft. Put in the fridge to cool, minimum one hour, but overnight is fine. Using a blender, regular or immersion, blend in batches until very smooth. Bring back up to heat in the pot, and taste for salt, pepper and nutmeg. Mix in heavy cream until the soup lightens one shade; go slow, you can always add more. Taste again for seasoning. Eat.

I have done this with both homemade stock and canned broth with equal success. I even did it with canned pumpkin once, and it still worked, just be careful to get pumpkin and not pumpkin pie filling. If using canned pumpkin, just add stock until the consistency seems thickly soupy. I pass it through a chinois (a commercial grade fine strainer) if I want that extra silkiness to the texture, but a little lumpy is okay too. You can garnish it *with everything from the sweet treats Adam prefers, to crème fraiche and chives, toasted pumpkin seeds tossed in curry powder, unsweetened whipped cream mixed with amaretti cookie crumbs, or white truffle shavings and extra-virgin olive oil. You can serve it in a mini roasted pumpkin. You can make it vegetarian with vegetable stock, or even vegan if you leave out the cream.*

Scene Two: Marie and Sally in a bookstore. Second floor.

Marie: So I just happen to see his American Express bill.

Sally: What do you mean you just *happen* to see it?

Marie: Well, he was shaving and... there it was in his briefcase.

Sally: What if he came out and saw you looking through his briefcase?

Marie: You're missing the point, I'm telling you what I found. He just spent a hundred and twenty dollars on a new nightgown for his wife. I don't think he's ever going to leave her.

Sally: No one thinks he's ever going to leave her.

Marie: You're right, you're right, I know you're right.

Adam takes the train to my place, which is right on the Blue O'Hare El Line, and amazes me with how great he looks. Adam is my polar opposite. Tall, thin, light brown bone-straight hair, natural athlete. Eats whatever he wants and never gains an ounce, the bastard. He is also sort of a numbers wunderkind, one of the few students accepted to the MBA program at Northwestern's Kellogg Business School right out of college. I, of course, can barely do long division. He got recruited right out of Kellogg to work in the Venture Capital department of a London bank, and since he seems to effortlessly know what new ideas are likely to take off, he has done very well for himself. He shares a great flat in Kensington with his friend Chase, and generally lives a life few mortals ever dare dream of. He is a little pasty—he is living in London after all—but I am relieved that he hasn't picked up some poncy accent, nor does he throw those little Briticisms into our conversation. Nothing is "brilliant," no one is "knackered," and he does not need to use the "loo," thank goodness. We get him settled, play generic catch-up over huge bowls of the tettrazini (no point in wasting it), and once done, I sit him down on the couch and begin my carefully rehearsed speech.

"I need you to be my best friend for a minute, not just my brother, and you have to be supportive of me while I do this, okay?"

"Okay."

"I have been seeing someone."

"That's great, Sid! I was hoping you were, you seem to have a twinkle about you. Why the secrecy? Is it a girl?"

"No, I am not a lesbian."

"Pity, they are very in vogue now, I would make huge trendy points with all my pals back over the pond!" He just got two ex-pat demerits for saying "over the pond," but I am inclined to forgive him for the moment. "So, how come I haven't gotten the juicy details yet? What is he, some old midlife crisis guy?"

Oy, gottenyu.

I must have blanched pretty good, because Adam starts laughing really hard.

"He IS! He IS some old midlife crisis guy! Sid, you sneaky bitch, who the hell is he?"

"Geoffrey Fahl."

"Why do I know that name?"

"Remember your father? Partner at Stein, Rachmann, Edison and *FAHL*?"

"Oh good lord, *MISTER* Fahl, I don't think I ever heard him referred to by a first name before! At least he is the youngest partner—I mean Edison is at least five years older than Dad, and Rachmann, well, Rachmann is just ugly."

"And gay."

"I always thought so, especially once you meet Mrs. Rachmann. Whatever, I can't believe you are banging Mr. Fahl! Does Dad know? He couldn't, I would have heard by now. So when did he divorce that chilly wench he was married to? What was her name? Cruella?"

"Her name is Sandra, and they are not divorced."

"Oh, Sidlet, please tell me they are separated."

"Nothing would give me greater pleasure. I have ambition to tell you those very words someday. But today, not so much."

"Uh-oh. Has he said he is going to leave her?"

"No."

"Wow, kiddo, that is deep. How long?"

"Eight months."

"But then…" He has done the math.

"I know." I don't want to deal with that part now, and Adam seems to sense it.

"Wow. WOW! I mean, damn. Sid this is sort of major, here, I am going to need a minute…. Do you love him?"

"I think I may be heading in that direction, yes."

"Does he love you?"

"I don't know, but I don't think so."

"Then he is an idiot."

"That is certainly up for discussion. You don't think I am an awful person?"

"Of course not. I am actually sort of impressed. I thought all those years with Mark just squeezed all the game slut out of you! Welcome home, Trampy!" Adam and I used to call each other Scampy and Trampy in high school, in acknowledgment of our mutual tendency toward ridiculous amorous adventures.

"Thank you very much."

"Wow, Mr. Fahl. I guess I can see how he is sort of attractive, I mean, not handsome, but attractive. I have to ask, tho', guy that age, I mean Sid, what is he, twenty years older than you?"

"Twenty-three."

"So, um, Viagra?" He really is a wicked boy, my brother.

"Like he would need that, hot as I am."

"Good point, I shouldn't have doubted you. How is it?"

"The sex? Bar none, he is the best lover I have ever had. It is unimaginably amazing."

"Good for you! Older women always were great in bed too, but you hear stories about guys not being up to snuff after fifty. Gives me hope! So what, do you really think you are some midlife thing to him? Cheaper than a Porsche?"

"Fuck you sideways."

"Okay, kidding, but really, I mean, do you think it is going somewhere?"

"I don't know. I want it to, I mean, I think I am falling really hard for him, and not in some transitional way, or some Electra thing, I mean, we are really great together."

"I am sure you are, but Sid…"

Here it comes, follow the bouncing ball, y'all…

"They never leave their wives."

Bastard.

"I know, I know."

"Look, if you are having fun, have fun. If you are having great sex, I am all for it! Just be careful. Are you dating anyone else?"

"No."

"Well, do."

"Adam…"

"DO! Don't date anyone exclusively who isn't dating you exclusively. That includes wives, Sid. You want to stick with him, fine, but don't shut any doors or windows because you think he is going to wake up one morning and realize he can't live without you. I mean, he should—you know he should. He is the luckiest asshole on the planet to have you, but he won't, they just don't."

"I know, I know."

"Cut that out, you sound like whats-her-name in that movie."

I swear the boy reads my goddamned mind. "Carrie Fisher. *When Harry Met Sally…*"

"EXACTLY! Hey, I love that movie…do you have it on tape?"

"Of course. Adam, NO!"

"Oh yeah, aversion therapy baby. True love wins in the end, the married guy loses to the single guy and you get to see Meg Ryan fake an orgasm. And I want popcorn." Shit.

Scene Three: A lanky man sits on a couch in a darkened Chicago living room next to his roly poly and adorable older sister. They share a big bowl of popcorn. Their faces are lit by the light of the television screen. In the background can be heard dialogue from the movie.

Sally:	You sent flowers to yourself.
Marie:	Sixty dollars I spent on this big stupid arrangement of flowers and I wrote a card that I planned to leave on the front table where Arthur would just happen to see it.
Sally:	What did the card say?
Marie:	"Please say yes. Love Jonathan."
Sally:	Did it work?
Marie:	He never even came over. He forgot this charity thing that his wife was a chairman of. He's never going to leave her!
Sally:	Of course he isn't.
Marie:	You're right, you're right, I know you're right. Where is this place?
Sally:	Somewhere in the next block.
Marie:	Uh… I can't believe I'm doing this.
Sally:	Look, Harry is one of my best friends and you are one of my best friends and if by some chance you two hit it off then we could all still be friends instead of drifting apart the way you do when

you get involved with someone who doesn't know your friends.

Marie: You and I haven't drifted apart since I started see-
         ing Arthur.

Sally: If Arthur ever left his wife and I actually met him
         I'm sure that you and I would drift apart.

Marie: He's never going to leave her.

Sally: Of course he isn't.

Marie: You're right, you're right, I know you're right.

The man elbows his sister, and the two of them laugh very hard. In the middle of laughing, she begins to cry. He moves the popcorn bowl, and puts his arm around her and pulls her close, stroking her hair.

FADE OUT.

chapter 12

between the lines

18 december 3:45 a.m.

Geoff—

Well, where else would I be in the middle of the night, but awake in front of the computer, thinking of you, wanting to speak my mind.

I am so very unsettled.

I have seen of late in your eyes the fear that will be our un-doing. Heard in your voice the discord of your thoughts, felt in your words the abandonment of our purpose. And while I am as prepared as I might be for a permanent decision to be at the end of what we have been, I need the comfort of the page to help me get my head around what I feel.

I write because I think you may choose to stop this train short of its ultimate destination. And I need to respond, need to use my words, manage my feelings in a time of rational thought, reasonable objectivity. I will not risk driving a wedge between us by trying to express myself in moments of limited clarity and maximum disappointment. I write because I know that tomorrow—well, actually today—I have to look into your eyes and say what is true for me, and I fear I will say it badly, I fear I will do it all wrong, and I have to know that when I am finished I can at the very least hand this to you as a sort of clarifying *Cliff Notes*. A study guide, if you will. By the time you read this I will have unburdened myself to you in whatever way I could manage. By the time you read this you will have given me some response, even if that response is that you have no idea what to do with what I have said. I hope that whatever occurred we are okay in the ways that are important.

The only thing I can ask of you is to comprehend that my intentions are simply openness; I am not looking for response, am not trying to alter where you are, am not asking for more than I was earlier.

Well, now that I look on it, that is a lie.

I do want to alter where you are. To make you undo the ending you have so carefully imposed, to pull your words out of the air where you launched them at me so kindly. I might not have even noticed how pointed they were, how likely to inflict wounds, until their barbs took hold in my skin, and would not be shaken off. I carry them still, can feel their prickling heat, can feel their subtle anguish, can feel their precious pain.

So yes I write to alter. And to honor, and to celebrate. And I suppose to beg you to read this, read me, and more than listen—hear. And I am too good for begging, I have too much pride. You know this, so pay attention to what it means for me to be on my knees on this page before you, asking you to know my mind.

I have to focus. I am trying so hard to tell you who I am, why this feels so important, why I have to be this honest, even knowing it may send you running from me. I have tried so hard to be good, to not push too hard, not ask too much. But I look at this possible ending, this thing which seems so unfinished, and I cannot help but want to reach out. To see if there has been anything in these months that has brought any clarity about what and why we were. To see if I have fallen out of favor, become regrettable. In all the things we talk about so freely, in all the discussions about life and love and joy and heartache, we don't talk about us. At least not beyond the things which make us problematic. We don't talk about what is good or right, and I think you know why I am more than willing, to move forward, but I do not know what is in your head, and I do not know what to do with the overabundance of what rails in mine.

How do I let go of the part of this relationship that lives outside what is rational or acceptable, and yet brings me such complete joy?

How do I tell you how insanely happy I am when we are together, without having you assume that I am after more than I claim?

How do I explain it to you without seeming melodramatic, or psychotic, or ridiculous?

How do I balance how afraid I am to push you away by sharing too much, with how afraid I am to let you leave without telling you what I feel?

I am going to have to be brave enough to try to tell you face to face, and I know there will be things I will forget to say in the nervousness of the moment. This letter is the coward's way out, but I can only add it to the list of offenses I am asking you to forgive.

I have talked with you a little about my faith in the universe, in my own instincts. I have learned hard lessons, have fine-tuned my ability to hear the inner voices, weed out what is most important. When I go with my gut, I am never wrong. Which is to say, even when I make mistakes, they are the mistakes I am supposed to make, and I make them for the right reasons. If I know nothing else, it is that all the wide world can do is send us the people we are supposed to know, whisper to us when they arrive. We have to want to hear it, have to trust in it, especially when it forces us to make choices. You, for me, are not a difficult choice. A complicated, inconvenient, honest choice, but never difficult.

You challenge me in all the ways I want and need to be challenged. You make me feel appreciated. You make me want to be a better person so that I feel worthier of you. You make me feel more attractive than I have a right to.

I try so hard to be beautiful for you. I know I shouldn't.

In its simplest terms, you make sense to me. In theory we couldn't be more wrong for each other, but in practice, I cannot help but focus on all that is right. I am never more myself, frankly and unabashedly me, than when we are together. And in the moments when you let yourself go, when you turn off the gears, I see you, everything you are. I can, and have, found the adjectives for all your wondrous qualities, but I see too all your faults, and I appreciate that the combination makes you who you are, and that I adore who you are. There is nothing about you I would change, with the notable exception of your willingness to be with me. The impact you have had on me is undeniable. I have never known anyone who makes me feel the way I do when we are together. I am attracted to you on so many levels—intellectually, emotionally, spiritually, psychologically, philosophically, physically—it makes my head swim.

This would have been enough, more than I could begin to thank anyone for in a lifetime of trying. I never would have believed that you might be attracted to me in return. That you might see in me any qualities that are as important and rare to you as yours are to me. Had we acknowledged this mutual attraction and never acted on it, I would still think myself incredibly lucky. But we did. And it wasn't purposeless. It wasn't without thought, or caution. We acted because when you recognize intriguing potential between you and someone you care about, someone you trust, you want more than anything to know. To be sure. I have never felt so safe in anyone's arms, in anyone's company. So cared for. No one in my life has ever found that perfect balance between passion and palliation. I am unequivocally contented when I am with you, whether we are talking over dinner, or making love, or just holding each other in silence.

And I cannot do this non-breakup breakup, even though last week it was what I asked for. I don't know what I am supposed to think or feel. I have spent these past nights trying not to think about the fact that perhaps we are over. That we can't really be paused, or on hold, unless we both agree that there is something here we will need to revisit. Not because we are definitely meant to be together, but because you cannot tell me with complete certainty that we aren't. I am not ready to let that go, not until it feels finished.

If you no longer find me interesting, or intellectually stimulating, or bright or witty or supportive, well, then okay. If you don't trust me, can't be yourself with me, then okay. If I no longer make you laugh, if you no longer find me attractive, then okay. I mean, it stings, but okay. I always assumed that it would probably happen eventually.

At the end of the day, your problematic relationship, my failed marriage, these were damaged before. Nothing that is wrong for either of us was created by our interest in each other, even if the expression of that interest makes us more conscious of the flaws. If either one of us had been happy, or fulfilled in what we had, we could never have gotten to here. And when we look at the trials and sorrows that have been sent to each of us over the past year, it becomes too easy to dismiss us as another problem. As something to be dealt with, simply because the timing seems so awfully bad.

But I will not look at you as a problem. I will continue to

see you, to see us, as a gift, to think of us as the balance for all that is wrong in the world. If you are about to make the same heartbreaking choice about your personal life as I have recently done, then I will look to us as a healing balm for those pains. If you are destined, as I was, to find yourself alone, after so much work, after so much time, then I will hope that I could help you through, keep you safe from harm and heartache. Perhaps the reason we are here is to acknowledge that when relationships end we become fragile, unsure of ourselves. That the time when it makes the least sense to be open to new people, is the time we are loneliest, and need to be held, to be cared for, the time when we need to be re-minded that we are worthy of love, that we can inspire at-traction and affection.

I thought I could continue with you just as we have been for the foreseeable future, with no complaints. I thought that if this were all you were able to offer me, then I would accept for as long as you were willing. But I have not been able to stop myself from wondering if there might not be more. I don't want or need promises from you, I don't need to jump to the head of the line, I have neither the time nor the inclination to attempt to be in the top five of your priorities. All I would ask is for recognition that things have been good. That they have been good enough to think that they might be good at the next level. I believe with everything I am that I could make you happy, so what I ask for is the opportunity and your per-mission to try. And the only commitment I want is that if I am successful today, that you give me the same opportunity and permission tomorrow. Tomorrow we can decide about the day after.

Perhaps it is not my wound to heal, not my place to make change. Perhaps all I am allowed to do is be good to you for as long as you will let me. And while I will fight for you to the end of these pages, perhaps the lesson I take is that if every-thing I have tried to be for you, everything we have been to each other, everything we might be can't bind you to me for any longer than this, if the possibility of happiness won't stop you, then these words won't make you change your mind.

Whatever happens after today, whether you decide that we can continue to explore what we are together, whether we really stay friends or you retreat to a place where we are simply friendly acquaintances, know that there is a part of me that you own, now and always. That no matter where you go or what you do, someone out in the world adores you, is thinking of you, wishing you happiness. And if you ever need anything, anything at all, come to me and I will help you in whatever way I can.

It is all in your hands. I will move ahead on the assumption that you understand me, that we are fine, that you know that any request for your time and company is simply about the continuation of a friendship that means the world to me. And I will expect the same of you, and assume that if you make an offer or accept an invitation, unless you tell me otherwise, it is just because I haven't completely overstepped my bounds and you can still suffer spending time with me as just good friends. If I have unintentionally made you feel uncomfortable, or awkward, you have my apologies. If you decide that you don't want to see me, even platonically, I will understand. I will be enormously heartbroken, but I will own the hurt, and let it make me real, and never, never regret for a moment that I allowed you into me so far that when you leave the hollow place you filled will miss you. It is the most exquisite pain I can imagine. It is what keeps me human, and in the end, I will be as full of gratitude for that gift as for any you have given me.

I am deeply sorry for dumping this on you, for saying and writing it wrong, for leaving out all the things I should have said, for keeping in the things I shouldn't. For everything.

I end with all good thoughts. With tremendous hope that I have not caused irreparable damage. And while I know you never seem to want to speak to me of these ridiculous letters I keep dropping on you, I am always willing to discuss, to clarify, to sit quiet and hear a response if you have one.

Whatever is in store, know this. I am forever changed by what we have shared, and the memories of what we have been will keep me warm on lonely nights for the rest of my life. I cannot begin to express what it means to me that, for a time at least, I was chosen. You are a little piece of heaven here on earth, and I am the luckiest girl ever.

So I say this, without reservation.

If you ever change your mind, ever in this life, don't hesitate. Come for me.

Ever,

Sidney

chapter 13

QUOTE OF THE DAY

Tomorrow is Saint Valentine's day,
All in the morning betime,
And I a maid at your window,
To be your Valentine.

—William Shakespeare
Hamlet: Ophelia, in madness, singing

I thought we were officially over, Geoff and I. I mean, I knew we were sort of over before Christmas, when I gave him my whole big speech about needing more from him, and wanting to make changes, and how exhausting it was working so hard at trying not to count on him, and when we agreed that we would just be done until Sandra left again, and then if he decided to come back to me, it would be with the understanding that we were in some way moving forward, and I know that I didn't share this speech with you, but it was hard enough to get it out the first time, and I did give you the endless letter from hell, so you must have some idea what was in the works.

To recap, after spending time talking it through with Adam over Thanksgiving, and via e-mail in the weeks following, it became clear that I needed Geoff to acknowledge me in ways that he wasn't currently, and that I needed to protect myself a bit from relying too much on him, and on us, and have a better picture of how he should fit into my life. So, on our last date before Sandra's return, knowing that it would be up to a couple of months before we had another chance to be alone, I took the opportunity at the end of an afternoon of playful bedroom romping to give him his Christmas presents (which he loved…an old gavel that had belonged to his favorite professor at law school, and a leather case for his squash racquet with his initials embossed on it), and forced him to listen to me for fifteen minutes while I talked at him about our relationship. He listened like a good boy, agreed that perhaps I was right about some issues, admitted that he didn't really have a response beyond having heard me, and knowing what was expected of him should he decide to continue with me in the New Year, and that we would just have to wait and see. He gave me a book, a pewter paperweight with a feather quill engraved on it, and one of those magnetic refrigerator poetry kits, (be still my heart, such overwhelming romance), a lovely kiss, a long hug, and then he left me.

I cried a lot. Not so anyone would notice, just little quiet breakdowns in my office, or sitting in the bath. I wept through an entire hour-long massage, but I think my masseuse just thought she was releasing toxins, and didn't comment on it. I missed him like a dull ache all day long and at night I dreamt of him and woke up lonely. He called the next week to wish me a lovely holiday season, and to tell me that he had read the whole letter.

"All I can say is thank you for writing it, and that I read it all, even though it took me a while, and I have heard everything you have said and written, and I think we should just both go off on our vacations and have a restful time, and when we get back we will get together and catch up, and see what we will see."

"Okay."

"It will all be all right, you know."

"I don't know what that means, exactly."

"It means whatever happens, it will be all right."

"If you say so."

"I do. And Sid?"

"Yes?"

"For future reference, I am an old man and I have a very limited attention span. A memo would have served." I can hear the smile.

"Are you actually criticizing me for verbosity?" He really is the most lovely boy ever. Even if he is breaking my heart into a bezillion pieces.

"Not criticizing, it was beautifully rendered, but two more pages and it would have been a novel, and you know men of my advancing years cannot keep focused for that long. Just bullet point it for me next time."

"What if there is no next time? Who says I ever intend on writing anything to you ever again?"

"All right then, it will just be redundant information."

"Duly noted."

"Have a good trip Sidney, I will see you when I get back."

"You too, and Geoff…"

"Yes?"

"Happy New Year, to us both."

"Indeed. To us both."

Sigh. Deep and mournful sigh.

So, I went away for two weeks with my folks and Adam for a little family vacation to St. Thomas, where Adam was wonderful about telling me I had done the right thing, and gave me all sorts of ideas about how to ease back into the dating world, all the while helping me keep up appearances so that my parents had no idea what I was going through, and after two weeks of fun and sun and snorkeling, I returned home tanned, rested, and with a brave face.

Geoff spent this time in Arizona with Sandra and another couple they know who own a home there. I returned, and he returned, and we did not communicate with each other, and I moved through January in something of a fog. I really only thought about him once a day, which is to say from about the minute I woke up until the moment I fell asleep. (You can't possibly imagine I was able to move on so quickly as all that; after all, it had been so few weeks since the last time he kissed me, the last time I felt his arms around me, the last time I felt his weight on me.)

But I did really think we were over. I mourned him as someone gone, I mourned us as ended, I grieved for what might have been, for the things I would never have. I privately bemoaned the fact that I would never know what it was to spend a whole night with him, that I would never be the one he turned to in his best and worst moments. I wrote very sad poems, which I will not foist upon you.

And I thought of our last conversation, the fact that he had said that if he returned to me in the New Year he would know what it was he was returning for, and remembering and clinging to that little if, in those moments I wrote hopeful poems, which again, I will spare you.

Mark came to town. It was awkward, even as it was nice to see him. We had dinner at home, and he commented on the changes I had effected in a most complimentary fashion, even though a lot of what I did was stuff he had nixed when we were together. He showed me pictures of his new place. He was enjoying the job. He was loving California. He was slightly tan, had lost a little weight, seemed happy. We didn't talk about dating, but I sensed he might have met someone. He was more self-assured than I remembered him. The whole experience was in soft focus. I am sure I am blocking it to a certain extent, and in any case, it is only the result that makes any difference. We agreed that we should file for divorce in the fall when our separation hit the one-year mark, that our current financial arrangement would suit, that we didn't need lawyers—we could just do it ourselves. It was and is hazy, the whole thing, as if it happened to someone else, and all I wanted was to talk to Geoff, to have his counsel, to see him. But I couldn't reach out, I couldn't ask for his time, especially knowing that Sandra was still in town. Then, I got an e-mail after Mark went back to California.

To: poetsid@aol.com
From: fahlguy1@aol.com
RE: good thoughts

Sidney—
Heard from your dad that Mark was in and you have officially decided to divorce. I know how hard it must have been, and I want you to know that I am so sorry for everything it must have dredged up for you. I am holding all good thoughts. You are one of the strongest, most self-reliant women I have ever known, and whatever you are feeling in this moment, I know you are going to be fine. More than fine, really great. There is a wonderful life full of possibility ahead of you. Let's have lunch or something soon.
Best,
Geoff

I didn't know what to say, didn't know how to reply. What could I write back? Thanks? Thanks for thinking nice thoughts for me? Thanks for seeing the wonderful life ahead of me which you have no desire to be a part of? Thanks for knowing I am in pain and not bothering to come to me and hold me and make it better? I wrote back only that it was nice to hear from him, that I was fine, that lunch would be lovely. What else could I say?

SIDEBAR

Okay, I know that this is all really whiny and sort of irritating to read, and that I am glossing over the whole Mark visit like it wasn't really much of anything, when it was in fact monumental. I know that a stronger person would be more forthcoming about the whole time period, and share with you the funny stories from the trip, like deep-sea fishing with my parents and watching my mother get all excited about catching things, but needing to throw all the fish back because the thought of killing them felt cruel. I know I should give you all the details about the four of us getting schickered on hurricanes and dancing in a little beachside shack with the locals. I should offer every detail of the discussion with Mark, the strange moment at the end of the evening when he made an offhand comment about us having sex for old times' sake like we would if we were in a movie, and how I actually almost considered it except I knew it would be a bad idea and that it would feel like I was cheating on Geoff who wasn't even in my life anymore, so I just laughed it off like he had been joking. I know I should tell you about my sister Naomi's long weekend in town while her husband Michael took the kids to see his parents in Florida, since up until now she has been an afterthought of a tertiary character, and you are probably wondering why I even bothered to include her at all, but it isn't like this weekend was any different than any other time she has visited, and we didn't have some big bonding event or anything. She came, we shopped, Mom took us for spa days at Kiva, we all found dresses to wear to Sarah's bat mitzvah this July, she left. It was good to see her, but we didn't really spend any time alone together, nor did we have any conversations worth noting. I should talk about work, the new semester, the eager young writers in my care, the fun I am having with my new co-teacher for the Classical Dramatic Texts seminar. I should, but I won't. And I won't defend it, except to say that I don't wanna. It is my story, and good or bad, I am going to tell it the way it occurs to me, and none of that wants to come out, because all I really want to talk about is Geoff. And I know that makes me a little bit weak, and that I should seem more well rounded, and that I am starting maybe to annoy you a little bit, like I am obsessing about him to the exclusion of all else. But guess what? I DON'T CARE. Because I am indeed obsessing about him, and if you are my friend, you will placate me a little bit here, knowing that it is helping me to vent. Besides, I really just want to get to the part where he comes back to me. (Don't you just adore blatant foreshadowing?)

Meanwhile, back at headquarters...

Geoff and I picked and discarded half a dozen possible lunch dates, until it became clear that a midday meeting seemed impossible with our schedules, and settled instead on drinks after work. It took us until the first week of February to make arrangements, and I didn't sleep very well for the three nights before meeting him. The bar across the street from his office seemed best; he had a late appointment in the building, and I was teaching at Columbia that afternoon so I was downtown anyway, and it was quiet and dark there. I arrived early to find that he had arrived even earlier, and secured a corner table for us.

He looked so good to me. Dark gray suit, white-and-gray striped shirt, the surprise of the lime green in the otherwise conservative power tie. He rose to meet me, a twinkle in his eyes, a smile slowly percolating beneath the patrician nose. He has grown a small, neatly trimmed goatee, which looks good on him. He has had a haircut recently; the salt in the salt-and-pepper mix always seems more prominent when he has had a haircut. How handsome he appears to me—not the cut of the clothes, or the well-maintained air, just the fact of him, again strikes me. This man I never would have looked at twice if I passed him on the street, utterly nondescript, yet he resonates in my heart like I am looking at Paul Newman in his prime. In fact, if Paul Newman in his prime were standing before me right this minute, offering me a life by his side, I would still pick Geoff. Which is a really easy statement to make, since Paul Newman then or now is not getting anywhere near me with offers, except for fifty cents off his newest salad dressing, but it feels good to think of it that way. And then of course it feels awful, because this strange man who I think is the most Adonis-like creature I could ever conjure up, he isn't here to make my dreams come true. He is here out of obligation. He is here because we spent nine months promising each other that we would be friends no matter what. He is here because he is too kind not to be here.

I kiss his cheek, inhale the scent of his cologne, which I love and which I always forgot to peek in the medicine cabinet to see what brand it was (in hindsight a good thing, because I know me, and in my current state I would for sure have bought a bottle to sprinkle on my pillow at night, like I need more help dreaming of him).

I sit on his right, order a glass of Pinot Noir, nibble at the little salty sweet Japanese cracker snack mix, try not to say anything dumb.

"How are you doing?" he begins.

"Okay. Hanging in there. You?" Friendship sucks rocks.

"Good. Busy. Sounds like you guys had a good trip, your dad said it was great to hang out with you and Adam." I wonder if we are automatically going to be boring now that we aren't sleeping together anymore.

"It was fun. You know Mom and Dad, no one lets loose on vacation better than the Steins."

"You still have a little color. It looks good on you." I think I look jaundiced with the last vestiges of my tan, but it is nice of him to say.

"Thanks. But you should have seen me when we got back. Brown as a berry, my mother always says. I like the beard."

"Do you? I didn't shave for a few days over vacation and then thought I would try it out. It came in a lot whiter than I would have liked, but I haven't had facial hair since the mustache in law school, so I thought it might be fun. Draw attention away from the rapid disappearance of what is on my head." He runs his hand over his balding pate, and smiles.

"Well, it suits you." This is without a doubt the most inane conversation I have ever had. Why can't we talk? Why is it so formal and stilted? Why is…the…hey…that is my KNEE!

There is the firm pressure of a hand on my left knee. I am assuming it is Geoff's, otherwise there is a very small person hiding under the table feeling me up.

"Yes? Can I help you? Something you wanted?"

"Sorry, I just wanted to touch you. I actually wanted to hold your hand for a minute, but both your hands are on top of the table, and I, well, I just…"

I reach down and cover the hand on my knee with my own, interlocking fingers, squeezing with gentle pressure.

"Hi." I smile at him.

"Hi." He smiles back.

We don't talk for a minute, just sit there, surreptitiously holding hands. I am DYING. What does it mean? Is he coming back to me? Is he leaving her? WHAT?

"Look Sid, I don't know what to say exactly. I haven't made any decision about Sandra. And while I appreciate your desire to have more from me, and it isn't that you don't deserve more, I don't think I can give much more than I am giving now. I do wish we could have more time together, I do wish we could go to a movie, or take a walk or go to a museum together. But we can't, it is too risky. And I do have to be a little selfish about my time. I have a lot of major obligations. If I have two nights free in a week and I spend one of them with you, that is half of my available quiet time. If I have one weekend day to myself, with no other obligations and I spend three or four hours of it with you, that is a full third of my 'me' time. Of course there are times I wish we could spend a whole day together, but it isn't like we can go run errands and get things done in tandem, so I have to protect some of my time for myself."

I hadn't really ever thought of it this way. I mean, don't get me wrong, it is still incredibly irritating, but it does start to make a little sense.

"Geoff, I don't want all your time. I just want to know that the time you do spend with me isn't accidental. I want some acknowledgment that I am not some awful thing that is happening to you. I want you to initiate more. I want you to at least TRY to stop threatening to break up with me on every date. I want to know that our next meeting is a when and not an if. I want to know that it is okay with you that I have feelings for you that are developing and growing. I want you to look at us and give some credence to the fact that you have chosen to continue this relationship for nearly a year!"

"You are right, and I can try, but I can't make any big promises Sid, I just can't. Sandra is leaving next week, she is resuming her normal travel schedule, and I do want to see you. And I will try to be mindful of you. I know what it is you offer me, Sidney, and I am very moved by it, but I can't do more right now."

"Okay. Baby steps."

"Baby steps. And Sid, about your letter…"

"Yes?"

"I am going to make a decision, I really am. I will not go into next year without knowing whether I am going to stay with her or get a divorce." Well, it is only February, so he has given himself plenty of time to avoid that decision, but I do allow myself a fleeting vision of Geoff and I next New Year's eve, under a full moon, on a beach somewhere, kissing at midnight, heading off towards our glorious future together… "But Sidney…"

"Yes?" That imagined moonlight still shining in my eyes.

"Whatever happens, you are going to have to understand that I cannot make you any promises about us." Scratch the moonlight. We may be back, but we are a long way from beach vacations. Then again, the important part is, we are back. Baby steps.

"Okay."

"Okay."

"But Geoff…"

"Yes?"

"There is something you do need to know."

"What is that?"

"They don't come any better than me. And I am a limited time offer."

"I am very aware of both of those things. We will just have to see what it is we see."

The rest of the conversation miraculously returns to our usual mode of ease and lightness. We talk about our respective vacations, I tell him about the new semester, he tells me about his big new estate client, a crotchety old woman with more money than God, looking to use her will to punish everyone who ever said boo to her. After a little over an hour, he asks for the check.

"Big plans tonight?"

"Meeting some theatre friends at a benefit."

"Sounds like fun."

"Should be okay. You?"

"Home, leftover Thai food, watch TV. Sandra has some meeting tonight."

"I know, my mom is at it."

This would be one of those moments we never seem to know if it is awkward, funny, or sad. We usually go with funny.

"Of course. I should have known. So, I will e-mail you, but dinner next week? Maybe Wednesday?"

"Sounds good. I have a haircut in the afternoon."

"Straight hair?"

"Yes, I will have straight hair." I can see him remembering the last time I had straight hair. And what I did with it.

"Well, we shouldn't let that go to waste."

"I should say not."

We get up, put coats on, walk over to the elevator, even

though it is only one flight down. Inside, he looks at me and smiles.

"I told you I would make you insane."

"Everyone has to be good at something."

"C'mere."

Geoffrey M. Fahl, Esq. is kissing me. His new facial hair is deliciously tickly. To say that I like it is the biggest understatement a girl could make.

We part ways after a short hug outside in the cold, he to go south toward his parking lot, me to head north toward my benefit. We are back. Somewhat better. Not fixed really, but better. I am very happy. I am so happy that while I am walking I call Adam on my cell phone, even knowing it will cost me eight thousand dollars in charges, even knowing that it is 1:30 in the morning in London, and he will be pissed off.

"Mmmmm… 'lo?"

"Scampy. It's me."

"He's back."

"How the hell did you know that?"

"Why else would you call me at this ungodly hour. Has he left her?"

"Of course not. But he is going to try and be a little better with me."

"He's a shit, Sid."

"He is not. This is very complicated. Can't you be happy for me?"

"Fine, on one condition."

"What?"

"Date other people. Actively pursue the dating of other people. Be open to meeting men who are single and want to date you. Keep it up with him if you want, but do not, under any circumstances, limit yourself to him unless he is doing the same. Do you hear me?"

"I hear you. And by the way, I am not an idiot. I would happily date other people if people were inclined to be dating me, which they are not at the moment."

"You come off unavailable. And people probably think you aren't ready. Show them that you are ready, got it?"

"Done. I promise."

"Okay, then. Send me an e-mail telling me all about how the boy came back to you, it isn't like I don't want to know, but Christ on a crutch, Sid, it is nearly two."

"Okay, sorry."

"And Sid, I am happy for you, I know you wanted this very badly, he is a very lucky man."

"Thank you."

"Okay, later gator."

"Bye."

By the time I have finished my conversation with Adam, I have walked the few blocks to my function, meeting up with a few colleagues from Columbia, some wine and cheese thing with a sad little silent auction, in support of a small community-based art center which provides after-school opportunities. It is a good thing I have the benefit of the really good glass of Pinot Noir I imbibed with Geoff, because the swill at this event is truly undrinkable. But the conversation is lively, and the jazz trio excellent. I am looking at an auction table and thinking I might bid on a handmade scarf as a gift for my mom, when a low voice behind me says, "Pardon me."

I turn, and find that I am looking at Joseph Edington, a local Chicago vocalist and voice-over guy, who I have met at least a dozen times over the past couple of years through my friend Robert. He never remembers me. This time is no different.

"Hi, Joe, I'm Sidney. Sidney Stein? Robert's friend?"

"Oh, yes, of course, how are you?"

"Fine, you?"

"Fine, I am here to fill in for the usual singer on the second set."

"Great, I haven't heard you since the last Notorious gig." Notorious, the small group that Joe sings with regularly, sort of a blend of standards, smart comedy songs, and original numbers, has become a favorite of mine, and their local shows on the bar circuit an occasional treat for me. Okay, and to be honest, I have always had something of a location crush on Joe. Site specific. When we are in the same room, I think he is totally cute. When I leave the room, I forget he exists. Besides, he is married.

"Oh yeah. Right. That was a good show." I am noticing a significant lack of wedding band. Then again, last time I saw him, I was wearing a ring too, and now, not so much.

"Anyway, it is good to see you again."

"Yeah, you too. I am sure I will see you around sometime."

"I am sure you will." I am equally sure you will not remember me. But that is okay.

"I'm going to go sing, you staying to listen?"

"Wouldn't miss it."

Joseph Edington smiles winningly at me, squeezes my arm, and goes to join the band up front. If I didn't know better, I would think he was flirting. Robert wanders over.

"Hey you."

"Hey."

"Saw you chatting with Joe."

"Yep. He never remembers me."

"He might this time."

"Why is that?"

"He is single now."

"I thought I noticed a ring missing."

"Yes, well, it is recent, and he has been playing the field more than a little. Plus, he does currently have a girlfriend. But he keeps claiming that they are just transitional, so I wouldn't put it past him to pursue you as well."

"Thanks for the heads-up."

"Just thought you should have the 4-1-1."

"You are so ghetto."

"I am a child of the streets." I laugh. Robert is a 48-year-old, five-foot-four, hundred-and-thirty pound white gay set designer originally from Scarsdale.

The set is good, Joe sings Sinatra in a way that makes me all warm and gooey, and makes the most delicious eye contact while doing it. And, flush with the return of my wayward boy, the wine, and the promise to Adam to keep my options open, I flirt back, thinking, what the hell? But my compatriots want to leave early, and since they are my ride, and I always dance with the date that brung me, I don't have an opportunity to re-connect with Joe before leaving.

Not that it matters, really. He won't remember me next time anyway.

Once home, the combination of the re-connection with Geoff and the interesting mild flirtation with Joe result in a poem both musical and cautiously optimistic. Very cautious. Because that is what it is about now, after all this time, it is about the knowing. It is about wanting to know and be known and be sure and not have this nagging doubt with me all the time. I cannot let myself believe in us completely, but I cannot deny that we are rare and exceptional and possibly important, and isn't that enough to move forward and find out?

chapter 14

QUOTE OF THE DAY

Don't be afraid to take a big step.
You can't cross a chasm in two small jumps.
—David Lloyd George

It has been far too long since I did girls' night with the gang.
Now, granted, I have been busy, what with my impending divorce, my secret affair, work on the book, my secret affair,
teaching, my secret affair, breathing in and out all day, my secret affair…no excuses. I have been neglecting my duties as gal
pal, and mean to rectify it tonight. Of course, I have a date with
Geoff tonight, but as all three of the girls in question (okay,
two actual girls and one gay man) are currently doing shows,
they are not coming over until eleven, so I have plenty of time
to see Geoff and still get home. A perfect two-act
evening…dinner and sex with my favorite boy, then home for
a late-night festival with friends. We are going to have one of
our famous Blahsmopolitan Extravaganzas, and watch the new
Sex and the City DVDs I bought last week, to catch some of

the episodes we have missed, and talk about boys. Geoff cannot understand my social calendar at all. If he isn't asleep by midnight, he is a mess the next day. I have tried to explain to him that my theatre background has trained me to be something of a vampire, and since I do not teach any morning classes, there is no need to get to bed early. My actor friends are all at work until ten or so, and then they want to wind down just like he does after his work day. Luckily for me, as it is a Friday night, I can stay up late with the gang without any worries about dragging tomorrow. And since none of them has Saturday matinees tomorrow, we are likely to be up very late indeed.

SIDEBAR

The Blahsmopolitan was invented in my house one week after Ocean Spray released their new White Cranberry Juice to the American public. I picked up a bottle to taste, and the next day Parker called to see if I was up for a long evening at home with Cosmopolitans...(both the drink and the Magazine, since we love to do the quiz and read the latest tips on how to make a man your bed slave) and I said we should try using the new juice as an experiment. Parker was hesitant; after all, he does love the way the regular Cosmo delivers a pink flush to his devastating cheekbones, but agreed it was easier than going out to buy different juice. This is what we came up with:

Chicago Style Blahsmopolitan
1 1/2 oz. SKYY Citrus Vodka
1/2 oz. Cointreau
1 oz. White Cranberry Juice
splash Rose's Lime
Shake vigorously with ice, strain into martini glass and garnish with piece of fresh lime.
We originally called them Blond Cosmopolitans, but after three

each all we could get out was "Blaahhhhzmopolitans" and then we re-
alized that their sweet and tangy fruity goodness was a surefire cure for
the blahs, so they became Blahsmopolitans ever after.

Geoff and I decide to stay in at his place, so I stop by Mag-
giano's on my way and pick up pasta and salad, and over glasses
of a really nice Shiraz that Geoff had lying around (in the aforementioned climate-controlled wine storage unit in his basement) we play a little catch-up with the Bulls game on in the
background.

"How are things at work?" he asks me around a mouthful of
Caesar salad.

"Good. Busy. I have three classes this quarter. The Beginning Poetry is unfortunately all freshman girls who are attempting to conscript Alanis Morissette's angry young lyrics,
but applying it to fairly mundane scenarios. No one needs to
read poetry about how 'fucking' oppressed they are, when the
oppression seems to stem mostly from their parents' unwillingness to buy them a car, or the way their roommate always
eats the last yogurt. I am trying to get them to pay attention to
their feelings, their surroundings, their fears, but I seem to spend
a lot of time listening to them bitch about stuff and not really
focus on the work. It feels a lot like group therapy. On the other
hand, the Advanced Seminar is going really well, only six students, all pretty focused, all with some talent and a desire to push
themselves. And the Dramatic Texts workshop is terrific. Ten
students, mostly third and fourth year acting majors, none of
whom has L.A. in their sights as the grand ambition. They all
seem to want to make a life in theatre and not television, and
so they are really tackling the text analysis and dramaturgical
work with real passion. Remember Jim Wickliffe?"

"The name sounds familiar, actor?"

"Yep. He did the lead in that staged reading we saw at the
Council for Jewish Elderly benefit."

"The one at the Auditorium?"

"Yes."

"Right, right, the tall guy with the impeccable dialect."

"Right. He is team teaching with me, and has a real gift for helping them pull the nuance out of the text without inventing extraneous character stuff."

"Meaning what, exactly?"

"Well, he won't let them do anything in their scenes without defending it as being supported by the text."

"How on earth do you do that?"

"Well, it is like, let's say you are a secondary character in a scene, maybe a messenger of some kind. You can't use as motivation a secret desire to kill the king, unless somewhere in the script or stage directions it gives you a reason to think that is true of your character. You can't invent too much, and so the performances that the students are giving are really subtle, honest, genuine and completely make sense within the story, which is a pretty tough thing to do with these ancient texts if you aren't used to it. It is a joy to work with him."

"Should I be jealous?" Geoff is smirking at me. I shift on the couch so that I am facing him, and he puts his arms around me.

"Yes, you should. You should be seething with envy. You should be making every effort to ensure that you are the only man in my heart." I begin to kiss him all over his face and neck with small little pecks.

"Well, at least I can try. Just don't call me Jim." Geoff puts his hands in my hair and pulls me in for a delicious kiss, all Italian spice and wine.

"I will never call you Jim." I kiss him back, a little harder, put my hands on the back of the couch, and without unlocking lips, get up on my knees and straddle him. He moans lightly into my mouth when he feels my weight settle on him, and pulls me very tightly to him, crushing my breasts against his chest.

Oh wow. I know I keep saying this, but you are just going to have to believe me, everything this man does to me makes me so hot for him.

"Bedroom," I manage to whisper when he lets me up for air.

"Bedroom." We get up, move upstairs, I can't be apart from him, not even as long as it takes to undress. I go over to him, touching him, kissing him, awkwardly taking off my own clothes, trying to take his off, until finally we are a mess of hands and buttons, and things half-on and half-off. He puts his hands on my shoulders, moves me back one step, and we simultaneously shake off our clothes and dive for the bed.

Geoff is very sweet tonight, it feels like lovemaking. He pets me and caresses me, taking his time as if we have forever. He makes me wish for forever. He uses his hand on me while kissing me, and then takes my hand in his, and watches me intently while I stroke myself. I was never really much for masturbating in front of lovers, I mean, it seems so silly when they are right there and are supposed to be participating, but Geoff loves to watch me, and I love how turned on he gets, and it isn't like it doesn't feel good. When it is clear that I am very tingly, Geoff wanders southerly, suckling at my breasts, nibbling my stomach, licking the insides of my thighs until I am absolutely begging him, saying, "Please, please, please," over and over, and trying to lift my hips up to meet his elusive mouth.

And then he requites me, most exquisitely. (This man's tongue should receive a Presidential commendation of some sort, the Congressional Medal of Honor at least.) I come almost too soon, but he doesn't stop, and suddenly I am in the throes of one of those formerly mythological multiple orgasms. Lying beside me, while I attempt to recover, Geoff looks down at me and smiles the sweetest, kindest, most loving smile I have ever seen, as if he is just tickled that he pleases me, happy for my happiness. He leans over and kisses me. I reach for him, and he is hard and throbbing in my hand, and I roll him onto his back, and make some effort to show my own prowess in the oral arena, adding in one of the best things about schlepping around a rack like mine, which is that it makes the simultaneous tit job/blow job a pretty easy task.

I get no complaints from my lover, who is beyond any words at all, except to tell me that he is going to come really soon.

Which he does.

Lying in bed, replete, his arms around me, his heartbeat under my cheek, the rise and fall of his chest, this is perfection. Nothing has ever been so good. I love him so much.

Shit.

Shit shit doubleshit.

Shitshitshitshitshitshitshitshitshit.

Crap on a cracker.

I love him.

I actually really and truly love him.

I absolutely for real way down where it is scary have fallen in love with him.

I am in deepest darkest doo-doo.

I lie in Geoff's arms while he naps, heart racing, completely mortified. I AM FREAKING OUT. But subtly, you know, quietly, so I don't disturb him. Eventually he rouses, smiles at me, kisses my forehead and wanders his fine naked self across the room. Damn that is a great ass. Not "great for an older man," just great period. I love his butt. I love him.

SHIT.

Stop that.

It is out of the question.

While he is in the bathroom, I dress quickly, tell him I am going to go back downstairs to use the powder room there, go into the den, chug the now warm remains of both previously abandoned glasses, and steal a cigarette. He seems surprised that I am already up and about, since usually I languish in the bed until he comes back, erroneously thinking that perhaps I look so fetching all rumpled in his covers that he will break down and ask me to stay. Tonight for the first time, I am desperate to leave. The walls are closing in. I can't breathe very well. I feel insane and all wobbly. Because I don't really want to go. EVER.

I want to stay here with him always. Because I love him so much I could just spit.

God dammit. God dammit all to hell.

I try to be casual. I try to be normal. I don't know if he senses anything.

"So what does your week look like?" (*read: I love you*)

"I think I should be open maybe on Thursday. If not, then Sunday for sure." *He doesn't seem suspicious.*

"Great." *I love you.* "I don't have anything, I will keep them open." *I love you.* "Don't suppose I can get an option on both?" *I LOVE YOU.*

"Let's play it by ear. Hey how is the book coming?" *Good God, fucking small talk? NOW?*

"So far so good." *I want to be with you forever and ever.* "My publishing company is switching some things around so it looks like I am going to be working with a new editor, and I am a little nervous about that." *Let's run off and get married and be bigamists and move to Montana.*

"I would think so, how long have you been working with your current editor?"

Why is there never a big earth-swallowing hole when you need one?

"Ever since the first book." *I have never nor will I ever love any man the way I love you.* "Amy is the best, and after six years, I am terrified to lose her." *Bullshit, it is you I don't want to lose.*

"I am sure it will be good, maybe it will add something to the process, I mean with a fresh perspective." *For the love of all that is good and holy on this our big blue marble in the sky will you please shut the fuck up and let me get out of here before I slip and say it out loud you silly old bear?*

"Could be." *I am so lost.* "I am trying to be hopeful, and put my faith in the universe that things will turn out for the best."

"I am sure it will."

The phone rings.

Baruch atah Adonai, eloheynu melech ha'aolom...blessed art

thou, Adonai, our god, king of the universe, who has saved me by the tolling of bells. The machine picks up. Sandra's voice, that pinched, slightly nasal, supercilious twang, can be heard drifting in from the foyer.

"Geoffrey, it's me. I assume you are still watching the game with Richard. I will try you on your cell phone." *Vey is mere. How ironical. Saved by my nemesis.*

"I have to call her back, which means I really do have to kick you out."

For the first time in eleven months and three weeks I am grateful to Sandra. Then I remember that if she didn't exist I wouldn't have to worry about having fallen in love with him. *Or would I? Stop thinking.*

"Okay, I will talk to you later this week." He escorts me to the back door, and holds it open for me.

"Okay, drive safe."

Off a bridge if I have any brains. "I will. Good night."

The door closes behind me. I start to leave. Then I turn around and face the barrier between my lover and me. I knock on it. Geoff opens, head tilted quizzically. I grab his face and kiss him hard. "Sorry, forgot to tell you that. Bye."

He laughs and goes back inside.

"And that I love you," I whisper at the door.

I am so fucked. And I nearly kill myself on the ride home about four times because I can't keep focused, and so I nearly run two stop signs, and then forget to go when the lights turn green, and I am an absolute mess.

Love. What the hell am I thinking of? What is the worst possible thing I could do in this situation? Focus, Sid, he is MARRIED. He is too old for you. He works with your dad. His wife is connected to your mother in eighty-five ways. It would never work. You'd be a laughingstock, people would think you a gold-digger or that you had some major Daddy fetish.

On the other hand, in twenty years you could get a group rate at the senior facility, and visit him and Mom and Dad every Sunday in one fell swoop.

Good lord, what a thought.

But we are so good together. And he is smart and funny and gets my jokes and makes me laugh and makes me feel special and the sex is so great.

But for how long? He is fifty-six years old. How long before it is all dentures and enlarged prostate and arthritis? How long before he needs Viagra to keep the juices flowing? How many years before you worry that if you are too passionate he will have a coronary? How well will he make love to you after the hip replacement? How many years of happiness before senility sets in and he thinks you are his second-grade teacher?

But I get him and he gets me and we are so lovely together, and wouldn't twenty or twenty-five great years with someone you love with your whole heart be better than a lifetime with anyone else? And he is a really healthy guy…what if he lives to be ninety or more? It could be thirty-plus years of love and laughter. And even sex between young people starts to significantly decrease after six or seven years of marriage, look at all we would be left with, this friendship, this intellectual compatibility, this profound connection! And from what I hear, Viagra works just fine, so who cares if he needs it eventually?

This is insane. You aren't even legally divorced. He is your transition guy, the one who keeps you perky while you are getting out of your marriage and into single life. He is a Band-Aid. A cold compress. Why would you even want to be with someone who cheated on his last wife with you? And on his first wife with anything that had a pulse? Could you ever even trust him? It doesn't matter anyway. The first guy after the break-up is never THE ONE, he isn't Mr. Right, he is Mr. Right Now. Isn't he?

But I love him with my whole self.

Fuck. Fuckety fuck fuck FUCK.

I get home at ten-thirty, jump in a quick shower to get the smell of him off me, get into my favorite lounging comfy clothes, lay out the cocktail supplies, throw some pretzels in a bowl, and go to the living room to wait for my compatriots. I am trying not to think about the dreaded and unwelcome epiphany of the evening, which is hard to do, because I have that little post-sex twinkle, the twinges in the nether regions, the littlest bit of whisker burn on the lips and chin, and all of that makes me think of Geoff, and every time I think of Geoff that little voice pipes up "*I love him*" in the most irritating way. Luckily, the doorbell rings after only three or four such musings, and I am immediately enveloped in the bliss of girlish adoration.

Now, Pam is a friend from Northwestern—insanely brilliant actor, total comic genius, bawdy bad girl to the nth degree, but with a healthy dose of earth mother. Nearly six feet tall in her stocking feet, built like an amazon goddess, wide gray eyes and full lips and the kind of nose that seems best suited for a Greek statue. Her voice has the most fabulous deep and resonant timbre, which is why she gets a lot of voice-over work. This is good, because as amazing as she is, her look is pretty specific, so theatre directors often have trouble casting her, and she works only sporadically onstage.

Bruce is a lithe little chameleon of an actor, half-Mexican, with brooding, nearly black eyes, thick dark hair, always perfectly tousled, maybe five-five or -six, whip-thin and specializing these days in brutal interpretations of contemporary drama as he segues more and more into directing. We met when I was teaching at the Montessori school, where he came in two mornings a week to teach drama, and fell madly in love in the way only gay men and straight women can. I introduced him to Pam one night a few months later, and within minutes a triumvirate had emerged. The only kind of ménage à trois that works, no one sexually interested in anyone else. We are completely addicted to each other, and yet, frequently go months without speaking, especially when we are mired in work.

Then, shortly after I started teaching at Columbia, I met Heather, a grad student in the English department who eventually dropped out because she was in such demand as a stage manager. Heather is the kind of girl who might normally piss me off. Her mom is African-American, her dad Jewish. She has skin the exact color of caramel, and curly hair like mine, only a half-shade lighter. Golden hazel eyes, full lips, five-foot seven and all legs. She has that natural athlete's physique, all tone without ever working out, and the wench eats like a frigging horse. Some things are truly unfair. She is also smart, really sweet, and a great friend, which is why you can't hate her. And even though she is the youngest at twenty-eight, with Pam and I both thirty-three and Bruce thirty-six, she has a quiet wisdom about her that makes her an easy fit with us, even if we do tease her mercilessly about being in her twenties.

The three of them have all arrived together, and for ten minutes there is a cacophony of hugging and shrieking and finally we go to the kitchen to make drinks. For over an hour we indulge in much drinking, much smoking, and much snacking—we decimate the pretzels and move on to my emergency stash of Peanut Butter Ritz Bits Sandwiches. We watch a re-run of *Queer as Folk* first, which just happens to be on, cheering our friend-by-proxy Scott Lowell, local Chicago boy who plays Ted, the adorable accountant/porn website guru, and is friends with a lot of our friends, even if not so much with us directly. No matter, we are always excited when one of our own makes it even semi-big, and for him to have landed a major supporting role on a big-time Showtime show, that is the best.

BACKSTORY

I met him once, a year or two ago, and had a mad crush on him. He is pretty cute on the show, but really totally yummy in person, and he has the most amazing eyes with fab lashes. For weeks after I kept asking my friend James, who is a good friend of his, how my new boyfriend

Scott Lowell was doing, and if he had mentioned me in any of his e-mails. Apparently he never did, and I have been healing gradually from the rejection ever since.

Meanwhile, back at the AA meeting...

After a quick refill all around, we watch one of the episodes of *Sex and the City* that we had missed that season. Carrie is having an affair with Mr. Big, who has married the evil and leggy Natasha, but he and Carrie can't stay away from each other. Chris Noth is dead sexy as Big, so even tho' we all love Aidan, Carrie's current boyfriend in this episode, we totally understand why Carrie can't help herself. Some of us understand more than others. Then, in a very touching scene, Carrie confesses to Samantha that she is seeing Big again, and Samantha is awfully supportive, and I don't know if it was the early part of the evening, or the two Blahsmopolitans, or the tender moment between fictional girlfriends, or just my life in general, but I start to cry, and then I sort of can't stop.

"Honey, what is it?" Pam puts her arm around my shoulder while Bruce stops the tape, and Heather, who has been sitting on the floor, starts rubbing my leg.

"Carrie. And. Big. Belong. Together. Don't. They?" I manage to hiccup.

"Damn woman, it is just a TV show." Bruce, despite the reputation of artistic type gay men, is not overly emotional. Or sensitive. Or even nice.

"No, I mean, it is possible that two people are supposed to be together, even if their circumstances are complicated, right?" I am getting control over myself by degrees.

"Of course it is." This from Heather, who is, after all, in her twenties and has the world's most perfect boyfriend.

"But unlikely, if you ask me." Bruce again, my little ray of sunshine.

"Who is he?" Pam always does know me best.

"I can't say." I swore I wouldn't do anything to jeopardize Geoff's identity, and even in my drunken, confused misery, I have to be true to that.

"Well, we will call him Mr. Big, then, how is that?" Pam is so understanding. And tall. Pam is so goddamn tall I can barely believe it, it is like being held by a man. And I can see right up her nose from this angle, and she has a really sort of enormous booger in her right nostril, and it makes me wonder if she can feel it in there…

"Sidney? You still there?" This tears me away from my nasal reveries.

"Yes," I whine miserably. "We can call him Mr. Big."

"Pam, how did you know? You are good, girl!" Heather is always easily impressed.

"Good God, if it is gonna be a 'very special episode of *Blossom'* in here, I am going to make more drinks." Bruce is a bitter little queen.

"Shut up Bruce," Pam says, "Sidney is having boy trouble. Sid, honey, how long have you been with him?"

"It. Will. Be. A. Year. Next. Week." I sound like a petulant four-year-old, even to myself.

Silence deafens.

"I know, okay, (hic) I am sorry I never said anything before, I know I am supposed to share everything, but it has been really confusing, (hic) and complicated, and I guess I am just the worst person ever, but I didn't want you to judge me (hic) or tell me not to be with him because it has been important to me to have him in my life, and I didn't want to have to defend myself (hic)."

"It's okay, sweetie, we are just surprised is all." Have I mentioned that I love Pam? I love gargantuan Pam, even with the booger. I even love Pam's booger. How can she not feel that thing in there, it is HUGE, I would have to get that stalactite out immediamente if it were my nose.

"And I suppose all this drama is because you love him." Why

do I even like Bruce? "And of course, they never leave their wives." Actually, I don't think I do like Bruce.

"Yes." I manage to get out before dissolving into tears again. Bruce hands me a fresh drink and a napkin.

I love Bruce.

"Tell us what you can tell us." Dear sweet Heather.

"It happened last St. Patrick's Day ...."

I tell them the whole story, minus anything that might identify Geoff as Geoff. At least I am pretty sure I did. After that third drink it got a lot fuzzy. And after the fourth, well, beyond fuzzy into swirly. I remember crying a lot and blowing my nose on my sleeve, and railing at the gods who have sent me such cruel luck. I remember talking about how bad I felt about Mark and how things ended, even though I was glad we were over. I don't remember anything else until I woke up in bed, clutching onto Pam, with Heather spooning me. It must have been five in the morning or so, and oddly bright in the room. My first thought is that I have the best friends in the whole world. My second thought, upon looking up, is that Pam's booger from another planet has mysteriously disappeared. My third thought is that it might be loose somewhere in the bed. This is when I realize that I am going to have to throw up.

I manage to extricate myself from all these tangly girl parts, and make it to the bathroom where I am gloriously and loudly sick. Twice. And I feel better for about thirty seconds, until I become aware that there is a marching band in golf shoes parading around my cerebellum. And that everything aches, either from the hangover or from sleeping weird. And that I still don't know where Pam's booger might be lurking to surprise me. Then I am sick again.

"Here, princess." Bruce hands me a glass of water, just the right level of cool but not cold, and wipes my forehead with a wet washcloth. "Better? Think we can stand up?"

"Yes. Thank you." Bruce really is quite dear in his way. He helps me off the bathroom floor, escorts me to the living room, hands me three Advil, two extra-strength Tums, and a fresh glass of water, then tucks the throw around me, as I am now shivery.

"So, kiddo, what'cha gonna do about this mess?"

"I have no idea."

"Well, do you think he loves you?"

"No. I don't think he does. But sometimes I think he could, you know, if he were free, if he were able to look at me as a possibility and not a liability."

"So if he leaves her, you think it might work."

"I think it could, yes. Twenty-three years isn't really so much. It isn't like he is in his 70s and me in my 20s. I am a grown-up. I am about to be a divorcée. I have a graduate degree. I am not some suicide blond bimbette with silicone boobs, I am a short, fat, smart girl, so publicly it won't look so bad."

"Do you really think it is as simple as all that?"

"Of course not, nothing ever is, but I have to believe that this is special, that what I feel is important, and when he talks about the things that his wife does that make him nuts, they are not things I do. And when he talks about the qualities he always wanted in a woman, they are things I possess in spades. Can I be certain we would work? No. But I wanna find out. Bruce, next Sunday it will be a YEAR. We have had some three dozen dates, and it is always wonderful, and always fun, and always so passionate and playful. I don't know if we could have a future, but I love him, and I want to know. Am I awful?"

"No, kiddo, just human. And stupid."

"Don't call me stupid." Damn, I feel like shit.

"Spade a spade, darling girl. You knew he was married when you started. He has been honest, from what I can decipher from your blubbering last night, about what he can offer you, what his situation is, and you have continued to be with him. That is your choice. The risk you knew you were taking was that somewhere along the way, you might fall for him, which you have, and you have no one to blame for your misery but yourself."

"You are a real crap weasel, you know that?"

"I am on your side, baby, you know I am. Look, if that man doesn't see what a rare and wonderful woman you are, if he doesn't know what it is he has when he has you, he is an addlepated fool." When was the last time someone used addlepated in a sentence, I wonder?

"I know. But you know what I think it is really?"

"I am all atwitter. What is it really?"

"I think that he is really messed up about women, and so he has always fallen for these needy, neurotic women who were wrong for him, thinking that he could fix them, you know? Even though it isn't really what he wants or needs, there is a sort of safety in that."

"I can't wait to hear how this turns out. Go on."

"Well, that way, even though he genuinely loves them, and even though it is painful when it ends, ultimately, it is always on his terms and due largely to their inability to be changed, so he always is in the power position, you know? When it ends, it is sad for him, it hurts him, but it doesn't break him."

"Okay, you have a point here?"

"Yes, if you will let me finish. I think that as far as I can tell from his own admittance, that I am about as close to the perfect woman for him as he has ever been involved with."

"You mean except for the age difference, his marriage, and his being your dad's business partner."

"Right. Wait. Did I say that about his being my dad's partner? I thought I hadn't said—"

"Don't worry, the girls didn't hear you. Heather went to check the messages on her cell phone, and Pam went to the toilet, and you mumbled something about him and your dad both suffering at work if you got caught, and from your descriptions of him, I assumed it wasn't some random paralegal. Don't worry kitten, it is safe with me, Mr. Big he remains."

"I am never drinking again."

"Until you do. Finish your theory, you are perfect for him, and...?"

"Oh, right. I am perfect for him, and he knows it, and it scares the bejesus out of him."

"Really?"

"Really, because if he leaves his wife, and we are together, REALLY TRULY together, he will fall totally in love with me and then I have the power to really hurt him. Then, if it doesn't work, it isn't because he fell for a loony, it is just him. And then he would be a sad and lonely old man. And because I would not be dependent on him for financial or emotional stability, and because I am so much younger, there is nothing keeping me from leaving him but his own behavior. So by keeping me in this box, by limiting the time he spends with me, by not ever spending the night, he prevents himself from loving me, because if he let himself love me, I could break him, and he cannot handle it." Not that I have been thinking about it at all.

"Interesting."

"That is all you have to say? Interesting?"

"I don't know the man, you could be brilliantly insightful, or you could be an idiot. You might have pegged his pathology perfectly, or you might have come up with the most asinine theory in the universe. The only thing that matters is that even if it is true, you know it, he doesn't, and there is a whole lot of other shit surrounding you that does not exactly make it tempting for him to explore it as possible."

"Have I mentioned that you are a crap weasel?"

"It came up earlier."

"Just checking."

"Dreamboat, you know I want you to have what you want. Hell, if I were straight, I'd be mad for you myself. All I have to go on is what you have told me, and so I believe he is a miracle man for you, and that your love for him is pure and true and good and that if he weren't such a frigging coward, the two of you could run off into the sunset and be blissful forever. Having said that, we both know it is highly unlikely. What is more likely is that he will keep you around for fun and companionship and sex until he tires of you, or until you confess to him that you have fallen for him, in which case he will break it off with you 'for your own good,' and imagine himself quite the big man, protecting you from his heartbreaking ways."

"I don't like the sound of that at all!"

"Look, there is officially no easy or pleasant way out of this. Keep seeing him if you want, just don't fool yourself that you are gonna get him for the long haul. Think of him as a favorite restaurant that has announced that it is closing, but with no set date yet. Eat there as often as you want, build as many memories as you think you need, but know that once it shuts its doors, you will have plenty of other places to find sustenance."

"You are worse with the metaphors than I am."

"I know."

"Bruce…thank you."

"Chica, when it is over, you call me. I may be a nasty and cynical old boy, but I promise I will not say I told you so."

"Would you really be in love with me if you were straight?"

"Truly, madly, deeply. To be frank, I am sort of in love with you anyway."

This makes me cry the littlest bit. Bruce gives me a big hug, hands me a tissue, and goes to make me tea and dry toast.

Pam and Heather wake up, both with far more mild hangovers than I, and the four of us end up sitting around my apartment all day watching a *Trading Spaces* marathon on The Learning Channel and eating takeout Chinese food from Far East, who does it better than anyone else. They leave around four in the afternoon, and I let myself take a long nap.

Next Sunday. I wonder if he knows it is our one-year anniversary. I wonder if he knew, would he care? I have a couple of small tokens for him, little nothing gifts, really, just Happy St. Patrick's Day stuff. It will be enough just to see him. I have to make it enough.

chapter 15

such a tangled web we weave

FACT OF THE DAY

The favorite horses of both Alexander the Great and Julius Caesar both had atavistic mutations—extra toes. Modern horses normally have only one toe per foot, but are descended from horses with three or four toes on each limb. It only goes to prove that sometimes extra isn't bad, just different, sometimes preferred, even if it strays from the widely accepted, and that what may result from abnormality can become the eventual norm.

I love May. Not just because my birthday is June 1, so May somehow always feels more like my birthday month, and not just because it is spring, but because there is something about Chicago in May that is inexplicable—you are just going to have to trust me. I finished my morning class last Wednesday and decided to take a walk over to Marshall Field's to try and find a gift for Mother's Day this weekend. The air is soft, the sun is shining, I am in a very good mood. I had seen Geoff the night before, and things are in a really good place for us. He hasn't threatened to break up with me once since our post-New-Year's-reconvening, in fact, he keeps letting things slip about him and Sandra being problematic and keeps making random references to the two of us in the future. Not having a future, you understand, but just knowing each other in the future. He remembered our anniversary, not in a monumental way, he actually just said, "It *was* today, wasn't it?" while we were in bed, and he didn't seem annoyed at my little presents. We are back to our once-a-week schedule, and all is fine.

I mean, of course, it isn't—I am totally in love with him and miss him like a virus when we aren't together, and think about him all the time, but you know, fine is relative, and relatively, we are fine. And in general I am just trying to focus my energy on letting it be whatever it will be, and follow the lead of the universe, wherever it is taking me.

I think it is this decision to not make any decision that has such a spring in my step this fine fair spring afternoon. I wander aimlessly around Marshall Field's, find a pretty robe for Mom in my general price range and look at all the new goodies in the cosmetics department. I am getting ready to leave, wandering past jewelry, when I see a vaguely familiar person walking toward me.

Joe Edington.

What the hell? I have nothing to lose....

"Hey, Joe, how are you?"

"Fine, um…" I told you he wouldn't remember me.

"Sidney. Sidney Stein. Friend of Robert's. We met at that benefit in February over at Gallery 37…" He makes me feel like a total idiot.

"Right! Gosh, I am sorry. Hi! How are you?"

"Fine, just getting something for Mother's Day. How are you?"

"Great, sort of same thing, not really for Mom, but for a sort of good friend slash mother figure. Hey, you're a girl!" Nice of him to notice. "What do you think of this?"

He opens his bag and shows me a scarf, not really my taste, but nice.

"It's beautiful. I am sure she will love it."

"Thanks, I am no good at this sort of thing, so it is great to have an outside opinion. My ex-wife used to take care of it."

"It is my pleasure to be of assistance. My ex-husband called me to get ideas for his mom, too." Okay, soon-to-be ex, the divorce papers won't go through till fall, but ex-enough.

"Well, it is good you guys are still friendly enough for him to get your advice on things."

"We really split up to save our friendship."

"That's so great, my ex and I really split up to prevent bloodshed."

"Ouch. Hey, how is everything going with Notorious? I haven't seen you guys in a while."

"Good, I guess. We have a show tomorrow night at the Beat Kitchen, if you are free."

"Sure, what time?"

"I think we start at nine. It would be so great if you could come. Bring friends!"

"I will try to make it." Provided wild beasts don't eat me in my sleep.

"Cool. Well, Sidney, it was great bumping into you, I will hope to see you tomorrow."

"Absolutely, see you around."

Hmmm.

Joseph Edington.

Let's have this moment. Cute, smart, single (albeit with possible girlfriend), and maybe the teensiest bit interested? Go to the show. Be adorable. You have a haircut in the afternoon anyway, shame for the sassy straight hair to go to waste, since Sandra is in town for the rest of the week. And didn't you promise Adam and Bruce you would make yourself available to other men? Win/win; if he is interested, it would be very healthy for you to be seeing someone, and if he isn't, it is really okay, because you are in love with Geoff, so it isn't like you are totally emotionally available. But it would be fun to be dating, in public, like a real person.

So I take my flippy hair to the Beat Kitchen to see the band. My friend Tracy is dating the bass player, so we hang out like groupies during the two sets, and after the show, Joe comes over to the table.

"Sidney, I am so glad you could make it!" He gives me a hug. Very nice. At least now we know he can remember me for a whole day.

"Wouldn't have missed it. You guys were great tonight. All my favorite stuff off the new album."

"You bought the album?"

"A few weeks ago."

BACKSTORY

The day after the benefit encounter, I went onto the Notorious Web site and ordered the latest CD. When it arrived, (return address Joe's house), it had a Post-it inside which said "Thanks for all your support, luv Joe Edington." Thinking he had recognized my name, I sent an e-mail to his address on the Web site, telling him that I was playing it in my office at Columbia and everyone really dug it, so that if he started getting a lot of orders, it was due to me, and perhaps they ought to think of thanking me in the next liner notes. He replied, "Thanks for all your support, luv Joe Edington." Which made me know that he had no idea who I was, which is good, because now I look like some stalker. I hope he doesn't remember it.

Meanwhile, back at the Beat Kitchen...

"Well then, thanks for your support." How original.

"My pleasure." A quick check of the watch proves that I should get going, as I am supposed to be meeting Parker at the Four Moon in fifteen minutes.

"Can I get you a drink?" He is really cute. But I have blown off Parker enough of late to accommodate Geoff's schedule, so he takes priority tonight.

"Thank you, but I am meeting someone at the Four Moon.

You guys are welcome to stop over if you want, the kitchen is open till one tonight, and Thursdays are a pretty fun crowd."

"I'll see what everyone wants to do, and maybe we will stop by."

"Well, if I don't see you, then thanks for telling me about the gig—I had a great time."

"Yeah, thank you so much for coming out. It is terrific to have friendly faces in the audience."

"Okay, then, see you around."

"Well, maybe later!" Joe then kisses me dead on the mouth.

Joseph Edington kissed me. And I am not quite sure how I feel about it.

I take my sassy self to the Four Moon. Parker is waiting for me at our usual table in the back.

"Look at your kicky new spring hair!" I love Parker. He is an astounding person. One of the most brilliant actors I have ever seen onstage, smart as a whip, kind and generous of spirit, and completely wickedly gorgeous in a rock star sort of way. He is reading the *Reader,* which came out today, and trying to convince me to place a Matches ad.

"I am not a personal ad type of girl."

"I think you should do it anyway. It could be fun! What do you have to lose?"

"My sanity? My dignity? My peace of mind? Look at those ads, all the men in the world are looking for tall, thin, beautiful girls to watch sunsets with. I mean, get real. Who the hell is going to answer my personal ad?"

"You never know until you try."

"I'll think about it."

"Good enough."

"Anyway, there is a sort of prospect on the horizon, maybe…"

"Really? Who?"

I tell Parker all about the random Joe meetings, remind him

of my previous crush-like tendencies, and he is sure that something is about to happen. I am not that optimistic, but at least I am finding it titillating to consider.

Some other folks begin to arrive after their shows, the table expands, the conversations get louder, and then suddenly a tap on my shoulder. Guess who?

"Mind if I join you?"

"Not at all, Joe, have a seat." OH. MY. GOD.

I introduce Joe around the table, he knows a few people from his voice-over work, and he insinuates himself easily into the conversation. He is funnier than I expect, and is flirting like mad with me, so I flirt back, having forgotten how much fun it is just to flirt. Pretty soon, we are just talking to each other, trading basic info, discovering how many people we have in common. I tease him for never remembering me and he promises never to let it happen again. He claims to be a frustrated writer, always starting stuff and never finishing it, and telling me maybe I can tutor him. We will see about that. When he leaves after an hour and a half or so, he kisses me again (again on the mouth, yummy!), and gives me his card.

"I am sorry, I don't have a card on me…."

"It's okay, call me or e-mail me or something, and remember to leave a number so I can get back to you."

"Will do."

Joe leaves, and Parker looks over at me and says "I think your kicky new spring hair just picked up that Notorious gentleman!"

Parker may not exactly be wrong about that. The whole thing is ved-dy int-er-est-ing. He wants me to get in touch. Hasn't mentioned that girlfriend—maybe they are over.

What about Geoff?

Shaddup. Geoff has a wife. You promised Adam, no dating anyone exclusively who isn't dating you exclusively—that includes wives.

But you are in love with someone else.

So what? This isn't about love, it is about dating. Getting out there. Testing the waters. Nothing serious, just fun. Besides he hasn't even asked me out yet, so deal with it when the time comes. You have had a crush on him for like three years, what is the harm in e-mailing him and finding out what his deal is? After all, you have a thousand friends in common; maybe he will just be a great friend.

I put the card in my coat pocket, and forget it.

Sunday afternoon (after Sandra leaves for the airport) Geoff comes over to my place to watch some World War II thing because I get the History Channel with my cable and he doesn't. (I actually think they ought to call the History Channel the World War II Channel, since I have never seen them show anything but WWII documentaries.) This, of course, doesn't last too long, since about ten minutes into the program, Geoff looks at me and says, "Would it be awfully forward of me to ask if we can go to bed right away?"

"Not at all. You leaving me earlier than expected, or am I just that irresistible?"

"The latter, I assure you."

LOVE HIM.

"Well then, come assure me like you mean it."

Which he does. Twice. And then we nap. And then we wake. And he assures me one last time for good measure. And then we are cuddling.

"Umm," I say, all snuggled up against him like a cat, "can't you stay? I hit the TiVo, so we can watch the rest of the documentary. "There is a new Italian place around the corner, just opened, food's good, we could have dinner…"

"It is very tempting, but I can't. I have to go back to the office."

"What on earth for?"

"Big annual meeting tomorrow, have to go look in on the stuff the associates did to make sure everything is in place."

"Don't you have an office manager for that?"

"She isn't really competent enough to cover it."

"That is shitty. You shouldn't have to go in on a Sunday to double check someone else's work."

"I know, I am trying to get rid of her. I promised myself that by next year's annual meeting, there will be someone in that job who will be able to take care of business so that I do not have to come in the day before."

"So next year, we can just spend the whole day in bed AND have dinner and not worry."

"Exactly."

Exactly? Exactly. EXACTLY. I just suggested us together a whole year from now, and he said EXACTLY! Wow. Totally wow. And may I just say, hallelujah.

Can I get a witness?

Geoff leaves, and I put on my bathrobe and go back to the living room, where, for no reason other than he wanted to see it, I watch the rest of the program. I find myself doing this more and more these days, tuning in to things that I normally wouldn't because I know he likes them. Not in that disgusting "I have to like everything my boyfriend likes" sycophantic way, but more out of a desire to know him better. To understand him better. To see things that I usually wouldn't bother with through his eyes. It is pretty well done, this movie, focusing on the African-American soldiers who were fighting against racial prejudice abroad and suffering it at home, and I am glad that I watched it, and grateful to Geoff for putting it in my mind.

Then I do something I am a little bit embarrassed by. I get out my PalmPilot, look up this same weekend next year, and put in a date with Geoff for the whole day Saturday. I wonder if I will be allowed to keep it there, or if I will have to erase it. Or if, in a totally unexpected turn of events, I will be replacing his name with someone else's.

chapter 16

QUOTE OF THE DAY

My merry, merry, merry roundelay
Concludes with Cupid's curse:
They that do change old love for new,
Pray gods, they change for worse!

—George Peele

When I got to Columbia today for office hours, I discovered Joe's card in my pocket. Hadn't really thought of him for the last couple of days, focused as I was on Geoff, but as he was leaving my place yesterday, Geoff announced that he is co-counsel on some big case with another firm in New York, and so will be traveling himself a bit in the coming weeks, in a very incompatible way with Sandra, and that it might be as long as a month before he could see me. One step forward, and two steps back.

I look at the card, and think about how much fun it was to hang out and flirt with Joe. I think about a month alone. I think about my promise to Adam. I think about Bruce's advice.

Joseph Edington Musician/Vocalist/Voice Over
home: 773-555-2754 fax: 312-555-3242
pager: 773-555-7987 cell phone: 630-555-1457
e-mail: Jedling@yahoo.com

What the hell. What have I got to lose?

To: Jedling@yahoo.com
From: poetsid@aol.com
RE: Hi.

Joe—
Hope you had a lovely weekend, I am sure you took advantage of the warm weather to knuckle down and get some serious writing done. :)

At any rate, I am most glad to have run into you last week (all those stalking classes are staring to pay off), the show Thursday night was exactly what the doctor ordered, and it was lovely to have a new face at the Four Moon. Mostly I am glad to have finally gotten a chance to have an actual conversation, I feel like we have been circling each other in this town for ages, all these people in common, etc....

Since your card is so forthcoming about how to get hold of you, I figured it was only fair to do a little quid pro quo, so if you have any need to get in touch, this is how:
home: 773-555-4187
work: 312-555-0855
Four Moon Tavern: 773-555-MOON
fax: 312-555-0811
pager: 312-555-5677
e-mail work: sidney_stein@columbiacollege.edu
e-mail home: poetsid@aol.com
send smoke signals or semaphore in the direction of Logan Square.
(Unfortunately my Morse code is a little rusty, so better avoid it in case of possible miscommunication).

By the bye, it might be a little much for you, but I often meet up with some folks at Sidetrack for Monday night showtunes, if you wanted to come warble along....

Okay, must stop procrastinating and get some work done. (It's that Gemini thing again.) Enjoy the sunshine today.
bisous,
Sidney

I settle down to paperwork, and about ten minutes later, my computer blings. I've got mail.

Hi Sidney,
It was good talking to you, too. Having a conversation with you and the fellas after the show reminded me what it was like to go out and toss back a few after doing theatre productions. It's been a long time since I did that, to be sure. Thanks to your encouraging words, maybe it won't be long before I enjoy that kind of activity with more liver-bashing regularity.
Your attendance and appreciation for our efforts was much appreciated at the Notorious show. Whatever happens with that group, we've certainly had a good time. And we've sure created a lot of songs; somehow I'll find something to do with all that dark jazzy comedy. Maybe there's an empty theatre in Branson looking for the kind of nonsense we can generate.
Thanks for the multiplicity of avenues for contact (too bad about the Morse code—I've developed impressive proficiency). Our paths will certainly cross again sometime soon!
Joe

Goodness, that was a fast reply.

SIDEBAR

This is where I admit to a not unusual affliction known as the Punchy Monday Syndrome, not to be confused with the "other" PMS. This usually simply results in major procrastination of any actual work due to a hatred of Mondays in general.

Which is why I e-mail him back again.

Joe—

Somehow, Morse proficiency doesn't really surprise me. I suppose you could always give me a brief refresher course...it is just my tendency toward verbosity always seems better served by communication of a more oral nature. (Okay, verbal might have been a slightly better choice, but one must do what one can to be intriguing and insouciant and just the slightest bit cheeky if one has any hope of a reply....)

I'll keep an eye out for those crossing paths...I have a bad habit of "roll and go" at intersections, and would hate to miss you. Meantime, I think you should definitely look into that Branson thing. That and perhaps adding some Cirque du Soleil moves to the act...it opens up the whole Disney/Vegas scene for you guys as well.

cheers,
Sidney

I don't hear from him again at work, but when I check at home before I go to bed, there is another e-mail waiting for me.

SS,

Hey, you're pretty funny—for a girl!

Sorry, you can take the boy out of the misogynist white trash neighborhood, but you can't take the misogyn—you know.

I'll talk to the boys about your suggested ideas for the act. They smack of greatness. Or they grate, like I'm on smack. I'm not sure.

Hey, Sidney, give me a call at home. I've kinda gotta tell you something.

yer pal, Joe

It is too late to call him tonight, so I decide to call in the morning, since I will be working at home anyway. The conversation is funny, really; he admits to still having the girlfriend, who he swears is a transitional thing, (which he is supposedly transitioning out of), and now he feels guilty for hitting on me. I tell him no harm no foul, admit to my old crush, let him know that it is no big deal, and that I would love to be friends. He says he won't be able to stop flirting with me, and I tell him to flirt all he wants—I will flirt back. He asks if I won't think him a cad, and I promise to only think lovely thoughts of him. He asks if he will be allowed to ask me out once he and his girl-friend are over, and I say of course, and that in the meantime, the flirting will keep us in touch. He really does have a great voice, and we talk for over an hour about all sorts of things. When we hang up, I send an e-mail to let him know that I really meant it about being friends, he is so much fun. And to be honest, I am a world-class flirt, especially with e-mail, and since I can't send flirty e-mails to Geoff, who gets paranoid about people being able to retrieve them off the computer, I might as well exploit this new connection.

J—

I should only ever talk to professional voice-over boys in the morning...there is just something about those deep and dulcet tones that perks me up so much better than caffeine. You're better than a latte. I suggest a wake-up call service as a side-line for you. I'd sure cough up a couple bucks in the a.m. to have you talk me awake. (Or nudge me, you know, whatever.)

In all seriousness, I really do appreciate your forthrightness about your situation. Lesser men always seem to either pretend they weren't flirting at all, or blame it on the beer, or wait until an innocent good-night kiss goes a little too far, and then make apologies. How refreshing to meet someone who is upfront, not just about acknowledging a little spark, but also willing to admit to historically less than honorable tendencies. (Feeds right into that base female instinct to snare the wicked

unavailable men who are sure to break one's heart eventually...
actually kind of a genius pick-up move on your part! There is
nothing quite so irresistible as a bad boy, especially one with
a mischievous smile and quick wit.)

xoxox (You put 'em where they will do you the most good.)

:) Sidney

He replies a mere fifteen minutes later.

Wow, Sidney,

You know, I have a real problem getting work done in my
life, and I'm simultaneously thrilled and chagrined to get to
know you better, because writing to you is going to be impossible to resist.

If only I could make a living by delivering flirtatious, sexy
phone calls to women like you. I could get rich by engaging
in my second favorite activity on earth. As it is, I have to struggle along earning my rent with voice-over work for commer-
cials, which only comes in at number three.

I have lots of friends, and not enough time for all of them.
And then I meet someone who writes e-mails like you do. Of
COURSE I'm going to keep in touch with you! What's more
fun than [see above]? Nothing.

I know you'll understand if my time gets limited sometimes. The girlfriend—okay, her name is Kim, she has a
name!—occupies a large space. Hmm...yes, I do feel like I'm
sneaking around a bit here. I was certainly in Sneak mode
when I was kinda sorta hitting on you the other night.

Thanks for some of the best e-mails I've ever received in
my young life!

Xoxo Joe

So much for work. I have to respond....

Wow yourself.

I have given up on work. It is Tuesday and the sun is shining and my head just ain't in it. Besides, it's almost lunch, I'm not really gonna get anything done until after that anyway.

And I love being irresistible, even if it is just in an e-mail sort of way.

:) unproductive little me.

Needless to say, Joe replies at the speed of sound.

We will talk soon. I'm not sure about tonight, but how late can I call?

ox

j

Gotcha. Have I mentioned how much fun this is? I convince myself that it is good for the writing...

j—

You can call as late as you like; I am a night owl. Never go to bed before 1 a.m. (Well, never go to SLEEP before 1...she says with a sly knowing wink.) I will be home most of the evening. But if the urge strikes you at 1:30 or 2, go for it...I can sleep when I'm dead.

I suppose in the interest of full disclosure, it is only fair to warn you that the fabulous, kicky Breck-Girl-pet-me-hair the other night was something of false advertising...in its natural state, nothing but curls. Nice, in their own way, but I didn't want you to harbor any illusions of silky tresses.

la di da.

I'd say I'd talk to you soon, but who am I kidding? The chances that there won't be at least one more e-mail before I leave for work are slim to none,

so,

more later,

(Insert seductive, yet totally platonic, I-really-am-a-good-girl-like-I-promised eyelash batting here.)
:) S

To which he responds…

friend in the bathroom
voice-over demo consulting
sigh—what a shame: I was only interested in speaking to you because of your silky, straight locks…
;-) later j

Which is when I give up any thought of decorum and send him:

Just checking…friends do on occasion inquire as to what their friends might be wearing when sending innocent little e-mails, do they not? Just for my own edification, you understand, not that I am ACTUALLY asking what you might be wearing, because that would be silly and a little seedy (boxers?) and we have firmly established (briefs?) that this is not that kind of (boxer briefs?) party. It is really just because I have this friend (fig leaf?) who is e-mailing this new friend, and she wants to know the protocol.
thanks.

It has started to get ridiculous. He of course comes back immediately with…

Sidney,
Tighty-whiteys.
I've heard that those are the garment of choice for gay men, especially when the wearer's body is also closely shaved and extremely well-built.

   doorbell
gotta go J

I leave, go to class, listen halfheartedly to my whiny beginning poets, go back to my office, get some work done, and before I head for home, I reply with...

Joe—
   I seem to remember that the current trend for gay men
is heather-gray boxer briefs, for support and for style.
Calvin Klein, if you can afford them, Hanes, if you are
below the poverty line. Surprisingly, body-shaving per-
centages are down in 2002, possibly because it finally occurred to them that full body whisker burn is less than
pleasant...
   Hope the voice consultation went well (is going well?)...do
you always consult in the bathroom? Is it because the acoustics
are better? Do you get in the shower to consult, or just mill
around the sink? What about shower singing consultation?
   I was actually reasonably productive for my three o'clock
class. I feel less guilty now.
bisous, Sidney

   And sure as anything, by the time I drive home and turn on
the computer...

S,
   No, she had just arrived, and so had to use the facilities before we started work. She's a nice lady with a great voice, but
I really had to beat her up a bit to get her to read the way I
wanted her to. Not easy, as she is a very attractive young
woman, so mostly I just wanted to be nice to her so she would
like me.
   Luckily, I am very good at controlling those impulses. I also
have giant bat wings and long silky green hair.

Have a good evening, my new friend...

J

Well I couldn't be expected to just let it go by, could I?

J—

Glad to know all your dangerous impulses are so well controlled these days. I will have no fear of inviting you over to my celibate little cell for scintillating conversation, tea and biscuits. I can pet your lovely wings and brush your viridian locks and you can teach me to sing in the shower and have no fear of anything unseemly occurring. What fun we shall have in our chaste little visits. Courtly love may not be dead after all. I'll give you a token for luck and we can exchange longing glances, and every now and again in the wee hours of the morning we can have a fond thought for each other....

If I don't speak with you later, then very soon.

S

My phone rings at midnight.

"Hello?"

"Sidney? It's Joe." Well, duh, big red truck...

"Hello. We are going to have to stop e-mailing, it is too distracting." I am a big fat liar.

"I know, I barely got anything useful done today."

"It was fun, tho."

"Absolutely, I don't know when I have had more fun e-mailing someone."

"Me either."

And so it goes. We talk about nothing in particular, and then he starts saying some really deeply flirtatious things, full of not-so-subtle entendre, and I know he is thinking perhaps that I might talk dirty to him, so I stop him.

"Joe, be a good boy."

"Whatever do you mean?"

"I am not having phone sex with you."

"I never said—"

"JOE. I am not having phone sex with you."

"Can't blame a guy for trying."

"No, and you can't blame a girl for saying no. It is for our own mutual good. You want to be faithful to Kim, and I want to not be with someone who is attached to someone else. If we get all hot and bothered on the phone, we are more likely to do something we will both ultimately regret."

"You are so right, thank you."

"So let's say good-night."

"Okay, I will talk to you tomorrow or something."

"Okay, good night Joe."

"Good night Sidney."

Vey is mere. Hadn't seen this coming.

Let's take stock. New boy, attraction for whom predates Geoff, is interested, but currently attached. (Please do not point out patterns to me, this is not therapy.) But, the e-mail and phone stuff is wicked and fun and pretty harmless. Geoff is out of my life temporarily, and unless something radical changes, he will never really belong to me, so…keep Joe in on deck. If he gets single and asks you out, brilliant. If not, it will still be a good distraction while you wait for Geoff to come back. Like Godot.

Like I said before, extra is not necessarily bad.

chapter 17

super powers

QUOTE OF THE DAY

The only way to get rid of a temptation is to yield to it.
—Oscar Wilde

My life as a queen of e-mail continues. Joe and I have had quite a week of communications. I began it the morning after the first phone call. I had dreamt of him, and not of Geoff for a change, and it seemed appropriate to share that information.

Heckyll—
Perhaps I should call you Jacob Marley, for all the visitations you made me last night. I am not so much of a humbug as to dismiss you as a bit of undigested beef, not in the least because I had chicken for dinner. I will instead hope that for whatever time you spent frolicking in my subconscious, that I in some way returned the favor.
(Insert deep and mournful, yet resigned sigh here.)
Anyhoo...it was great to chat with you, how interesting it

is that we have so many things in common, and we have only begun to scratch the surface. So, if you want to write me back, send the following information:

1. Something about you that is surprising or unexpected.
2. A list of three skills you have that I wouldn't already know about. (Assume I credit you already with all sorts of gift-edness in the naked categories, and keep it clean...I am trying to get some work done today.)
3. The one recording artist you cannot live without.
4. The one place you know well that you want to show me.
5. The one place you have never been that you want me to show you.

My answers to these five are listed below...you can add other questions to your list if there is stuff that you are curious about.

1. I have 2 tattoos.
2. I am a gourmet chef. I was a ninth bar sharpshooter with a 22-caliber rifle at 50 yards. I speak French.
3. Louis Armstrong.
4. My parents' weekend house.
5. Montana.
Off to a lunch meeting. Catch you later.
yours,
Jeckyll

I got this after aforementioned lunch meeting.

Sturm,
It was very difficult for me to end our phone conversation also, but of course I understood perfectly. I'm sure you'll hear from me again some night, possibly for innocent sharing, but being the kind of person I am, possibly for not-so-innocent, coordinated activity. You'll gracefully turn me to proper path-

ways, or weakly acquiesce, as the mood strikes you. Both are acceptable, forever.

1. I would have said that the surprising thing about me is that voracious sexual appetite with a tendency toward having a foul mouth, but that's no longer a surprise. (Sorry about some of this racier stuff. I know you didn't want to be distracted today, but it was bound to come up.) My yodeling ability surprises some. Hmm...it's surprising how little is surprising about me. Okay. My middle name is Storm.

2. Extensive computer skills, including digital audio recording. The ability to balance a yardstick on my nose indefinitely. Pretty good tennis player.

3. (Impossible to choose one.) Robbie Fulks. Nat King Cole. Buck Owens. Frank Sinatra.

4. Have you been to Uncle Fun, the collectible store on Belmont? A great breakfast place in my neighborhood? I'm not a native Chicagoan, I've lived in Missouri and Arizona and a lot in Ohio, none of which I recommend highly or remember well, and I've only been to Europe twice.

5. Your parents' weekend house.

I may now be too boring for our friendship to continue. (Sigh.) It's been good knowing you!

yers,

Drang

Talk about fuel for the fire.

Benedick—

Is your middle name really and truly Storm? It makes you like a superhero. Mild-mannered voice-over actor and singer by day, by night using his sexual prowess to keep the women of the world safe from harm. Slower than molasses in Alaska, smoother than a 25-year-old single malt, able to hit the smallest G-spot from fifty paces...hmm. I wanna be your sidekick.

Make the world safe for democracy and the American way and multiple orgasms.

I LOVE Uncle Fun, one of my favorite places to find the perfect gifts for the people who are impossible to shop for. I don't know that I have been to any great breakfast places in your neighborhood, do you burn the toast, or is your place a good breakfast place? My place is an excellent breakfast place. Except for coffee. I make lousy coffee. One might be surprised that a chef who can whip up a nine-course, wine-matched dinner for 12 without too many problems has trouble with coffee, but I do. Luckily there is a Starbucks on the corner.

You aren't boring in the least.

(Okay, I'll admit to a slight twinge of disappointment that you didn't ask if you could see my tattoos. I'll let you make it up to me.)

One of these nights I'm gonna ask you to sing me to sleep, so get your lullabies ready. If it has to be over the phone I am okay with that.

bisous, cherie.

Your Beatrice

Told you I was good. He replied immediately if not sooner.

Innie,

Yes, it's cheating to even think the things I'm thinking. But you know it, and I know it. Sometime, somewhere the two of us will need to explore carnal landscapes together. It could be sooner, it could be later, but two people with minds like ours and the curiosity our communication has created will certainly not be allowed to resist that satisfaction. Of our curiosity.

(So he writes. Then, of course, he's unavailable for the entire weekend.)

I love your superhero scenario. Storm with his sidekick Lightning Girl. He, an intrepid sexual adventurer. She, his faithful foil and sidekick, his invaluable resource for all things female. "On the outer islands of Borneo, I was faced with a puzzling carnal conundrum, for which even I was at a loss, Lightning Girl! Tell me—how does it feel when I do THIS??"

I expect to see your tattoos. Are they in places easily revealed in public? I'm guessing they are...

I'm very good at coffee.

I will sing you to sleep sometime. My pleasure, ma'am.

Yours,
Outie

Ma'am? Shucks...

As I am crafting a reply, I get another e-mail, this one from Geoff saying that he has an unexpected window of opportunity this evening if I am available. As if he has to ask. I agree to see him at my place at eight, and go back to my note for Joe.

Algernon—

Lightning Girl I like. Makes me all electric.

Tattoo #1 is easily accessible in public, #2 is in a slightly more private location. You can see the former next time I see you, the latter when we are dipping in that warm pool you mentioned.

By the bye, I am listening to your album. And looking at your autographed Post-it which I stuck to my computer when it arrived. This apparently makes me 12 years old. If I send a note that asks you to check off boxes indicating how much you like me and whether you want to save me a dance at the mixer next week, please remind me that I am a grown woman with a Master's Degree and an almost ex-husband and I should be SO above this by now. How the heck am I gonna concentrate on my date tonight?

Cecily

Figure it doesn't hurt to let him know that I am not waiting for him.

And he notices....

Ooby,
  You have a date tonight?! Excellent! Are you interested? Excited? Motivated? Expectant?
  And if I start drawing race cars on the back of my notebook, we'll stop all communication immediately. But yes, count on me for the next mixer. I'm the one with the bad skin and the Jackson Browne long hair parted in the middle.
love,
Dooby

Wheee. What a trip. I stop working and e-mailing because now I suddenly have a date tonight with my man, and since I hadn't anticipated it, there is much preparation to be done. While I am showering and primping for Geoff, I find myself thinking about possible outcomes for this current situation. On the one hand, everything is theoretical, as I have been very clear with Joe about not playing second fiddle to anyone. I can't think about handling that with two guys at once. But, let's say that Joe isn't lying, that he really does think he and Kim will be breaking up in the near future. Then I have them both. Sort of perfect really, Joe for fun and play and attentiveness, Geoff, well, for being Geoff and because I love him. Once-a-week-dates with the man of my dreams and the rest of the time with someone who I can take out in public. Adam and my friends will be appeased, my parents will be happy that I am dating, I won't be so lonely...
  Hmm.
  I guess I am actually lonely. I hadn't really thought about it much. I mean, I teach and work during the day, I go out with friends a couple of nights a week, see my folks one night a week, see Geoff one night a week, have some quiet time at home the other nights. So I am plenty busy. I have plenty of contact with the outside world. But it is true; I get into bed every night and wish Geoff was there.

What a hot mess.

Piffle.

Whatever.

I hate all that woe is me bullshit. I have a hell of an upside right now. Geoff is sweet and adorable and has made some strides in the areas I asked him to, and Joe is a riot and making me feel like the fabulous seductress I actually am. I am gonna have them both. Decision made. After all, I am a modern woman, and there are no strings on me. I am feeling suddenly very much like Samantha on *Sex and the City.* All the men and sex and passion she can handle, with no guilt, no concern. I love her character—strong, smart, sexy, in charge. My new role model. I am gonna get everything I want and more. A new convert to Samanthism. I am pumped. So much so, that I shake myself a Blahsmopolitan, which I drink while I am waiting for Geoff. A big one. Which accounts for the thought that it is a good decision to greet him at the door wearing my sassiest black underwear with a men's white buttondown thrown over it, or in this case, an unbuttoned-down.

"I guess we aren't going to dinner," my lover says, smiling and shaking his head, as he moves into my living room.

"You are looking at dinner." (Okay, it was more like one and a half Blahsmopolitans, I made too much for one, and it would have been a shame to let the rest go to waste, all melty in the shaker.)

"Well well well." He kisses me. The kiss sends the drinks right to my brain, and I am all atingle everywhere else. He bites at my neck, pinches my nipples, puts a knee between my legs and kisses me even harder. I grab his tie and drag him into the bedroom where we make a four-course meal of each other.

"Are you drunk?" He asks me, when we are all tangled in the bed together, post-romp.

"A little tipsy. I had a drink while I was waiting for you."

"That was incredible."

"It most certainly was."

His stomach growls loudly. We laugh. Mine answers it. We laugh harder.

"You go watch TV, I'll be right in. History Channel is 78."

I put the shirt back on, buttoned this time, with a pair of black leggings, and go to the kitchen. I put water on the stove to boil, and pull a lemon, two eggs, a piece of parmesan, butter and cream out of the fridge. Two egg yolks, whisked with cheese, cream, and lemon (both zest and juice), a little salt and some chopped parsley, the most perfect after-sex pasta sauce ever. The water boils, I throw in cappellini, which cooks in about two minutes, drain it, throw it back in the pot with a hunk of butter, and once the butter is coating all the pasta, dump in the lemon cream sauce. A quick toss, and in a bowl, with more grated cheese and parsley on top, and two forks.

SIDEBAR

I saw Nigella Lawson do a version of this on her cooking show, and since I have a nonsexual crush on her, and since she is one hot mama AND all her recipes turn out, I have co-opted it. If you are looking for a great cookbook that won't have you pulling your hair out, I can highly recommend both How To Eat *and* Nigella Bites *without hesitation. And the TV show is like soft core food porn. Love it.*

Total time in kitchen, 12 minutes. I grab a beer out of the fridge for Geoff, a Perrier for me, and head to the living room where he is sitting on the couch in his underwear and shirt and socks, hair mussed, History Channel on some show about ancient Rome, cigarette smoking itself to the filter in the ashtray, head thrown back, asleep. I could cry I love him so much. I set the bowl and bottles down on the coffee table. I put out the cigarette. I lower myself gently to the couch beside him and snuggle up, kissing him gently below his right ear. He wakes, stretches like a cat, and pulls me close for a really great hug. Then he smiles at me.

"I smell something yummy."

"I made pasta."

"I think it is you." He kisses me.

"You are incorrigible." I kiss him back.

"Insatiable." He puts his hand up my shirt.

The pasta was really good. Even if we did have to microwave it.

Later, when I walked him to the door, he reminded me that scheduling would still be tough for a few more weeks, but said he would get in touch regardless.

"Look, I don't know what I am going to do about Sandra, but the plan right now is to spend more time together. And if history serves, we only really fight when we are together, so maybe it will be the best thing overall. I just don't know. But I guess, expect the unexpected. After all, I'm here now."

I don't want to say that it sounds like he is leaning toward leaving her, but it sort of sounds like he is considering it, at least superficially. And I can't help but remember what he said back in February about not going into next year without a firm decision.

"Well, I will be here for whatever time you can offer me."

"I know. We'll just have to see how it all plays out."

He let me know that he is crazed with work these days, and obviously we won't be able to manage a date-date any time soon, but that if worse came to worst we could at least have lunch or something, maybe for my birthday, which is in two weeks. I told him we could play it by ear, but that I would love to see him whenever he had time. I am secretly thrilled that he has remembered my birthday, and wonder if there will be gifts involved. He kissed my forehead, and then put his hand on my neck, cupping just under my right ear, his thumb stroking my cheek. Then he kissed me gently on the lips, and left.

Sigh.

I tidied up, washed the dishes, had a cigarette, and went to the computer. I am gonna miss him so bad.

what will I do with the days before me?

so unlike that first time
last time
any time
I am beyond my own control

there are no words for what he puts me through
and if there were
my mouth would refuse to scream them for me

I will always remember
what he tastes like
in darkness

his pulse
on my back
one half—note off—tempo
from my own
and yet
not awkward

I learned soon
to leave
when the heartbeats
begin to deafen
and ache

I do not break
I bruise

the air is crisp and cool
blows my fears around me
to collect at my feet like autumn leaves
loose
fluid
no skeletal constraints

arms
hips
head thrown back
I dance with the breezes
let them know my secret name

light
diffused through city air
is neither warm
nor cold
cannot be felt on the skin
does not force the shielding of eyes
genuine as a picture of light
evoking as much emotion

touches us both
this plastic sun
glints off the tips of his hair
bristling in the whites of his eyes
at a distance
he becomes a study in geometry
round head
square shoulders
triangular hips
bathed in this sunlight
which gives me no warmth
casts no shadows

half asleep
in the shower
I heighten my senses
to the beat of the water
constant liquid heat
flows in rivulets
over white skin
trying desperately
to awaken for

be awakened by
you

this morning I opened the drain
let myself
swirl away
with the bathwater

do not touch
the lost soul
vellum heart
on cold mornings
does not bleed

the words that got me through today
will be my downfall tomorrow
I am
learning to believe
in oblivion
doubt not
the dubious nature
irrevocable mindslide
intimate emptiness
reaching for nameless
faceless
saints
ecstasy of revolt
kicking in my chest
sharp slow breathing
thumping thunderous organ
visionary and prophet
leaving myself behind
careful of my new raw skin
hearing everything with virgin ears

I heal slowly

on these mornings
leaving the last answer
in silence
zenith
over yesterday's
killing hours
the vastness of the night
a most perfect vice
a most holy sin

I am in pieces
seeking wholeness
wherever I sit or stand
I am unsafe

I seek him behind closed doors
listen for his words
placed around voice and naked rhythm

in the degenerate state
the victim of society
becomes merely a thinker
or still worse
the parrot of other's thinking

I will not squawk your thoughts back at you
in attempt of proving us incomparable

but instead
will give voice to what thinking you spark in me
with such sweet surety
that you will find us agreeable
even when we disagree

for when you put your hand
unexpected

on the side of my neck
with a touch intimate and transparent

I smiled.

I did too, you know. I smiled with my whole heart. And remembered the touch there, and loved him for it. Loved him for himself. Loved him, in spite of the complete and utter insanity of loving him at all. And wondered what was next.

What is going to happen? Will Lightning Girl and Storm consummate their passion for each other? Will Lawyer Boy leave his wife, and if he does, will he choose Lightning Girl? Will the cable man show up before 5? Will anyone ever find a way to have their cake and eat it too? Will anyone get out alive? Tune in next week when we discover what happens next, same Lightning Time, same Lightning Station.

more of the same only different

QUESTION OF THE DAY

Where the hell are all the baby pigeons? I have never in my life seen a baby pigeon, and I live in a big city with flocks and flocks of the adults milling about everywhere, and yet, no babies, no nests, nothing. Where are all the pigeons breeding? Do they live in secret underground lairs and only come out into the sun when they are fully grown? Are the babies invisible to ensure perpetuation of the species? Is there something very very wrong with me that I think of these questions at all?

I was in my office at Columbia when my friend Robert, the same Robert who is also friends with Joe, called me to catch up. We chatted about work and shows we had seen, I told him that my new editor seemed to be sort of blowing me off and not wanting to nail down a meeting, which was very frustrating, he told me that his car was acting up and that he didn't have the money to get it checked out, you know, yadda yadda yadda. I told him that Joe and I were communicating, and he thought it was pretty cool, but I didn't mention the ridiculously flirtatious nature of those communications. After we finished talking, I immediately sent Joe an e-mail.

Stormlet—
    Just spoke with Robert Leonetti, who was so glad to hear

we ran into each other and have had opportunity to communicate, as he has always thought we would get along famously. (I doubt he would feel the same if he had any idea of
the nature of that communication, but then again, it's none
of his business, if nothing else, he is unexpectedly correct...we
do get along famously, or infamously.)

And since you do like a girl with a big vocabulary, here are
some words I really like:

desire longing acquiescence carnal licentious concupiscent unchaste propensity ardor inclination lubricity sedulous
prurience libidinous lickerish quenchless extortionate lover
unconstricted breath caresses enter lascivious kiss subliminal yes

and my most favorite ever:

salacity

:) LG

Since we seem to use e-mail much like instant messaging, I
get a reply in a few minutes.

Sidney,

Robert is just a basically great, nice guy. He and I have had
many long in-depth conversations, so he might well anticipate
that we're hitting it off as well as we are.

It's been rare to find a woman with a larger vocabulary than
my own. Language is pretty important to me, I guess. I love
your word list. I believe I will claim it for my own. Allow me to
pronounce them to you one by one, very soon.

J.

La di da, so much more fun than actually working...

Agathon—

So I don't know what your schedule is looking like, but as
it is Thursday (and therefore our two week anniversary) I am

planning on going to the Four Moon, and would be most happy for your convivial company were you to be so inclined....
—Socrates

His reply is much more serious than I expected.

Hey Sidney,
   I look forward to a long interchange with you soon, but I'm going into being-with-girlfriend mode. I do apologize—I know I don't need to but I do. Had a strange, awkward conversation with Kim last night. We should be able to patch it up tonight. Going to an annual party at a good friend of mine's house. Jenny, my ex-wife, will be there also, which may be a little awkward too. Had a long lunch talk with a friend today about relationships in general and Kim in particular. And then on a long drive today I imagined what I would do if we broke up. Which we will eventually, of course. We have plane tickets for an event in August. I'm watching her dog on Sunday and Monday. I'm—
   My connection to you has very greatly distracted me and made me think of so many things. Some of the things on my mind you're no doubt aware of. Others have to do with how I am with women and what I want and where I'm going...
   Not as much time to type now as I'd like. Just a rush of emotion and mental processes.
   You won't see me tonight at Four Moon, unless I'm single. Then you'll see me. You'll also see me drink.
Talk to you soon, Joe

Poor guy. This love and dating business is such a pain in the ass. I have to remember that he and I are attempting a friendship, even if there is a mutual attraction underscoring it.

J—
   What can I say except that I am sorry for whatever difficulties you are going through... the certainty of an ending

may be freeing during a relationship, but there are no guarantees that when the ending comes it is by mutual agreement as to when and how. If what you want is to patch things up, then this is what I wish for you. If what you want is to be free, then I hope you can manage that in a way that is the least painful thing for you both. Based on the tone in your note, I will say that I hope I do not see you tonight, since the requirements for that seem beyond what you want for now. If I do see you, I will leave it to you to tell me what I can do to help.

Get in touch when you can, when you want...I am thinking of you and wishing you all good things.

yours,

Sidney

I went to see Parker play the most perfect Algernon ever, in a very good production of "The Importance of Being Earnest" and we went to the Moon after for a drink and a late nosh. We bumped into Leo Januscz, a director friend of ours, and I regaled them both with the developments in the Joe arena.

Parker is tired and wants to go home early, and I find that I am a little bored and my contacts are bothering me from the smoke, and by midnight it seems clear that Joe and Kim haven't broken up tonight, so I pack it in and go home. Lying in bed, thoughts of Joe and the certainty of his breakup make me think abut Geoff and the uncertainty of his.

I close my eyes and imagine it. *The phone rings. It is Geoff. He is coming over. He and Sandra have called it quits. He loves me. He needs me. We are going to figure out how to be together. I should pack an overnight bag, we can escape to my folks' place in Wisconsin for the weekend. And then monkeys will fly out of my butt.*

I am pondering this, the being together part—not the flying monkey butt part—when the phone rings.

Oh my dear lord in heaven.

"Sid?" It's Joe. I am trying not to be disappointed that it isn't Geoff. Geoff, after all, is working on the damn case in New York.

"Hey, Joe, how are you?" Sigh. Bird in the hand and all that.

"Fine. Guess where?"

"Oh no, Four Moon?"

"Yep."

"Baby, I am so sorry."

"Well, no, I mean, we didn't break up, but she didn't want me to stay over, and I didn't want to go home, so I came here, but they said you left like forty minutes ago."

"Yeah, it was kinda dead. I could come back…" I don't really relish this, as I have already gotten into comfy clothes and taken out my contacts and taken off my make-up etc.

"No, that seems silly. Is there someplace near you for a drink?"

"Not really. I mean I have drinks here, but you said you couldn't come over…"

"True. I would totally jump you. But, I mean, do you have a porch or something?" Odd one, this Joe. Then again, it is nice to know someone wants to jump me.

"I have a front stoop, if that would serve."

"Sounds good, I mean, if it is okay with you."

"What the hell."

I give him directions, put on a bra, decide to bag prettying up for him, and meet him outside. We sit on my stoop and talk for a half hour or so. He tells me about his problems with Kim and I tell him enough about Geoff that he understands why I can't be the other woman again. I don't tell him that Geoff and I are still together. He can't believe we haven't ever spent a whole night together after fourteen months. To be honest, neither can I.

"I really want to kiss you." Bless his heart. And to be frank, I really sort of want him to kiss me. So I decide, maybe a compromise.

"Look, Joe, you can kiss me—kissing is lovely. But I have to be very clear about this, you don't get to second base unless you are single. We can't get into too much trouble if we limit it to kissing, but it goes no further, deal?"

"Deal."

And then he kisses me.

Joseph Edington is kissing me. And I like it well enough. But it isn't Geoff, not by a long shot.

I get a call from Geoff the next morning. All is well. He is wrapping things up and should be back home by Saturday. He asks if I am going to be at the Columbia Theatre opening on Monday. He knows that I usually have to attend. Geoff and Sandra have been invited to be guests of one of the college trustees, and he wanted me to have a heads-up that they would be there.

Damn it all to hell. I mean, I usually love opening nights, and I have a lot of friends that are likely to be there, but it is really going to suck to be faced with Geoff and Sandra, especially the way she hangs on him in public.

Crap-o-rama.

Lightbulb.

J—

Thank you for an unexpected and most pleasurable visit last night. (Who'd have thought it was gonna be about you getting me OUT of bed!) Take this the right way, you were totally worth getting dressed for. :)

If it is looking like Storm might be available Monday night for a covert operation with Lightning Girl, let me know, mission dispatch coming under separate heading.....

Hope your audition is going well.

talk soon,

Sidney

MISSION DISPATCH

Storm—

As you know, my day job as Poetry and Dramatic Texts Professor at Columbia College requires that I occasionally abandon you and our nightly patrols to attend public events. This coming Monday, our theatre department has an opening of the last mainstage show of their season, which I, of course, must participate in. I have recently received word that my former mentor, Count Love-'em-and-leave-'em will be in attendance with his wife, the Countess Frigid de Bitchy, which means that I am destined to have a miserable, self-loathing, upsetting evening. That is, unless my fearless partner is willing to escort me to said event, and remind me as tangibly as possible that I am as fabulous as they come, and keep me laughing and distracted, and turn a potentially awful night into a great one.

The essence of this mission, and the only reason it could work, is that you would need to know that it is not about any attempt to incite jealousy in the aforementioned Count, (although, if seeing me in the company of a handsome fellow who looks at me like I am a Sunday buffet and makes me laugh all night gives him a twinge of pain, I won't lose sleep) but rather, just enough self-knowledge that my poor little brain will not be able to shake off the blows if I am there alone, and that of all the lovely boys in my life, you are currently the most lovely and my first choice.

Due to the sensitive nature of the Count's public position, his identity will need to remain classified, simply know that he is there, and his presence turns little twisted pins in my poor battered heart, and that I need good reason to not look at him.

Be my reason?

There is a very heartfelt good-night kiss in it for you, that I can promise.

Inform at your leisure. This message will self-destruct as soon as you hit the delete key.

yours,

Lightning Girl

Okay, you and I both know this is bullshit. I am really only interested in Joe being there to make Geoff sick with jealousy. Which he won't be, but still. I just hope that trying to make Geoff jealous isn't the only reason I am interested in Joe, period. I mean it is one thing to trot a man out and parade him in front of your periodically insensitive lover for effect, it is quite another to pursue an entire relationship on the off chance that the aforementioned lover might even care. Which he might not.

Turns out it doesn't matter even a little bit. Joe can't make it, he is going to be with Kim. I dress to the nines, get myself all steeled for the party, and Geoff shows up without Sandra, who was called out of town for a meeting in Detroit, and got delayed coming back. Of course, he completely ignores me all night, afraid to be seen even chatting with me, and then, to add insult to injury, the technical elements of the show get all cocked up, so everything goes wrong, and everyone is on edge, and by the time I play nice to all the right people at the party, Geoff has left without even saying goodbye.

A week passes pretty uneventfully, classes are over for the summer, and I find that my heart isn't much in the book these days, as my new editor is still keeping me on the back burner, so I find my days pretty dull. Geoff can't seem to get our birthday lunch date organized, but I get a gift from him in the mail. A boxed set of classical CDs performed by the Chicago Symphony Orchestra, and the new W. S. Merwin translation of Dante's *Inferno*, signed by Merwin, who in addition to being an amazing translator, is my favorite poet of all time. Thoughtful, beautiful, and somehow so empty without him. E-mailing with Joe helps some, even if he and Kim are still together.

Re: ee mail

j

i am very bored right now
i am so bored
that i
may have inadvertently
become a direct channel
for ee cummings
because i
cannot seem to muster
any energy
for capital letters
or punctuation
or work

i feel near to bursting
with things to tell you
and i kinda sorta miss you
in an odd little way
like just because i havent really talked
or e mailed
or seen you in a few days
seems somehow awful
and yet
at the same time
i feel nearly completely ridiculous
for feeling that way in the first place

this is the part where you make a mental note to be sure and tell
me that if i am ridiculous then so are you because you miss me
the tiniest bit too and that you too have been saving all the best
stories and funniest moments from the last few days to tell me
about and make me laugh the next time we can manage it

it is coming up on five thirty
i am leaving work soon
i am having dinner with a friend who is in from milwaukee for the
night
she is staying with me
but she goes to bed early
in case you wanted to call
or drop by
or something

all the flowers are off the tree in the front yard
        and shriveled to sticky little brown things
so it is not quite as lovely a place as it was last week
but if i knew someone was coming
at a particular hour of the evening
i might mention that i have
an extra parking space
behind my house
and a back entrance
where i might be sitting
by premeditated and prearranged coincidence
on my back porch
where there is a pretty good view of the moon
which
though one day past full
is still pretty big
and is at the other end of the house from the guest room
and therefore
quite safe
aurally speaking
since speaking orally
will not disturb sleeping guest types
you know
in case you wanted to
i dont know

see me
i guess
you know
if you wanted

if not
then
sometime
soon
i hope

later lover
me

Sidney—

Does anyone write more beautiful e-mail than you? I don't think so. Not that I've ever read.

Yes, you are just a bit ridiculous, and so am I. Yes, I do miss you sometimes. Sometimes a little. Sometimes not at all. And sometimes a lot with extreme prejudice and obvious physical manifestations, based on mere assumptions and fantasies, and now unfairly stated. Because... No! I'm not yet free. Last night I was alternately glad of that and not glad of that. Then at about four o'clock in the morning I was chased out of bed by snoring and I was miserable and awake and angry and feeling trapped. I lay in bed in her house thinking of you (and others, in the past). And I was really not happy to be with her and with her. Whither? Wither?

And then she drove me home and kissed me goodbye and we made more plans.

And I came home and sat down at my computer and did some stuff and wrote a sick friend. And then checked my e-mail, about ten minutes too late. And read your e-mail. Does anyone write more beautiful messages than you? No.

talk to you. soon. in person.
Lv j

Sigh. Anyone have any information on those baby pigeons yet?

chapter 19

QUOTE OF THE DAY

The pleasure of love is in loving.
We are much happier in the passion we feel
than in that we inspire.
—Francis, Duc de La Rochefoucauld: Maxim 259.
(Author's note: BULLSHIT.)

TIME: 1:45 a.m. PLACE: Home Office

Joe just left. We spent the better part of the last two hours talking, cuddling, and kissing like twelve-year-olds on my back porch in the moonlight. He serenaded me. Sigh. But I was firm in my resolve and did not invite him in, and when he tried to move things beyond kissing I reminded him clearly that until he is free, we go no further. He talked about Kim, told me that he has been a heartbreaker in the past and didn't want to hurt either of us, and I said in all honesty that I thought it sounded like they should be over, but that obviously I shouldn't be any part of that decision. Sound familiar? I feel like I am from the Department of Redundancy Department. Why is it always the unavailable guys than end up in my lap? Yeesh.

SIDEBAR

*Having said that, what the heck is all this "heartbreaker" business?
I swear, someone ought to tell men in general that they should never,
EVER tell any woman that they are no-good low-down scoundrels. I
once had a guy actually say, OUT LOUD… "I worry for you. Don't
go getting all crazy about me, I'm dangerous." If I hadn't been so tired,
I would have laughed in his face. Puh-leese. You aren't the fucking Lone
Ranger. And just so you boys know, it is an instantaneous way to kill
any attraction a rational intelligent woman might have been harboring
for you. And the kind of gal who will hear that and swoon, she ain't
the kind of gal you want hangin' round, if you get my drift.*

Joe called me in the morning, and we had a good long talk.
He asked hypothetically about dating other people if we were
dating each other, and seemed surprised that I said it was fine.

"But if we can date other people and each other, why won't
you date me while I am with Kim?"

Not that I should have to explain the nuances to him, but…

"I need an even playing field. Kim is your girlfriend. She gets
first priority. Can't have that. And I can't imagine her agreeing
to your seeing me, so that makes me the secret other woman,
and we know I am not doing that! If you and Kim break up, and
we date casually, and we are both seeing other people, then
everyone is even until someone feels like there is a chance or need
to pursue an exclusive relationship. That, I can handle. Gladly."

"Wow. That is something I never considered."

I give his relationship with Kim another month at most. Especially now that he knows he has me in the wings AND an option on other women. Men are so predictable sometimes.

"Can I see you tonight?"

"Of course. I'll be home, just give me a call."

"Okay, talk to you later."

Hee hee. I do feel sort of wicked….

Next morning...

Sidney—
    Just wanted to send a brief note thanking you again for a lovely evening. Great conversation, superlative gin, and wonderful, vigorous necking.
love,
Joe

Joe—
    ditto ditto ditto ditto.
    I am really so glad we finally met. (Or at least, that you finally remembered me.)
    Meanwhile, if you remember my little happy word list, it has become a poem. For your reading enjoyment see below....
xoxox ss

Desideratum

when did longing become ancient
sacred
when did the mundane daily words

lose their power

was it in the moment of acquiescence?
was it in the carnal gaze?
was it in the way he made me licentious
concupiscent
unchaste?

my propensity for ardor surprises even me
the inclination to lubricity
sedulous prurience
I have become
libidinous

lickerish
quenchless
extortionate

these eyes meet his in eager empressement
across crowded rooms
my ghost lover
who can touch me through walls
from across town
across time
unconstricted by the physics of the flesh
I lie in the darkness
of a lonely night
and can feel the lips pressed against mine
the quiet breath on my neck
the light fingertip caresses
I can feel him enter me
become lascivious with the thickened air
knowing the witchcraft of his kisses
the voodoo of his embrace
his subliminal presence
the apparition of emotion
the specter of the promise he will not offer me

he has become
my omnipresent familiar
keeping watch
not to protect
but to ensure
ensnare
to lay claim to this earthly heart
which knows salacity

from the Latin

meaning fond of leaping

Okay, I know I keep sending him poems I write for Geoff, but I can't send them to Geoff and it is nice to get feedback on them. Joe is always so impressed with my work. He probably thinks this song is about him, and all that Carly Simon stuff, but I like the compliments anyway. I don't get to see him for a couple of weeks, as he goes home for a visit, followed by a class reunion. On the other front, Sandra has changed her travel schedule for the summer to be mostly local day trips, so that she and Geoff can spend more time together, making my social calendar with him more like once every three to four weeks, which, let me be frank, sucks out loud. But tomorrow, at least, Joe comes back. A lovely distraction. He left me a message while he was out of town, without a return number, so I send a note in reply.

Storm—

Hope your travels to the center of the Midwest were interesting and enjoyable, and that Dad was good, and that your male classmates were all paunchy and balding and boring and the female classmates all adoring and attractive and pliable.

Anyhoo, I have no idea when exactly you are getting back, but whenever it is, I look forward to catching up whenever we get around to it...

(You are required to miss me the tiniest bit, tho...just for my ego's sake.)

XOXOXOXOXOX

(Deep long slow wet kisses full of promise and potential.)
your Lightning Girl

But his reply, I wasn't prepared for.

DAMN, Sidney.

I'd love to talk to you, but I don't think I should. I'm sorry (even though you've told me I shouldn't be!) but I think it would be best until this is over. Yes! I miss you, talking to you, especially after a message like this one, but I feel myself pulled in two directions, and I really I need to focus.

In fact, very little of anything comes to mind today. I spent about 12 hours yesterday sitting on my cousins' front porch and talking to my relatives. Relaxing, in its way, but not recommended for honing one's wits.

After talking to Kim a few times on the phone today, I sense she's somewhat tentative and strange about us, too. She definitely knows that I've been having problems, but I can't tell whether she's trying to hold on or give me permission to go away or pushing me away. Right now, I want to hold on, so I hope she does too.

I do miss you, more than the tiniest bit. I look forward to talking to you and writing to you again. Thank you for understanding and forgiving me, whether there's anything to forgive or whether blah-blah....

(Heartfelt hugs, with all body parts below the waist separated by an American Amish Society approved six inches, as the pulse races and blood is unwillingly diverted.)
J. Storm

Figures. No Geoff, now no kissing playmate. Still, must try to be supportive friend type...

Joe—

I wish you all good things.

So, as per what I decipher as your request, this will be my last communication with you until you green-light a renewal. I do understand, and I hope whatever it is you need to figure out, that you do it in a way that makes you certain of who you are and what you want and what you need and what is best for you both short and long term. It is healthy of you to do so, and I wish you all clarity.

I am out in the world, waiting for news of you, and hoping it is good. Be well, my dearest boy.

Be very well indeed.

Yours,

Sidney

When the computer blings, I assume it is a reply from him, so I am shocked to see a note from Geoff. It appears that Sandra's one-day meeting got heated (some major marketing fuck-up or something) and that she missed the last available flight home, so she will be gone for the night, and he wants to see me. (I try not to wonder about the fact that she is in Dallas, and whether she really missed her flight on purpose.) Closed door, open window, it all works! We agree on a little Mexican place up the street from my house. I spend the night in my usual whirlwind of cleaning on his behalf, and attending to various personal hygiene details.

Geoff is a little weird and distant when he gets to my place, but we haven't seen much of each other since early May, and as it is now late June, that means nearly 2 months since our last date (a frigging mind-numbing ETERNITY) so I pay it no mind. We walk to the restaurant, and get a table inside (for the air-conditioning), but by the window (for the view), order a half pitcher of margaritas (for the buzz), and Geoff loosens up a bit, and soon we are conversing with our usual aplomb.

He really is my favorite person in the whole world.

After dinner, we retrace our steps along the boulevard, looking at all the old Victorian mansions, now condos and apartments, and the pink-orange light of the setting summer sun, and I am terribly contented.

We get inside, and I thank him again for dinner, and move toward him for a kiss. He steps back.

"Look, I have to be honest about something here, things with Sandra have been better. Not perfect, and not great, but much better, so I don't really know what direction that is heading. Her company is making some major changes in her travel responsibilities in light of the impact 9/11 has had on their bottom line, so she will be working here most of the time, and you know I am in no position to see you when she is in town. I just don't know what any of this is going to turn out to be, but I am going to have to say that for the time being, we will just have to play everything by ear and be flexible."

Crap-a-zilla.

Not just that they are doing better, but now she isn't going to be traveling. Then again, how great can it be if he hightails it to me the second she leaves town? And businesses change their mind every ten minutes, she might be back to her old schedule in no time. And last time he did say that they only fight when she is in town, so maybe her being here permanently is really the surest way to be rid of her altogether. I think quickly about my response. If I say the wrong thing, I may be screwed. Or rather, not, which is SO not in the plan right now. I land on flippant as the right tone.

"That's sweet. You gonna take me to bed, or what?"

He smiles and shakes his head.

"I just wanted you to know where I was coming from."

"I thank you. Now I know. Can we get naked now?"

He steps forward and kisses me. "Absolutely."

We repair to the bedroom. Clothes are eliminated quickly. We are both slicked in a light dew of sweat, but neither of us cares. I lick his neck and shoulders, loving the salty-sweetness of him. He pushes me on the bed, on top of the covers, and begins to ravish me with his mouth and hands. I cannot think about anything except his touch and the sensations he creates and how much I love him and how much I have missed him, and I quickly find myself in the throes of a toe-curling orgasm. I want to sing. I want to weep. I want, I want, I want—

He moves up the bed, and lies beside me, stroking my face and hair and shoulders and breasts, and kissing me lightly. I reach for him, and pull him on top of me, and he enters me like a warm fog. I am transported back to our second date, lo these many moons ago, and how surprised I was at how perfectly made for each other we seemed to be. How can it be that now, fifteen months later, he is still a wonderful surprise for me? And, if I dare to imagine, I for him? How is it possible that after all this time, all the hours we have spent in bed together, that every kiss, every caress feels as electric as the first ones? How can it always be so comfortable and yet so subtly different every time? He is getting close to coming, and just the look on his face, the movement of his body, his weight on me, I know that I am going to come again, an almost intellectual orgasm, if such a thing is possible, since as we all know, most women can't get there from intercourse alone. But my brain and my heart are suddenly hard-wired to my clit, and even though the current position of his body means that he is nowhere near it, it jumps and tingles as if it is being stroked, and when he moans, and I feel the warmth spread inside me, I lose myself in a release that seems at once wonderfully impossible and impossibly wonderful.

He collapses beside me, and I wrap the blanket around us like a sticky, panting burrito, glad that I always buy king-size linens for my queen-size bed so that we don't have to get up and get underneath the covers. I have a brief, disjointed thought about the telltale stains that are likely to be discovered later on this expanse of chenille, and the fortune it is going to cost me in dry cleaning, but I don't really care. Not right now.

We rest for a while, and then Geoff asks if I would give him a quick back rub, which I am happy to do, since I love the feel of his strong back and shoulders under my hands. He sits up, and I kneel behind him, and begin kneading his neck and shoulders, while he moans happily. I love him so very much. And I have missed him so very much. And I will be missing him so very much. And I have no idea when I am going to see him again, and before I know it, the tears are pricking my eyes like hot little arrows. I close them, and shake my head to try and stop it, but the movement makes Geoff turn around, and he catches me.

"Are you all right?"

"I am working on it." It is the only thing I can think to say. He nods, rises, and walks to the bathroom. I wipe away the tears, confused, wondering why he barely acknowledged them, wondering where my hug was, my soothing words, my comfort? He returns and begins to dress, and I go to the bathroom, where I wash my face and get hold of myself. Or try to. When I get out, he is sitting in the living room already, smoking. I throw on my clothes and go to join him. He doesn't look at me.

"I can just leave if you want." Why won't he look at me?

"I don't ever want you to leave. Isn't that the point?"

"I understand that, but if you want, I can just leave right now. If it would be easier."

"No, I don't want you to leave." What is he doing? Why is he so cold? Jesus, a few little tears, they don't contain a viral contagion! He gets up off the couch where I have sat next to him, and begins to pace, not looking me in the face. He looks like he wants to run away.

"You know, we could just have dinner. We don't have to…I mean, we could just, you know…"

"I'm sorry, I didn't mean to cry, I just— It was such a wonderful night, and I was thinking how much I have missed you and how much I am going to miss you, and I couldn't help it, I am so sorry. Really, let's just forget it." Why am I apologizing? WHY? I have done nothing wrong! But I can't stop. "Please, I'm sorry, I didn't mean to make you uncomfortable."

"I am not uncomfortable."

"You are pacing like you can't wait to get out of here! Please, let's forget it happened, let's not let it ruin a perfect night." WHAT THE FUCK AM I TALKING ABOUT? Perfect? What is perfect about waiting two months for dinner and ninety minutes of sex, however amazing that sex is? What is perfect about three hours with the man you love, followed by what could be months of separation? What is perfect about the night you are about to spend alone in a bed that smells of the lover who will not deign to stay the night with you after fifteen months? UNDER A $350 CHENILLE BLANKET COVERED IN CUM STAINS THAT WILL NOW COST YOU SEVENTY-FIVE DOLLARS TO HAVE REMOVED BY SOME RANDOM DRY CLEANERS (since you can't take such nastiness to your usual place, too mortifying) WHO WILL PROBABLY CALL YOU A WHORE IN KOREAN WHEN YOU GO PICK IT UP!!!!!

"Look, I know this is hard on you, but I was honest when I got here, and I know that it is too much to ask, but there is a part of me that wishes that as my friend you might be happy for me that things are going better at home."

You have got to be kidding me.

"Excuse me?"

"I know."

"I can't be glad for you, because I know all too well why things are better, and I cannot trust the motivations behind it. And I can't pretend I don't know the things I know."

"Look, maybe you are just going to have to trust me that no one really knows what goes on except me and Sandra, and if I say it is better, then it is better, and I am the only one who can be an accurate judge of that."

"Fine." What else am I supposed to say?

"I don't know what is going to happen."

"I know, I'm sorry, I don't want to fight. Please can't we just forget the whole thing? I just want to go back to how things were, I want to know that we are fine." I am a complete and utter doormat. I am an idiot of the highest degree. He should be begging my forgiveness, not the other way around! Who is this woman, and where the hell did she put her BACKBONE?

"We are fine. Everything is fine. Everything is as it was. Don't worry." Right.

"I worry, I do worry."

"Well, don't. I really do have to go." Want to go, you mean, can't wait to go, desperately ITCHING to go.

I stand up. I am numb. I feel like someone has beaten me with a sock full of lead weights, no outward sign of injury, but all internally bleeding and bruised. I walk over to where he is, trying not to cry again. He gives me an awkward half hug, and kisses my forehead.

"Everything is fine." Bullshit. Everything is broken.

We walk to the door. He exits, I watch him leave, and at the landing, he turns and looks at me.

"Smile? Smile?"

And then he is gone.

I close the door. I walk inside. A bolt of electricity which has been sparked in the molten nickel core of the earth shoots up through the layers of stone and water and lime and coal and fossilized creatures and people and places, and enters my feet, gains momentum in the speeding of my blood, and hits my vocal cords where it takes a shape and exits my mouth in a fury of sound that I cannot believe is coming from me. A wailing, keening howl of deepest anguish and darkest anger, a noise somewhere between a mourning elephant and a nuclear warning siren. It is a pitch of profound despair, and it is a noise I have never heard before, let alone made. I stand in the living room, and the sound segues into the kind of sobbing one usually only sees in movies or at funerals for children. I have lost him. My stomach churns in sorrow. I know I am going to be sick. I make it to the bathroom in the nick of time. Everyone to the lifeboats. Margaritas and dinner first, watch your step, no pushing please, the M&M's and tea from your four o'clock break, then whatever remains of lunch, no waiting, room for everyone. I get up off the floor. Run a glass of water. Drink it. Turn right around and vomit it up, still cool leaving me, one of the oddest sensations I have ever felt. Finally dry heaves. I expect to see the remains of my heart floating in the bowl, all wasted, shredded, unusable, unwanted flesh.

I get up again, shakier, cold sweat, hands trembling, slightly dizzy. My knees buckle a little, then catch and support me. The tears won't stop. My cheeks are soaked, my shirt front damp. I hiccup and cough, but cannot stop crying. I have never felt so empty.

I take ten deep breaths, then ten more. I pick up the phone and call Parker.

"Hello?"

"It's me. Can you come over?"

"What happened?"

"I. Can't. Say. Can. You. Just. Please. Come. Over."

"On my way, sit tight baby girl, I am coming right now."

Parker is coming. This makes me feel better. I wipe my face. The breeze feels good.

The breeze. Feels good.

The summer breeze. Through my open windows. In the living room.

The windows underneath which, by my quick mental calculations, Geoff must have been standing when I made that preternatural noise.

Take a minute, it will hit you.

Ah HA! See what I am driving at, people? He had to have heard me. The whole neighborhood had to have heard me. People in SPACE had to have heard me! He knew. The bastard KNEW that I was inside having a meltdown, and did not, I repeat, DID NOT COME BACK TO SEE IF I WAS OKAY! Bad enough that he behaved so awfully when I had just lost my hold on a little basic wan eye leakage, but to hear that sound and not come back, I am so flabbergasted that I stop crying.

UNTRAINED POP-PSYCHOLOGYCAL ANALYSIS

Now, I have some theories about his personal aversion to tears, from what I can piece together from the information I have gleaned in our time together, I conjecture that other women in his life have used tears as a manipulation tool with him, and that his reaction is a combination of general discomfort with emotion and a feeling that the display might be forced, or dishonest or calculated in some way. I also happen to believe that it is entirely possible, despite the incredulous response I am likely to get from you, that he is afraid that he might cry as well, and I happen to think if he started, he might never stop. Doubt me if you like, but there is deep pain in that man which he has been masking and pushing into little corners for years, and I happen to think that if he let himself cry, REALLY CRY, it would be like Victoria Falls for several hours, and then off to a little padded room to relax for a couple days. You can have your own opinion.

I can't believe he didn't come back. And if he was too much of a fucking coward to face me, I can't believe he didn't at least call to see if I was okay. It has been nearly twenty minutes— what with all the throwing up, plenty of time give a little ringy-dingy and see how I am faring.

What an asshole. What an unmitigated ASSHOLE! I am furious. I am seething! I am on fire with indignation and rage and hurt and disgust and and and...

BZZZZZZZZZZZZZZZ!

Doorbell.

I go to the door, and Parker, wonderful glorious Parker comes in and puts his arms around me, and hugs me tight, and I dissolve in another bout of weeping. Finally I pull back, and he smiles at me.

"Rough night?" This makes me laugh, and then we are both laughing and then I am crying and laughing and Parker goes to fetch Kleenex. Good thing, because I am one big snotty mess.

"Date?"

"Yes."

"What happened."

I give him the highlights, and he nods a lot.

"I mean, it was like, the minute I had some emotion where he was concerned, he totally fucking shut down, like he was angry with me for having feelings, you know? And he couldn't stop for ten seconds just to comfort me, just to tell me he understood how hard this is on me. I mean I was NAKED, sitting beside him, weeping, and he didn't even give me a hug or hold me or anything! Any stranger on the street would have offered some sort of gesture, and this is my friend, my lover of FIFTEEN MONTHS, and he couldn't be bothered to even be human! He just got up, and paced and ranted, he scolded me for not being HAPPY FOR HIM!"

"He is a shit."

"That is an insult to feces everywhere!"

This makes us laugh again.

"How can I be so in love with someone who thinks that little of me? How can I be in love with someone who is so cruel, when I have never been anything but supportive and good to him? How can I be in love with someone who doesn't value me enough to be bothered to wipe a few tears away for me? What kind of fucking idiot must I be to have fallen head over heels in love with such an ASSHOLE?!"

"You are human. And from all you have told me about him, tonight aside, in the important ways, you are very good together. You have intellectual equality, philosophical and humoristic compatibility, and most important, the sex of your lives. Of course you fell in love with him. He is the one who gave you the strength to get out of your marriage, which we both know was a long time coming. He reminded you that you are one hot tamale, that you are an object of desire, he made you feel possible, isn't that what you said?"

"Yes. I should have left it at that. Friendship, great sex, no strings. Why did I have to go and fall in love with him? It fucks everything up."

"You can't control that. You got free, you could allow yourself to imagine him in your life in a real way. You liked how that looked, you saw potential, you fell in love. It isn't miraculous or unexpected. Just human."

"Why doesn't he love me? Why can't I ever get it right? What on earth could be so wrong about me that he would rather stay with that cold, manipulative, gold-digging, ambitious TWAT who makes him anywhere from irritated to genuinely unhappy the majority of the time, than be with me who loves him as he is and only wants to make him happy?"

"This isn't about you, this is about him. This is about his comfort level. He is more comfortable unhappy, or he wouldn't work so hard to stay that way. And if he took ten seconds to think about you, and what you are offering him, who you are, and the life he might have with you, he would lose his mind."

"I don't believe you. He has to know. He has to be aware that this is not some fluke, that girls like me don't just come along around every corner. He isn't stupid, Park, he has to know on some level that he is never ever going to find a young, beautiful, sexy, smart, funny woman who will fall this hard for him, and not want to change him, and not need his money or his power or prestige, and wants only to spend a large portion of her time trying to make him happy. She doesn't exist! It is me, just me, that's all! One of a kind! Once in a lifetime opportunity kicking at the door and leaning on the bell and screaming to be let in. Why won't he let me in?"

"I don't know, sweetheart, I just don't know."

I wipe away the tears for the umpteenth time. "Well, fuck him."

"Right on!"

"FUCK HIM! Fuck them both. She wants to be queen of the world, and be afforded her lifestyle, and cuckold him with people's cousins when she is out of town, and be evil to people he likes and respects, and he is willing to let her— so, fine! She can have him. He wants to spend the rest of his life with that bloodless cunt, his choice. He doesn't have the balls to choose life and love and laughter and passion because it might damage his precious reputation, as if he would be the first older man of power to trade a wife in for a newer model, why should I allow myself to become the butt of trophy wife jokes? For what? Some old man who will make me a widow when I am in my fifties, if I am lucky enough to get him for even that long? For maybe ten to fifteen decent years before his mind starts to go, and the body begins to fail? I should be grateful to him for showing me his true colors! I should call and thank him for letting me know exactly how selfish, indifferent, coldhearted and cruel he can be before I wasted any more time loving him. I should be thanking my lucky stars that he isn't in love with me, so I won't have to work very hard to extricate myself from his grasp. I will have a life of wonder and joy with a man who will appreciate me and remind me every day that he knows how blessed he is to have me, and in the next five years Sandra will find some other more powerful, younger, handsomer, richer man, and leave him anyway, and then he will be a sad lonely old fuck with no one to love him, and I will have moved so far down my own path that he will never catch up to me. FUCK HIM!"

"Brava! Hallelujah!!! EXACTLY TRUE!!!!" Parker applauds my little monologue energetically.

"Parker, it's all bullshit, and you know it, and I don't mean any of it, really. I love him so much, what the hell am I going to do?"

"Cry. A lot. And write. A lot. And take some time to see what the next few weeks bring. Maybe he will apologize, or do something to acknowledge that he was harsh. Maybe his reaction was because you are forcing him to face the realities of this situation and he needs time to process it all before he can have any sort of rational response to things, and in a while he will come around. In the meantime, sad as you are, you have got to put some energy into getting into the whole dating scene, and getting yourself out there, and meeting some men."

"Jesus, Parker, I can't think about that right now."

"Wrong answer. And don't even talk to me about this whole Joe business, because I don't care how much you kiss that man or how many flirty e-mails you send him, he was a safe choice because he has a girlfriend and so you don't have to be real with him. I mean real dating. Single men. Men who are physically and emotionally available. DATING. For real. Do it."

"I don't exactly see you getting yourself out there...." Parker's recent history with men is his own to tell, so I will not go into details here, but there are many reasons that of all my friends, even the select few who actually know about Geoff, he was the one I called first. 'Nough said.

"I was on a date when you called me."

"Oh no, Parker, really?"

"Really. So there."

"With who?"

"That guy I met at Sidetrack last week."

"The really cute one with the smile who was trying to pick you up by listing all the shows he has seen you in?"

"That is the one."

"You minx! Why didn't you tell me?"

"You sounded desperate, and so I just wanted to get over here."

"I am such a shit, I ruined your date."

"Actually, I think it was a good thing."

"Why, wasn't it going well?"

"It was great, actually. He picked up picnic food, and we went down to Buckingham fountain, and ate, and talked and laughed and walked around, and he kissed me a couple of times."

"Good kisser?"

"Very."

"Excellent."

"And then you called and I told him I had to go because one of my best friends was in crisis and that you had been there for me through all the worst of my worst times, so that I had to get to you right away."

"You are such an amazing friend. Thank you."

"Damn, girl, it isn't like I don't owe you at least a dozen more of these, although I hope you never have need to cash in on them. Anyway, he now knows that I am very committed to my friends, and that I am a very caring person, AND I got to avoid the whole decision about whether to sleep with him, so there will be no regrets tomorrow morning!"

"I love you."

"I love you too. So what are we going to say in your ad?"

"What ad?"

"Your *Reader* ad."

"Not gonna happen, my friend."

"Gonna happen indeed. Look, it won't go in until next week, so by the time people start to call you, you will have had some time to recover from tonight's massacre. And you said yourself, even if it isn't over, it is certainly on sabbatical, so take the time away from him to get out in the world and just see who is there. You have nothing to lose. And many many free drinks to gain."

"Fine."

"Fine."

We go to the computer. I log on to the internet. Parker guides me to the Reader Matches, where, apparently, I can place a fifty-word ad for free which will run two weeks. I cannot believe I am going to do this.

Let's recap, shall we? I don't exactly think my ad can say, "Brokenhearted poet needs new muse. Legally separated WF, 33, 5'3", 260, brown/blue, currently in love w/MWM who is a shithead, but trying to move on. ISO S/D/WWM, 35-45, for long walks (on the beach, or all over me), theatre, candlelit dinners, and great conversation. Ability to sleep over essential."

"What should we say?" Parker seems overly excited about this.

"Good God, I have no idea."

"Well, what would you want someone to know?"

"I dunno, I think it is more about the kind of man I want to attract."

"So how do you attract the right kind of man?"

"If I knew that, I wouldn't be in this pickle!"

"I mean with words. Jesus, for a writer, fifty words sure has you stumped."

Let me just say that one can challenge me on a lot of things. My political views, my grading curve, the choices I make about my wardrobe. But no one—and I mean no one—challenges me on my ability to write to the occasion. Not even my best friends. ESPECIALLY not my best friends.

READER MATCHES *Thursday July 4th*

Women Seeking Men

PLEASE LIMIT YOURSELF TO TWO CARRY-ON BAGS. Life is short, we should be abundant with each other. SWF, 33, Rubenesque in truest sense, i.e. cute enough to inspire painting, ISO S/D/WWM 34-45, for friendship, intelligent conversation, convivial company. Seeking blended Cary Grant, William Powell, David Letterman and W. S. Merwin.

Happy Independence Day to me. Let the games begin.

chapter 20

an embarrassment of riches, or:
waiting for david letterman

QUOTE OF THE DAY

"You have nineteen new messages."
—*The Reader* automated Matches phone system

Nineteen new messages. NINETEEN NEW MESSAGES?
Good lord in heaven, what the hell am I going to do with nineteen new messages? To be frank, I wasn't really expecting any messages. After all, anyone who has ever read the "Men Seeking Women" area of the Reader Matches knows one thing, big girls are not in fashion. Euphemisms abound. Athletic. Fit. Slim. Slender. Active. Height-weight proportionate. Petite. Likes to work out. Even the dreaded "no fatties please." The few ads requesting larger gals all seem to be from African-American men in their 50s looking for "thick" women, or "big legs." This is not a derogatory remark, nor a sweeping generalization, nor an attempt to denigrate or perpetuate stereotype of any kind. I simply tell it as I see it, and in the world of personal ads, one gets the hang of things pretty quickly.

Let's bring you up to speed a bit, since I certainly must sound a little loony, considering two short weeks ago I was a woman on the verge of a nervous breakdown. Today I am a woman on the verge of...well, I'm actually not sure. I'll get back to you before the end of the chapter.

Anyway, the night of the June Massacre, as it will forever be known in the vernacular of my nearest and dearest, Parker stayed over and in the morning, we went out for brunch, indulged in mimosas galore, and immediately went back to my place for a nap. We watched TV. We talked about boys. I cried some. They talk about the five stages of grief, from denial through acceptance; I hit them all about once an hour. I let myself be angry. I let myself be sad. I imagined how he would come back to me and beg my forgiveness and profess his undying love. I wrote my very first no-holds-barred-you-have-really-fucked-up-badly poem about him. Parker thought it was a good step. Parker also thought it was more of a psst-by-the-way-in-case-you-didn't-notice-you-sort-of-hurt-my-feelings-but-don't-worry-your-pretty-little-butt-about-it poem, but I will let you give it your own long and ridiculously hyphenated descriptor.

seeing red

oh mister man
you have cut me so deep
I am beyond bleeding

how could you
in my quiet moment of despair
in my shaking need
in my tangible anguish
how could you
run away?

if the days and weeks and months
that came before

had not
if the laughter and music and passion
that preceded
disappeared
if those nights we lay tangled naked together
and kissed so deeply
and were so open to each other
became as so much mist
even then
if I weren't what I have been
but simply someone
anyone
any stranger on the street
would you not have offered some comfort
to one who sat before you
heart in hands
tears on cheeks
asking only for understanding
for soothing

how dare you

how dare you look at your friend
your lover
in pain
and not put aside your own petty paranoiac need
to abandon her
and simply accept your basic human responsibility
to hold her
to wipe her salty sorrows away
to tell her you knew why she cried
that there was compassion in you
for what she faced
that it was okay for her to be a bit broken

how dare you look at this woman
who had given you all of herself
asked for only what you might manage to offer in return
this woman who believed in you
beyond your capacity to believe in yourself
who forgave you
beyond your ability to forgive yourself
who loved you with her whole heart
and only wanted to make you happy
who sat naked and weeping before you
and turn away

how dare you lecture her
and rant
and pace like a caged animal
spewing the same ancient bullshit
about making your own decisions
about not being pushed
about how much better things have gotten
and have the unmitigated gall
to ask for her happiness
that you have found such improvement in your life without her

it was unconscionable
it was inhumane
it was unfriendly
it was unwarranted

and while you were being forgiven
even as you were killing me
while you were excused
even as my heart was shattering into a thousand bits of sorrow
it will not be forgotten

not the way the air chilled
nor the way your eyes chilled

nor the way you turned from me and calmly left me in my anguish
opened the door
and asked me to smile
as you walked away

you asked me to smile

Parker made me read it over and over out loud till I was practically screaming. He stayed over a second night to be sure I was okay. That is the thing about friends, they know how to ease you back into the world.

I almost forgot about the ad, to be honest, everything was so blurry. But then I got a letter with instructions on how to set up my voice-mailbox. Oy. What an exercise. Press 1 for single, 2 for divorced, 3 for widowed, 4 for out of your fucking mind. I recorded answers to inane questions so that people interested in knowing more about me than the fifty words in the ad could express, could hear my voice and judge whether my ideal Sunday activities and their ideal Sunday activities made us a possible match. I called Parker and yelled at him for making me do it, and he made me promise to take the exercise seriously, I didn't want bad *Reader* ad karma. So I did. I answered all the questions like a good girl, which took me over forty-five minutes because I didn't want to sound like I was reading a script, hence I kept messing up and needing to start over so I didn't sound like an idiot either. A total waste of time, after all, no one was going to call in and listen to it anyway, right?

Wrong. Oh so very wrong.

I didn't call in to check my mailbox for six days. I wasn't going to appear desperate; after all, this was just a dare, a lark, I had better things to do. But when I realized that tomorrow morning the ad was going to appear for its second week, I thought I had better look into it, just in case.

"You have nineteen new messages."

I got a piece of paper and a pen, and prepared to take notes.

Here goes…

Of the nineteen messages, all fairly long and detailed, three were from men who had at best an indifferent grasp on the English language; two were over the age of 60; one was a self-proclaimed "Switch Dom" looking for a Domina to help him explore his submissive side; one was an unemployed, divorced father of three currently living in a room over his parents' garage; one was an "unhappily married" fire chief in the suburbs looking for a city girl playmate; two were in their early twenties; and one sounded an awful lot like my cousin Andrew, which was significantly creepy.

This left me with eight prospects. I went back and listened to their messages again, and then looked at my notes.

Contestant number one: Michael, 43, attorney, divorced, three kids, love of literature.

Contestant number two: Bob, 37, works in theatre on the technical side.

Contestant number three: Michael, 36, divorced, father of one, working on his Doctor of Divinity at University of Chicago.

Contestant number four: Gary, 45, career naval officer, divorced, father of two.

Contestant number five: Dave, 40, computer guy.

Contestant number six: Brian (or Ryan, can't really hear much, called from a cell phone) 36, sales rep.

Contestant number seven: Michael, 34, CPA/attorney, divorced.

Contestant number eight: you guessed it, Michael, 40, musician, divorced, father of one.

What is it with guys named Michael? Are all men named Michael currently single, or was there Michael-specific subliminal messaging in my ad that I am unaware of? They have all left me their phone numbers. Numbers one, two, four, seven and eight have ads of their own. I call in and listen to their messages. They all seem reasonably normal. I don't really know what I am supposed to do with the information I have, but my mother would be disappointed if I didn't return my phone calls, so I do. I call them all. I wait till Friday morning, but then I call. Every last one of them. I do this late morning when I am reasonably certain they will not be home. I am a very smart girl, eight phone calls, eight answering machines. I leave a simple straightforward message, "This is Sidney, thanks for the call, here is my number, I look forward to chatting with you soon."

My stomach is in knots.

I immediately go out for the rest of the day, otherwise I may be home if and when they call, and I don't know that I am ready for that. And a good thing too, because five of them do leave me messages while I am schmying around. Two Michaels, Brian/Ryan, Bob and Gary all leave messages looking forward to talking to me. I don't know which Michaels, as no one has left a last name. While I am pondering whether it is better to call them back tonight, especially as it is already after nine, the phone rings.

"Hello?"

"Hi, is Sidney there?"

Oh sweet jesus.

"This is Sidney." Please be an overzealous telemarketer.

"Sidney, this is Michael, from the *Reader?*"

Of course it is. Who else would it be?

"Hi, thanks for calling me back."

"No problem, is this an okay time?"

"Sure, it's fine." I have no idea how to do this.

"So how are you doing?"

"Fine." Mortified, but fine.

"Have you done this before? The ad, I mean."

"Nope, first time."

"Well, it isn't so bad. Have you talked to many people?"

"You are the first." Why would I say that?

"I promise to go easy on you. Take a deep breath. It isn't nearly as painful as you think it is going to be."

I laugh. He's sort of funny, and he has a nice voice.

"Besides, you can always hang up on me as a last resort."

"Do you get that a lot? Hanging up I mean?"

"Hardly ever. So, I wanted to tell you I really liked your ad."

"Thanks. It was sort of a dare, late at night, I don't even really remember what it says to be honest."

"It was good, caught my eye. None of the usual inanity."

"What do you mean?"

"Well, you didn't say anything about long walks on the beach, Ravinia, candlelit dinners, or taking advantage of the city's great museums. If half the people in the *Reader* really were doing all that, then I wouldn't have so much trouble getting into a Saturday-night movie."

He's really funny, I had noticed those standard claims myself. So I quip back.

"You forgot that everyone is as comfortable in formalwear as they are in blue jeans."

"Exactly! And everyone is very good-looking."

"And everyone is professional!" This isn't so hard after all.

"Professional what, I always wonder?"

"I don't think I want to know."

"Probably best. It is amazing we don't see more people in tuxedos and blue jeans walking along the beach after their candlelit dinners."

"They are all at Ravinia, probably. Being professional."

"So, the best way to handle these calls is to just be yourself, don't put any pressure on it, and don't reveal anything which makes you uncomfortable, and don't agree to meet anyone unless you really want to."

"You sound like an expert."

"This is my fourth time in two years."

"Take this the right way, that is not exactly a rousing endorsement of success."

"I know, it sounds bad. I actually did have a relationship for almost ten months with a woman I met in this manner, so that was pretty good, I think."

"What happened? Sorry, that was rude…"

"Not at all. Just didn't work out. And don't worry about protocol—it is a little bit about revealing information sooner than one might usually. After all, even though it is an incredibly inorganic way to meet someone, it helps with the numbers game."

"The numbers game?"

"Well, think about how many people you have met in your whole life. What percentage were people you liked enough to be friends? What percentage of those were you attracted to? What percentage of those were attracted back? Finding someone is all about the numbers, if you meet enough people, make enough friends, eventually you will be attracted to someone who is attracted to you and off you go."

"An interesting theory. Makes a lot of sense."

"Or I could be full of crap, that is a distinct possibility as well."

This makes me giggle.

"You have a very nice laugh."

"Thank you." Maybe this wasn't such a bad idea after all…

Flash Forward

I can't sleep. It is nearly four-thirty in the morning and I cannot sleep even a little bit. I keep thinking about my conversation with Mike (as he prefers to be called). And how he made me laugh. I laughed a lot, actually, while we talked. And I mean TALKED. Once we got rolling it was insane, we shared our histories and talked about movies and books and childhood stuff, it was like we had known each other for years, we were practically finishing each other's sentences.

We talked for a very long time.

I am a little embarrassed to admit how long.

Okay, but don't make fun of me.

Five hours.

Yes, okay, we talked for five hours. Stop laughing. That isn't polite. CUT IT OUT, he was very nice! By the time it got to be 2:00 a.m. he asked if he could take me out. I said sure. He asked

if I was busy tonight (as it was already Saturday morning) and I
said I had plans to meet some friends for drinks late, but was free
in the early part of the evening. He said how about a drink at
seven. I said sure. He said how about the Signature Room on the
95th floor of the Hancock building, and I said that sounded
great—one of my favorites. We agreed to meet in the lounge
nearest the elevators. And then we hung up. And now I can't sleep.
Turns out he is the Michael with the three kids, 11, 14 and 16,
very friendly with his ex-wife, lawyer specializing in copyright
infringement, sidelines as a musician. He seems so amazing. Normal. Smart and funny and sweet. He described himself as five-
eleven, light brown hair, blue eyes, slender build, Irish looking. I
do have a little thing for those Irish boys, I must admit, that fair
skin and light eyes combo always seems so attractive. I am not
going to be cute enough for him. He is going to be disappointed, and I am going to be heartbroken. But what if he likes
me? After all, such an amazing connection, I mean five hours flew
by on the phone, and we like all the same silly things, what if we
are really totally great together? I fantasize about Parker toasting
us at our wedding, taking credit for making me place the ad that
brought us together. I fantasize about the look on Geoff's face
when he hears from my dad at work that I am madly in love. I
fantasize about how much his kids are going to adore me. It is
almost five, and the sky is lightening and what the hell am I going
to wear tonight? What do you wear to meet your future? What
do you say when he tells you at the end of the evening that he
intends to marry you? And more importantly, do you sleep with
him on the first date? What. do. you…zzzzzzzzzz (finally).

Eventually, sheer exhaustion will always win.

I wake up just after noon and call Parker. He tells me to wear
the dark gray skirt with the sassy black zip-up shirt and my little pointy-toed Richard Tyler Mary Janes with the spiky heel.
Sexy, but not over the top, urbane, a little funky, and totally me.
I indulge in afternoon quality time at home, take a long bath,
read, gradually getting physically and mentally prepared for

tonight. Before I get dressed, I masturbate quickly; it is like a kind of pep talk from myself and, besides, it puts a great flush in my cheeks and is rumored to jump-start pheromone production and make you irresistible. Certainly doesn't hurt, that is for sure. My timing is good, I am not ready too early and watching the clock, my hair is behaving, I am damned cute in my little outfit, and the night is perfect, a balmy July evening with a cool breeze and little humidity. I get to the 95th floor at seven on the dot, and look around. He said he would be wearing black pants and a blue button-down, little black-rimmed glasses. I scan the area. I think I beat him. There is a chair here, so I sit, mostly because my knees are a tiny bit wobbly. My heart is racing. Seven-oh-three. My watch could be a little fast. Seven-oh-six. Never know about traffic, he was coming from Rogers Park way on the North side. Seven-oh-nine. Please don't let me get stood up on my first actual date-date since my separation. (No, Geoff doesn't count, I mean a real date with an available man.) Seven-eleven. Deep breath, anyone can get hung up, twenty minutes is the max before lateness is rudeness unless there is a timing issue like a movie or theatre tickets. Seven-fourteen. I am looking at my watch, and am noticing a pair of shiny black shoes stationed in front of me. From the vague area above the shoes I hear...

"Sidney?"

Oy.

My eyes travel up the shoes to the crisply tailored black pants, up past the chic flat-front (don't look at his crotch for lord's sake), the simple elegance of the silver buckle on the black leather belt, the deep midnight blue of the shirt, wrinkle-less over a trim midriff, up to the slight hint of skin at the unbuttoned collar to...sigh.

I am looking into an open face, smiling expectantly at me, with, as promised, little black-rimmed glasses over blue eyes. I smile back. I am hoping my disappointment is not clearly obvious.

"Mike." I rise from my chair, and extend my hand, which he

grasps warmly as he leans in to kiss my cheek. "How nice to meet you in person." I want to cry. It isn't that he is ugly, he is just…not for me, really, you know?

"I am so sorry I am late, traffic was a little tight getting into downtown, and…"

He is talking and gently guiding me by the elbow to a small table near the windows, a breathtaking view of the Chicago city lights. I cannot concentrate. Why did I let myself get all worked up about him? Why did I spend so much time worrying that I wouldn't be cute enough for him, and never wondered if he would be cute enough for me? I mean, Geoff isn't exactly devastatingly handsome (except to me, not that he cares), and Mark was no George Clooney look-alike. I just, well, sometimes you just know that someone isn't going to do it for you. Not in a shallow way, just in a resigned way. Mike, who is happily babbling away about his kids for the moment, has a head shaped vaguely like a squashed peanut. You know the kind, pointy chin, full cheeks, weird indentation at the temples, then swollen forehead. A great expanse of forehead. The eyes are blue, close-set and a little watery.

All of this could be gotten around, I suppose, if it weren't for the smile. Thin lips—not that sexy Kenneth Branagh no-lip— just thin lines with no definition. Also not insurmountable. But he won't stop smiling at me, and I really wish he would, because Mike, the fantasy man of my dreams, has terrible teeth. Again, not that quirky imperfect crooked of pre-braces Tom Cruise, or the British style we're-just-so-glad-they-aren't-green-and-mossy snaggle of Hugh Grant, not even the who-gives-a-shit-he's-sexy-anyway orthodontic nightmare of Alan Rickman—no, Mike looks sort of like a jack-o'-lantern. His top teeth are smallish, uneven in size, excessive of gum, canines freakishly pointy to the point of nearly being fangs, and there are large gaps between each of the front six, while the lower teeth seem to have all tried to grow at once out of the foremost inch of space, and are crammed in there higgledy-piggledy.

A gap in the middle can be charming, case in point David Letterman, who I think is just dreamy (more on that later), but five gaps is too much, particularly if the space could obviously be put to good use elsewhere. I can't imagine kissing that mouth. I can't imagine that mouth kissing me. And don't you go passing judgment on my passing of judgment, you all think about whether you want someone to kiss you in the first few minutes yourselves, not a set in stone yes I will or no I won't, but it at least crosses your mind. But he looks like he could bite and cause damage. He makes me want to find my orthodontist, Dr. de Sade, and thanks him for the five years of torture that I endured, apparently, just for this purpose, that I will never ever cause disgust with my smile.

"Can I get you something?" A kindly-looking waitress has appeared, interrupting Mike's discussion of how he passed the day with his youngest daughter, he looks at me, and asks what I might like. All my friends have counseled me on the dating rules, and rule number one is only order wine on a first date, and only two glasses, max. Elegant, adult, you don't look like a lush, and two is enough to settle the nerves, but not get stupid.

"I'll have a Grey Goose martini, up, three olives." Fuck the rules, those teeth require serious lubrication.

"Sam Adams. Thanks." Mike turns his attention back to me. "So, enough of me babbling, how was your day?"

Okay, Sid, go for it. You liked this guy. He is smart and made you laugh, and was really nice and you have a great deal in common. Don't be shallow, just give him a shot. Maybe he will be so great you won't even notice after a while.

"Well, I was a little tired…"

"I can't imagine why!" He smiles. Where the hell is that wench with the martini?

I discover something important. When I talk about myself, my work, whatever, Mike listens intently. When he listens, he doesn't smile. This is good. I begin to outline everything from my teaching philosophies, to my writing methods, anything to keep him listening. He is a good listener, a lot of nodding and um-hmming. The martini goes down like water. The beer appears to make him sweat, but still, sweaty forehead keeps attention away from barracuda jaws, so not a bad trade-off. I am not exactly sure what I am waxing on about when the waitress reappears.

"Can I bring you another round?"

Mike looks at me and says "You want to get out of here?" God yes.

"Sure."

"Just a check please."

Excellent. It is a little after eight. Enough time to have fulfilled obligation. We can leave, I can meet up with Parker and the gang at Four Moon, and the evening will be over.

"You up for a bite?" EEEEEK! Oh, he means food. I don't know what to say. Be kind, Sidney, he is a very nice man, and he is treating you well, and you should give him a chance at least. Just tell him you should probably get ready to meet up with your friends if that is okay with him.

"Sure, maybe a quick something." THAT IS NOT THE ANSWER WE AGREED ON, YOU NINNY!

"Great."

The waitress comes back with the check, and Mike waves off my offer of financial participation. We walk through the bar, his hand lightly on the small of my back, and ride the elevator down ninety-five floors while my ears pop. The air outside feels good, and Mike flags a cab.

"Do you like tapas?"

Tapas is one of my favorite foods, damn his eyes. "Sure, love it."

"Café Ba-Ba-Reeba at Halsted and Armitage please," Mike tells the driver.

The sangria doesn't help my lack of attraction, and unfortunately neither does the conversation. It is a pity really, because this is a truly nice guy. Résumé Boy. The kind of guy who has it all on paper. Excellent boyfriend material. But I cannot manufacture chemistry no matter how hard I try, no matter how much I drink. And which is worse, he is looking across the table at me like I am the future stepmother of his children. Ironic, isn't it? Not remotely pleasant, but ironic nonetheless.

He orders for us both. Baked goat cheese, Spanish Tortilla omelet, garlic aioli potatoes, beef skewers. Somewhere in the middle of dinner my stomach turns over. The vodka, the wine, the heavy rich food, the heat of a crowded restaurant—I am suddenly very queasy. I have a sensitive stomach, and it is displeased. I need air. Quickly. Technology to the rescue. I jump like something has tickled me suddenly. I grab for my pager, and ask Mike if he will excuse me, it is the friends I am supposed to be meeting later. I take my cell phone and run outside to fake a call. I eat some Tums. I pace a bit in the cool air. Better. Not great, but better.

"Mike, I am so sorry, I hate it when people jump for their phones, I just wanted to be sure of the plan."

"Not at all, you said last night that I could only have you for the beginning of the evening, is everything set?"

"They are on their way to the bar, just wanted me to know."

"Well then, why don't I get the check so that you can meet up with them."

He is so sweet. "Thank you, I didn't mean to rush you."

"Not at all, I am glad that you were available as long as this, I never thought I would get the pleasure of your company for dinner." Have I mentioned that he is really deeply truly such a very nice man? Dating sucks rocks.

"It has been lovely, thanks."

He pays the check, again refusing my offer of money, and when he finds out that I have left my car at the Hancock Building, he flags a cab, and gets in to escort me back. I didn't even think there were such gentlemen in the world, and when he gets out of the cab to escort me to my car, I know there aren't.

I look at him once more to see if I can generate any spark at all for him. Nope. Sigh.

"Thank you for a wonderful evening."

"Thank you, the pleasure was truly all mine."

More true than you know, at any rate.

"Have a great time with your friends, I'll call you tomorrow if that is okay."

I don't know what to say. "Okay."

He leans in to kiss me, and I nearly give myself whiplash turning my head so that he catches the cheek.

"Good night, thanks again."

Driving out of the parking lot, I realize that my stomach is not going to be able to handle a smoky bar, and people eating fried food in front of me would be the end of everything, so I call Parker and beg off. I tell him about the evening and he tells me not to berate myself; chemistry is intangible, can't be forced, he is proud of me for giving it a shot, and reminds me that there are seven other prospects, and a whole week of the ad still running. This is not exactly a comfort to me.

I get home and change into my pajamas. I make a cup of chamomile tea and take some more Tums. I settle on the couch, and the phone rings. It is him, I just know it, so I let the machine pick up.

Beep. "Sidney, this is Mike. I hope you and your friends are having a grand old time. I know that first meetings are awkward and difficult, even if there are five hours on the phone preceding them. But I think there was definitely enough to warrant a second date, and if you would be interested in that, I would love to take you out again. I was a little nervous, so I hope that you take tonight with a grain of salt. Anyway, I think I forgot to tell you how exquisitely beautiful you looked tonight. When I got off the elevator and saw you sitting there, my heart knew it was you, but my head couldn't conceive that such a stunning creature was waiting for me. Anyway, you have my number, I hope you call, but if you don't, I still want you to know what an amazing time I had tonight and what an extraordinary woman I think you are. Talk to you soon, I hope. Bye." Beep.

Fifteen months, and I don't think Geoff ever said anything remotely that lovely to me, and I know he never told me he thought I was beautiful. Attractive, yes, that he was attracted to me, yes, but never beautiful. Never extraordinary. Bastard.

I will call Mike tomorrow and let him know that I am trying to see some of the other guys who answered my ad. Hopefully he will understand. I wish I liked him, I truly do. I turn on the TV, and flip to Letterman. It is so strange how the mind works. There, on my television, is a man of no less quirky attributes than Mike. But never even having met David Letterman, I have a solidly grounded and not insignificant passion for him in theory that I know in a million years I would never have for Mike in the concrete. What is that about I wonder?

SIDEBAR

Okay, the Letterman fetish. Actually a lot of women I know find him hot hot hot, and none of us falls into the traditional star-fuck mentality, nor the residual Teen Beat ideal that says that celebrity itself is attractive. But I have had a major league crush on David Letterman for twenty years now, and I think I finally have a handle on why. The year he premiered, I was twelve. Now in Chicago, the show came on past my prescribed bedtime. But I was a natural night owl from day one, and bedtime was always a struggle between my parents and myself. So for my twelfth birthday, they made me a deal. No bedtime. BUT, I had to get myself up in the morning to get to school with no prodding from them. If I was late even once, I would have proven myself too irresponsible for no bedtime, and would have to go back to the old system. I felt very sassy. Especially for the first couple of weeks, when I would proudly say good-night to them as they went upstairs to bed and I stayed downstairs in the den in front of the TV. Those first weeks were really hard. I stayed up way too late, and it was hell getting up in the morning, but get up I did. After all, I just needed to settle into a schedule. I finally did figure out that if I got to bed before midnight, I was fine in the morning. If I got to bed before one, I was tired, but not unmanageably so. Anytime after one and I would be having a very rough day following.

When I discovered the lovely Mr. L, it was like all the pieces fell into place. His show was over early enough to still get enough sleep. He was smart and funny, and precocious thing that I was, I loved that his humor was at once silly and adult, urbane and accessible. Watching Letterman made me feel grown up, clued in, strangely proud. And I liked that he seemed kind. That the person he mostly made fun of was himself. That he never seemed to choose humor over humanity during his interviews. That he seemed always to put his guests at ease, and let them be themselves for the rest of us to watch. That he never seemed intimidated by even the biggest names. Crush seeds planted, watered, fertilized.

Now the interesting thing is, the passions of our youth rarely follow us through the ages. Our tastes change, our need to like the same guys all our girlfriends like disappears. Think of some of the mad infatuations of your twelfth and thirteenth year and how ridiculous—sometimes downright unattractive—those people are to you today. But not David. No sirree, my love for that tall drink of Hoosier with a khaki chaser has grown undiminished to nearly insane proportions. Over the years, I have continued to watch him, not fanatically, but if I am home at that hour, he is who I have on, and I enjoy his work tremendously. I have never written him a letter, nor tried to get in to see the show, despite once or twice yearly trips to New York. I don't own any memorabilia. I have met some celebrity types, people I am pretty sure know him, and never tried to finagle an introduction. We have never been in the same room, David and I, but of one thing I am sure. We would fall madly in love. First meeting love. I would make him laugh, and he would make me think, and we would be so ridiculously compatible that in short order some sort of major commitment would need to be made. And yes, I am aware that he has a longtime girlfriend, so essentially this is just one more unavailable older man to obsess about, but no, I am not particularly interested in your thoughts on that matter.

Think I am crazy? Probably. But I don't care. That man looks bet-

ter in a double breasted jacket than anyone I ever saw. And the goofy, youthful appeal he had when I was twelve has matured into a very adult respect and attraction. I think he gets better looking with age. I love the way he is keeping his hair so short these days. I think he has amazing hands. And though it is a fair certainty that we will never meet, I know in my heart that if we did, we could stop the turning of the world with our love. You can believe it or not as you choose.

And if you happen to be one of his bookers reading this, and thinking that I would make a witty and wonderful guest, please do me the great courtesy of ensuring that he isn't dating anyone at the time. Or at the very least, please ensure that if he is still attached, that his significant other isn't someone you want to protect from being brokenhearted, because as we have clearly established, I am not necessarily so good with boundaries, and therefore won't be in much position to respect her prior claim, nor will I have enough willpower to discourage the undeniable attraction he will be feeling. A show where the other guests are all middle-aged men wouldn't hurt my feelings either. We sisters have to stick together.

Meanwhile, back in Readerland....

I call in for new messages. There are seven more. I take my little notes. I have learned a very important lesson. Do not talk to anyone for longer than twenty minutes. Long enough to establish rapport, not so long as to induce overwhelming fantasy. Limit the first date plans to either coffee or drinks, with a pre-established time limit. Do not, under any circumstances, allow yourself to fantasize about a man unless you have met him in person. Unless it is David Letterman, in which case, go with God.

SIDEBAR, THE SEQUEL

You know, if David Letterman would just come to Chicago and randomly run into me somewhere, all this business would be over anyway. Maybe that will be the sequel. Hell, that guy wrote "Being John Malkovich," and before you know it he was making a movie with John

Malkovich. I'll just write Falling in Love with David Letterman, *and someone will option it for a movie, and I will write the screenplay, and I will get to meet David at long last and stop all this dating once and for all.*

Okay, shaddup.

If I have to go on some dozen more of these damnable Reader *dates, and be out in the world making myself available for the dregs of the dating pool, I have to hold some beliefs sacred. And David Letterman is my frigging holy grail, thank you very much, and no amount of sniggering at me or shaking your head in disbelief is going to change that. Mark and I didn't work, that is a cookie crumbling. Geoff didn't have enough guts or brains or balls to choose me, well, another cookie. Someday I will find the man with enough of everything, and if it isn't David Letterman, well then, David Letterman better hope he doesn't ever meet me, because he is going to fall head over heels and pine for me forever. Got it?*

In the remaining few days of my ad, I garner an additional twenty-six calls. Eighteen of them make the first cut, with the seven from the previous week making it an even twenty-five in the hopper. A round of phone calls narrows this to sixteen. Sixteen dates. Even scarier than nineteen messages. And considering the roller-coaster that the first date turned out to be, I may need to get some Dramamine for the ride.

chapter 21

a storm approacheth

QUOTE OF THE DAY

Cras amet qui numquam amavit;
Quique amavit, cras amet.
Let him love to-morrow who never loved before;
and he as well who has loved, let him love to-morrow.
> —Written in the time of Julius Cæsar,
> ascribed to Catullus

My PalmPilot informs me this lovely summer morning that tonight Joe is performing at a small local club. I must have entered it when we were doing our weird sort of courting dance, saving the date for him. I wonder how he is? I wonder how things are going with Kim? I have been a very good girl, and haven't written or called at all since our last communication, but with all this *Reader* ad bad dating business, I sort of miss him. At least I miss the potential we seemed to have. And the kissing. I really miss kissing. I mostly miss kissing Geoff, but I am trying not to think about it. And I am succeeding, sort of—I have gone as long as four hours in a row without thinking of him. Not often, but it has happened. Plus I have been very busy with this *Reader* stuff. I have had six more dates since Michael the First.

First was afternoon coffee with Michael the Second, the future Minister. 'Nough said.

Then a lovely drink with Gary, former Navy fighter pilot, which segued nicely into a friendly dinner, but he hadn't realized how old I was, or more to the point, how young I was, when we began talking, since I am "so mature," and when he made the connection that I am only a few years older than his oldest daughter, he got a little uncomfortable. This discomfort was fine, since as pleasant as the conversation was, I wasn't feeling any real spark.

Michael the Third, also known as Michael the Miserly, asked me out for a drink at the very swank Fulton Lounge, regaled me with his business acumen as both an attorney and a CPA, and when the bill came, proudly placed enough cash to cover his share on top, and looked at me expectantly. I smiled, covered my single glass of wine plus a far more generous tip than he had allowed, shook his hand, and politely declined his request for a second date.

Drinks with Brian (not Ryan) was unbelievably painful. This is the date where we learn to take everything someone says with a grain of salt. And that people who e-mail you photos may not be mailing you CURRENT photos. With Brian we learn that some men believe that if they are five nine, they are within their rights to self-describe as "almost six feet tall." That if they "love the theatre," it means their parents took them to see *A Christmas Carol* at The Goodman once or twice as a kid, and that they haven't been inside a theatre since. That their "interest in film" apparently doesn't need to include anything produced in black-and-white, with subtitles, with actresses unimproved by silicone or without car chases. That when they send you a picture of themselves via e-mail that shows a trim physique and a full head of hair, that photo may in fact be over ten years old, and the man who shows up is likely to be paunchy and bald. With Brian we learn that listening to the ins and outs of selling cellular phones is just as flipping boring as it sounds, despite the salesman's bizarre passion for it.

We learn that a gentleman can meet you for the first time and spend the first half hour talking directly to your cleavage without ever making eye contact, and the rest of the date talking at you while never looking away from the baseball game showing on the bar television above your head. We learn that in spite of a complete lack of anything in common, and an hour and a half of stilted and awkward conversation, the Brians of the world will not only ask you for a lift home, but will tell you how well they think it went, what a "cool chick" they think you are, ask you out on another date and try to score a goodnight kiss. You will claim a busy schedule, but they will not hear you, and will continue to call you thrice daily for a week until you finally tell them you have rekindled an old flame.

Good God.

Then there was Michael the Fourth, also known as Michael the Not Really Actually Divorced in the Legal Sense. Sometimes referred to as Michael the Big Fat Liar. Also referred to as Michael the Really Good Kisser, which I am not going to get into, but I was drunk, and didn't have all the vital information until after I let him kiss me. Another mistake I will not be making again, to be certain.

Bob only needed a second phone call to ascertain that a meeting was unnecessary, his technical work in "theatre" turned out to be lighting work for the *Jenny Jones* show, and from the fifteen-minute description he gave me of Ms. Jones, I have no doubt that any girl he might date will be called Jenny in a crucial intimate moment. This freed up an evening to have drinks with Dave the Computer Guy.

Dave the Computer Guy arrived at the bar of the W hotel apologizing for the fact that he was still wearing his Star Trek uniform, but apparently his meeting with the rest of the crew of the *Enterprise* ran late, and didn't have time to go home and change. I smiled sweetly at him, told him it was no problem at all, excused myself to the ladies' room, and left Captain Kirk to ponder the universe while I got the hell out of there at hyperspeed. I know it is awful to ditch someone, but not any more awful than showing up on a first date squeezed into a polyester replica of a sci-fi television show costume. I figure we are even on that one.

Seven dates in twelve days. I am exhausted. I am disgruntled. I have nine more possibles, and am beginning to dread them in a major way.

So I send Joe an e-mail.

Joe—

I know we are not in current communication, but when I turned my PalmPilot on today it reminded me that you are singing tonite at the Elbo Room, and I wanted to tell you to break a leg. I am sure it will go swimmingly. And if you do any material from my hero Mr. Sinatra, know that somewhere my heart hears it and I am smiling.

No reply necessary, I hope you are well....
ever,
Sidney

Hi Sidney,

Yes, I am indeed giving my all in the service of saloon singing under the harsh glare of whomever stumbles into the Elbo Room Cabaret between 9:00 and 11:00 tonight.

After a wonderful couple of days of really incredible closeness and togetherness, Kim is wending her way to London, by way of New York and Berlin. She'll be back on August 4th. Shortly after that we spend the weekend together in Wisconsin, and then a few days in Chicago. After that, she goes out of town, and we break up, stop being a couple. That's our current plan.

If you want to come by tonight, I'd love to see you, but that's up to you. I'm sure I'll be talking to you in the next couple of weeks.

I love the Palm operating system.
love, Joe

Well, that is more like it!

J—

As long as we have established that my earlier message was in no way an attempt to lure you into my web or renew unwanted distraction...you know I would love to see you. I have tentative plans with a friend, but haven't gotten confirmation yet. If I am not there, however, I will be home by 11 and would love to hear what I missed, so you could call me there when you are done. Maybe stop by for a brief celebratory gin or something on your way home.

Miss your face. (Hope it's okay to say that.)
Maybe later?
Sidney

Sidney,

No, I do not feel like you purposely drew me into your nefarious dealings. I've been thinking about you today, wondering whether I should invite you or not. I think I ultimately felt too guilty to contact you. Then I returned your message. I know I will not be able to be with you without kissing you, and that thought makes me feel guilty, as I've said. But you know the kind of person I am, so it will not be shocking to you to hear that the possibility of kissing you thrills me quite a bit, too.
Maybe later... Joe

I called Parker, filled him in, and he told me to go to see Joe. I decide not to be too saucy, and don't go overboard on preparations. I call him and let him know I will be there, and he offers to leave my name on the list at the door.

The Elbo Room is actually not too crowded, and I wander over to where Joe will be performing. The minute I am in the room, I am glad I came, since there are only five other people here, and three of them are drunk and obnoxious, and completely ignoring the performance. As the show itself became more and more moot, Joe started singing things just for me, which was terribly intoxicating. Lots of Sinatra, practically the whole *Wee Small Hours* album in fact, full of meaningful eye contact. We hang out for a bit after, and then he invites himself over for a drink. I happily acquiesce, drive him to his car, and then watch him mug in my rearview mirror as he follows me home. What a lovely silly boy he is, and for the first time in weeks I am feeling almost happy, almost hopeful.

I let him in, ply him with Tanqueray Ten, and we relax on the couch to play a little catch-up. I ask what he meant about the impending breakup, and he explains as best he can. They have agreed that things aren't going to move forward. It is winding down. But there were plans made before that realization which seem silly to cancel, especially as they aren't miserable together. So, he and Kim have decided to break up after they have completed their previously agreed-upon travel plans. End on a high note, friends and no hard feelings. It seems weird to me, but then again, it is nice to hear that some people actually do get out of relationships that aren't working the way they should.

Bitter, party of one?

Then he kisses me. Well, you didn't think I was going to not kiss him, not after all those tedious dates? Of course I let him kiss me! For two hours. There are times when my life makes very little sense to me. This is one of them. But I am not complaining. Just before I fall asleep, the phone rings.

"I had to hear your voice one more time before I went to sleep."

"You are such a goofball."

"But I am a good kisser."

"You are a lovely kisser. But next time, shave, my chin is lacking at least three layers of skin."

"Poor baby, want me to come back and kiss it to make it better?" I actually sort of do, but I have sworn that I will not sleep with him until he is single, and I have been very proud of the way that I have been sticking to that plan.

"Thanks for the offer, but I will just heal in peace."

"Probably better that way, at least for another couple of weeks. If I came back tonight, there are all sorts of places I would have to kiss you to make you feel better." Oh my. This makes me all tingly. After all, it has been several weeks since my last date with Geoff, and no nookie makes Sidney a dull girl. Plus I have been drinking gin and kissing and it is nearly two in the morning...

"Where would you kiss me?"

"Oh my darling Lightning Girl, I would start at the top of your sweet little head, kissing you all around your hairline..."

Let's just say that while Joe didn't get past first base while he was here in the flesh, we now have carnal knowledge of the verbal type. And for the first night in months, I fell asleep without thinking of Geoff.

Sidney—

Just wanted to drop a note to tell you what a lovely time I had with you last night. It was incredibly sweet of you to come see my little show, and then to give me top shelf gin and many, many kisses. What a lucky boy I am!

As I said to you when I was very close to your face last night, you are fabulous.

It's good to know that you agree with me!

In fact I seem to recall you agreeing with me a lot in the later part of the evening, I am looking forward to making you agree with me for hours on end in the very near future.

love

Joe

I'd be lying if I said I wasn't looking forward to that very thing myself.

Storm—
My own little kumquat, it was definitely a treat to see you, I am so glad my plans for the evening rescheduled, and I am always most grateful for your congenial company, and good humor, and many many lovely kisses. And the bedtime story was an unexpected delight. I have an early date tonight for cocktails after work, but will be home by 8-ish and in for the evening, as it is too hot to venture much outside the range of the air conditioner. I will probably indulge in a movie. If you are free and want to join me, you are most welcome. Just a thought. If not tonight, I'll see you later I am sure. I have a date tomorrow night, and family night on Sunday, but I think the early part of next week isn't too bad.
I am now, as I have always been, even in absence,
Your Lightning Girl

He should know I am not waiting around for him. With all the kissing there wasn't much opportunity to tell him about my adventures in Readerland, but I have continued to schedule myself into a corner, determined to get through the irritation of meeting all these men. Then maybe Parker will shut the hell up.

Tonight's contestant is Peter, who is a writer supporting himself as the night shift operator at a small local halfway house. We are meeting for drinks in the hour between the end of my workday and the beginning of his. He picks Chief O'Neill's, great Irish pub not too far from my apartment. He is clean-cut, 38, well-spoken, generically fine-looking in a nondescript nonthreatening sort of way. Our conversation progresses with a certain amount of ease. In fact I am thinking that this might be going well until the waitress brings him his drink. He sips it, grimaces, and waves her back over.

"This isn't Macallan 18, this is the 12, and I know the fucking difference. So don't think you are going to pull one over on me, when I said I wanted an 18-year-old single malt, I meant it! You had better sashay yourself back over to the bar and get me what I ordered, or I will need to have a chat with your manager about the way you and the bartender are colluding to deceive the patrons for your own financial gain."

I wish it had been me that threw the drink in his face.

When the manager arrived at the table to escort my dripping, sputtering, red-faced suitor out the door, he gave me a look that seemed to say "You are one dumb broad to put up with this guy." Peter shook off the manager's hand and announced that he needed no assistance with his departure. Then he looked at me and said "C'mon, let's get out of here." So not gonna happen, my friend.

"I have a better idea, you get out of here. Go look for your manners, you seem to have misplaced them. And lose my number."

I have never been applauded by a whole pub before. Peter started to shout something at me as he was leaving, but I couldn't hear it over the din. I moved to the bar. The bartender put down a glass of ice in front of me. Then he grabbed the Macallan 25 and poured me a healthy slug. "On the house, darlin'."

"Thank you." The whiskey is dreamy. Some music starts coming from the back room. I order fish and chips.

"Where did you find that schmuck?"

This unexpected observation comes from my left, and when I turn to look, to see who it is speaking Yiddish to me in an Irish pub, I find a vaguely familiar face smiling at me. I can't place where I know him from.

"The *Reader* personals, actually, and he found me."

"What is Columbia's favorite daughter doing with an ad in the *Reader?*"

Duh. Columbia. Teaches in the music program, I think.

"A friend dared me. I am proving him wrong. Looking forward to a big fat I-told-you-so."

"I see, do you get to call him tonight with that message?"

"Unfortunately no, I have eight more dates to get through before I can make that call."

"Eight more? How many have you had already?"

"Tonight was eight. I am officially halfway done. On the downhill slope."

"Wow. That is a lot of dates, were they all that bad?"

"No, tonight was probably in the top three in terms of awfulness."

"I am afraid to ask."

I give him the rundown. It makes him laugh. He tells me I am a natural raconteur. My food comes, the portions are enormous, so I offer to share. I am remembering his name is Jeremy something. He picks at my fries and we chat about Columbia. We have a few students in common. He is cute, sort of. Has that sort of scruffy absentminded musician/professor look about him. Tall, thin, dark wavy hair in need of cutting, tweedy-looking. But nice. Funny. We are having a great time. This is the date I am supposed to be on. He touches my arm when he talks, he makes great eye contact, I am having a wonderful time.

That is, until his girlfriend arrives.

Sonuvabitch.

SIDEBAR

Bet you thought this was the one, right? The one I would meet randomly who would sweep me off my feet and save me from dating forever. Sorry, that is only in the other kind of book, the one where everything gets wrapped neatly up in the final chapters so that no one has to entertain the thought that perhaps the heroine ends up, gasp! ALONE. Man-less. Unmarried. Unloved. It is unthinkable, right? You are nervously flipping ahead, only a few chapters left, I had bet-

*ter get on that meeting Mr. Right thing, I am RUNNING OUT
OF TIME! Deep breath. I am not going to spoil the ending for you
just yet, but however it ends, it will be okay. For both of us.*

Alicia is a perky, willowy, blond graduate student with breasts
that defy gravity and an air of easy grace. Your basic horror
show. Also, she is smart, and really nice, and the three of us spend
the next two hours hanging out and talking, and all in all, despite my initial disappointment that Jeremy wasn't my next big
thing, it was a pretty cool evening. I am glad I stayed.

My answering machine is flashing its head off. This puts me
in a minor panic state, considering the people leaving messages
these days all seem to result in tedious evenings. But I am lucky.
There is a message from Joe. He apologizes for not being able to
see me tonight. He says he will call me soon, most likely after he
and Kim have ended things once and for all. He can't stop thinking about me, and he hopes it is okay to say that his first order of
business post-breakup is to prove that he was worth waiting for.

We shall see.

There is also a message from Geoff. Checking in. Wanted to
tell me about some Ernie Kovacs documentary that is on tomorrow. Hoped I was doing okay. Was going to the benefit next
week for Writer's Theatre, didn't know if I would be there, but
would look forward to maybe seeing me.

Whatever. Shithead.

A message from Parker, wanting the lowdown on the date
of the moment, I can't wait to tell him about this one.

A message from Adam, telling me that he doesn't think he
can make it to the impending bat mitzvah of the New York
niece, and how do I think Mom is going to take the news?

I will miss Adam, he was a really great brother.

A message from my mother, asking if it will be okay if Adam
and I share a hotel room for the aforementioned bat mitzvah
since neither of us is bringing anybody. He is SO SCREWED.
Poor baby.

Finally, a message that makes me sit down in surprise.

"Sid, it's Josh. Your cousin. I wanted to give you a heads up, I ran into Doug Hullter today, and it turns out he has moved back to the city, and is living in your neighborhood. He and Brenda got divorced. Anyway, when he said where he had moved, I mentioned that you were just a couple of blocks from there, and that you and Mark had also split, and he asked for your number, so if you hear from him, I am how he tracked you down. Hope it was okay to do that. See you in New York!"

Wow.

Doug Hullter.

BACKSTORY

The summer after junior year of high school, my cousin Josh and I both worked for my dad at the firm. That summer, the offices were expanding to take over the rest of the floor, and the project manager overseeing the construction was Doug Hullter. Doug was maybe the best looking man I had ever known personally. Dead ringer for Dennis Quaid. I was smitten with him on first glance. We started chatting a bit, taking lunch at the same time, and he turned out to be this totally amazing guy. Very smart, had majored in Philosophy and Art History in college, but went into his dad's construction business because he loved working with his hands and building things. He wrote poetry. He was teaching himself the guitar. We laughed a lot, and became sort of friends. After work on Fridays, he and his guys would all head over to a local bar to hang out, and they started asking Josh and me to come with.

Now, Josh was in college, thinking of applying to law school, and had turned twenty-one in the spring. But I was just seventeen. Not that anyone cared, especially me. I was the only girl, a ratio I like, and we would hang out, drink beer and tell stories, and I never had a better summer, not ever. I fell madly in love with Doug, who was twenty-seven at the time, but as far as I ever got with him was the occasional spontaneous turn on the dance floor if a song he liked happened to come on the jukebox. He was an amazing dancer. Sigh. Anyway, it was fun to hang out with the guys. They all treated me like more of a mascot than anything else, but I didn't care, it was too wickedly joyful. Josh kept teasing me about my pining for Doug, but I told him I was just interested in his friendship. We both pretended to believe me.

Doug and I actually did stay in touch after the summer, talked on the phone every once in a while, met up for coffee or a beer here and there. He never treated me like a kid, but he also never made a pass at me either. Pity.

Then he met Brenda. Blond, beautiful, kindergarten teacher Brenda. Wide hazel eyes, pert button nose, a shiksa goddess. They were engaged within six months. I was beyond heartbroken. I wallowed in misery. Doug bought a tiny house in the far western suburbs. I cried myself to sleep nightly. Doug invited me over to check out the new digs, and we had pizza and beer just the two of us in his new living room surrounded by boxes labeled in Brenda's flowing handwriting. It was the best worst night ever. When I left I gave him a letter confessing my abiding love, and including two poems I had written for him. He called me the next day to tell me how flattered he was, how much my words meant to him, that if I had been older or he younger that we absolutely might have been together, that he would keep the poems forever. I think he was being kind, but I needed those phrases anyway, and so I believed them.

They had an engagement party, and invited me and Josh. I got drunk and had furtive and awkward sex with one of the guys from Doug's crew that I had never paid much attention to before. In his truck. In the parking lot. Ew.

They got married. I was not invited. I spent the day of the wedding throwing up, and pretending I had the flu. There is no angst like eighteen-year-old angst. They settled down for a suburban life, and we fell out of touch once I left for college. The last time I saw him was at a Christmas party during my freshman year winter vacation.

Doug Hullter. I haven't thought about him in ages. Divorced. Living in my area. Wanted my number. Let's see, he would be about forty-three or so now. No longer such a big age difference. Amazing what fifteen years can do. Whatever, Sid, don't be a moron. He probably just asked to be polite. If he bothers to call at all it will just be because he knows Josh will tell me they ran into each other and it would be rude not to call. We'll get together for a drink, tell some old stories, share our marital woes, and then run out of things to say. He won't be nearly the same man I remember, and I won't bear any resemblance to the girl I was, and we will promise to get together again soon, but we never will. This is how things go. And if he never calls, it doesn't matter.

I wonder if he will call.

It would be really nice if he would call.

I want to kill Josh for leaving me that message, it would have been so much better to be surprised by Doug calling, as opposed to knowing that he could call and might not.

My phone rings. I jump out of my skin.

"Hello?"

"I can't go a whole day without hearing your voice."

"Hi Joe, how are you?"

"I miss you."

"No, you don't, you're just horny."

"Well, that is a form of missing you."

"And I am very flattered. But I think we should keep things chaste until you and Kim are done. The other night was a fluke, a special treat, but we should back off and let you finish things without distraction." Not planning on being a booty call, even if it is just over the phone.

"You are right, once again. We will be good little campers until my life is squared away, and then we will be bad little campers until we are half-dead from ecstasy."

"Deal."

"Good night sweetheart."

"Good night darlin'."

He really is a lovely boy. A bit mad, but in a nice way.

Then again, Doug Hullter asked for my number. Didn't tell Josh to say hello from him, didn't say he would probably bump into me around the neighborhood, no, he asked for my number.

Hmm.

Don't it just make you all warm and fuzzy?

And curious. Very very curious.

chapter 22

quality time

QUOTE OF THE DAY

All happy families resemble one another;
every unhappy family is unhappy in its own way.
—Tolstoy: *Anna Karénina*

I somehow think that my particular happy family falls outside this astute observation. We are happy, assuredly, but I have never seen our like in anyone else's household, if my meaning is clear. It has been an extraordinarily long week.

I will attempt to recap as concisely as possible, since I feel like I have packed an entire month's worth of intrigue and drama into seven short days.

MONDAY: Monday I met my mother for finalization shopping. This means that we go to the same places we went over Thanksgiving, and buy all sorts of stuff, but most importantly new bat mitzvah outfits since neither of us can refrain from wearing clothes before the event for which they are acquired, and now we have been seen in public in said items, which will not do. I am amazed neither of us broke down and wore our

wedding gowns before the big day. No complaints from me—
Mom is buying, plus she is really fun to shop with. When I got
home Monday night, the following message awaited me:

"Sidney, this is, um, Doug. Doug Hullter. I don't know if Josh
mentioned it, but I am back in the city, and I guess we are in
the same area, small world, and anyway, he gave me your number and I thought, well, maybe you might want to get together
and have a drink or something, so if you get a chance give me
a call. 773-555-5683. Hope to talk to you soon. Bye."

Wow.

WOW.

I can't believe he called. I am so excited that he called. I am,
well, just, I don't even know what, that is how excited I am.

I take a deep breath. I go to the bathroom and pee. I come
back to the bedroom and listen to the message again. I write
down the number. I go back to the bathroom and pee again,
because sometimes you forget to wait for those last few drops,
and then they come back to haunt you. I go back to the bedroom and listen to the message again. I put away my new purchases. I listen to the message again. Then I pick up the phone.
Then I hang up the phone. Then I pick up the phone. Then
I hang up the phone. Then I go to the kitchen and drink a
glass of water since my mouth is suddenly all dry. Then I go
to the living room, since I think I shouldn't call from my bedroom. I don't know why exactly I suddenly think I shouldn't
call from the bedroom, but since when do you look to me for
logical behavior?

I pick up the phone.

I dial.

"Hello?"

"Parker, it's me." I chickened out. I need moral support first.

"Hey kitten, 'sup?"

"He called."

"Narrow it down for me, you have more than one boy on
deck these days."

"Doug."

"The ancient unrequited love? The one who got away?"

"The same."

"Excellent! Did he ask you out?"

"Sort of, I mean I was out, so it is just a message. He suggested getting together for drinks or something."

"That counts. Totally. Let me hear the message."

I take the cordless back into the bedroom and hold it over the answering machine for Parker to hear.

"He sounds HOT!"

"You can't tell that over the phone, you goof."

"Hey, remember last week when you said that *Reader* guy sounded short over the phone, and then Mini Me showed up? He sounds hot. Don't sweat me."

"You do have a point. You were the only one who believed me when I said he sounded short, everyone mocked me. How does someone sound short? they all asked me. But I could TELL, and then who comes bopping into the bar right on time, a member of the Lollypop Gang."

Parker is laughing. "At least he was old to boot!"

"That sonuvabitch was sixty if he was a day! Forty-six my ass! Only if he is dyslexic! I mean give me a break, liver spots for chrissakes. All over his totally bald little head."

Now we are both laughing.

"Pumpkin, I am so sorry, but I am so glad I made you take out that ad, it is endlessly amusing."

"Oh yeah. A fucking party and a half. Focus for me, what do I do about Doug?"

"Call him."

"And say what?"

"You had me at hello?"

"Parker..."

"Come over here right now and prove that you were worth waiting fifteen years for, you big handsome lummox."

"You aren't helping."

"I've got it! Just go over to his place and stand outside with your boombox hoisted over your head and play Peter Gabriel's 'In Your Eyes.'"

"Fuck you."

"If we could do that, neither one of us would be worried about what you were going to say to Doug."

"FO-CUS. Doug. I call. Do I talk on the phone, or just a quick hit to make plans?"

"Tell him you just have a few minutes, but wanted to get back to him and that a drink sounds lovely. Make the date. Tell him you are looking forward to it. Then get the hell out of there before you say something stupid."

"I love your confidence in me."

"Okay, get off the phone before HE says something stupid, and the magic is lost altogether."

"That is a much better point."

"And then call me back and let me know what happened."

"Hokay, Meester. I call jhoo back."

"Hokay, Messus."

"Bye."

"Bye."

I hang up the phone. I listen to the message again. I go back to the bathroom and pee again, wondering if my bladder is the size of a pea. Then I think pee/pea, and this makes me laugh. I have been living alone too long.

"Hello?"

Parker is right. He does sound hot.

"Doug? It's Sidney, returning your call."

"Sidney. Sid Sid Sid."

"Doug Doug Doug."

"How are you?"

"Not bad, you?"

"Not bad."

"Well then, I am glad we got that cleared up. Talk to you in another fifteen years?"

"Give a guy a break, Sidley. It is bound to be awkward for a minute."

Sigh. I forgot he used to call me Sidley. I loved having a pet name.

"I'm just busting your chops a little."

"I know, I know. Is it weird that I called?"

"A little. Did it feel weird calling?"

"Not really, no."

"Well, that is something, I guess."

"Yeah. So Josh said we are neighbors."

"He mentioned it to me as well, where are you?"

"Maplewood and Altgeld. You?"

"Closer to Rockwell, on the boulevard."

"Nice. And not far at all."

"Yep, very close."

"Sid, this is dumb, if we ran into each other on the street unexpectedly it would be easier than this. What is it about the phone that makes everything odd and stilted?"

"I dunno. I really don't."

"We were friends once upon a time."

"Yes, we were."

"I thought perhaps we might be friends again."

"It isn't so far-fetched."

"I don't know about you, but I am feeling these days like I can use all the friends I can get."

"Very true. Something in the air."

"Do you have any desire to get together and catch up in person?"

"I would like that. Really."

"Good, me too. What does your week look like?"

"I am free Thursday night, is that okay for you?"

"Great. Seven?"

"Sure."

"I can walk over and pick you up, maybe we can head up to the Boulevard Café?"

"Sounds good."

"That wasn't so hard."

"Not at all. Nearly painless."

"Whew. I have to admit I am kind of relieved."

"Me too."

Then we started to laugh. The whole ridiculous thing hit us both at once, and pretty soon we were giggling up a storm.

"Okay, Doug, I should go, but Thursday, seven?"

"Right. I will see you then."

"Okay. And Doug?"

"Yeah?"

"I am really glad you called."

"Me too. See you Thursday."

"Bye."

"Bye."

And can I just say, whoo-hoo?!

TUESDAY: When I got up, I sent a quick e-mail to Joe, who had mentioned the possibility of a Wednesday night movie date, whereupon I promptly invited myself over, since I have not yet seen the inside of Storm's hideout.

Joeyface—

I have at long last scheduled a meeting this afternoon with my new editor. She seems completely disinterested in meeting me, and less than lukewarm about my work in general. I am afraid I may be told that they are not moving forward on the new book. And if I am moving forward, this new lady may make the process significantly unpleasant. I have no idea what is likely to happen.

I hope your auditions etc. are going well, and that I will be alive to indulge in our movie date tomorrow (by the bye, we can watch at my place if you want, I wasn't trying to finagle an invite if you weren't ready to host me at your place).

Pray for me.
Yours,
Sidney

Sidney,

Have you felt my thoughts and prayers? I sincerely hope you come through today's meeting relatively unscathed, your flesh unmarred, your heart unbowed. Heartless she-devil that you are, I know that you have the strength to survive much. Go with God.

There may be a glitch for tomorrow night. I'm going to be going out to Oak Lawn to record this pharmaceutical dude, and I'm not sure when my client will want me to generate something they can listen to. If they need a clean, edited version of what I recorded, I may need to spend my time Wednesday night doing that. Heartless, racy, he-devil that I am, can you allow me to keep you on the bubble until I call you Wednesday evening? If you're not home, I'll leave a message on your machine.

I'm perfectly comfortable watching the movie at my house. I've got central air and popcorn and 32 inches. Of flat-screen tv. Measured diagonally.
luv
Joe

Joe—

Were those thoughts and prayers I was feeling? Tingly.

As to tomorrow, later is better for me. I have girls nite including dinner until 9 or 9:30ish, but since I am a night owl and do not have much of anything on Thursday morning, I don't mind starting late if you don't... I will remain on the bubble, as you say, with all fond hopes for a rendezvous tomorrow. And yes, you are a he-devil. And heartless. But as I have never kissed you in central air conditioning in the pale flick-

ering light of a 32-inch screen, I can do nothing except wait
and pray.

xoxoxoxoxox (Tiny fluttery kisses for your sweet little face.)
:) Sidney

Then I got ready and went into the Loop for my meeting with
the new editor. Let's just call her Ms. Ogilvie. We will call her
this since it is her name, and it will be much less confusing for
me that way. She kept me waiting nearly forty minutes in the reception area, perched on a folding chair. Anyone with an ass wider
than a handspan will feel my pain. When she finally deigned to
see me, I almost laughed in shock. Groomed to within an inch
of her life, hair pulled so tightly into a bun that the very follicles
seemed to be only barely hanging on. All knife-edge cheekbones,
and thin lips with nude matte lipstick, and a nose job that had
seen better days. The navy blue suit could have been KGB issue,
as could the clunky black lace-up shoes, but the blouse, sad shiny
rayon with the attached bow circa 1984, that was a touch straight
out of a movie. This is a central casting divorcée turned librar-
ian turned editor, and she is looking at me as if I might eat her.

"Ms. Stein, I am so sorry to have kept you waiting, I was on
a conference with the New York office and it ran a little late,
I hope it wasn't a terrible inconvenience." She gestures me into
a chair in her dingy little office.

"Not at all." I sit, she retreats behind the desk.

"I also wanted to explain why it has taken me so long to
arrange this meeting. When Amy was moved into the nonfic-
tion division, and I came on board, she made very clear to me
the direction that she had taken with you, and your history together. I wanted to be sure before we met that I had become
more than just surface-familiar with your past work, and that I
spent some serious time on the pieces you have sent in to date
for the new anthology, so that we can try and make the transition as seamless as possible. Amy was originally scheduled to be

here today to talk with us, but unfortunately seems to have acquired a summer cold, so you and I are on our own."

"It's fine, and I thank you for taking such care to be prepared, but to be frank, I am hoping that your new perspective will perhaps assist me in taking the work in a new direction, and the fresher you are when you come to it, the better for me in the long run."

"Well. I am no expert by any stretch, but I think we will do just fine. Tea? Coffee?"

"Tea is fine, thank you."

"I'll grab it and we can get to work."

"Great, thanks."

Phew. Double phew. Maybe in a few months she'll let me take her for a makeover.

The rest of the afternoon flew by, Ms. O. had some really great insight on the stuff I had already sent in, and I left the balance of the book with her to go over before the next meeting. I also left her the first few pieces of the Journal Poetry I had been writing, and gave her a little explanation of the genesis of the work. She seemed to like the idea, and said she would give it a look-see, and would call me if she thought the company might want to pursue it.

After the meeting, I went home, changed and headed over to the posh Marché for the Writer's Theatre benefit. Elegant, non-stuffy, excellent mix of people, and the first time I have been in a room with Geoff since the June Massacre. It was, sadly, sort of wonderful.

Sandra, though in town, was not in attendance. The crowd was not the usual suspects of their circle, so he spent most of his time hanging out with me. Casual, fun, a little flirty, as if to say that he was sorry and wanted to pretend the abomination that was our last date never happened. I wanted to stay mad. I wanted to tell him to fuck off. I wanted to really, really badly, but I couldn't. The problem with loving someone, with being in love with them, is that you forgive them even when they are their most cruel. You forgive them and let the pain go away, because what other choice do you have? If you don't forgive them, then you are in love with an unforgivable asshole, and what does that say about you?

He told me he had been really busy, and hadn't been ignoring me on purpose. I said that ignoring me accidentally was fine, as long as he had been busy. We didn't talk about us, we just talked. And he made all the little jokes he makes to keep me laughing. And I laughed in spite of myself. And at the end of the evening he squeezed my arm, and kissed my cheek and told me he would talk to me soon.

WEDNESDAY: Nothing much really happened on Wednesday. I did some writing, had lunch with Parker, who is absolutely convinced that Doug is going to be THE ONE, and helped me make some decisions about my wardrobe for tomorrow evening. Had dinner with Pam, Heather and Bruce and got them all caught up on my recent dating travails, then zipped home, looking forward to my movie date with Joe.

Except Joe left me a message that he couldn't make it, so I spent the evening instead straightening up the apartment, and doing all the quiet cliché girly things one does when an unexpected night in presents itself. Doug called to reconfirm, and I started getting organized for the trip to Westchester this weekend. Adam called to inform me that he couldn't believe Mom guilted him into coming, especially as his work schedule didn't allow for much time off, so he is getting in on Friday, and leaving Sunday night, needing to go straight to work from the airport Monday morning. I tell him he is a pussy and that he should walk it off. He tells me he is going to short sheet my bed.

I love Adam.

THURSDAY: I could go into some long description of my daily activities, but let's be frank, there is only one thing that matters about Thursday, and that is Doug.

My doorbell rang at precisely six-fifty-nine. I take a deep breath, check my reflection in the foyer mirror, and open the door. He is older than the man I knew, obviously, but just as handsome. The once sandy-brown hair is shot through with gray, the laugh lines are more pronounced and he is wearing little rectangular glasses over the eyes of robin's-egg blue, but it is the same man. He smiles at me.

"Hi."

I smile back.

"Hi."

He steps forward with his arms wide and pulls me into the most delicious hug ever. He is wearing the same Hugo Boss cologne that I remember. He lets me go. I let him in.

"Wow, great place."

"Thanks, I love it here."

"All these old Victorians are terrific, new construction can't touch them. I have really been enjoying the neighborhood."

"It is a super area, I've been here a decade, and I keep liking it more and more."

I give him the quick tour, and then we leave to walk to dinner. He offers me his arm as we stroll down Logan Boulevard, and within four blocks, we are talking like the old friends we are. He has caught up with Josh already, fills me in on some of the guys I might remember, and by the time we are seated outside at the café, he has begun to tell me about his breakup with Brenda.

"I think she wanted to get married, I don't think she wanted to be married. Once Jesse was born, that was it, she was Supermommy, and I was just this annoying man who lived in the house. We talked about splitting when Jesse was four, but then a random night of reconciliation turned out to be Jenny, so that put things off again. The business took off, so I was working longer and longer hours, trying to not go home probably, and one day I woke up and it was our thirteenth wedding anniversary."

"Unlucky number."

"You aren't kidding. She forgot."

"No."

"Oh yeah. Completely slipped her mind."

"And women complain about men forgetting special dates."

"I know! Anyway, Jesse was nine, Jenny was five, I barely knew them, and I was happiest at work. I talked to Brenda after the kids were asleep, and she didn't seem remotely surprised or upset that I wanted to leave. She immediately went to the computer and started ordering books about talking to kids about divorce, and how to parent as a unit after the breakup. I sat in the bedroom crying at my failure as a husband, and she did research with dry eyes."

"I am so sorry, that must have been awful."

"It was. I got an apartment out there for the first year and a half, but about six months ago a buddy of mine told me about the house over on Maplewood. A friend of his mother's was going into a retirement facility and needed to sell, and I thought about being back in the city, and it felt like a fresher start. So here I am."

"Wow. Is it hard being away from the kids?"

"Yes. And no. It is better now because they are still young enough that the two weekends a month they spend in the city with me feel like an adventure, and we don't get distracted by being near their mom and their friends. But I know in a few years it is going to be difficult."

I told him about the breakup with Mark, that I would be getting the papers sent to me in a couple of months, but that it seemed like just a legality, and that in fact, I hadn't really felt married in years. We ate, we drank, we talked about how weird it was to be dating again, he paid and we walked back to my place. This time, instead of offering his arm, he took my hand.

Shazam.

At my door, I invited him in for a drink, and he politely declined. Early morning. But I could tell there was something else.

"Sid, when I called, it was really just to catch up, just to have a friend in the neighborhood. I didn't think it was going to be a date-date, you know?" Of course not. Why would I be surprised? What on earth in my history would make me think that he would be interested in me? WHY DON'T I EVER EVER GET WHAT I WANT?

"Sure, Doug, no big deal, I was just inviting you in for a drink. You aren't THAT irresistible you know."

"I know, I just, I'm totally fucking this up. Look, Sid, once upon a time you were a girl with a crush, and I was very flattered to be the object of that affection. But back then, I never really looked at you in that way—you were always just a great person that I liked hanging out with. When I ran into Josh, the only thing I could think was that it would be so great to get that back. You know, friend in the area, brunches, drinks?"

"Doug, it's fine. Truly. I'm not seventeen anymore. I didn't think this was some big deal, I am glad you called, I am glad we still get along, and I hope that we are going to be friends again and hang out."

"You aren't hearing me Sid. You have grown up. Into this amazing woman. You were always pretty, but you have a serenity about your beauty now, a maturity. You are so smart and so funny, and all night I kept looking at your smile and your mesmerizing eyes and thinking that I really wanted to kiss you."

Ohmygod.

"Really?"

"Really. And it scares me a little."

"Why is that?"

"Because I don't want to fulfill some ancient fantasy for you. I don't want to consummate what never was. I want to know that if I kiss you, if we become involved that it is because you want to be with the me I am now, not the guy you remember. I am not the guy you remember, Sid."

He is so sweet I could cry.

"Doug, the girl I was really loved the man you were, in her way, and wanted to be with him. But the woman I am now doesn't want a cocky twenty-seven year old. The guy you were then would be too young for me now, and couldn't possibly hold my attention. But the man you are now, he is someone I am very glad to have met, and if there was no history between us, if we had just bumped into each other in line at Starbucks and struck up a conversation, I would have been interested. If we had been strangers before tonight, but had passed the evening the way we just did, I would want to get to know you better. I would see the potential for romantic involvement. The only thing that is different is that we do have some history, and that makes our friendship a little more important, and therefore I think if we are smart, and you think we should pursue this, we should take it slow, let it develop organically, be mindful of each other, and just see what happens."

"Really?"

"Really."

"It doesn't make me some sort of cad to say that I may need to take things SERIOUSLY slowly?"

"Not at all."

"Thank you, Sid."

"Thank you."

"When are you back from New York?"

"Sunday night."

"Okay, I have a crazy week coming up, and next weekend I have my kids, but I'll call you and we can maybe do something early the following week?"

"I would love that."

"Okay. Well, have a safe trip, and I will talk to you when you get back."

"Okay. Thank you for a wonderful evening, Doug."

"Thank you."

Doug gave me a big hug and a quick peck on the mouth, and then turned back down my stoop, and walked toward home.

I hope he doesn't take things too slowly. A girl can only be expected to have so much patience.

Inside, at the computer, as I am wont to do, I begin. A new

poem for Doug, the first in so many years, I let go of the past
and look to the future. And look to the future and see my past.

possible

a quick and quiet joy
ascends the spine
reaches the brain
with a white warmth
oils the gears
nestles in the throat like a whiskey tickle
careens in the bloodstream
hides behind the
reasonable heart
is silent
still
the breath
expires
nothing contains the sentient exquisite hum
elusive ecstatic beat
nothing

for there in the ending of an evening
is the tease of a beginning
there
in the absence of promise
lives potential
and we will find that
our greatest strength
is in acknowledging
the power we gain
in yielding

And then I pack for the weekend.

FRIDAY: The phone wakes me from a dead sleep. It is 7:00 a.m.

"Sidney? It's Geoff."

"I know your voice."

"Did I wake you?"

"Nah. I had to get up to answer the phone."

"I'm sorry, I know it's early."

"Where are you?"

"At the airport."

"Where are you going?"

"New York."

"Business?"

"Yep."

"Over the weekend?"

"I have meetings both today and Monday, so it seemed silly to fly back and forth."

"I see."

"The thing is, Sid, your dad invited me to the bat mitzvah festivities, since I am going to be in town."

"I see."

"I have to call him back and say yes or no, and I wanted to ask you first."

"Why?"

"To see how you would feel about my being around this weekend."

He wants to know how I feel? All of a sudden, my feelings are important to him?

"Do you want to come?"

"It would be nice to have some things to do."

Yeah, 'cause New York is so frigging BORING, one cannot find ways to fill your time. Why can't he just say he wants to see me? Why is that so hard? Well, I am taking the calm route.

"Well, then you should come. It will be fun."

"Okay then, I will call and let him know."

"Okay."

"Then I will see you later tonight."

"Looks that way. Have a good flight."

"You too, Sid."

"Bye."

"Go back to sleep, kiddo, I'm sorry I woke you."

"S'okay. I'll see you later."

"Okay, bye then."

But I cannot go back to sleep. I have to repack for the weekend. Nicer underwear. Sassier clothes for tonight and Sunday. More beauty products. My heart runneth over. I am one dumb bitch. I try not to think too much about that last part, though.

The car comes at nine-fifteen containing my parents and their luggage, and we three embark on the tedium that is travel. I should thank Geoff for waking me, it means I can sleep on the plane. There is a car waiting on the other end, and off we go to sunny Westchester county. I have no idea how people live this whole suburban lifestyle. I am here only minutes and already I am dying to jump a train back into Manhattan. We check into the Ramada in New Rochelle, and find little goody bags from Naomi awaiting us. Or rather, awaiting my parents, since apparently Adam has checked in already and taken our goody bag to the room. Wait till he hears that Geoff is coming.

"Honey, go unpack, and grab Adam and come to our suite to hang out." Mom and Dad have reserved a hospitality suite, and are hosting cocktails for the out-of-town guests before tonight's shabbat dinner.

"Okay Mom. Give us a half hour or so."

"Okay sweetheart. Number 1519."

"We'll be there."

Adam and I are in 627. I knock, and then use the key. Adam is crashed out on one of the beds, snoring away. I think about not waking him. Then I think better of it. I jump on the bed next to him. He yells.

"Hello handsome brother."

"Sid, I am going to fucking kill you. Do you have any idea how exhausted I am?"

"Too bad. Mom and Dad want us unpacked, dressed for dinner and in their suite pronto."

"Good God, it is beginning already."

"I know. But wake up, because I have news."

"This cannot be good."

"Guess who is coming?"

"Mark?"

"No, silly, Naomi never liked him anyway."

"She's a pill. I give, who?"

"She's not a pill, she's just old and suburban."

"She's a pill, Sid, love her, would do anything for her, but she's a pill."

"Okay, she's sort of a pill, but she can't help it."

"Fair enough. Who is coming?"

"Geoff."

"Oh Christ, Sid. What are you doing?"

"What do you mean? Dad invited him."

"Whatever, that isn't the point. Actually, I take that back, it IS the point. DAD INVITED HIM. Dad's business partner. Dad's married business partner. Not his son-in-law. Not even his daughter's boyfriend. Just his business partner. Why are you all aglow that he is coming anyway? Need I remind you of the June Massacre?"

"No, you needn't remind me, I am well aware of what has happened. But do you really think he would be coming here if he didn't want to see me?"

"OF COURSE HE WANTS TO SEE YOU. Sid, he's human. He's not dead. Out of town for the weekend, who doesn't want to get laid?"

"It isn't like that."

"Isn't it?"

"Okay, maybe it is a little bit like that, but what if I want to get laid?"

"You can't."

"Why not?"

"Because you are in love with him. He can get laid. YOU make love. He gets off. YOU get hurt. That man isn't ever going to choose you. He is a shitheel, and I wish I could take him aside and beat the ever-loving crap out of him and tell him I know what he has done, but I can't. All I can do is tell you to leave it alone. Let it be over."

"I don't know if I can, Adam. I want him so bad."

"Aren't you the one who always says it is good to want things?"

"Shut up."

"You shut up."

"No YOU shut up!"

"No, YOU shut up!"

Muffled from through the wall we hear, "Why don't you both shut up!"

This makes us laugh really hard. Then there is a knock on the door.

"Jesus you two are a pain." Cousin Josh is apparently our disgruntled neighbor.

"Shut up!" Adam says, grabbing him in a manly cousinly sort of hug.

"You shut up!" he replies, walking over to kiss me on the cheek. "Hey, did Doug ever call you?"

"Doug?" asks Adam.

"Yes he did, we went out last night." This makes me smile, and forget the Geoff thing for a minute.

"Wait, who is Doug?" Adam is confused and feeling left out.

"Remember that construction guy Sid was so hot on, from the summer we were at the firm?"

"Vaguely. Was he the one that she got all moody about when he got married?"

I hate these boys.

"That's the one. He's divorced now, ran into him last week,

he asked for Sid's number, so perhaps after all this time she will get the guy." Josh is grinning like an idiot.

"Okay, SHE is in the room, and SHE has had enough of this nonsense for one day. Yes, Doug called, yes, we went out for dinner last night, and yes, we had a nice time. No, I did not sleep with him, but yes, there may be some possibility of actual dating, we are going to get to know each other again as adults and take things slow and see what happens. Is that enough information for the two of you?"

Adam and Josh look at each other. They nod. Then they both grab me and throw me on the bed where Adam tickles my ribs while Josh tries to hold my feet down.

We finish unpacking, spruce up a bit for the evening, and head upstairs to my parents' suite. Soon, some of the other out-of-town relatives and guests begin to arrive, and by five o'clock the place is jumping. The shabbat dinner is scheduled for seven-thirty. Everyone should be well lubricated by then. I see Naomi's in-laws, who I have not seen since Naomi's wedding. They are looking at me and whispering. Divorce is not a popular concept with Westchester Jews. I decide against going over to talk to them. A lot of the East Coast cousins are there. There is much laughter and story-telling and kissing and hugging and general frivolity. All over the suite people are looking at brag books full of picture of new kids, grandkids, houses or boats. Then at six-thirty, Adam elbows my ribs. I turn around to see my dad patting Geoff on the shoulder. My heart swells. Dad escorts him over to say hi.

"Geoff, you remember my boy Adam?"

"Of course, how are things going for you in London?"

"Very well thank you, sir."

Sir?

"And of course you know Sid." If you only knew, Dad. Adam snorts loudly into his drink.

"Always good to see you Sidney." Geoff leans over and kisses my cheek. Adam snorts again. I step back onto his foot. He pokes my ribs until I get off him. I can tell already it is going to be a long weekend.

Geoff is seated at our table for the dinner, the evening is uneventful, full of casual conversations and catching up with family. After dinner we all go back to the hotel bar and hang out. At around eleven Geoff goes up to bed. He shockingly leaves his cell phone on the table. I wait ten minutes before officially publicly noticing it, and announce that I am going up to return it to him. Adam rolls his eyes.

At eleven fifteen, having ascertained that no one I know is about in the halls, I knock on Geoff's door. He answers, lets me in, and smiles.

Just before one, I tiptoe into my room, fumble a bit in the dark for my pajamas, make a hasty and quiet toilette in the bathroom. When I come out, a voice in the darkness greets me.

"Slut."

"Sorry I woke you."

"I can't sleep anyway, jet lag. How was it?"

"It's over."

"Right."

"I ended it."

"Right."

"I told him I can't sleep with him anymore, not unless we are making a decision to be together. I told him that his behavior back in June was a wake-up call for me, and that I will not be some sideline plaything. I told him that if he and Sandra break up and he wants to begin again with me, if I am available, I will be open to that, but that I will no longer subjugate myself to his wants and needs for so little return. I told him that I love him, but it is too hard."

Adam turns on the light and looks at me. He sees the red eyes, the resigned mouth. He knows that it is the truth. Then he notices the rumpled hair.

"Before or after you had sex with him?" He knows me too well.

"After. I was lying in his arms, and it just felt empty. I wanted to stay and I knew he would never let me, not just tonight, but not ever. And I thought about everything that has happened in the last sixteen months and how hard it has been, and I just felt done. Finis. So I took a deep breath and I got up and got dressed and told him it was over."

"You okay?"

"I dunno."

"C'mere."

I stand up, walk across the brief distance and climb in with Adam, who holds me very tightly while I cry.

"I am very very proud of you Sid. It is the right thing. And on your terms, your decision. You are the bravest person I know."

"I don't feel brave, I feel very small and frightened."

"That will pass."

"I hope so."

I get up, and go over to my bed. Adam has short sheeted it.

"Asshole."

"Can't say I didn't warn you."

We giggled for a long time. Between the jet lag and the heart lag, I don't think either one of us slept much.

SATURDAY: The bat mitzvah service was lovely, and Rachel did very well, and we all got up on the bima and offered our blessings. Geoff looked tired all day, and kept giving me sidelong glances as if to try and read my mind. There was a light lunch at the temple, and then we went back to the hotel to take naps before the big evening party. Josh and Adam and I watched a pay-per-view movie, but we all fell asleep and missed the ending. We assume Sandra Bullock got the guy, she always does.

Then party time. To be honest, everything happened really fast. The food was good, there was a lot of dancing, a record-breaking eighteen-minute horah, a lot of twelve- and thirteen-year-old girls dancing way too sexily to songs like the remake of "Lady Marmalade," and a lot of twelve- and thirteen-year-old boys watching them with utterly rapt confusion. They played a set of Motown for the older folks, and my parents and Adam and Naomi and I all danced together in a circle the way we always do at these events. During one of the few slow songs, I danced with my dad, and Geoff danced with my mom, and halfway through we bumped into each other, and Geoff looked at my dad and said, "I'll trade you."

I had never danced with him before. He was a little stiff, but it was nice anyway. I am really going to miss him.

"Are you okay?" There is something in his eyes I have never seen there before.

"I think so. Are you okay?"

"I don't know."

"I thought you would be relieved."

"So did I. There have been so many times I have wanted you to say that, to save me from myself, to make it easier."

"But?"

"But I didn't know how it would make me feel to actually hear it."

"And how did it make you feel?"

"Shitty."

"I'm sorry."

"Me too. For everything."

"No regrets, Mister Man. I have none."

"Regrets no, but sorry, yes."

"I know."

"Can I still see you? Friendly like?"

"I would like that."

"I may have moments of weakness, just slap me and keep me on the straight and narrow."

"I'll do what I can."

The song ended. Literally and metaphorically.

SUNDAY: Family brunch. Geoff was invited, but went back to the city early instead. While saying goodbye he made me promise him a lunch date next week. I agreed, wondering if we will be able to maintain the friendship or if we will just fade away. Worse comes to worst I can always use a free lunch. We all headed to the airport en masse and said our goodbyes. Adam whispered again that he was proud of me. I slept on the way home. My folks dropped me off with kisses and I congratulated them on a lovely weekend. Here are the messages that awaited me when I got home this evening.

- Naomi, thanking me for all my help over the weekend and apologizing for not having more time to spend with me.
- Parker, telling me he met a new boy, and needs to dish.
- Doug, telling me he hopes I had a good weekend, and that things are even crazier than he thought this week, but that next week looked pretty good after Wednesday.
- Geoff, telling me that he wants to have lunch on Thursday if that suits my schedule.
- Joe, telling me that he and Kim decided not to wait till August, and that he is officially single, and wants to take me out Friday for our first real actual date.

See what I meant by a long week? Yeesh.

chapter 23

be careful what you wish for

QUOTE OF THE DAY

Reason's whole pleasure, all the joys of sense,
Lie in three words,—health, peace, and competence.
                                        —Alexander Pope

"Sidney, your father and I are concerned about you." Thursday morning breakfast with Mom. Not eating much, as I have the first post-breakup lunch date with Geoff.

"What are you concerned about, Mom?"

"You seem distant." Oy.

"In what way?"

"In the way that you don't tell us what is going on with you. We don't hear much about the new book, we don't hear much about your plans when the school year starts next month, we haven't heard about any men in your life, you don't talk about Mark at all."

"I'm sorry, Mom, I don't mean to be cryptic. Mark is okay, we talk every other week or so, and sometimes e-mail, we are really just fine and both of us are feeling very positive about all the decision making, and I think our friendship is very secure. I have been dating, but really only guys with not much potential, so I haven't been talking much about it. There are a couple of guys I know that I like, but I don't know what is going to happen, and I am trying not to focus too much on finding some big new relationship. I have a meeting next week at Columbia to discuss the upcoming year, but as far as I know I will have the same schedule as last year. The book is with my new editor, and I think she has some really great ideas. I am working on another one, which is a concept piece."

"What does that mean, a concept piece?"

"Well, you know how sometimes rock bands put together an album that seems to tell a story, almost like the score of a musical?"

"Like TOMMY or THE WALL?"

I often forget that my mother was alive and well and young in the sixties and seventies.

"Exactly. This is sort of like that."

"What is the concept?"

Here goes…

"Well, it is the journal of a woman having an affair with a married man."

"Is it dirty?"

"No, but there are some poems that are sexy. It is really just a different sort of love poetry. Most anthologies of love poems are about the exploration of conventional love between two people. But in this day and age, boy meets girl poetry isn't quite so simple. Heck, boy meets girl period isn't quite so simple. So I thought about what changes would happen in the way the words come together if the writer is talking about an unconventional, even unethical or immoral in the eyes of some, progression of love."

"Sounds interesting. I don't know that I have ever heard of anything quite like it."

"That was sort of the point."

"And these new guys you are talking about?"

I tell Mom about both Joe and Doug, and she gives me the most interesting advice I think my mother has ever given me.

"Date them both."

"What?"

"Date them both. I mean it sounds like this Doug fellow, I seem to remember your father being very impressed with him if memory serves, it sounds like he is more your speed in terms of a serious relationship, but Joe, he sounds like fun for just casual dating. So date them both. If you start to have feelings for one or the other, you can make it exclusive, but there is no harm in keeping all your options open. After all, I was still dating Issac Kroner when I accepted your father's invitation to the Alpha Epsilon Pi formal." There is a twinkle in her eye.

"I love you, Mom."

"I love you too, kiddo."

We finish breakfast, and I walk her to her car. She gives me a big hug, enveloping me in a cloud of Chanel No. 5.

"And Sidney..."

"Yeah, Mom?"

"They never leave their wives."

"WHAT?"

"For the new book, in my experience, they never leave their wives. I think you should know that statistically married men stay married, even if they cheat. Even if they fall in love. They stay married."

"I'll keep that in mind." My mother places her perfectly manicured hands on either side of my face and smiles at me warmly.

"You do that. I love you."

"Love you too."

Have I mentioned that my mother is about the coolest chick I know? Issac Kroner indeed.

★ ★ ★

I run a few errands, stop by Barnes & Noble to pick up the latest Li Young Lee anthology, as he is one of my favorite contemporary poets, end up buying about eight new CDs that I really can't afford, and go to Bistro Campagne to meet Geoff. Even in the middle of a workday, his nervousness requires a trip out to Oak Park to eliminate the chance of being spotted. For the first time, he is waiting for me. The place is empty, and I wonder for the zillionth time how it is they stay in business.

"Hello you." I walk over to the bar, and accept the kiss on my cheek.

"How are you?"

"Good, you?"

"Okay. A little stressed, lots going on at work, just keeping my head above water."

"Everything okay?"

"Sure, sure, just busy, that's all."

We head to our table in the corner, Geoff orders a half bottle of my favorite Pinot Noir, and we look over the menu.

"We've never been here for lunch, the menu is so different." He looks nervous.

"Yeah, much lighter, the rabbit sounds good."

"I never could eat rabbit. I had one as a pet when I was a kid, too creepy."

"Will it bother you if I order it?"

"Of course not."

Geoff decides on the hanger steak with frites, I get the rabbit, we decide to split a simple salad.

"Sandra has received a job offer with a new company."

"Wow, is she going to take it?"

"We are discussing it. It means going back to traveling a lot. But it is a good career move for her."

"I see."

"On the one hand, it feels like it would be okay for her to

start traveling again, but on the other hand, since things have been better for us with her home these past seven months, it feels like it could be detrimental too."

"That is a tough decision. What do you think she is going to do?"

"I think she is probably going to take it."

"And how do you feel about it?"

"I don't know. To be honest, I was going to tell you about it last weekend in New York. I was feeling okay about it, since I thought it would make things easier for you and I, but now I don't know."

"Made it easier to contemplate if you were going to have me around for company."

"Sort of, I guess. Makes me kind of a schmuck, huh?"

"Kind of. But not in a terminal way."

"You are very kind."

"Yes, I am."

"I don't suppose that you would reconsider, in light of recent events?"

My whole heart goes out to him. And breaks a little. Because I really do love him, and I really do miss him, and I still long for him physically and emotionally. But I think about my breakfast with Mom, and the life that I want, and the life I want doesn't seem to have space for him anymore.

"No, I don't think so. If she were going away never to return, that would be different, if you were leaving her, it would be different. But I can't go back to what we have been, Geoff, I deserve more."

"I know you do. You really do. What if I could offer more?"

"What could you possibly offer if you have a wife?"

"We could see each other more often."

"Not enough."

"I could spend the night." Wow. Only been waiting nearly a year and a half to hear that.

"Not enough."

"I thought that was such a big deal for you, the sleeping over thing?"

"It was. It is. But Geoff, the only thing I ever wanted more than for you to stay over or ask me to stay, was for you to want it. I hated that it was the place you drew a line in the sand, but at the end of the day, I know that you never spent a night with me out of obligation, or as some sort of reward for me. I always knew that if you ever stayed the night, it would be because you had realized that to leave would be unbearable. I will always be sorry that I never woke up in your arms, but I will always be glad that I never had to question the time we spent together."

"I feel like something is wrong, but I can't pinpoint what it is."

"You are just unsettled. You never thought it would happen this way. This is the hardest thing I have ever had to do, Geoff, every fiber of my being wants to say the hell with it and agree. My heart wants so much to take advantage of your offer, to spend more time, to spend whole nights with you. But I know me, and I know you. I would convince myself that we were moving toward a life together, and you would start to feel smothered. I would start wanting whole weekends, and you would get more and more paranoid about getting caught. I would start pushing you to divorce, and you would shut down and get defensive. I love you. Part of me will always love you. Part of me will always wonder what we might have had if we had been given the opportunity. But what you offer is simply not enough. I want the moon, Geoff. I want it all. And you cannot offer me the moon. If you want to have dinner or hang out when Sandra is out of town, I would love to see you. But we are friends, no more. I want you in my life, but not my bed, Geoff, I just can't."

"I hear you."

"Are we okay?"

"We are fine. I want you to have everything you want Sid. It is going to kill me when you finally get it, but I want it for you."

"Thank you for that."

"I know I never said it back, but in my own fucked up way, I do love you Sidney."

Good lord, please give me the strength to maintain.

"And I love you, Geoff. Always."

He walked me to my car. He kissed my forehead and held me very tightly. He said he would call to have dinner or something in the coming week or two. I wondered if he actually would. And then I went home. The computer offers some solace.

shhhhh

there is nothing which doesn't spark fear in me
but I imprison it in my secret soul
I do not want this knowledge imparted
my heart trapped
reaching inside to myself

afraid of the nakedness of truth
I dance and spin for you
gambol and sing
mug and grin behind Salome's seven veils
behind the harlequin's mask
beneath the Lone Ranger's cape
frightened that I am hollow
transparent
unworthy
that you will see through me
my brave brave face
and extricate yourself from my embrace
so I costume myself in wit
cloak myself in pride
pull on the pretty glamours
and speak my sharp confidences

the picture of security without
the trembling whimpering child within

the days and hours become a slick oily gamesters play
the repartee
the badinage
the whisper of trusting you with all of what doesn't matter
none of what is most real

it isn't that I take pleasure in the deceit
there is no ease of breath
when lungs give weight to triviality

I always thought
if it would come down to begging
the request would be for love
for comfort
for arms around me
sweet words in my ears
sweet hands on my skin
for waking breath
and sleeping safety

but what I beg of you
goes beyond those petty politics
don't just love me
hear me
know me
don't see the jester
but the soul behind the smile
don't take the words as complete
listen to what I don't say
the words I cannot find
the wishes in the spaces between what I can muster and what I
can manage

there are volumes there

it isn't that I want to deny the spontaneity in me
that I don't appreciate who I am
I need you to remind me that I am possible
to shore up my heart
which beats for you
in ecstasy full of trepidation
in broken rhythm
in limping trust

if choosing me is in you
then choose me
choose definitively
fill the air around me
with softness and warmth
that I might blossom in your care

scale this fortress
these years of self-doubt
self-denial
take the walls down
with gentle hands
cradle each brick like a babe in your arms
and lay them to rest beyond my reach
that I may not build them up again

and if ever you need to know
the deep identity
the me in me
I am everywhere in everyone
and deep in you
I am so deep in you.

That is sort of the way it is, after all, the fear of loneliness, the fear that we may become lost in our love for another, that all our strength is a mask, a put-on. And yet our basic human reality is that those feelings are the common link between us, that those fears are the thing we have that most connects us to each other. I hated looking at my lover of nearly a year and a half and saying no. Saying that what he offered wasn't nearly enough. Because the no wasn't fully fleshed within me, the strength was in many ways borrowed strength. Pieced together from my friends and family and what they wanted for me, what they expected from me. I hate that I am in so many ways exactly what I fear, weak, easily manipulated. I hate that I would willingly, gladly, alter myself, suppress my needs, just to be with this man. I hate that I question what I might have done or said that might have made him come for me in a real way. And at the same time, I am feeling flush with what he did offer, with the steps he tried to take.

After all, he feels some loss, he tried to win me back in his way, and whether it is the deep-down truth or just what he felt he should say, his declaration of love, watered down and insufficient as it was, touches my very soul with a small and simple joy. I loved him in my way and he loved me in his and for a time we were possible.

I had pretty much stopped crying when the phone rang.

SIDEBAR

C'mon, you didn't think I was going to get through all of that without a couple of hours of weeping and fighting with myself not to call him back and say "the hell with it, I'm yours," did you? What are you, new? Don't you know me at all? I wrote the poem, then called Parker, then called Adam—hell, I called everyone who I knew would tell me I had done the right thing. I was duly impressed with myself, and put on my bravest strongest face.

Then I cried like the little girl I am.

Meanwhile, back at the set of The Dating Game...

"Sidney my darling."

"Hello Joseph."

"I love it when you call me Joseph. Are we on for tomorrow?"

Abso-fucking-lutely. "We are."

"Pick you up at eight?"

"Fine."

"How about that Italian place on California?"

"Perfect."

"No, you're perfect."

"Thank you."

"I will see you tomorrow."

"You most certainly will."

Well, here we go.

Flash Forward

Joe and I are sitting on my couch. We have had a lovely dinner, have shared wine and laughter, there is an ease between us that acknowledges the weeks of odd courtship that have preceded tonight, and the strange hum of electricity that comes with the knowledge that we are taking a step forward.

Joe moves toward me on the couch and smiles.

"Hey pretty lady."

"Hello there." He kisses me gently.

"You taste good."

"Thank you."

He kisses me again.

"You are the most funnest kisser I have ever known." Sweet boy.

"And you have a loose grasp on grammar, but I am inclined to forgive you."

"I appreciate that."

He kisses me harder and longer. And longer and harder. And

then he moves his hand over my left breast and kneads it lightly. Then he stops, and pulls back.

"You aren't stopping me?" His look is a little puzzled.

"No I am not."

"Why come?"

"I told you, no second base unless you are single. Are you single?"

"I am indeed."

"Then have at it." I am such a lady, aren't I?

Joe smiles broadly, leans in, and kisses me even harder.

Now, in all fairness, it has been a whirlwind couple of weeks, and my brain is in a bit of a tumult. I am trying very hard not to think of either Geoff or Doug while Joe is kissing me. I am trying to relax, to just get out of my head and enjoy myself. But something is happening, and I am not exactly sure what to make of it. Joe's kisses, always perfectly pleasant, (if never really a match for the pleasant perfection of Geoff's kisses), have suddenly become intensely aggressive. There is a level of tongue involvement that is nearly oppressive. There is a licking and sucking of my neck that is registering like a weird sort of primal bathing ritual as opposed to the sexy nibbling I prefer, the whole thing has become, well, sloppy. My chin is wet, my neck is wet, and which is worse, in his ardor, Joe has managed to maneuver himself so that I am on my back on the couch, he has one leg between my legs, knee pressed against a tender spot which needs no such attention, and he is literally kissing my head into the crevice between the sofa cushions. Plus he is working both my breasts like they are bread dough, and in general I am feeling more assaulted than seduced.

I place both hands on Joe's chest and push him off me a bit to get some air.

"Easy tiger!"

"Sorry, was I getting too carried away?"

"Just a little intense is all. Relax, I am not going anywhere."

"Sorry darling, I have just been waiting so long to be with you, my passion is overwhelming me."

Well, it is nice to be wanted. And I do like him.

"Sidney?"

"Yes?"

"I would very much like to spend the night with you, if that is okay."

Spend the night. On the first real date, he wants to spend the night. I think about how nice it would be to actually sleep in someone's arms, to wake up with someone. And to be frank, I can't think of a good reason not to sleep with him. Geoff and I are over, Doug and I haven't really begun, Joe and I have been doing this dance for so long, plus, to be honest, I think it would be smart for me to sleep with him. To tangibly physically move forward. To take one more step on the healing process to getting over Geoff. Not to mention the fact that I really want to have sex. With a live person. I am wearying quickly of battery-operated lovers, and yesterday morning opened my ridiculously well-equipped nightstand drawer and, gazing over the assortment of toys, thought, "I am so bored with all of you," before abandoning the idea of getting off and opting for a Milky Way bar instead.

"Yes, Joe, you can spend the night if you like."

His grin is blinding. He gets up, takes my hand, walks with me to my bedroom.

SIDEBAR

Now, I am a smart girl, and all smart girls know that your first time, sometimes even your first couple times with a new lover, well, things are usually far from perfect. I mean, everyone is different, a new body to get acclimated to, different things which work for one or the other, none of the smart girls that I know expect fireworks first time out of the box. Even my experience with Geoff reinforced this for me, the exception proving the rule. After all, for a woman of 34, I have had a very respectable (or embarrassing, depending how you look at it) cadre of lovers. I won't divulge how many, a lady doesn't keep running tallies. Let's just say that it is a number somewhere significantly more than Prude and significantly less than Skank-Ho. Yes, I am in double digits. And with the notable exception of Geoff, none of the first encounters with any of these lovers was exactly life-altering. They have ranged from deeply mediocre to pretty damn good, and I assume that I too have fallen somewhere in those categories. Although, if any of them are to be believed, I generally err on the side of pretty damn good, if I do say so myself.

The point, and yes I do have one, is that a smart girl takes her new lover to the bedroom with romance in her heart, but realism on her mind. We expect to have fun. We expect to see some potential. We do not expect to achieve orgasm, nor do we plan to fake it unless our compatriot is of the single-minded-no-one-sleeps-until-everyone-comes-really-I-can-do-this sort, in which case we play like Meg Ryan so that we can get some rest. But none of the smart girls think that we are going to recreate the Dennis Quaid-Ellen Barkin heat from The Big Easy *on night one. Hopefully night two or three, once we are a little comfortable, once we know each other a little better, once we have established some trust and rapport.*

Having said that, when a smart girl takes on a new lover, particularly in her thirties, particularly with a man who has had his share of partners himself, we do expect basic competence. We expect him to know where everything is and have a general sense of what to do with it. We do expect that he will be attentive to whatever guidance we offer. We do expect that we will not feel extraneous. We have these expectations. We are sometimes disappointed.

Joe gets into my bedroom, and immediately begins to strip down. This is somewhat abrupt, but I suppose once we are in bed there will be time for some exploration, and to be honest, I tend to get irritated by fooling around while standing up, so while I might have preferred some tender mutual undressing, I am not particularly offended by the pedestrian shedding of clothing, and follow suit.

Joe's body isn't really what I expected, to be honest. He has sort of a concave-ish chest, with a little potbelly sticking out roundly in front. His legs are somewhat bowed, giving him an air that is minimally simian. I try to get the thought of Geoff's long lean body out of my head, I look instead at his face. This is Joe. Cute, sweet Joe of the fabulous e-mails. The boy who makes me melt when he sings, three years of location crush to support me, nearly three and a half months of courting, literally hours of face-chafing kissing, one night of really hot phone sex, Joe. You want him. He wants you. Just relax and let it happen.

We repair to the bed. Joe sighs deeply, as does anyone who hits those featherbeds for the first time. He rolls toward me, and begins to kiss me. Once again, he quickly manages to trap me underneath him, and begins that same haphazard tongue action that so stunned me on the couch. He is everywhere at once, all hands and mouth, but no nuance, no subtlety, no tender foreplay, just strange uncoordinated attacks on all the usual strongholds. I am stunned. I am astonished, actually, a little flabbergasted. After all, this man had described in great and titillating detail all the things he was going to do to me, except he isn't doing any of them, and what he is doing is really mostly irritating. And suffocating, because the oral attack seems to be interested in my actual tonsils, and that tongue from hell is valiantly trying to take up residence somewhere halfway down my esophagus. If he doesn't stop soon, we may have a problem, because I have a reasonably sensitive gag reflex, and he is getting a little too close for comfort. I manage to get my arms loose, and grab his head between my hands and pull him away. Apparently Joe assumes that I mean for him to take those skills and migrate southerly with them, although mostly I just need a breather.

"Yes my darling. I want to taste you." He sounds ridiculous. Sort of a soft-core porno endearment. I kind of want to giggle, but I don't think he would approve. He begins to kiss and nibble at my breasts, but really as more of a perfunctory hello before lodging himself definitively betwixt my thighs. I am not exactly sure what he is doing down there. More to the point,

I don't think he is exactly sure what he is doing down there. One thing he is definitely doing is drooling a great deal, I can feel a small puddle forming under me, and this makes me a little annoyed, since it means I will be sleeping in the wet spot from hell. There is odd licking, random sucking, and occasionally I can feel a hand fumbling around, but all in all, it feels like a small blind sea creature has accidentally become lodged in my crotch, and is trying frantically to find its way out. Every now and again there is something that can only be a nose or a chin, and I am pretty sure I don't want to know which, or what he thinks it is doing for me.

Now, as I mentioned before, I am a smart girl. I do not expect a man to have ESP when it comes to my sexual preferences. Perhaps Kim loved this sort of attention. I try to offer some encouragement, some guidance. I whisper, "Gently. Gently," as he batters me with his fingers. I whisper, "Slow circles," when he licks crazily all over the place. I take my hand and try to guide him, and he pushes it away, and continues the barrage. I give up. He clearly thinks he knows best, and I am too tired to argue with him. I think about Geoff, but instead of the fantasy helping me to get excited, the oral impudence of my new lover is too distracting to allow me to conjure Geoff up in a real enough way to be of assistance. You would think Joe might have noticed that I wasn't really moving much, and that I certainly wasn't making any happy noises, but to be honest, I think at that moment I might have been anyone, I was just a strange sort of vessel, and Joe wasn't really thinking about me at all. I was contemplating my deep need to do laundry, when he came up for air.

"Yes, darling, so good." He looks like he was hit in the face with a jellyfish. "I want to be inside you now."

Whatever. It has got to be better than what has preceded it.

Joe looms over me, takes my hand and puts it on his erection as he grabs the condom from the bedside table. I am surprised by its contours, so very different from Geoff. Its presence in my hand seems, well, inconsequential. But I am no size queen, motion of the ocean and all that, and luckily for me (and my partners) I am not exactly a woman of capacious nether measurements. In fact, while my outer bulk might belie the idea, I actually take the smallest diaphragm they manufacture without having to have one specially made. So one does not exactly need to be hung like Jeff Stryker to be of use to me, and let's be clear, there is only so much real estate a gal needs. But Joe, is, well, small.

Small enough that we are in fact, apparently, having sex before I notice anything. Actually, I don't notice anything. I just shift my hips a little because he is pressing uncomfortably on one thigh, and Joe says, "Hold on, slipped out," and I think You were IN? Once I concentrated I could feel something, so I tried to participate, you know, move around, join in, but Joe has no discernible rhythm, so every time I move, he (apparently) slips out, but then who could notice because I have had bigger tampons in me!

Joseph Edington is fucking me. And I do not like it. Not one little bit.

Finally, I just lay back and let him go, all these weird and random thrusts, side to side, back and forth, he fucks like a one-armed spastic hitting a bongo. He fucks like Elaine danced on *Seinfeld*. He fucks like someone who has only ever been with women who want a man in their life more than they want orgasms. I can't believe someone married him. I can't believe anyone dated him for longer than a minute. I am trying to squelch the bitter vitriol that is rising in me. After all, it isn't a federal offense to be a lousy lay. But I can't really help it. I am tired. I am damp. I am, well, actually, tremendously pissed off and put out.

For this I waited? All the weeks of being a good girl, and playing and kissing, and sending my best e-mails and thinking how nice it would be to have a good casual transition guy, and this is what I get? This sexual incompetent? I am, as Chekhov once wrote, in mourning for my life. I want him to finish. I want him to go home. I want Geoff back. I want Doug to step it up so I can stop wanting Geoff back. But mostly, I WANT THIS SLIPPERY-SWEATY-NO-RHYTHM-HAVING-TINY-LITTLE-DICK-M★★★★★-F★★★★★ TO GET THE HELL OFF ME!!!! Luckily what he lacks in length and girth he makes up for with brevity, so my suffering ends a few seconds after I have that thought. Except when he is finished, he wants to know that I have come too. He begins to work at me with his hand, but there is just no way I am ever going to get there, so I reach down, move him out of the way, make some noise, wriggle around a bit, and fake a small one just to make him stop. Which, blissfully, he does.

Then he falls asleep.

Thank God.

When I hear snoring, I get up, and go to the shower. The hot water feels lovely, and it is good to get the sweat and spit off me. Usually I like to languish with my lover, usually I like that slightly sticky warm feeling of having just made love, but tonight I am looking for a baptism.

Oy. What a mess.

I sneak quietly back to the bed, and, as softly as possible, slide in. Joe rolls over and spoons me, which actually feels pretty good, and I manage to doze off. But then, just as I am getting into actual REM sleep, I feel Joe begin to grind against me. Oh no. Good God. He is kissing the back of my neck, and running his hands over my body, and I am just too tired and too disappointed to stop him. I roll over at his insistence, and he reaches for another condom. At least he isn't going to try and give me head again. Second verse, same as the first, a little bit quicker, a whole lot worse. This proves it, without a doubt.

Joseph Edington is, bar none, the worst lover I have ever had. Ever.

And one thing is for sure, I am going to have to break up with him immediately if not sooner. Because no amount of flirting and fun e-mailing will ever make me suffer through another night of this. Life is too short. And I know that may sound harsh, and I know that many many of you will scold me for writing him off so soon, for not at least attempting to have some conversation about it with him, to be more adamant about making him hear from me what I want and need, but to be perfectly frank, I don't care. I am an educator all day, I do not want to have to teach some putz how to screw. And it really isn't that my expectations are too high because of Geoff, if anything, they are more realistic. I knew for a fact that the first lover, probably all the lovers, after Geoff would pale in comparison. That is okay with me, everyone can only have one "best ever," and I got mine for sixteen months, so my memory banks are quite full, thank you. But Joe, he pales in comparison to Kendrick Sloane, the guy I painfully lost my virginity to in the borrowed apartment of an out-of-town friend, and trust me kids, that was no joyride.

In the morning, I pretend to be asleep while Joe quietly wanders around. I hear him in the shower. I peek through slitted eyelids as he walks back to the bedroom stark naked, that tiny little thing flopping around. A towel might not have been a bad idea, just a thought. He comes over to the bed and half lays on top of me, and I mumble something about being very very tired. He kisses my forehead and says he has to go, brunch with Mom, but he will call me later. I hear him getting dressed, and then, at long last the door opens and closes and he is gone.

Dating sucks.

I roll over and grab my favorite vibrator out of the nightstand. Suddenly I am not so disenchanted with the nightstand playmates after all. I bought this one because its size and shape reminded me of Geoff. How's that for both obsessive and depressive? Doesn't matter today though, we have a lovely few minutes together, and then I go back to sleep.

I don't answer my phone all day. Joe calls three times. Wants to see me tonight. I have to think up a plan, and in the meantime, I am playing possum.

Trust me, you'd do the same.

chapter 24

breaking up isn't hard to do

QUOTE OF THE DAY

Yet tears to human suffering are due;
And mortal hopes defeated and o'erthrown
Are mourned by man, and not by man alone.
                                        —William Wordsworth

Actually, dealing with Joe is surprisingly simple. Luckily for me, we both have crazy scheduling weeks immediately after the bedroom debacle, including out-of-town guests and family obligations, so it is nearly nine days before we are able to arrange a date. He comes over. I make him dinner, figuring I owe him at least that. Roasted chicken with an herbed yogurt sauce, wild rice pilaf with currants and pistachios and fresh mint, sautéed baby spinach. We talk and laugh, and I feel bad, because he is dropping all sorts of references to us going places and doing things together and all I can think is what a totally great guy he is. Then I remember his itty bitty little willy and what he did with it, and my resolve returns. After dinner, I begin to do the dishes and Joe sidles up behind me and slips his arms around my waist, nuzzling into my neck.

"Delicious dinner, just like the chef."

I figure this is as good a time as any, and put my master plan into play.

STEP ONE: CRYING

I look down at the soapy water in the sink and think of Geoff. It is shitty, I know, but these days, all I have to do to conjure up some very genuine tears is remind myself that I wasn't good enough, that he didn't choose me, that we would never ever belong to each other. Presto chango, ladies and gentlemen, we now have some lovely full orbs of water gliding over the perfect cheeks of our hapless heroine, which is to say, as we have mentioned before, myself. I indulge in one little sniff. Joe, good boy that he is, notices. He turns me gently toward him. I keep looking down. He places a fingertip under my chin, and raises my head to look into my face. His eyes are full of concern.

"Baby, what's the matter?" He pulls me close. I sniff again. It is time for step two.

STEP TWO: LYING

"Joe, I am so sorry, I don't think it is a good idea for us to see each other romantically."

Joe looks perplexed. Concerned. Confused.

"Why? I thought we were having such a great night?"

"We are, we were, I just…" pause for dramatic wiping of tears, "I just can't. It isn't fair to you, and I am so sorry, I really didn't mean…" I let myself trail off, and lower my head again in my misery.

"Hey hey, easy, tell me what's going on, it can't be that bad."

Actually Joe, it can. Just not the way you think.

I take a deep breath, I wipe the tears again, I look him in the face.

SIDEBAR

Remember kids, before you try this at home, the key to a good lie is a whole lot of truth. As much truth as you can possibly muster. Lots of truth, little bit of bullshit, easier to remember and plausible deniability all in one. They will believe you, I guarantee it. Just watch:

"Joe I like you, and I care about you, and I thought I was ready to be with you (TRUE). But the truth is, I am still in love with someone else (TRUE). You know all about my lover, and things are definitely over with him (TRUE). And I thought after all the time you and I had spent leading up to this that I was in a great place to move forward with you (TRUE). But I know now that I can't be with you (TRUE). Because after the other night was over I felt awful (TRUE). And I realized that however ready I thought I was, in fact, moving forward conceptually and moving forward in reality are two different things (TRUE). Joe, you are great (MOSTLY TRUE). And the other night was very special to me (★★★BIG FAT LIE!★★★ taa daaa!). But I have had some important time to think things over, and I realize that even though we are not together anymore, I still belong to him (TRUE). And it would be unconscionable to make love with you with another man in my heart or on my mind. (Well, technically TRUE, but the fact is that any man of even minimal sexual prowess can make a woman forget the one that got away for at least an hour or two, so LIE OF OMISSION OR MANIPULATION OF FACTS.) I am really very sorry. (TRUE, very sorry I slept with you.) I never meant to hurt you (TRUE). And I hope that we can still be friends, even though that sounds like the biggest stupidest cliché ever (TRUE)."

Joe looks at me with tender kindness, and smiles. Step three is up to him, but if you have done one and two correctly, he will jump right in.

STEP THREE: MAKE HIM COMFORT YOU FOR BREAKING UP WITH HIM

"Of course we are friends, poor baby, I am sorry that guy has messed you up so bad. And of course I'm disappointed, but I understand completely. And you are right, you can't know how long it takes to get over a heartbreak. I am just so worried about you, you have such emotional investment in this man who has hurt you so badly."

Bingo.

"Thank you for that, I know now that I just have to spend some time alone, and get myself figured out a bit. You have been really super, Joe, really, I am very lucky to know you."

"No problem, sweetie."

Joe hugs me again. We finish washing up, and then he leaves.

Thank God, because he is no sooner out the door than my phone rings.

"Sidley." Maybe the Gods are rewarding me for recent miseries.

"Douglas."

"How are you?"

"Good, you?"

"Good. Actually, I have the munchies."

"Have you been smoking?"

"No, just those late-night-want-something-sweet sort of munchies."

"I get those."

"Wanna go get ice cream?"

"I can't think of anything I would like better."

"I'll pick you up in five minutes."

Wheee!

Doug pulls up in front of my house in his Land Rover, and I jump in. Well, I don't exactly jump. I'm only 5'3", remember, so hauling my carcass into these tall trucklike SUV urban assault vehicles is a less-than-graceful endeavor. He leans over and kisses me briefly on the lips, and I am most grateful for the little tingles it causes. We drive up to Wilson Avenue, and he heads east to Ravenswood. The Zephyr is a grand old art deco ice cream parlor, and I don't think I have been here since high school. The choice makes me very happy.

I order a hot fudge sundae, and Doug orders caramel, and we tuck in like little kids. Doug tells me about work, and his kids, and passes along hellos from a couple of the guys he still works with that remember me from that long-ago summer, including the one I slept with at the engagement party. Ew. I tell him about my work, and my plans for the upcoming semester, and before we know it, they are cleaning up around us, and putting chairs on tables.

"Guess we should probably go." He waves over our waiter and gets the check.

"This was great, thanks for thinking of it. I love this place."

"Well, thanks for being up for a spontaneous ice cream abduction."

"You can abduct me for ice cream any time you like."

Doug pays the bill, and takes my hand as we walk to the car. On the ride home, we spot a couple of kids necking in a car next to us at a stoplight. He is wearing a black coat, and she seems terribly trendy, both dark-haired and attractive. I say that they look a lot like Christian Slater and Winona Ryder looked in *Heathers*. He says he never saw the movie. I wax a little poetic about the film, and he says he should see it. I tell him that I have it on DVD, and offer to loan it to him. He says he would rather watch it with me, and I ask if he is up for it tonight or if we should do it another time.

"What the hell, I'm not particularly tired. I mean if you actually would be interested."

"Tonight is all about spontaneity."

"Well then, let's go for it!"

In spite of the ice cream, we both need popcorn, which I make while Doug goes through the movie library in my office.

"My kids would go nuts here—you have every children's movie ever made in there!"

"Well if you ever want to borrow some for a weekend, just let me know."

We settle in on the couch, and I start the movie. We finish most of the popcorn. Doug shifts and puts his arm around my shoulders. I lean against him like this is the most natural thing in the world. Somewhere in the last twenty minutes, all the warm comfort of leaning against Doug and the good food in my tummy, everything sort of hits me at once, and I fall asleep.

When I open my eyes the TV screen is a dead blue, and the clock reads 2:36. Doug is sound asleep next to me on the couch. He looks good to me. I am grateful for how good. I lean over and kiss him gently on the cheek. He stirs.

"Mmm. Fell asleep. Sorry."

"It's okay, sweetie, but we should shift to something more comfortable, or you will be crippled in the morning."

"I can go home."

"Do you want to go home?"

"Not really. Do you want me to go home?"

"Not really."

"But Sid, I still think…"

"I know, just sleep. We'll keep our clothes on."

"Okay."

"Okay."

I get up and turn, and offer him my hand. He takes it and I help him off the couch. We walk to my bedroom, and climb on top of the covers, still dressed. I curl up against him, and he kisses the top of my head. And we fall back to sleep.

chapter 25

happily ever after, or:
epilogue

QUOTE OF THE DAY

How We Are Spared
At midsummer before dawn
an orange light returns to the mountains like a great
weight
and the small birds cry out
and bear it up

—W. S. Merwin

I am relaxing at home the night before the wedding. Everything is on schedule, the girls have their perfect little dresses and
beribboned baskets at the ready, all the details have been covered. It will be small, but beautiful. The ceremony will be private, just immediate family in the chambers of a judge friend
of Dad's, the reception at 160 Blue with the extended nearest
and dearest. Doug and I will leave this weekend for eight days
on Petit St. Vincent in the Caribbean, and then my parents and
Doug's girls and Naomi and her brood will fly down and meet
us for five days of family fun in Disney World. I have purchased
my first-ever bikini for the trip, still getting used to my new size
twelve frame. I am looking at my dress, a simple ivory satin
sheath, much in the mode of a classic 1950s silhouette, off the
shoulder with a wide cuff, three-quarter sleeves. A costume de-

signer friend made it for me, and I do feel like a princess look-ing at it. I am stirred from my reveries by my doorbell.

"Hi." Goodness gracious me.

"Geoff, what are you doing here?"

"I left Sandra."

"What?"

"I left Sandra. I want you back. I need you. Don't get mar-ried tomorrow, run away with me tonight and marry me in-stead. I love you."

"I don't believe this."

"Believe it. It is you I should be making a life with, we are great together, we always were, I just didn't have the guts to admit it, but the thought of you actually marrying someone else, it is killing me. Please. I will make you so happy."

I cannot answer him, as behind him up my front porch Mark suddenly appears.

"Mark?!"

"Don't get married. I still love you. Come back to me."

This is when I wake up.

I really have GOT to not eat sausage pizza at two in the morning, my dreams get all fucked up.

You didn't really think I was going out like that, do you? Please. Have you learned nothing after all this? Haven't you been paying the slightest bit of attention? I am essentially exactly who I was in the last chapter, and every chapter before that. Short, fat, soon to be divorced, slowly healing broken heart.

But, since you are insisting upon some sort of closure, I will offer you the following.

It is Labor Day weekend. I am spending most of this week-end in preparations for the semester which is upon me. There will be dinner and a movie on Saturday night with Doug, and brunch with my parents on Sunday. Geoff wanted to have lunch on Monday, but I put him off a bit, opting instead for a day of fun and festivities with Pam, Heather, Bruce and Parker. We are beginning the rounds of testing for a new drink for fall, as the Blahsmopolitan is a little too fruity for football season. It is arduous work, but someone has to do it. In the meantime, I put the final touch on the Journal Poems. A little more storytelling than I usually indulge in, but it wanted to be written, so I let it come, and actually, while it is really different for me, I kinda like it. We will see what old Ogilvie has to say about it.

soul mating

the old woman lives
as old women do
in a tedium of routine
she rises
bathes
dresses
breaks fast
keeps house
tends her garden
tends the garden of her mind
which does not blossom
in the practiced way it once did

She is content.

it does not bother her
the way it might you or I
she is unemotional
about the loss of detail
the slippery ways a word
or a memory
might elude her

she has lived for over four hundred years
the keeper of soul stories

as was her mother
and her mother's mother before her
back generations
to the time
when mortals and gods lived together
as twins in the womb of their mother earth

and if you travel
to the foothills of the mountains
where what we know as Europe was born
and find the valley
where the full moon
casts a shadow of a hunter
on the mountain face behind it
follow the point of the hunter's arrow
to a grove of blue pines
you will see her small simple house
her small simple garden
she will ask you in
brew you a tea your tongue will remember
but you know not from where or when

And she will tell you this legend.

when all the energy of the world was new
and the electric pulse we know as life force
was gathering itself together
light and dark formed a bond that was inseparable
for whether they lived together or apart
one did not exist without the other

we have come to define all sorts of explanations
both scientific and mystic
to correlate with this

positive and negative
male and female
concave and convex
however you
or your ancestors
named it
it is still light and dark

and when man arrived in the world
the life force came into him
to make him breathe
whether you believe that force is a soul
or merely a series of logical and mundane impulses
encoded on the genetic map
it is what makes us real

it became apparent
in short order
that the world in which we lived
was made up of these dualities.
these twinnings,
the existence of each
mutually exclusive to the existence
of the other
we began to seek out similar pairings
in our relationship to other people
the concept of soul mate
arrived with the creation of gods we could name
for we cannot fathom the gods in their reality
only in ours
the idea that someone or something
made us
made us complete in heaven
separated by our birth into humanity
forever seeking our other half

light to our dark
but each soul is complete
and finite
and does not need another
to make it so

we may meet
and love
and live with someone
who is so perfect for us
that we feel a magical
almost sacred bond
but it is the expression
of our personal mythology
that makes it thus
not a godly act
not a force of nature
the longing we feel
is not for a soul mate
but for a womb mate

A twin.

not a completion
of two halves making wholeness
but of two wholes
creating divinity
while we all long for that
whether we know so or not
it is only possible for one pair in a million
if in your first human birthing
for we all will have many
you were a twin
only then is it possible
through the generations

to find your mate
and you are destined to find one another
not in every lifetime
but often enough on your journey
that you know them
when they come to you
A sibling.
A parent.
A peerless friend.
A perfect lover.

you will meet
and live
and love
and lose one another
until the end of time as we know it.
and if you are lucky
you will share
more laughter than sorrow
over your centuries together
only one pair in a million
their destiny
written
with a pen of pure darkness
and ink of pure light
on the newborn sky
and in the smallest part
of the cells that make up their blood
and when they meet again
as they are destined to do
more often than not
the secret language they used
to communicate
in that first

and most ancient womb
becomes fluent again in their hearts

whether you come to her in flesh
or as a spirit borne on your dreams
whether you walk her valley in daylight
the weight of your pack
anchoring you to what is real
or in darkness
on wings that know the way
of their own memory
the story is the same

its meaning inevitable

the burden becomes yours

was she real?

did you create her?

is her story true
or merely a fairy tale
to while away an hour?

and did she tell you
because you are one in a million?

or because you are not
and knowing the statistics
may help you stop searching
for someone or something
you are not destined to have

The answers are all yes.

The burden becomes yours, and mine. Destiny only does so much, after all. So while I do not come to this ending engaged, thin, rich or famous, I do come to this ending happy. Because essentially, it isn't really an ending at all. I didn't wake up this morning and think, here is where it ends, I just thought, here is where today begins. My divorce papers will arrive next week. I feel very okay about that, but when they show up, I may very well have a meltdown. I will most certainly have a cocktail. Maybe four.

Geoff and I have managed these past weeks to segue into fairly genuine and mostly platonic friendship, save one very small slip last week when a good-night kiss got slightly out of hand, but we didn't sleep together, and he promised to behave himself. I actually do think he and Sandra might someday split up after all. Her new job sends her to Dallas quite a bit, and according to Mrs. Rachmann via my mother, Sari Ketzelman's cousin is thrilled about seeing her when she is back in his neck of the woods. If they divorce, I wonder if he will come for me. I don't think I would go with him, after everything that has happened; I am stronger in my resolve where he is concerned. Plus, I never wanted him by default. I am no consolation prize after all. He should have chosen me definitively when he had the chance, silly rabbit. Then again, who knows, if I am available, (and let's be honest, if I am horny) and he comes sniffing around all free and single-like, my resolve may resolve to be unresolved, if you get my meaning.

Doug and I are taking things very slowly, really getting to know one another. He is sweet and funny and I like him very much. I sort of assumed I would fall madly in love with him right away, as if the ardor of my youth had just been dehydrated over the years and would reconstitute itself immediately. But I am not in love with him, at least not yet. Our strange night of sleeping together hasn't been repeated, with or without clothes. It is sort of charming, really, he is very concerned about protecting both our friendship and our slightly war-scarred hearts. He knows all about Geoff, he even knows about Joe (well, not the details, just that he existed), and he doesn't seem to mind any of it. We have had three more dates since the ice cream night, and there have been some kisses and petting that are rife with potential. I think that maybe on Saturday night we may take that next carnal step, and may I just ask that considering the last time, you all pray for me. Pray very very hard.

And as of this week, David Letterman has announced his impending fatherhood, making his "longtime girlfriend" the "mother of his child," which is much harder to get around, so I have been a little in mourning for him.

But nothing is really tidy. By all technical standards, I am alone. And actually, I am really okay with that. If Doug turns out to be something, that will happen or not at the discretion of the universe. And if he doesn't, well, then someone else will show up. Or not.

I suppose the moral of my story, if one is to be articulated in any sense, is that in general, I really do like my life a whole lot. I know who I am, which is proving to be terribly helpful, since it is obviously confusing enough trying to figure other people out. I like the color of my hair, thanks to a devoted and gifted stylist. I like meeting new people and finding out what they like, since so many of the best things in my life are things that some wonderful person brought to me as their passion, and that in turn made me passionate about it.

As to aspirations for the future, I hope that the universe continues to send me a path that is interesting, challenging and full of joy. I hope to continue to get my writing published, but less than I hope I am still inspired to write. I hope to continue to enjoy success and upward mobility in my teaching career, but less than I hope that I live a good life and leave the world the minutest bit better than I found it. I hope to find someone special to share the life I lead, but less than I hope to maintain the sense of self that makes me okay even when I am alone.

The important part is that really and truly, the answers are all yes.

For all of us.

And that is enough.

In May Red Dress Ink
brings you tales of modern love—
from the male perspective.

Girl Boy Etc.

by Michael Weinreb

Girl Boy Etc. delves into the inner lives of young single
men as they weather the uncertainties of modern
relationships, and teems with perceptions as sharp as
the shooting pain of a hangover headache and as
familiar as the feeling of being dumped.

"The brilliance—and humor—of this collection comes
from Weinreb's white-knuckled grasp of how it feels
to want the kind of love that does not exist, which is
the only love anyone wants, really."—Chuck
Klosterman, author of *Sex, Drugs, and Cocoa Puffs*.

RED DRESS INK
™